# THE MAN WHO WANTED TO SMELL BOOKS
## AND OTHER STORIES

Born in Kilmarnock in 1919 to a Scottish father and a
Canadian mother, Elspeth Dryer spent the early years of
her childhood in England. When she was nine her parents
returned to Scotland and she continued her schooling at
George Watson's Ladies' College in Edinburgh. From there
she went to study Fine Arts, English and Philosophy at
Edinburgh University before moving to Edinburgh College
of Art where she took a Diploma in Art. After graduating she
taught painting for several years in the Borders, Aberdeen
and Northern Ireland. She married the philosopher George
Elder Davie in 1944 (he was teaching at Queen's University
Belfast) and a daughter was born to them in 1946.

The family returned to Scotland and settled in Edinburgh
which provided the scene and the material for much of
Elspeth Davie's writing from then on, with her perceptive
eye for the disturbing nuances of apparently banal and
everyday happenings. Davie had written short stories as a
teenager, but her first book was a novel, *Providings*, published
in 1965. Her second book was a collection called *The Spark
and Other Stories* (1968). Three more novels were published
over the years; *Creating a Scene* (1971) which deals with
teaching art and received a Scottish Arts Council Award;
*Climbers on a Stair* (1978) and *Coming to Light* (1989). But it
was Elspeth Davie's short fiction which brought her particular success with readers and critics alike, and her stories
appeared in *The London Magazine, Cornhill, Transatlantic
Review* and numerous anthologies. She received another
Scottish Arts Council Award in 1977 and the prestigious
Katherine Mansfield Prize in 1978. Her stories appeared in
*The High Tide Talker and Other Stories* (1976), *The Night of
the Funny Hats* (1980), *A Traveller's Room* (1985) and *Death
of a Doctor and Other Stories* (1992). Elspeth Davie died in
1995.

ELSPETH DAVIE

# The Man Who Wanted
# to Smell Books

*and other stories*

*Introduced by Giles Gordon*

★

CANONGATE
CLASSICS
101

This edition first published as a Canongate Classic in 2001 by Canongate Books Ltd, 14 High Street, Edinburgh, EH1 1TE. The stories in this selection were first published in volume form as follows: 'Family House', 'The Spark' and 'A Visit to the Zoo' in *The Spark and other stories* (Calder and Boyars, 1968); 'The Snow Heart', 'The Colour', 'Waiting for the Sun', 'Allergy', 'The High Tide Talker' and 'The Bookstall' in *The High Tide Talker and other stories* (Hamish Hamilton, 1976); 'The Night of the Funny Hats', 'Pedestrian', 'The Time-Keeper', 'Concerto' and 'The Swans' from *The Night of the Funny Hats* (Hamish Hamilton, 1980); 'Lines', 'Security', 'A Field in Space', 'Out of Order', 'Bulbs', 'Shoe in the Sand', 'Couchettes', 'Thorns and Gifts' and 'Accompanists' from *A Traveller's Room* (Hamish Hamilton, 1985); 'Death of a Doctor', 'The Man Who Wanted to Smell Books', 'Choirmaster', 'Through the Forest' and 'The Morning Mare' from *Death of a Doctor and other stories* (Sinclair-Stevenson, 1992). 'Family House', 'The Spark' and 'A Visit to the Zoo' copyright © The Calder Educational Trust. Reproduced by permission. Copyright © Elspeth Davie 1968, 1976, 1980, 1984, 1985, 1992. This selection copyright © The Estate of Elspeth Davie, 2001. Introduction copyright © Giles Gordon, 2001.

The 28 stories in this volume are printed more or less in order of when they were written, and in the order in which they were first published in volume form.

The publishers gratefully acknowledge general subsidy from the Scottish Arts Council towards the Canongate Classics series and a specific grant towards the publication of this volume.

Typeset by Hewer Text Ltd, Edinburgh
Printed and bound by Omnia Books Ltd, Glasgow

10 9 8 7 6 5 4 3 2 1

*British Library Cataloguing-in-Publication Data*
A catalogue record for this book
is available from the British Library

ISBN 1 84195 200 1

www.canongate.net

# Contents

# Introduction

'Finally, I would say that writers – for all that they are supposed to have this so-called and greatly over-rated "knowledge of human nature" – are not necessarily better equipped than any other persons for knowing themselves. Indeed, they need all the help they can get. The camera may sometimes provide this.'[1]

The stern, severe, intelligent face intense, searchlight eyes; prominent nose; tight but wide lips; compassionate, strong chin – is topped by a sensible fringe and Mrs Davie wears a black, halter-neck jumper. Hers is a latter-day Presbyterian visage with a vengeance.

She eschewed biography, thinking it irrelevant to the work, and, perhaps surprisingly, was reluctant to reveal, at least in print, her date of birth. A touch of female vanity? I suspect rather it was a touch of reticence, modesty.

The facts of her life that she chose to reveal, here modestly embellished, are simple: born Elspeth Dryer on 20th March 1919 in Kilmarnock, she went to school in Edinburgh, studied at the capital's university and college of art and taught painting for several years thereafter. This professional involvement with the fine arts I take to be crucial to her writing. She then lived for a while in Ireland, with her husband, who taught at Queen's University, Belfast before returning to Scotland.

In Ireland she became friendly with a general practitioner Dr Pat Strang, later married to the poet Richard Murphy, with whom she discussed literature seriously once a week. She also knew Philip Larkin, who was assistant librarian at the university. She painted there and sold quite a few canvases, mainly landscapes in what her husband describes as 'the French Impressionist style'. They married in October 1944 and a daughter, Anne, was born in January 1946. She didn't, in the biographical notes accompanying her short stories in anthologies, or on the back flaps of the jackets of her five collections of short stories or four novels, reveal that her husband was George Davie, one of Scotland's most distinguished philosophers and the author of that fundamental and key work, *The Democratic Intellect: Scotland and her universities in the nineteenth century* (1961).

Dr Davie told me that Elspeth's parents were living in England until she was nine, and she went to school there. She was taught how to write but not how to join up letters, and throughout her life her meticulous, neat epistles written to family, friends and other correspondents in blue biro did not have the words joined up. When her parents (father Scottish, mother Canadian) came back to Scotland Elspeth was sent to George Watson's Ladies' College. She was addicted to *Beowulf* which she was taught at a tender age when in England. Dr Davie remarked, 'Elspeth didn't care much for Scottish education,' and he told me that her comment on his seminal book was that it was 'surprisingly well written' for an academic.

She spent two years studying Fine Art, English and Philosophy at Edinburgh University but left then as she wasn't up to speed with mathematics and couldn't have taken a degree. She then took a DA at Edinburgh College of Art.

Her writing style was formed by the time she was sixteen when she began to publish short stories in the school magazine. When she reprinted some of these stories later she changed them very little. She received Scottish Arts Council awards in 1971 and 1977, and won the prestigious Katherine Mansfield short story prize in 1978 for 'The High Tide Talker', the title story of one of her collections. One of the judges was V.S. Pritchett, who was much taken with her stance on Presbyterianism.

In the early 1950s two Edinburgh writers were among the

prizewinners of the *Observer*'s rather famous short story competition, and they neatly represent the two facets of 'modernist' Scottish writing. The winner was the stylish, mercurial Muriel Spark (born a year earlier) – Jewish become Roman Catholic; the runner-up, the Calvinist, Knoxian Elspeth Davie. The colourful Spark is today rather more widely read than the somewhat monochromatic Davie ever was, but the current (posterity is likely to regard Davie far more highly than the present does) imbalance in their readership does a singular injustice to the precision, exactitude, sly humour and socialist compassion of the latter writer. Spark and Davie are two of the best, most idiosyncratic and original Scottish prose writers since Robert Louis Stevenson.

A further parallel between Spark and Davie is provided by the fact that for many years Davie and her husband lived in a flat overlooking Bruntsfield Meadows, within view and sound of James Gillespie's school where girls of slender means would toil under the tutelage of Miss Jean Brodie's successors. That Davie's first collection of stories should have been entitled *The Spark* was not intentionally homage to her contemporary.

She published four novels – *Providings* (1965), *Creating a Scene* (1971), *Climbers on a Stair*, about tenement life in Scotland's capital (1978) and *Coming to Light* (1989), a kind of masterpiece of the kaleidoscopic Presbyterian consciousness, the progress of a soul in collusion with the stratosphere. It was as a short story writer, however, that she achieved her finest results.

The novel, as E.M. Forster and more than a few others have suggested, tells a story, and is about people. Even at its most quixotic, moralistic, when rendered in literary form (*Tristram Shandy*, say, or the work of B.S. Johnson) it depicts the vagaries of individuals wrestling with life and making, or failing to make, inroads upon it. This doesn't much happen in Davie's novels. Her characters are stoics, their lives preserved in aspic, getting on with a mundane everyday.

Paintings do various things, one of which – unless, sometimes but not always, they are abstract – is to tell a story. Or, rather, a story – plot, narrative, situation – may be deduced from the visual images. Davie the short story writer wrote as if she were a painter. Her published stories delineate the worlds she explored to a considerable degree as if the language she used was pigment. Rather like John Berger's important art criticism derived from a solemn sense of morality (which Davie must have been aware of), the language of the story – unlike Spark's – is less concerned with a Firbankian elegance than a Calvinist, Cubist truth. And she was impressed (if not dazzled) by the colour and shapes, angles upon reality of the Scottish Colourists.

'The difficulty with the artist, and particularly the writer, is that much of his work has its roots in the unconscious', she wrote in a note which accompanies in an anthology two of her best stories – 'Concerto' and 'Allergy'.

> There is little to show apart from the finished product. So, instead, he may start talking and answering questions and perhaps find himself giving hard-edged and conclusive statements about things he has not considered in that particular way. He is not always at ease in this, for part of his business as writer, in an age of form-filling and labelling, curt questions and short answers, is to see that the silent uniqueness of persons and situations, their essence if you like, doesn't get lost amongst the files. It's his job to recognize and preserve the more secret side of life. The writers who chiefly interest me are those who strike in at an angle to experience rather than going along parallel to it . . . The desolating and the unfamiliar is happening continually between our getting up and our going to bed . . . It is of this day-to-day business of living, its mysteriousness and its absurdity, that I would like to write.[2]

And she did. These sentences describe precisely the effect of her writing upon her readers. To suggest that, along with the cautious, austere Presbyterianism of her intellect she employed a fragmentary, Cubist approach deconstructing her characters by way of X-raying their consciousness, might imply a certain pretentiousness, but this is the opposite of the case: her prose is utterly down to earth. Yet there is something of Cubism in her work, the way in which she breaks down characters and situations to reconstruct and illuminate them, although this is always compassionate and 'human', never merely theoretical. In all her writing there is an essential fastidious balance between intellect and eye (or eye and intellect). She writes as an artist, a painter with a literary mind.

Not only is her art influenced by painters and painting, some of her best stories are about painting, or inspired by it, including here 'The Colour'. Music also was fundamental to her and acknowledged in such stories as 'Choirmaster', 'Concerto' and 'Accompanists', the latter story in addition being notable for a touch of feminism (also found in the clever story 'The Bookstall').

Her first publisher was John Calder, and the Scottish Elspeth Davie was very much at home and in appropriate company with such French writers on the Calder and Boyars list as Beckett, Nathalie Sarraute, Marguerite Duras, Robert Pinget and, particularly, Alain Robbe-Grillet. The latter's *Snapshots and Towards a New Novel* (Calder and Boyars, 1965) was the most exhilarating theoretical book on contemporary fiction in years and Davie was very much a disciple. Robbe-Grillet posited a world where to a degree human beings were dominated and ruled by objects (Davie's first novel is about that) – by buildings, furniture, *things*. Davie's characters, likewise, are restricted by their environments, physical as much as social context, pre-ordained inevitability. She wrote less about the anxieties of the individual though than of the ways in which everyday life conspires against our best-laid plans and obsessions.

Thus she was writing in, and out of, a European tradition. As the English novelist B.S. Johnson wrote in his introduc-

tion to *Aren't You Rather Young to be Writing Your Memoirs?*
(1973), 'It is a fact of crucial significance in the history of the
novel that James Joyce opened the first cinema in Dublin in
1909. Joyce saw very early on that film must usurp some of
the prerogatives which until then had belonged almost ex-
clusively to the novelist. Films could tell a story more
directly.' In other words, the role of the fiction writer, the
fiction writer as serious artist, whether he or she liked it or not
– had changed. It didn't make artistic sense to pretend that
Joyce, Eliot and the other prophets of modernism hadn't
existed. The planet, post the world wars, had changed
fundamentally and art had to reflect that. Elspeth Davie
held all these concerns in her artistic credo.

Her short stories, eighty or so, were collected in five
volumes: *The Spark* (1969); *The High Tide Talker* (1976);
*The Night of the Funny Hats* (1980); *A Traveller's Room*
(1985); and *Death of a Doctor* (1992), the latter four books
published by Christopher Sinclair-Stevenson, first at Hamish Hamilton, then under his eponymous imprint. Stories
from all these books are represented in this selection.

It is invidious perhaps to single out one story as her best
as her work has such unity as well as authority but 'Concerto' is superb. It is about a commotion caused by a
member of the audience during a concert and the effect
it has on the rest of the listeners and on the music being
essayed. There is a dangerous dry humour to it as the
mundane threatens the sublime. Can those merely listening
to a piece of music experience the condition of the com-
poser when he created the sounds, and if so can they hold
on to this experience and temperament (emotional intelligence) when the external world is mitigating against it?

The title story of this selection, 'The Man Who Wanted to
Smell Books', is indirect homage to another great modernist
writer she admired, the Argentinian Borges. On the one
hand, it mocks the way in which printed books, repositories
of wisdom, can in a thoroughly 'trendy' way become part of a

system – a library, no less – which eschews human beings and would deny them access. As I write, it is announced that a memorial to Donald Dewar, first First Minister of the Scottish Executive, will be a library in Queensberry House, but the library is likely to have the books on computer screens: Elspeth Davie got there first, with this story (1990). She and Mr Dewar must be spinning wryly in their graves.

Elspeth Davie was, as George Davie wrote in a letter to the present writer dated 1st March 1997, 'very often scathing about modern nonsense but the strength of another story, "Family House", is that it shows up the sense in which opposition to modern nonsense can be taken too far and so as to bring about its own undoing'. Many of her stories, and the authorial imagination behind them, are slightly sceptical of what Dr Davie calls 'overdone modernity'.

Mercifully, Davie owes nothing to the Kailyard, or for that matter to the Scottish 'Renaissance'. It seems extraordinary that she was producing the inspired metaphysical and profoundly moral work she was when the likes of Compton Mackenzie, Eric Linklater and even James Kennaway were stylistically still adhering to the modes of the traditional novel in English. She would obviously never be a 'popular' or 'commercial' novelist or fiction writer. It is unlikely that readers of Irvine Welsh would take to her but admirers of Alasdair Gray, James Kelman and particularly A.L. Kennedy should, and Gray and Kelman admired her work.

And yet she is no abstractionist. Always writing in English, not in Scots, synthetic or otherwise, her characters are verily the children of John Knox, weighed down by guilt, weariness and struggling to survive, more partly living than living. The bleakness of northern Presbyterianism fills their lives with puzzling foreboding as the light and shade of Edinburgh, which she captures perfectly, lifts them up.

George Davie, in the letter previously cited, writes:

In all the stories the crucial illustration of your Knoxian thesis – an illustration capable of silencing the
puzzlement which some people have felt of the asso-
ciation of Elspeth with Protestantism or rather Presbyterianism – is found in the story 'Choirmaster'. It
was, interestingly, the only story she ever wrote which
she talked about with some satisfaction in her writing,
calling it her 'story about God'. It hasn't been much
liked by Catholics, they tend to be shocked by her
treatment of Jesus whose high point to them seems to
be the crucified Christ, perhaps the bleeding heart.
This was very far from Elspeth's tastes and one might
venture the idea that she would be much nearer to
what MacDiarmid calls 'the saying of Christ long kept
dim, that who so follows me, things of like nature will
do, and greater'.

Elspeth Davie is a Scottish writer of universality and high
aspiration. Unlike so many of her contemporaries and successors, she believed, albeit perhaps with a certain trepida-
tion, that art – literature – might usefully be 'difficult'. Yet she
wrote less about the anxieties of the individual than of the
ways by which everyday life conspires against the individual's
modest ambitions, hopes and obsessions, and her stories
remain entirely grounded in what she called 'this day-to-day
business of living, its mysteriousness and its absurdity'.

Giles Gordon

NOTES

1    Thus the always modest Elspeth Davie in a note opposite a
     photograph of her in Angela Catlin, *Natural Light: Portraits of
     Scottish Writers* (Paul Harris Publishing, 1985).
2    Elspeth Davie in *Beyond the Words: Eleven Writers in Search of
     a New Fiction* edited by Giles Gordon (Hutchinson, 1975).

# Family House

ANYONE VISITING THIS house for the first time found himself unexpectedly and uncomfortably exposed before going a step from the iron gates. Tough soles and a thick skin were needed from the moment when, turning in from a soft, country road, he would find the thickly-sown, cutting little stones of the drive working their way over the tops of his shoes and through his shoelaces. And if, while removing them, he were to raise his eyes, he would meet the unbroken, aggressive glare of rows of unscreened windows. For there was no hiding from this place. The gravel was not only harsh but also noisy underfoot. There were no soft bushes to screen the visitor while he made his way to the front door, and nothing about the place made a concession to nerves, withdrawals or second thoughts of any kind. It was a large house – not distinguished by age or design, but formidably plain and square, built in a smooth, grey stone which had begun to take on the polish of marble simply through the care spent on it since it was first built. No one, after meeting the people who lived in it, could think of it again as a house which was owned. It was not owned, but painfully served. It existed not for shelter or comfort, but to announce its own immense gravity and the fact that it was packed from top to bottom with a massive deposit of possessions. The foundations of any ordinary house would have sunk askew, the walls and roof, long before this, have bulged and cracked under the strain.

A family of five lived there – two sisters and three brothers who had been together since they were children. Although the men went back and forth to offices in the city and the women went down to the village with shopping-bags like other housewives, they had no real communication with anyone else, but remained in their tight group – all five of them – thin, anxious people who, like their parents, uncles and aunts before them, had hurried up and down in service to the house. The brothers – Joseph, James and Edgar Findlay, seemed to have effaced themselves so completely in the world that they had become almost indistinguishable to outsiders. They were tall, gaunt men – dark without being interesting, and with a melancholy so grey and unromantic that people did not in the least wish to enquire what might be behind it. There were a few years between them in age, Joseph, who was fifty-nine, being the eldest, but they might have been triplets for all the interest that was taken in them as separate individuals. They were seldom described by name or profession, and any epithet, good or bad, which came their way, did for the three of them and sometimes for all five. The women were never apart and were not expected to need the luxury of their Christian names, Edith and Clara, to distinguish them. They were conveniently known as the Findlay sisters and could be told apart, when necessary, by the fact that Edith, who was oldest of the family, had grey hair, streaked with black, and Clara, who was the youngest, had fairish hair, going grey.

But the house was never spoken of except by name. It had a definite position on the map and in guidebooks; it stood high up and could be seen from a long distance, and the paths, the lines of trees and hedges, the position of the long, wedge-shaped flower-beds surrounding it had all been designed, from the beginning, to point out the house dramatically and give it an importance which it might well have lost as time went on. For the family who made their pilgrimage daily up and down over the thick layer of sharp-edged stones had never asked why this house and everything in it must be cherished long after it had ceased to provide any comfort for themselves. Habits laid down long before they were born had become laws for them, and because a time was coming when there would be no one left to whom this special care could be handed on, the house exacted from them – the last of the family – a greater effort than had ever been made before. As it grew older it was merciless in its demands. Year after year it was buttressed and strengthened. Ladders were never away from the walls while it was painted, pointed and chiselled. There was a continual scraping, hammering and screwing going on inside and out. Yet underneath it all remained the gnawing anxiety that some day something would begin to crumble or rot, that something absolutely essential to the safety of the house would start to rattle or swing suddenly loose. Ivy, too eager to hide the sharpness of its staring eyes, was torn from around the windows. Hedges were continually being cut back so that its view should be unimpeded, and the branches of old trees, dripping too near the roof, were lopped back to raw stumps at the first patch of damp which appeared on the ceilings.

The family who lived in the house made no demands for themselves. In their own eyes they had very little importance at all, and compared to the house and the heavy accumulation of stuff which it contained, they felt themselves to be lightweights. Their modesty was unnatural; they had never been noticed and did not wish to be, and most of their leisure time was spent inside the house, as though, if they were seen too often, their peculiar lack of distinction might take something from the importance of the place, and let down those people who stared confidently at them from their frames on mantelpieces and the tops of writing-desks. Yet inside the house there was little room for the five of them. It was not so large, after all, and every room was crammed with the possessions of those ancestors and relations who had been a great deal wealthier, more popular, generous, artistic, more widely travelled and more extraordinary in every way than themselves. People had obviously strewn gifts on them wherever they went, had photographed them leaning against giant tree-trunks in California, holding their hats on the decks of Atlantic liners, sitting at the centre of intimate picnic parties on the banks of unknown rivers, or smiling and waving from the windows of train carriages. If they had also sacrificed themselves to a house, then the service had taken the form of a perpetual treasure-hunt and they showed no signs of the strain, except for a wanness under tropical skies, or a certain puffiness about the eyes owing to the difficulties and uncertainties of getting the kind of food they were accustomed to. Most of the time, however, they had been flamboyant creatures, always on the move; and as though to carry on this tradition in the only way possible, the two sisters kept the treasures which had belonged to them always in motion so that, with constant shifting and re-arranging, the objects might still seem to have a restless life of their own.

So they polished and dusted, and carried the fragile tables, jingling with curios, from one corner to the other; or placed some ornament nearer the window at a certain time of day so that the sunlight might, for an hour or two, strike the rare metal or glass; or turned some piece of china round into the shadow so that a chip or crack might be hidden. They knelt, side by side, both straining at the handles of huge bottom drawers which held leaden wads of white linen, yards of lace and silk, and the caps and aprons, tunics, collars, petticoats and stockings of national costumes from all over the world. These they were constantly folding and shaking and wrapping up with fresh supplies of mothball, and when the time came to shut the drawer again, they would push with their heads down, gasping, and straining the muscles of their stomachs in order to confine the bulging piles of stuff to their former space. The pressure behind the door of every cupboard and beneath the lids of chests was terrifying even to those who were used to it. At times the five of them could feel the pressure inside their own heads, and a suffocating weight would lie on their chests when they woke in the night and thought of the straining house ready, perhaps, to split, ready to crack if it were not carefully handled. When, on stormy nights, they thought of the fragile things poised on tables, and the heavy objects hanging from the walls on old cords, every nerve in their bodies would tighten with the effort which, even flat on their backs, they made to resist the fraying and the splintering which might be going on there in the darkness. Above all, it was the long attic at the top of the house which crushed them. In the daytime they were conscious of it, like a great layer of heavy atmosphere. But at night, alone in their own rooms, staring at the ceiling, they felt their own identity lost under the mass of stuff up there which weighed on their lids even when they had shut their eyes, and bulged through grotesquely into their dreams when they were asleep.

The family seldom took a holiday away from the house, and to one another they showed the special loyalty of a group of people living under a tyrant whom they respected and even reverenced. The rigid timetable which they kept to, and the discomforts which they endured for the sake of the house, had kept down all superfluous flesh and feeling and prevented any extravagance showing in their expressions or behaviour. They were all silent people, chillingly resigned – the men, relieved to be away from one another in the daytime, were also relieved to be back again in the evening to a relationship which seemed to go on forever, safely, monotonously, unlike the precarious relationships which they caught glimpses of on their way back and forth to the house. There had been certain incidents in the past – times when someone had tried to advise or interfere, or shown some sneering disregard for the house and its property by trying to remove one of them away from the others into marriage or to some prosperous post abroad, or into debts just deep enough to give a taste of risk and pleasure. But all that was a long time ago. No interference from without had come for many years.

It was from inside the house, however, that the greatest disturbance was to come – beginning with an unimportant incident which occurred in its pressure-centre – the attic. It was a mild Autumn afternoon, and the elder sister, Edith, had gone up to look for a small table-lamp which she knew had been lying for many years under a heap of unidentified stuff. Indeed, nothing had been moved in the attic for a long time except the soft, outer layer of cloths, pillows and bedspreads which covered the broken, upturned furniture and the tangle of springs and wire like flesh covering the sensitive bones and nerves of an old invalid. In the course of years, however, one or two lanes had been hollowed out through the pile and one deep cave made out of two sides of tightly-wedged furniture, covered over at the top with various lighter objects which included folded tents and fishing rods, umbrellas, golf clubs, curtain-rails and a pair of broken crutches. Over everything else were two heavy lids of linoleum which had, at one time, been sliced into curious shapes to fit the awkward cupboards under the stair. At the far end of this hollow Edith had found the lamp she was looking for, but in pulling the flex she had also dislodged a heavy, mantelpiece clock. The square block of black marble and metal, built with side pillars to resemble a Greek temple, fell across her foot, all its machinery jangling and whirring for a second as she screamed.

It was nearly suppertime. The whole family had been sitting together downstairs waiting for her to come down, and now they came up to the attic – not quickly, for that was not their habit, but close on one another's heels, and apprehensively. They noticed, before anything else, that their sister was angry, and because they had never before seen an expression like this on her face, it appeared to them more like some momentary madness, caused by the pain. Two brothers bent over to examine her foot – the others bent with equal solicitude over the clock which chimed softly, once, as it was gently lifted and put into a safe corner.

'Not even the glass smashed,' murmured the younger sister as she peered into its face and ran her fingers round the rim. Edith now began to sob wildly, and three of them helped her down the attic stairs to her bedroom, as one ran to phone the doctor. They were now amazed and alarmed at this breakdown of her reserve. It was, after all, nothing so serious, as the doctor assured them later that evening. She must lie up for a day or two and have her foot bound – three days at the most, if she wished to be on the safe side.

It was very soon clear that Edith not only wanted to be on the safe side, but that she had made up her mind to stay there indefinitely. She rested for three days and, when her foot was healed, discovered that she was far too tired to move the rest of her body. With the voice of authority which belonged to her as the oldest of the family, but which she had never used before, she informed her brothers and sister that she had decided to stay in bed and regain some of the strength which she had lost in the house over a great number of years. They accepted the announcement silently and did not discuss it any more than they had thought of discussing other unaccountable things which had happened to them. By keeping silent, and simply not paying too much attention, they had vanquished all sorts of mysteries – from the appearance of apparitions to the turning up of unexpected visitors. Nevertheless, coming from within the family, Edith's words struck them as ominous.

On the day after this – a Sunday – the four of them went up and down many times during the afternoon and evening to visit her. Propped bolt upright against her pillows, and framed by the gilt, knobbed bedhead, their sister allowed herself to be identified for the first time. So this was Edith –

this stern woman in the fancy bedjacket who stared back at them without a hint of guilt or misgiving in her blue eyes. On the days following they came in with their trays and books and newspapers, on tiptoe or shuffling awkwardly according to their moods, but as time went on they became more wary under her gaze.

For Edith, who had seldom sat down in her life except to get nearer some bit of work, now seemed to want only to lie and watch them coming and going, following all their movements with a close attention embarrassing to people who were unused to walking sympathetically in and out of sickrooms. She would discuss the affairs of the day with them, or listen to the account of some mishap in house or office, but not as though she could ever be involved herself again. Though looking attentively, while they spoke, at their faces, she gave the impression that she was studying the movements of their lips and eyes with amusement, rather as a foreigner might listen to a language he does not quite understand, while unwilling to be done altogether out of his entertainment.

After ten days, when Edith's foot had long been completely healed, her sister sat down on the edge of the bed one afternoon when she had removed the tea-tray, and carefully took Edith's hand in her own. It was not easy to take this hand for it was a large one, and felt hard and strong under Clara's timid fingers. But, flushing slightly, she kept an awkward grip on it.

'Now, Edith,' she said, smiling gravely at the space of wall directly above her sister's head, 'you will tell me what is wrong, will you not? There is something wrong, of course, or else you would not stay in bed long after the doctor has said you may get up – you would not cause us such serious worry for nothing. No, Edith, you would not, and you must tell me at once what is the matter!'

Her voice, slow and persuasive at the beginning, ended quickly on a note of nervous disapproval. Edith, meantime, had withdrawn her hand to flick up the lace of her collar, and answered calmly enough.

'Why, of course I will tell you, Clara. But surely I have told you all often enough what is the matter. I will tell you again, if it is any help. I am seriously tired – that is all. I have been like that for years, so I did not expect any of you to notice. But lately the pressure has grown worse, much worse, so there is nothing for it but to give up for a while until something can be done about it.'

'Well, I am glad you have told me at last,' replied her sister, smiling her strained and patient smile. Not finding Edith's hand again on the coverlet, she smoothed her own mechanically as she talked. 'Of course we can take life more easily after this – I shall see to it. You will rest in the afternoons, and Martha can stay later. But, at any rate, I can relieve your mind on one thing. The blood-pressure you mentioned just now; do you think Dr Fisher has taken no account of these things, or that we should ever let him overlook anything as important as that?' Clara leaned forward, widening her tired eyes in an effort to make them look triumphant. She spoke slowly and emphatically: 'No, Edith – the last time the doctor was here he said that there was absolutely nothing wrong with your lungs, your heart or your blood-pressure. Everything is normal. It is nerves, Edith. There – I've told you now. It is only right you should know what he said – just a little worry about yourself after the shock of your accident. You have given yourself too much time to brood, that is all. And you must not talk about this blood-pressure again!'

'Oh, but I didn't say *blood*-pressure!' exclaimed Edith with a frown. 'It is not a pressure from inside at all. It is from outside – from the house. Don't say you haven't felt the weight of all that junk, Clara! Don't tell me you are going to put up with it indefinitely – that ton weight on top of us till we die!'

Clara shuddered at 'junk' as though her sister had spoken

an obscene word. Never, not in the worst moments of the
spring-cleaning, had such a word been even whispered
between them, and, seriously alarmed, she got up swiftly
and began to arrange the little objects on the mantelpiece,
with her back to Edith as though she had not heard.

'Moving them about will not help in the least, Clara, as
you know,' Edith remarked quietly, as she watched her.
'We have been doing it for years to try and relieve the
pressure. There is not a thing in this house which has ever
been in the same place for more than an hour at a time. But
it does no good. The only way is to get rid of it all. Indeed, it
must be done, and I will not be able to get out of bed until it
is!'

When the doctor came on a special visit the next afternoon he was in no hurry to be away. He went softly about
the large bedroom, looking about him easily and picking up
various objects from desk and mantelpiece which he said
were of rare value – collectors' pieces, he called them as he
turned them about in his hands admiringly. He studied the
photographs for a long time and asked about the relations,
and as he crossed over to the bed, he tapped the chairs with
his fingers and slid his hand down the length of the wardrobe with an envious sigh. It might have been the house
which he had come to examine and to praise for its
excellent health and appearance, and he seemed almost
reluctant to have to turn his attention to Edith.

It was not an uncommon thing, he told her, when he had
settled down at last, to feel, in certain cases of mild nervous
disorder, the kind of symptoms which she had described to
her sister. On the contrary, it was quite a common experience to have the feeling of heaviness in the limbs – a
sensation of pressure in the chest or head – yes, and even
a feeling of suffocation – of being unable to breathe freely
for the weight on the chest – a sensation, perhaps, of cramp
about the heart. He smiled, and stretched his fingers tightly
across his chest, then bound them around his head to

express the familiar meaning. In most cases, he assured her, after a little rest, these common nervous symptoms disappeared very quickly – once the patient showed herself willing to get up and get on with her normal work. And this – he impressed it upon her as he got to his feet briskly – was the most important part of what he had to say. For there was absolutely nothing organically wrong with her. He repeated this as he went out of the door, and again to the family who were waiting downstairs to hear his verdict. But he was in a hurry now, and no longer took any notice of the precious things which jingled along the shelves of the hall as he strode past with his heavy tread.

A few days later Clara was having supper upstairs alone with her sister. A heavy responsibility had fallen on her not only for the whole house and its upkeep, but also for the care of a woman whose thoughts, day and night, were now directed on this house with a ruthlessness never before known to the family. Edith's eyes could no longer be said to rest on objects; she now raked through them with a glance so reckless and scathing that the more fragile stuff could not be expected to last long under it. This evening, however, after the meal, she lay for some time with her eyes shut, and Clara, praying that the obsession was passing, drew in deep breaths at the open window. It was a beautiful October evening. Below her the weekly gardener was brushing up the leaves, and soon the smoke from his bonfire drifted through the room. To Clara the smell was a narcotic, reminiscent of autumn days stretching back through monotonous years, and of the blue haze which hung in the wintry, upper rooms of the house – scarcely opened except for the spring and autumn cleaning. But Edith opened her eyes and sniffed the air with triumph.

'You must begin with this room, Clara,' she cried, suddenly sitting up straight and staring about her sharply. 'That bureau over there has worried me for a long time. You see how it is packed with letters and papers which must be burned at once. No, of course they are not valuable. Why should they be? I don't intend to look over them. They must simply be taken out, bundle by bundle, and put on that bonfire. It is better than choking the chimney. Yes, Clara, of course I mean what I am saying! I am not ill and I am not joking.'

Just before darkness fell that evening, Clara came slowly from the bedroom and down the stairs with her arms full of papers. Her brothers followed her out into the garden, keeping some little distance from her, like sober attendants on a bride, and automatically catching at the white strips and ribbons of paper which blew about her in the wind. At first the flames did not seem strong enough to consume the dense wads of superior notepaper, but after a while the sheets blew open, revealing for a glaring second time-honoured secrets of home and business, scraps of ancient family scandal and a smattering of long-forgotten endearments. Exclamation marks and question marks quivered together on the paper, and formidable lists of figures curled up swiftly into scrolls of fire. When the flames died down there was nothing left but some flimsy black scales floating in the air, and a grey ash on the ground.

The fire had not brought any colour to Clara's face. She was paler than ever as she walked upstairs again to Edith's room. It was her sister who was flushed, as though the flames had burned her cheeks.

'The men can help you tomorrow,' was all she said. 'It is a beginning, anyway.' She turned to the wall without another word and Clara left the room.

'The doctor said it was particularly important not to give in to her,' she said to her brothers as she wished them goodnight. They could not tell from her voice whether this was an apology or a challenge, and she looked preoccupied – uncertainly opening and shutting drawers and continually glancing about the room as she spoke as though sizing the place up after a long absence.

'What is this?' she asked, picking up an object from the sideboard as she was turning to leave.

'What is that?' replied James, looking uneasily at it. 'Why, Clara – what are you talking about? You can see it is a brush with a curved handle. It has been there for years – and with a tray to match. There are two others like it in the drawer.'

'Yes, that is true – and what are they all *for*?' said Clara with unaccustomed sharpness.

'What are they for? Why, surely they are crumb-brushes, Clara. You must have known they were for brushing crumbs off a tea-table!'

'Then must there be three of them?' exclaimed Clara. 'Do we make more crumbs than anybody else, in this house? Is it likely that this one will get worn out with brushing in our lifetime – that there must always be two in reserve? It is very unlikely that I, at any rate shall use another brush while I live – far less the two of them. Do you even know how old I am?'

'But of course, Clara,' her brother replied hurriedly, 'and there are certainly not an excessive quantity of crumbs about the place. Why must we discuss the brushes, if it upsets you? They were not ours, in the first place. You have forgotten that they came to us with the napkin rings and hot water bottles when Aunt Helen gave up her house. If they are not used, they can be handed down. What has your age to do with it, Clara? You are too sensitive about that. We remember you are the youngest. And we do not expect you to use three crumb-brushes.'

Clara tossed her head and left the room. But her brothers remained standing together long afterwards, apprehensively staring about them, and puzzling over the meaning of various objects which they had caught sight of for the first time.

Two days later, in the absence of the gardener, Clara made her own bonfire – a magnificent affair, far bigger than the last, and lighting the whole garden up to the tops of the highest trees. When the three brothers came out of the house to see it they exclaimed in admiration. This time they could show little interest in what was being burned, for great flames destroyed the boxes and packets before they could be identified, but they drew nearer, step by step, to warm themselves, and their eyes shone outrageously in the light. Every now and then, as the garden grew darker, the fire threw a shimmer of light upon the front of the house. When this happened the woman and the three men stood motionless to stare at the quivering windows and wagging chimneys and at the grey stone which swelled and trembled as though it were no more solid than parchment. Now Joseph, the oldest man, went striding off quickly towards the house and returned in a few minutes with a heap of papers which the flames tore from his hands and devoured with a roar as soon as he had thrown them down.

'Papers are not enough to keep it going,' said Clara as the fire subsided again. She went back to the house, running this time, and returned, out of breath, with a couple of heavy wooden trays.

'There was no time to pick and choose,' she explained. 'I took the largest of the half-dozen behind the sideboard. At any rate they will keep it going while we find more stuff.'

They waited for a moment to see the flames lick round the tray-handles which were carved in the shape of crouching monkeys, gripping melons between their fingers.

'What a sin to waste them – and all the people who must be wanting trays!' cried Clara, shuddering with disgust and pleasure. All four of them now started to run towards the house, looking back over their shoulders to judge how long the fire might last. Clara sped upstairs – but not to her sister's room. For the moment she had almost forgotten about Edith. Instead she ran to a spare bedroom, and opening the drawers of a large chest, she began to shake out rolls of cloth and undo the great bags of woollen underwear. Mothballs bounced about the floor as she dug down into the piles with her fingers, but at last she had pulled out as big an armful as she could carry. The men were in the garden before her, however, making for the corner where a thin smoke still rose, and carrying between them as many inflammable objects as they had been able to lay hands on. With their awkward loads and anxious faces, they had the look of people working to save their possessions from a burning house, having caught up the first things which came to hand. James, in the lead, was carrying a basket-chair, piled up with raffia table-mats which he tossed on, one after the other, when he was still some distance away from the fire. Bursts of flame and a crackling like a forest going up forced them to stand aside when the chair went on; and the work-baskets, tea-cosies, clothes-brushes and picture-frames which followed the chair were lost at once in a blaze which sent sparks flying far above the chimneys of the house. This was no ordinary fire. It was more exhilarating than an explosion of sky-rockets. Beyond the vibrating circle where they stood, they caught glimpses of a house which appeared to rock gently on the quaking ground. Clouds, flowers and iron railings trembled together, and the agitation of their own faces made them appear to one another like persons undergoing, moment by moment, the most violent changes of emotion from quivering despair to the wildest glee. When the time came for Clara to unwrap her bundles of underwear their spirits were dampened.

'Perhaps they will smother the fire,' said Clara as she threw on the pants, vests and combinations bequeathed from uncles and great uncles who had died young, long before they could wear a hole in the wool. But when she saw the flames slowly eating through the outer layer she added: 'There must be thousands of people who could do with them – people without a stitch to their backs. What a waste and a sin!'

But the sin and the shame of it stirred them to even greater efforts, and they prodded at the fire until it leapt up again to devour a clothes-horse and a couple of small wooden cake-stands in a matter of minutes.

It was dark before the fire at last fell apart into a smouldering heap of ashes. Clara and her brothers were so exhausted with their orgy of destruction that they could scarcely stand upright, but as they approached the house they lifted their heads and stared up at it boldly. A little of the stuffing had already been taken out of it – even through the darkness they could feel that. The stone did not seem as smooth to them now. They could imagine it dented, here and there, where the surface caved in over certain hollow patches, odd corners which were not packed so tightly as before, and in spite of their exhaustion they felt a quiet satisfaction in the evening's work.

After super Clara went up to see her sister. She was sitting up in bed, reading, looking fresh-cheeked and rested, and she glanced up with a smile when her sister came in. There was no mention of bonfires, but Clara asked casually, as she drew the curtains: 'I suppose you will be getting up tomorrow?'

'Hardly so soon,' replied Edith. 'No, not yet – it is not quite time for me to get up and come downstairs, if that is what you mean. But I will certainly dress and get up for tea in my bedroom. That will be a beginning and help to cheer you all up.'

They were not cheerful as they brought up the heavy trays to her room next afternoon, but they sat with an expectant air, talking absentmindedly and listening for the sound of the lorry which arrived at this hour every week to remove the rubbish. They heard it at last a long distance away, coming up the steep road below their garden wall, and while it laboriously turned the corner of their drive, they excused themselves one by one and went out to meet it, accompanying it for the last few yards of the way as though guiding a triumphal car to the chosen place. When the three dustbin men saw this place – not the mean pair of ashcans, nor the paltry pile of tins, papers and grass-cuttings, but a great hillock of soft stuff, studded with glinting ornaments – they stopped some distance off and approached it reverently on foot. In five minutes, having prodded through the top layer, they returned to the family who were waiting nearby.

'Say – what's going on, here?' asked one, pointing to what he held up in his other hand – a green china mermaid, who also pointed with a puzzled air to the wave on which she sat. 'Are you moving off or what? Sure, that's a funny way to be doing it – clearing out all the fancy stuff and hanging on to the plain. Maybe you've made a mistake, folks. We're not buying and we're not selling and we're not mending and we're not shifting the stuff to any other place. There, it's on the lorry – Cleansing Department – and that's us. In other words – your things are for the dump!'

But as they only backed away, nodding and smiling, he went after them.

'Tell us what's up,' he shouted. 'For all I know you've got heirlooms and all tucked away under that little pile! And what about *her*?' He brandished the mermaid in front of them, but James waved him back nervously and angrily, exclaiming: 'Take it away! Take them all away! There is nothing to discuss. There is illness here – a nervous breakdown in the house. The things are to be removed in the normal way, and there is nothing more to be said!' Still shouting he disappeared with the rest of them inside the house.

The men now got to work on the pile with gusto and without wasting further words. The inmates of the house might be cracked, but the stuff they unearthed was unbelievably whole – basins and ewers, teapots and metal trays which had not taken a dint or a crack in fifty years, china baskets of unchipped violets and draped dancing figures without a pointed toe or finger missing. They lay together, smugly shining there amongst beaded shoes and piled soup-plates, as though on their usual spring-clean outing.

The family did not come out again, but the men worked on in frenzied enthusiasm in case they might suddenly appear with a changed mind about their possessions. They now went at the pile without plan or method, scarcely looking at the stuff, but grimly lifting up the clinking armfuls towards the lorry. Small ornaments fell and were ground underfoot as they staggered about, and they began to shout and threaten one another over each coveted piece. Like some deep archaeological site, the heap revealed layers of life in the history of the house – layers which, although only laid down that morning, contained objects which had not, before that, seen the light of day for a generation. The flimsier stuff, skimmed from the tops of drawers and shelves, had been deposited first, and this the rising wind took up and whirled along with the dust and leaves. Clawing at the ground, the men ran, shouting, after ghostly, lacey evening gloves which spread themselves against tree-trunks, and oriental fruit-baskets and initialled collar-boxes which bowled, lightly as hoops, in front of them.

At last, the furious slamming of the lorry doors brought the whole family to the windows in time to see the men drive off at a breakneck pace down the drive and around the corner. Behind them, where the dazzling hillock had stood, there was now only a churned-up patch of ground where fragments of glass and china lay, and on the long grass nearby stray ribbons and tassels hung mournfully. When the dust from the lorry had settled, the others looked at Edith who had stood beside them in her dressing-gown and was now turning to go back to her room.

'You are surely not going back to bed, Edith,' said Edgar reprovingly. 'Not now. Not after you have seen all the changes that are going on these days. Will we expect you down for supper tonight? Surely you will dress and come down for a little while and tomorrow you will feel yourself again. Don't pretend you haven't noticed the gaps in the cupboards and the open space on the top landing. We have heard you opening and shutting the drawers all morning.'

'I feel a different person – I admit it,' Edith replied as she walked away, '– different, but not absolutely better yet. You certainly cannot hurry an illness like mine, Edgar. In a day or so. One more day, perhaps, will make all the difference. It depends on so many things.' Her eyes rested for a moment on the things as she looked back from her bedroom. Calmly she stared through the other doors and at the heavy brass lamp on which a nymph, still smiling, writhed in an effort to hold up the fringed parchment shade, and beyond that to a massive wardrobe with its magnificent false top, and at the bursting trunks wedged so tightly under the beds that the mattresses above had grown hideously deformed over the years. Finally she lifted her head and gazed, without hatred, up the steep stairs towards the attic. They noticed then what they had never seen before – the extraordinary determination of her chin, so like the chins in all the framed photos of the house, but now to be seen jutting out with a witch-like ruthlessness which outdid all the rest.

'Sell or burn.' She murmured these words, as she gently closed the door behind her. Less than a week ago it would have seemed as though the devil himself had spoken, but now they stood around savouring them, listening for more. But there was silence in the house, except for the sly creaking of the bed as Edith climbed into it again.

The auctioneer's men started to work early the next afternoon. The gaps in corridors and cupboards widened behind them as they tramped about, and great spaces opened out in the rooms whose surfaces had already been smoothed of ornament. They worked slowly and cautiously, half expecting that the inmates of the house, who stood about crossing items off lists, would change their minds, or stampede to the front steps to say a last goodbye. But there was no interruption, and when they came to the attic they had the place to themselves.

Downstairs, the family – all five of them – were sitting round the table in the dining-room. There was nothing on the table, and they sat silently in the fading light, looking before them and listening as intently as people at a séance, waiting for the vibrations to start. The first indication of movement in the attic was the faint smell of dust which sifted down to them from three floors above – a familiar enough smell, but one which this evening gave to their nostrils a sensation lively as the tingle of snuff. Then they knew that the soft quilt of stuff on top was being gradually moved. It was not much yet, but they could feel it slowly lifting from them, as though a heavy swathe of hair was being lifted up and cut from their aching heads. Next they heard the grinding of things being forced painfully from the positions they had held for years, and the formidable thud and rattle as they were dragged down from stair to stair on to the landing below. It seemed as though the whole house was splitting from the top; and automatically the family below raised their hands to their heads. When they removed them again the noise overhead had stopped. Up there was silence and emptiness. Still the grinding and thudding went on in the corridor beside them, but a pressure had been removed from the top of their skulls and from the nerves at the back of their necks. It was even easier to hold up their heads, they discovered, and they lifted them quickly now to watch Edith who had got up from the table and was whipping off the photos from the mantelpiece and windowsill, from desks and bookcases and the tops of china-cupboards. In a few seconds the eyes which had not wavered for years – eyes grave, wistful, stern and piercing, but all terrible in their watchfulness – and disappeared. The photos, in a neat pile with faces down, had been placed in a corner of the sideboard. It was as easy as that to be rid of onlookers. The people round the table allowed themselves to smile at the audacity of this idea, but nevertheless a conspirator's brightness shone from their own eyes as they glanced about.

Though relieved of the pressure in their chests and heads, they slept badly that night. Like people unused to a rarefied atmosphere, they were restless and their nerves were on edge; and after twelve o'clock the wind began. At first it was only a breeze from the open windows – a welcome fluttering of curtains and loose papers breaking the stillness. In half an hour the wind had risen to a hysterical note, and gusts of rain, sharp as nails, struck tiles and windows and swept through the chips of gravel on the path, grinding them together with a sound like pebbles grinding on the shore. In the early hours of the morning, when the gale was at its height, the house, without its ballast, shook like a hollow ship at sea, and from all parts came a drumming, a rattling and a banging as though doors and windows had been suddenly prised open to let the furies in. But nobody got up to investigate. As though by a mutual agreement from they day before, they lay rigid the whole night through – letting the house rip.

In the morning Edith was up first. The others, waking slowly from their first, deep sleep, heard her voice calling to them from overhead, and giving themselves time for only a glance at the flooded garden, they dressed and went up to find her. She stood in a corner of the empty attic, sur-rounded by all the buckets and basins she had collected together and listening with interest to the variation of notes struck from them by the rapid drops of water falling from the roof. Craters and grey rings of damp covered the celling and the floor was thick with drifts of plaster which had blown far and wide, so that even the webs in distant corners were hung with a fine white dust.

'But there is more to see down below,' said Edith, after

they had listened to a full range of musical notes for some time. Following her down through the house, they were soon aware that, in the attic, they had only seen where the softening-up had taken place – a crumbling at the top which had convulsed the body of the building with more spectacular results.

The house had plainly given up. It had allowed the screws to loosen and the hinges to crack, and let the watery blisters rise under the face of paint. Tiles, sticking grimly to the roof through the storms of years, had been lifted in a matter of minutes, like slices of bread off a board. The glass lay everywhere. Long splinters were piled under the broken windows, and shining crumbs of it, fine as sugar, crunched under their feet in odd corners as they moved about. Throughout the morning they came on the fragments inside old shoes or in the folds of newspapers. They cut their fingers on it in the fringes of rugs and down the sides of armchairs. In every fireplace a heap of soot had fallen and lay, thickly quilting hearths and rugs and thinning out to sift with the leaves and plaster around passages where the cold wind still blew. It was difficult, they discovered, to get out of their own front door. Pushing against a bank of sodden leaves and twigs, they came face to face with a great, jagged branch which had fallen against the steps, and was still quivering and clawing at the door with a persistency which made them draw back at once into the hall with a feeling of panic. For as long as the scraping went on they remained inside, whispering and peering occasionally out into the garden through the slot of the letter-box.

Only when the wind had died down did they begin to hear the complaint of the house itself. There was a creaking and a wheezing about them, and a far-off rattling of un-identified broken things from places which they had not yet investigated. They could hear the heavy shifting of the house through all its loosened boards and joints, like a patient cautiously turning over to feel which of his limbs pain him most, and from overhead a faint whine and whistle in the chimneys and a half-hearted hiss as another puff of soot came down. But above all it was the huge sighing of the building which they heard, as a last gust of wind blew through it from end to end. They recognized it at once as a sigh which came from the bottom of its heart – a heart from which, in the last week, they had extracted as much life-blood as it was possible to take away without a complete collapse ensuing. The foreboding which, since morning, had increased in all of them except Edith, they now diagnosed in one another as the growing pangs of guilt.

Edith had now to work harder than she had ever done before to disperse the atmosphere of this guilt which hung about the place and threatened to thicken and congeal in the empty spaces where they had felt such light-heartedness only a few days before. She set about the task bravely, but at times it was too much even for her.

'It is a case of complete breakdown, I am sorry to say,' she would remark, as she came across further signs of damage in the next few days. 'We have done everything we could for it all these years. No people could have done more. But now is the time to make a change. Luckily for us, we have done most of the moving already – we have only ourselves to take away now. If other people can move themselves, so can we.'

But they were not convinced. Indeed if they had taken pickaxes and sledge-hammers to the house, they could not have felt more responsible for the damage. Nevertheless, it could perhaps be patched and propped again. The harm was extensive but not, after all, so serious. If necessary they could even pack the place up with furniture again – they could replace and rebuild and reorganize, and in a few years they might manage to make up to the house something of what it had lost and suffered at their hands. They would take it upon themselves.

'We will take it upon ourselves.' This was the phrase they repeated over and over again in answer to all the consolation and suggestion which Edith offered them. Already they were sagging under the weight. Again they had begun to assume the resigned, identical expressions of a united family – still shaken, but ready for their folly to be forgiven and forgotten. Very soon they would try to go back, not to where they had started, but far further back to a state of absolute and unquestioning innocence. Decidedly, they were to give up the rest of their lives to regain favour with God and house.

Their elder sister now began to search the place methodically from top to bottom, as though her own life depended on it. She would disappear early in the day, to be found hours later, moving about on her knees in some dark corner, or lying flat on her back, prodding and knocking on a low slant of roof above her head; or they would hear her in some distant part of the house, stamping slowly about in a circle, as though engaged in some ritual dance of her own. There were times when they wondered whether she might be searching for hidden treasure, known only to herself, or thumping the walls to find some secret cupboard where the family fortune lay. Most of the time, however, they took little notice and seldom mentioned it amongst themselves. The possibilities in human nature had only lately been opened up to them, and it was a discovery which, given time and their usual routine, they hoped would one day be completely forgotten as though it had never been made.

Meantime Edith appeared to have lost interest in the damage in the house. She passed by the wastes of damp, the cracking plaster and broken windows many times every day, with scarcely a glance, and made no comment when, after six days, slater and plasterer had failed to turn up. Nor did she comment on the limitations of her three brothers who stood about much of the time with their loose, clean hands at their sides or deep in the pockets of jackets which they had never removed. She had nothing to say about all this because she had better things to hope for. She was hoping in fact for bigger and deeper damage – damage long-standing, spectacular and terrible to cure. Dry rot was her aim.

She found what she was looking for one evening in a small unused bedroom downstairs, which until lately had contained a chest-of-drawers, a bed, and a marble washstand with ewers. There was nothing here now except one cane chair against the wall and a picture over the fireplace. Where the furniture had been, pale shapes, complete with knobs and spirals, were traced on the wallpaper, and above them, one long rectangular strip where a school photo had hung, keeping in living memory for over sixty years two hundred boys in striped blazers and tabbed socks. The remaining picture was a sombre reproduction in brown and white, but its subject was a garden in midsummer, where a family of young men and women were giving a tea party to their friends. There was nothing sombre about these people; they were obviously a frolicking crowd with generous and careless habits. Fruit of all kinds had been allowed to spill from baskets into the grass where tame birds pecked at it. A puppy was lapping up the milk running from a jug which had been knocked over in the midst of some game, or perhaps by the foot of the girl in a white dress who was swinging in a hammock above. Behind her in the distance could be seen an imposing house, not unlike their own, and at the gate stood an eager young man, identical with the other men in the picture, but showing by his anxious face and his untidy necktie that he had seen the world and found it wanting, and was now only too thankful to be back. As she stared at this picture – *A Homecoming* – Edith stamped mechanically but strenuously at the floorboards beneath it.

She did not need to stamp long. After a minute her foot went softly through the crumbling wood and a long piece of boarding fell in, covered on its inner side with a thick web of greyish-white strands, blotched here and there with blue and yellow patches. Edith fell on her knees and peered down into the area which had suddenly split open under her eyes. It was a place of primeval dampness and darkness, smelling of must and decay, but seeming, at first sight, to be nothing more than a disagreeable hollow under the floor. As she became accustomed to the darkness, however, she saw that what she stared into was not an empty hole but a world, well-established and powerful, where a secret growth had been going on, over months or years, spreading insidiously about the roots of the house. Here and there, springing out of the darkness, white blotches could be seen, stuck like tufts of cotton wool to the rotting wood, and between the black cracks spongey, yellowing mushrooms grew out. Further down, spread widely over the level places, was a layer of poisonous-looking red powder. Only one corner had been opened up, but Edith knew she knelt over a place where life had spawned and spread in the darkness over a vast area, wider and deeper than anything she had imagined during her rapping and stamping of the past week.

'This, at any rate, had nothing to do with us,' said Edith, when she had summoned the family together. 'The place will die of it sooner or later, if nothing is done. No doubt something will be done. But not by us. We brought it safely through its choked drains and its damp spots. We patched it up where it was thin. Pruned it down where it bulged. We can't forget the money spent to give it space to expand at the back, the cost of the paint it soaked up, year after year, to prevent the rust from getting it! But the cure of this is beyond us. We have our own health to think of. We are not surgeons or nurses to stand by at operations of this scale! Let it go to somebody else. As for us, there is nothing else for it – we must get out and stay out!'

As they stepped forward, one after the other, to look down into the opening, they breathed an air which smelt not only of decay, but also of certain freedom. This time they saw there was nothing more for them to do. Under these boards conscience could be finally buried. They would pack up and leave the place forever.

On a dark morning in the middle of November, they stood together for the last time outside the front door of the house.

'We have everything to look forward to!' exclaimed Edith after a long silence, while they braced themselves for the final departure. It was true, at any rate, that they were looking straight in front of them now – down the stony drive, and beyond it to the bleak stretches of empty fields, already beginning to darken under the rain. It was not, after all, the whole world which was before them, but a small hotel nearby, from where they would carry on the long-drawn-out negotiations over the head of the house. California and the decks of the ocean liners were as far off as they had ever been, and it was too late to group themselves, as their relations had done many times before them, for an exuberant send-off photo on the front steps of the house. The men required every scrap of jauntiness still left in them simply to carry the luggage down to the gates, and the women, worn out with their own displays of excitement and enthusiasm, had let their faces fall again, and now longed only to settle as soon as possible under some other roof.

They did not look back when they came to the gates, and when they were beyond them they did not immediately shake the dust of the place from their feet, for nothing as soft as dust had been under them. But the three men put down their cases and sat down outside to remove, for the last time, the cruel pieces of gravel which had lodged in the heels of their shoes. This done, and walking with greater confidence and dignity, they passed out of sight of the house forever.

# The Spark

'I FIND IT strange, Mr Abson, that your face doesn't change much at the things I've been telling you. But you do listen, don't you?'

'I listen, Mrs Imrie. I find what you say very interesting.'

' "Interesting"! But you do *feel* what I'm saying to you? About the little puffs of smoke between the tiles . . . the dog howling at the back?'

Abson was thoughtful for a few minutes, his round, black eyebrows raised, melancholy eyes fixed on the floor.

'Later, Mrs Imrie. Things come over me later. When I've had time.'

'When you've had time? But you have lots of time, Mr Abson. Who's disturbing us? You're a person of feeling, aren't you? A person would need to be inhuman not to respond to what I've just told you.'

'That's how I'm made, Mrs Imrie.'

'How? Not inhuman, I hope?'

'I mean I go over things later.'

'Later? How late?'

'Indeed I am not!' exclaimed a girl who had just opened the door. 'It's all your crazy clocks running on again!'

'I'm not referring to you, Brenda,' said her mother. 'I'm talking to Mr Abson here who feels everything later than other people.'

The girl shrugged herself through the room and over to a corner where she hung up her coat and stared close and long at a small mirror. As she watched her daughter combing out her hair the woman at the table seemed at ease, as though her own nerves were being combed out strand by strand from the knotted frizzle they had got into while sitting too long with the passive Mr Abson. But after a while she turned to him again, speaking, however, in a more patient and relaxed tone.

'How late do you mean, Mr Abson?'

The man gave his peculiar half-sigh. That is to say, he drew in his breath, held it for a while, and expelled it almost without a sound. But, halved like this, it was also irritating, as though he had no wish to give generously of his feelings – even feelings of desperation – like other people.

'How late, then?' Mrs Imrie repeated.

'At night. When I go to my own room. In bed probably. I go over things when I'm in bed. I suppose that's what I usually do.'

It was quieter in the room. The girl had stopped combing her hair, or she was combing it very lightly. The woman took up some sewing again. 'You mean things don't strike you right off? Even funny things you see or hear?' Mr Abson turned his eyes towards the window, but said nothing.

'I suppose that means you don't sleep well.'

'Not always.'

'I'm glad I'm not troubled like that. With me it's when my head touches the pillow. Or when would I ever get my work done next day? I've no time to think day *or* night, it seems!' She sewed steadily for a bit, and once she whispered: 'The whole roof caving in . . !'

After a while Mr Abson gathered up some papers from the table into a brief-case and prepared to go into the other room which was officially his for the evenings if the family were not entertaining visitors in there. They had only a very hazy idea of his job for he had not talked much about this. But they knew his firm made tiles and pots and mugs, and they associated him with a peculiar foreign jar they had once seen there – long, black and white, narrowing at the top to show that nothing was to be got out of it and nothing

put in except perhaps a bare twig or two. And yet with a
mournful, drooping lip to it.

'Don't go unless you must,' said Mrs Imrie. 'It'll probably take a bit to heat up in there. Jim and May will be back
soon and we'll have a cup then.'

'I'll come back later then, if I may,' said Abson. He went
out and they heard the door of the other room close behind
him.

'Always later!' exclaimed Mrs Imrie. 'I'm afraid later's
not much use to me. I've got to have the laughs on the dot,
and the crying too. And I like a gasp when it's tragedy –
even a blink would be enough. *Something*. When I told the
butcher about them throwing the twin babies out of the
window and the fireman nearly gone himself with the
smoke, he doubled over as though he'd a pain here –
doubled over his knife. Mrs Liddel did more. She wailed
out loud.'

'There *was* a safety-net, wasn't there?'

'Has the world gone quite heartless? Yes, there *was* a
safety-net. And lots of people down below, including that
mother – watching her two babies being thrown, one after
the other, out of a fourth-storey window!'

'Anyway, they're safe. No damage done.'

'Talk about sleeping! Imagine that poor woman's dreams
when she does close her eyes. Will she ever get it out of her
head? No she will not. Some people have reason to lie
awake at night.'

'We don't know what's in Mr Abson's head.'

'No, we don't. Whatever it is, it doesn't show on the face.
The strangest thing about buildings when they collapse is
the slowness. It's like a slow-motion picture. A sag here and
a bulging there, and a slow, slow puff of dust.'

'I've seen something like it on TV.'

'The sparks are dangerous. I believe they can travel
miles.'

'And still keep alive?'

'Seemingly. In a wind.'

'Surely not miles?'

'A long distance. You think they're dead, and the next thing you know there's a fire blazing away miles from the first place.'

'A single spark,' said the girl.

'But if it's alive, after all – and travelling fast.'

'A dark spark,' said the girl again, brooding on it.

'And more dangerous for not shining,' said her mother.

They sat in silence for a few minutes till the girl took up her comb again and began on her hair. This time there was a faint cracking and she laughed. 'More sparks,' she said, drawing out a strand and letting it float free from her head.

'Look, leave your hair alone,' said her mother, 'and get that comb away from the table.'

Later on, twenty minutes or so before her brother was due back, the girl knocked on the door opposite and opened it. Mr Abson was sitting there with his papers at a small table. The room had not heated up and as she spoke she could see the little white puffs of breath before her in the air.

'You haven't put on the light yet. Shall I come in?'

'Yes, come in,' said Abson. 'Have your brother and his fiancée arrived?'

'Not yet. "Fiancée" is idiotic. Why do you keep using that word?'

'I took it for granted.'

'Well don't. You haven't been here long or you'd know the number of girls he's brought home already. We keep off the word.'

'What is the play they're rehearsing?'

'I'm not very interested to talk about them. I don't know what it is. All I know is he's a sailor and she's a schoolmistress. Have you noticed how nearly all the women in these plays turn out to be teachers? Last year he was a painter and she taught Algebra. In the end they show they can take off their glasses and everything else the same as other women. But of course only for sailors, painters or murderers. Is that fair? Never for anyone else – never a male teacher, for instance.'

'Is your brother a good actor, then?'

'I'm not interested in that. But there's one thing. I've been behind the scenes when they're taking the paint off.'

'Yes?'

'It's strange, frightening maybe. They take a blob of grease and wipe off a pair of round, black eyebrows, or a frown or a luscious pair of lips. They can clear patches of white fright from their cheeks in one stroke – grease off a blush as quickly as you'd wipe round a dinner-plate, and underneath, when they've wiped off every mark, their faces are dull . . . dull!'

'It's not that. But undramatic perhaps. Unexaggerated.'

'No. Dull. When you take off eyebrows, for instance, the surprise goes out of the face. Yours is the opposite.'

'Mine. My what?'

'Your face, Mr Abson. When you wipe it off, yours must be exciting.'

There was silence in the room. The man turned his eyes slowly, still keeping his head stiff.

'When I say "wipe off" I'm not referring to paint, with you, of course.'

'No? What, then, could I wipe off?'

'I've no idea what it could be.'

'I take it you find the surface dull – no dramatic eyes or lips?'

'But underneath – exciting.'

'Where exactly does it break through?'

'It doesn't. But I can infer it, from what you say. At night, for instance, in your own room.'

'Miss Imrie, if you're trying to make up for anything your mother said – don't bother. She's been good to me. She likes me well enough even if I do get on her nerves. And I'm not to be here long. Why bother yourself?'

'Miss Imrie! Part of your trouble's politeness. Like fiancée. Politeness dulls the face. It's nothing to do with my mother, though naturally she likes excitement. She imagined that being abroad so long you'd have lots to talk about. But it hasn't worked like that and she doesn't hold it against you. It's a dull street, that's all. A dull street, a dull town, a dull country. We're pretty dull here compared with lots of them, aren't we?'

'And she has a feeling for drama like your brother?'

'She likes the applause and the gasps when she has something good to tell.'

'Something good?'

'Ah, you know what I mean. Don't fold up. Don't start moralising. I mean good and bad at the same time. Everyone likes sparks and fire-bells. Why else would they come running?'

'And the screams?'

'There were no screams. And no one was hurt.'

'There would be bigger crowds for screams, I can tell you that.'

The girl sat still and watched him. After a while she sighed, took the comb from the pocket of her jacket and drew it smoothly down one side of her head from the middle parting, bending her head right over so that the hair swung out away from her neck and ear. Her upturned eyes showed a rim of white round the lower lid and gave her a look of fixed surprise.

'It's not quite dark enough yet,' she said, 'and maybe not the right sort of day – but often, when I do this, I can get not just crackling, but actual sparks as well. Frost and darkness are the best. I know,' she smiled, 'that it can't happen often with men. There's got to be plenty of hair for it – something you haven't got. But more spectacular still . . .' she paused and smiled again into the dim room, 'is the last thing I take off at night. It's not just sparks but flashes. The quicker it's done, the brighter. If I rip off the vest and toss it away I can get great, blue flashes that sting my arms and back. And if the room is absolutely black it's like lightning – crackling, stinging lightning. But the stuff's got to be silky, nylon and that sort of thing. Nothing dull or thick. Not everyone believes this. People can get very stuffy about electricity too, you know, as though it ought to be confined solely to lamp-bulbs.'

'There's your brother now,' said the man, unstiffening to the sound of the key in the front door.

'Is it? There's another thing. Some people think you're getting sexy if you say "sparks in the hair". "Electricity" is as good as an invitation, and if it's electricity and underwear they're waiting to be eaten up.'

'Yes, it *is* them,' said the man. 'I can hear the girl too.'

'. . . Waiting to be eaten alive or ready to pounce themselves. It comes to the same thing,' said the girl. 'No, that's my mother's cousin. She's got a key and comes in on Tuesday nights if there's anything she wants to watch. No, it's early for them yet. The sad thing about those ones – whether they're waiting or pouncing – is they're still dull, terribly dull and sad.'

'You've little idea at your age how tired people can become,' said the man.

'At my age! Some of my friends are as tired right now as they'll ever be. Tireder, for instance, than my mother ever was or ever will be. Tired wasn't what I was talking about. It was dullness. A mean, suspicious, greedy, beady-eyed dullness, if you can imagine that!'

The man gave a laugh. He put his hands to his face and rubbed it hard for a moment, first his forehead, then his cheeks. He was breathing quickly.

'What's that for? Are you cold?'

'Maybe. I'm trying to wake up, warm up. Anything to scrub off those words.'

'Those words were meant to go over your head. They're nothing to do with you. Not one of them landed on you – so you can stop scrubbing.'

Abson's hands were suddenly still, his fists clenched at the sides of his head. He turned on her angrily exclaiming: 'And you! Look – you can stop nagging! Stop lecturing me!'

'That's better,' said the girl, leaning her elbow on the table so that now the other wing of hair hung down to touch his papers. 'I don't mean to nag. I think a lot *of* you, and a lot about you. And do you know *how* I think of you? I think of you as a sort of dark spark.'

There was a tremendous crash from the outer door on the word 'spark' and a sound of voices filled the hall. The wall behind them rattled with the buttons of overcoats being flung at the pegs on the other side, and there was a thumping on the wainscoting where heavy shoes were kicked off.

'That can't be just the two of them,' said the girl, straightening up and folding her hair back behind her ears. 'Maybe they've brought the whole group back. There's five there at least. Do you hear five?'

'But have they *got* to have the wind through the whole scene?' a voice was calling out plaintively in the hall. 'And has it got to be a *gale*? Two pages! Tenderly! Have you ever tried speaking *tenderly* with a howling gale at your ear?'

'A dark what?' said Abson.

'It's the last scene,' said the girl. 'They're talking about the bit where the two of them – I told you about the sailor and this woman – they're waiting for news of his son in the storm. There's a bridge been blown down or something.'

'A dark *what* did you say I was?' said the man.

'Just a minute,' said the girl. 'Listen! How many actually are there? I'm not going out there till I know. If it's five then it means Ben's around. I'm not going out there if that Ben has attached himself again. Well, it can't be helped. I'll never know if I don't look, will I? Are you coming out?'

'Not yet,' said Abson.

'Later then,' said the girl. When she opened the door a brilliant shaft of light and noise cut through the dark room.

The man inside had a glimpse of a boy sitting on the bottom stair taking his boots off and a young woman leaning against the wall unknotting a headscarf. The girl's sudden appearance in the hall caused a moment's silence then a burst of acclaim from at least five voices. She passed through them, leading the way into the other room and they went after, dropping the boots and waterproofs, shaking the rain from their hair. They followed her and the door closed beyond. Suddenly the hall was silent. It was quite silent and empty.

A long time later the group in the sitting-room heard steps going upstairs – or rather the boy who had sat taking his boots off on the stairs heard them. He was now leaning with his elbow on the hearthrug eating toast and he held up his knife with the butter on it for silence.

'Who is it?' he asked.

'I'll get him,' said Mrs Imrie, and she went out to find him already round the corner of the stairs. 'Why, you can't go up yet. It's early. Aren't you taking a cup with us before you disappear?'

'For a few minutes – with pleasure,' said Abson, coming down slowly.

Like her daughter, Mrs Imrie felt that politeness at this moment was a mistake. Why 'pleasure' with his face? With his reluctant steps? She had once had someone who, called down like this, had stuck his head in the door, made hideous faces at a group of old ladies and withdrawn. And been loved for it.

'Creaks on the stairs,' remarked the boy at the fireplace, watching Mr Abson who was now sitting with a cup of tea in his hand. 'That reminds me.'

'Go on!' voices encouraged him. 'Give us the story!'

'No, it's not a story. There's nothing to it.'

'Go on!' they shouted.

'Not a story – not an experience even. A sensation. A stirring of the hairs of the head. It was this perfectly

ordinary suburban villa belonging to a schoolfriend's family
– an ordinary red and yellow brick affair.'

'All right. Don't worry,' said someone. 'It was ordinary.
We got that.'

'I was staying the weekend. I had my dog with me. Well,
each evening at the same time – eight o'clock – footsteps
going upstairs. The first time I said "Who is it?" – nobody'd heard them. And the second night: "Who is it?"
Nobody heard them. The third night – same thing. No one
had ever heard them except me.'

'The dog?' murmured someone who'd heard the story.

'I'm coming to that. Each time it happened the dog
would get up and whine at the door of this room until I let
him out. We'd both stand at the foot of the stairs waiting for
the last creaks going up at the top. Then the dog would give
one yelp, turn his back to the stairs and sit huddled up to
me without moving a muscle. It happened three times. In
the end the family, including the schoolfriend, had taken an
intense dislike to both of us. Can you blame them? Each
time they came out of their cosy, plush drawing-room they
saw me gaping up the stairs and the dog hunched round the
other way. They could hardly wait to get rid of us. In the
end I had to carry my own suitcase to the station in the
pouring rain. I can still see myself trudging past their long,
cream car at the front gate. The schoolfriend hardly spoke
to me again – avoided me as though I had the plague. Well –
there you are. A gloomy silence in the audience. Didn't I
tell you you'd be disappointed?'

'No, not a bit,' said a girl from the other side of the room.
'The fact that it lacks all drama makes it more real. Now I
know it happened.'

'Thanks.'

'Even in spite of, or because of the dog. Because prowl-
ing, howling dogs are common in ghost stories. But yours
just sits there on the mat. He's a pet. He's sweet. I know
him.'

'Thanks again. His name is Brown. I suspected it was a boring little tale.'

'Surely not just Brown?'

'Simply and literally Brown. Nothing more nor less.'

'Well anyway, I liked the way you made nothing of your sensations. I think that's drama, or is it anti-drama? Nothing more about your hair rising. Or your sweaty palms.'

'I don't know what it is, but whatever it is, it hasn't got over the footlights.'

'I adore ghost stories!' exclaimed Mrs Imrie.

'Mr Abson,' the boy said, 'did you ever do any acting when you were young?' He was leaning against the fireside wall with his knees drawn up and he now gave his full attention to the older man. This attention was compelling as though silently, deliberately, almost while they were unaware, he had smoothly pivoted the focus of the whole room round in one direction. By the steadiness of his eyes, the absolute stillness of his thin hands – clasped together and just touching his lips as though he were preparing for an absorbing story – he silenced the rest of the group. They might have been under iron command not to move. Nobody moved or spoke.

'No, I never did,' replied Abson. Mrs Imrie gave a faint, a very faint, exasperated sigh.

'Well no, I suppose that's not absolutely correct,' said Abson, nervously smiling. 'I was, as a boy, I remember, once given the part of a tree in some play or other.'

'Yes?' came the boy's voice, quick and serious. There was unusual power in this young man. By split-second timing, by the sheer force of his expression and tone of voice, he had prevented a burst of laughter from the rest of the room.

'Well, I suppose you wouldn't really call it a play – it was probably a kind of ballet,' said Mr Abson, still smiling, though there were no answering smiles from the others. 'It didn't, you'll agree, need great dramatic gifts.'

'On the contrary,' said the young man at once.

'I beg your pardon?' Abson looked surprised.

'On the contrary it would need rather special dramatic gifts to express this.'

'Well, hardly human ones.'

'Superhuman, then. Did you enjoy it?'

'I think I did, now that you remind me. I'd really absolutely forgotten the experience.'

'Perhaps there were others.'

'Others?'

'Perhaps there were other parts?'

'I don't think so – unless you count noises off. Anything I was asked to do was strictly non-human or background.'

'To do a tree you've got to be more human, not less. You've got to be so human you can reach people and even go beyond them. That way you might just hope to arrive at your trees and rocks. Isn't that so?'

'Yes, that's an interesting point,' said Mr Abson.

'What kind of tree was it?' asked the young man.

'An apple tree,' said Abson. There were still no smiles.

'In blossom or with apples?' asked the young man.

'Just leaves,' said Mr Abson, remembering so much now that his face was warm for once. His eyes stared from a nucleus of shadowy, scalloped green. 'And an interesting thing I remember – it was not to be a tree in the wind. That was definitely ruled out. Yet you'd have thought they'd have insisted on wind to make absolutely sure people knew what they were looking at.'

'No, too obvious. All that thrashing and swooshing about, as though all trees must be in perpetual gales to show they really are trees. What rot!'

'Well, maybe you're right. Anyway, I had to make only the smallest movements – a kind of microscopic growing.'

'Oh God – that's difficult enough!'

'Not much more than a vibration – I'm not sure about this.'

'Your producer was a master then?'

'He was quite a talented young man, I think,' said Abson mildly. 'A vibration, or was it perhaps the dry bark cracking a bit in the sun?'

'God knows!' exclaimed the young man, at last permitting himself to smile. At once the rest of the group released themselves from his control. The red-haired girl put her head back on to the knee of the man behind who after simply lifting up strands of the long hair and letting them drop, began plunging his fingers up from the roots, tugging so roughly through the knots that the girl had her eyes screwed up each time his hand came down. It looked like torture but when her eyes were open the expression was blissful. Mrs Imrie put the cup she had been holding all this time down on to its saucer. Neither the ghost nor the tree had exactly electrified the atmosphere for her. She decided that at a suitable moment she would give them the roof crashing in the night with the sparks flying off, and the butcher bent double over his bloody trembling knife.

'Well, I suppose I should be getting up now,' said Mr Abson. 'I've very much enjoyed . . . but I think I'd better . . .'

'With your early start in the morning . . .' Mrs Imrie agreed, rising briskly to accompany him to the hall. But the boy who sat at the fire was before her. It was now almost an acrobatic feat to cross the room over the outstretched legs but he was up and out at the same moment as Mr Abson started to go slowly up, one hand on the banister. Through the open door they saw the young man go round to the side of the staircase and walk down the passage, sliding his own hand up the banister as far as it would go. For the last few inches he had to stand on his toes reaching out, his long fingers stretched hard against the wood, his body, straight and tense from head to foot, leaning forward at an angle along the banister. This sight gave the one or two who were

watching a strange frisson of dread or elation. They
watched a contact missed by inches, an effort to reach still
further, doomed. Mr Abson's hand moved smoothly on up
the banister. He disappeared round the bend of the stairs
without looking back. For a few moments longer the boy
remained stretched out. Then his arm dropped like a
weight. Mrs Imrie's daughter joined him in the hall.

'Poor ghost,' said the young man, turning slowly from
the stairs. 'One of you should take a look at him now and
then. Just once in a while – look at him, will you?'

'I do. Honestly I do. Before you all arrived we were
having a long talk.'

'Or he'll fade out. He'll absolutely fade out.'

'Don't you think we look after him well?'

'Look after – yes. Look *at* him!'

'Why should he fade out? I see him as a sort of dark
spark. He can be brought to life all right. But it takes
constant fanning. Bellows even.'

'Use them then!' He went quickly past her into the room
where Mrs Imrie had already started the conflagration.
Chimneys were crashing in the street, red, green and
orange flames unravelled from window to window, and
from one a white bundle dropped, then another, to the
gasping crowd below. Great swirls of living sparks were
being blown for miles along the rooftops. No gush of water
could quench these. No hosepipe, however long, catch up
with them.

Mr Abson stayed with the Imries for two months more
and then his work, whatever it was, took him to a neighbouring town where he remained another three months.
And there he died. Three months ago. They had almost
forgotten him. Or at any rate his face was not absolutely
clear any more. But the manner of his death which they
found in a newspaper, hearing further details from an
acquaintance who lived in that town, jolted their memory
in a peculiar way. He had failed to get out of the way of a

lorry, the paper said. He had stepped out, said a witness, and stood still.

'No, it was not deliberate, if that's what you mean,' said Mrs Imrie to a friend who had come in. 'If it says "failed to get out of the way" then that's exactly what it means. I wouldn't say, now I come to think of it, that I ever saw him do *anything* exactly deliberately, would you, Brenda?'

'Never. It would be that he didn't know whether to put his feet backwards or forwards. I've seen him do just that on the thresholds of doors.'

'You will never really know, will you?' said the friend.

'Never know what?'

'Nothing. It's all right.'

'It's terrible,' said Mrs Imrie. 'Poor man, he should have shown more in his face. That would have helped him. It would have helped people to take notice of him too.'

'He would be clear enough to the lorry-driver,' said her son. 'It's going to add another ghastly hazard to life if you're only visible to motorists if you've got an interesting expression.'

'He only thought of things later when he was in his own room. That wasn't good for him, was it? Like secret drinking or something. I should have interrupted him oftener.'

'Why are we talking like this? Could we help that bloody great lorry bearing down on him?'

'Oh, how I sometimes wanted to give him a push!' exclaimed Mrs Imrie. 'If I could have given him a push when he was standing there – one hard push – it would have saved him!'

'Rooted. Rooted to the spot,' said the girl. 'What does that remind you of? Are you thinking of a tree?'

'Am I *what*?' said her mother.

'If he'd even learnt to dance, oddly enough,' said the girl. 'There are people who learn to dance simply to help them move their feet properly – to balance themselves. Did you know that? Hospitals send them.'

'Hospitals now!' cried Mrs Imrie, holding her hand to her head. 'So now you make out he was a sort of patient. Some kind of case, I suppose.'

'It never even crossed my mind. I simply remember he sometimes asked about dances I'd been to.'

'Near enough a case,' said the friend, 'if he just stood there.'

'What are we talking about now?' said Mrs Imrie. 'Has it come round to this again? "Failed to get out of the way" – I interpret that simply as I see it set down on the page.'

'If you can see it simply,' the friend said.

During the next few days they could have been no more acutely aware of Abson had be been following them around from room to room over the whole house. His death lit him up for them. He flickered with a red, unnatural light which flared or sank as their feelings about him flared or died. He was not silent. His identity demanded constant discussion and examination. Yet what did they know about him? They had scraped their memories. At the end of the week the girl, for the second time, rang the young man who had sat by the fire.

'You'll come round and help us out, won't you?'

'If I can. Are you still brooding?'

'Oh, we're stuck. It's hateful. We'd almost forgotten him. And now this. We've got to start again, and there's nothing to go on. He didn't talk about himself and neither did we.'

'Why not forget him again?'

'How can I? I've got to get him clear first, if he's to be properly washed out. What was he like?'

'Look – I met him once only – at your house.'

'But you had a feeling for him. Say something about him.'

'It's you who must say it. Or you'll be haunted.'

'Haunted by nothing! All I can think of is a spark and a tree. And don't ask why. I don't remember how they came in or when.'

'Well think of them, then. Think hard!'

Later that evening, still having nothing to go on, she did think of them; for she was standing outside the open door of his room looking in at the place where, according to him, he had gone over and over things. What things? It was bare-looking now – a small room but with a high ceiling speckled in minute and scabby stars. A tree might grow in here. With an effort she could see it – this dry, grey tree with branches twisted at right angles round the corners of the ceiling and roots that had to bend back to fit the wainscoting. A rustling, creaking, cracking thing, dry to its sapless marrow. At first the dark spark settled lightly there like a crumb of dry ash, dead in the dead, bedroom air. Nothing kindled it here. It needed nothing, but took its life from some stupendous unknown fire blazing away miles from here. And gradually a microscopic speck of red began to burn at its centre. No movement fanned it, but still it expanded, fraying at its edges into palpitating spangles of rose-colour. Suddenly it rup-tured, falling away into other sparks which went rolling and spinning along the branches, dropping down and falling apart again, multiplying, sprouting buds and shoots, roots, leaves, blossoms and fruits of green and yellow fire. The tree burned in silence. No part of it was reflected on the walls or the star-scabbed ceiling, and not a spark or speck of ash fell to the ground. At last a single white flame burst from the root and ripped up the length of the tree, reducing it in one flash, like the slashing upstroke of a knife, to ash and blackness. Then to nothing. Spark and tree went out.

'I feel better about him now,' the girl told her mother and brother that night after supper. 'I can put him out of my mind.'

'How's that?' her mother asked.

'When you put everything together, looking back, you can see he was really alive.'

'Was he?' said her brother. 'But now he's dead.'

'He wasn't dead all the time though. Not grey as we

thought. If he'd been dead alive as well as dead dead – that
would finish me! But I can forget him!'

'But he's dead *now*,' said her brother. 'He stepped off a
pavement.'

'I prefer to think of it as going up in flame,' said the girl.
'It suits him – the way I'm thinking about him now. The
way he was really alive all the time.'

'Prefer all you like,' said her brother, 'but that's the way it
was. He stepped off a pavement.'

'Don't remind me of that fire,' said her mother with a
shudder. 'Don't ever bring that up again.'

# A Visit to the Zoo

THE SHOCKING TITLE, stinging us instantly to attention, was read out one afternoon amongst the usual fortnightly choice of essay subjects: *A Visit to the Zoo*. We were in the highest class of boys and due to leave school in a few months. After a stunned silence these words were greeted with incredulous whistlings, loud and prolonged hoots, sickened groans and a great shuffling and stamping from the back seats where young men with brilliantined hair and narrow shoes were sitting, casually hacking great slivers from the underside of their desks with outsized penknives. Our English master, who was new to the job and unsure of himself, quickly withdrew the subject, explaining that it had got mixed in with a set from some lower form. But the damage was done and it was a long time before the class settled down. A sense of outrage hung menacingly around, ready to ignite explosively with the chalk and dust in the dried-out air at the first hint of further offence. Gradually, however, still muttering savage threats, we sank heavily to the business of writing, after making our reluctant choice between *The Advantages and Disadvantages of a Political Career* and *The Dangers and Benefits of the Space Age* – giving only a scornful glance at *Whirlpool* which had been thrown in as the sop to those who had more imagination than knowledge. Yet throughout the whole hour from its blank beginning to the frenzied bout of last-minute writing, I felt the impact of that subject which had been withdrawn. It was indeed the one topic which for a long time I had been at pains to avoid, but here it was now forcing itself up unexpectedly like something painfully green and fresh amongst all those stony opinions which I was doggedly setting down on paper.

Almost three years before a young woman had come to live with my family for several weeks. I knew nothing about her except that she was a cousin of my mother's, that she was convalescing from a serious illness and that she expected to be left quite free all day to go out and in as she pleased. Two or three bottles of brilliant-coloured tonics, placed there by my mother, appeared on the bathroom shelf amongst our normal collection of dingy brown ones, throwing stained-glass wedges of light into the bath on sunny days but remaining corked throughout her visit. Nor did she appear to follow up any of the suggestions being offered on all sides as to the best method of 'taking her out of herself'. For it turned out that the one and only cure she had chosen for herself was to go often and alone to the zoo which was on the other side of the city.

I was on holiday – the only young person in the house and it seemed obvious that, sooner or later, she would ask me to accompany her. At first I was both surprised and thankful that she did not; then I grew angry. Later, however, as I watched her going off day after day by herself, I believed that by not taking it for granted that I would have to be asked she had given me a certain value apart from the family and had somehow included me in the adult world where people could be free and separate from one another if they wished to be, with no reasons given. In this way I gradually, silently came closer to her, and indeed believed that I could share the emotions which kept her all day and in all weathers restlessly on the move.

Then one day while casually drawing on her gloves she flatly enquired with an indifferent glance directed beyond me into the hall mirror: 'And are you coming out today?' We walked together to the centre of the city, moving silently and apart, going our separate ways with our own thoughts until we came to the junction of roads where a policeman directed three great streams of traffic. This place where there was hardly a person to be seen but only a steady whirl of glittering cars had for me an unreal and precarious brilliance that afternoon. Even the policeman seemed to take on the authority and abandon of some white-gloved clown who can draw a crazy collection of vehicles after him with a wave of the hand or keep them circling dizzily until he has decided at what corner he will point his finger. I followed with my eyes the direction of that hand down one broad street as far as the eye could see to where it narrowed and a faint green of trees could be seen. They were still the dusty city trees, sparsely planted, and the zoo was still a long way beyond them, but that day, for the first time, I saw this greenness with a painful shock of pleasure.

Now, day after day, we went to the zoo. Sometimes it was wet and we would be almost alone there, and on the stormiest days gusts of rain fell against the metal roofs of the monkey-houses like handfuls of sharp nails and even the enclosed pools were raked into miniature waves on which old crusts, orange peel and dusty feathers rocked desolately together. Sometimes it was so hot that after we had made a tour of the lower houses we climbed no higher but sat for a long time on a bench beside three empty cages which stood on their own in the shade of the only group of trees in that part of the garden. These cages had no labels; there was no way of knowing whether the animals there had died or been moved to some other part or whether the place was being prepared for new arrivals. In the heat we sat and stared at the dusty straw and the empty troughs wondering what the inmates had looked like, and my eyes would climb up and down the wire netting behind the bars as my imagination moved from ostriches and giraffes down to some almost invisible rodent hiding in the straw.

'I wonder how old you are,' she said one afternoon as we were sitting in the half-empty tea-house. It was unlike any other restaurant. Half of the roof was glass and on hot days

there was an almost tropical atmosphere about the place.
All round the walls grew tubs of tall, waxy green plants
whose leaves were always damp from the quantities of
steam which rose from the tea-urns at one end of the room.
The concrete floor was sandy and children would pad
silently back and forth carrying flashing glasses of lemonade
which they drank holding them above the table, the straws
tilted at an angle – thus keeping their chins high enough to
see what was going on out of the windows. The smell of
elephants penetrated to this place and above the high
bushes one could catch an occasional glimpse of the two
rows of children rocking by, perched back to back on an
ornamental tray which swung like a hammock at every step.
Long ago, in another age, I also had swung there. Now I
was sitting silently at table opposite a young woman who
had been watching me intently for some time while I
finished my tea.

'I'm fifteen,' I replied, abruptly pushing my plate away
from me.

'Yes, I know that,' she said, 'but I'm wondering how old
you are in other ways. I mean,' she went on, leaning her
elbows on the table, 'what do you know about people –
about men and women? Do you know, for instance, that
they can illumine the most dense, the most boring objects
or places or people for one another, and then, by one word
or even one look, turn the whole world to iron?'

I looked up quickly. But she was smiling slightly as
though to take back a little of the impenetrable hardness,
the numbing coldness she had put into that last word, at the
same time looking aside again through the hedges, to imply
that it was not after all a real question which required an
answer but simply a statement of fact which needed only
mutual recognition. I had not taken my eyes off her, but
now she appeared, in the space of a few seconds, to be quite
changed. She was a person who had at last spoken directly
to me, who had broken through the restless, drifting

indifference of the last few days with something un-
equivocal as a shout or a fierce gesture of the hands, and
I tried to hold her there at the point where this momentary
and precarious contact had been made by taking a more
careful note of her appearance.

Her hair was straight and dark, with a faint bronzing of
lighter colour at the back of her head where it was intri-
cately plaited and twisted up into a heavy coil like a great
unripened blackberry. In front it was brushed well back
from a smooth, narrow brow which, while absorbed in
some thought, she would often touch, tapping her fingers
gently between the eyebrows, then drawing them firmly up
over her brow and carefully round the temple down to the
cheekbone, as though she found deep lines there corresponding with certain ineradicable grievances in her own
heart. She had fine dark eyes but most of the time she
seemed to look at things with a peculiarly blank and fixed
stare as though she would not bother to see objects unless
they presented themselves within a very limited field of
vision which for her was usually straight ahead. One had the
impression that only at this particular spot were human
beings clear or even human before disappearing into the
amorphous background from which they had emerged. She
seldom followed them with her eyes. Occasionally she
would drop her head and tuck her chin down into the
folds of a broad scarf of blue silk which she wore even on
warm days and drew up over her head if it was wet or
windy. In this position, and without moving her head, she
would stare up and down her person from toes to bosom
with the same blank indifference with which she might look
down at a flat and uninteresting landscape. I remembered
all these things clearly now. I also knew in a flash that the
extra bottles in the bathroom – the tonics, the laxatives, the
vitamin pills – were all nonsense; my mother's insistence on
gritty brown bread, her references to deeper sleep, extra
milk and fresh air – meaningless. All these were no more a

likely cure for love than a bandage over the finger for some internal injury.

From that afternoon all the childishness of the zoo disappeared for me, and as the days went by its whole character changed; its cruelty and beauty, its strident colours and harsh cries gradually took the place of all those mild and comic impressions I had experienced there as a child. Now something savage and sad brooded far back in the darkness of the cages we passed. When I stopped to listen I would hear sounds I had not been aware of before – strange rustlings and whistlings from hidden birds, those unidentified croakings and hoots belonging rather to midnight than to noon; and sometimes there came a howl, heart-freezing, yet so distant that it seemed to come, not from the trim confines of the garden, but through the black arctic air and across miles and miles of snow-covered plain.

Everything that had been associated with earlier visits faded out. The animals themselves had changed. Now it was horrible to remember that I had ever expected them to clown for my entertainment – painful even to stare too long at the yawnings and scratchings, the sudden blows and caresses, or to meet the brooding, yellow eyes which stared back, unblinking, at grimacing human faces. Even the seals, flopping off the hot boulders, or rocking from side to side on their flippers ready for a fish to come hurtling through the air, looked mournfully out of place. No longer hypnotised by the velvety backwards and forwards padding of the lioness, I waited only for the slow, swinging turn she would make at each end of the narrow cell, and heard, with a sinking of the stomach, the soft swish of her great shoulder as over and over again with sickening regularity it brushed the same spot on the wall.

As the days went by and our outings never varied I began to wonder if the likeness of the man she loved might not, after all, be found in one of these animals at which we stared so long and gloomily; depending on my ever-changing feelings towards him I would find him on certain days amongst the monkeys, on others amongst the brilliant and talkative birds, and occasionally, when the thought of him began to bore me, I found him in a tank of brown, wrinkle-headed fish, gaping coldly at us like some jaded business man sealed inside the plate-glass of his office. One day I caught a spark of interest in her eyes for the first time as she looked after a well-dressed man who was strolling by himself round a pond of black and green ducks – a spark instantly extinguished when he turned his head; but from that moment I quickly removed this man of hers, whoever he was, from any likeness to certain of the monkey race – those tousled ones, shamelessly unbuttoned, who wore frayed fur round wrists and neck or, worse, patches of bare, scarlet skin on their backs. There were other elegant species to which he might still belong: monkeys with silky chestnut hair parted in the middle and falling smoothly over cleanshaven cheeks, whose fingers were long and delicate, rosy-pink on the inside. But the most likely place for him was still amongst the stylish birds; even if he was fat and formal it was possible to find him amongst the penguins who could stand for great lengths of time, tilted backwards, presenting plump, snowy shirt-fronts to the admiring crowds.

One afternoon I was peering into a cage which had seemed empty, but hearing a rustling in the inner passage I had put my head against the cold bars with both hands grasping them on either side. For a long time I stared but nothing appeared except a mouse which darted across and disappeared into a pile of straw. A chill disappointment had been growing in me for the whole of that day and now it was a raging discontent. Long ago I had lost the early liberties and privileges of this zoo and now, coming back again, had found nothing to put in their place. It was becoming clear to me that I was not to be allotted any of the responsibilities of being a real companion to this woman who stood behind me at this moment. She might speak flippantly about herself, but she did not bother with any comments I might make. She asked questions without expecting an answer; and sometimes after sitting silently for a long time she would give a deep sigh which she cancelled out immediately by a loud burst of laughter, at the same time turning her head away as though any reaction which might come from me was the last thing she could endure. The holidays were nearly over. That particular afternoon the zoo was almost deserted and inside me and around me was emptiness, a feeling that everything was already falling from my grasp. I hung on grimly to the bars as I spoke:

'Why don't you do something about it? Go after him, if that's how you feel – or find somebody else! Anything's better than wandering about day after day! Why did you choose us anyway? We're no use to you and you know it. You even show it – yes, that's true – you don't even bother to hide it – you've shown it all along!'

I shouted these last words in such a desperate voice that somewhere nearby but out of sight, the steady raking of a gravel path which had been going on for some time in the background ceased for a few seconds. Indeed at that moment everything seemed dead silent over the whole zoo.

She stepped forward quickly and put her hand round mine which was still holding the bar – grasping it so hard that the fingers were crushed about the iron in an instant's bone-cracking pain. The ache of iron was in my wrist, in my arm; cold iron was moving towards my chest when she dropped her hand. Mine remained on the bar until slowly, with the greatest caution, I withdrew it and held it up before me, still painfully curled and shaking slightly from its rigid grip. Slowly I stretched it out, finger by finger, and finally brought it close and peered into the palm which still held a blurred white bar-mark. No sooner had I seen this mark than I clenched my hand again as though concealing a painfully won prize and thrust it deep down into the pocket of my raincoat. We walked on without a word.

A few yards away was a signpost bristling with half-a-dozen white-painted arms pointing in all directions and on which were inscribed: Giraffe, Monkeys, Wolves, Gents, Reptiles, Elephant. Cautiously taking the middle path between the Reptiles and the Wolves I arrived at a small pavilion hidden behind bushes and here I sat down wearily on the short flight of wooden steps which led up to it. There was nobody about. I sat perhaps for ten minutes wondering if I would always be tired now, if perhaps this heaviness in the limbs and the slight giddiness which I felt as I bent to tie up a shoe-lace were the characteristic signs of maturity, and though I welcomed these, I wanted nothing better than to return for a few moments to my normal state. It was a relief to turn my eyes, hot with staring at fantastic birds, to the few dusty sparrows hopping about near my feet amongst leaves and stones which concealed only the common spiders and beetles which I could have found any day in my own back-garden. There was no mystery here and no glory. Not far away a gardener, clipping back a high hedge, kept the distant howlings at bay.

I had imagined that when I went back to the main path I should find her sitting on some nearby bench, or perhaps walking slowly on ahead, waiting for me to catch up. But when I at last emerged I saw her far off in the distance, already at the entrance gates. She turned once and waved – a friendly but casual gesture which slowed me down immediately, so clearly did it indicate that our afternoon together was at an end. I decided there and then that from that day I would leave nothing to chance. She would see that it was no dumb schoolboy she had on her hands. I would break ruthlessly through silences. If need be, in the days ahead, I could shift the whole scene of action to some entirely new and less disturbing territory.

But there were to be no more days. The next afternoon

was hot and thundery; I was outside the front door of the house, casually turning over the pages of a newspaper which lay on the steps and occasionally flicking away the flies which zigzagged erratically across the avenues of black print. Although seemingly absorbed, I was only awaiting the one cool look from her which was the usual signal that she was ready to go if I wished to join her. I waited a long time, and at last she came out. But the look was not casual. Instead, I saw with terror that her expression was kind. She paused, looked down at my paper in silence for a moment as though something of interest had caught her eye. Then she said, pointing, still with her head bent:

'They're absolutely wrong about that because I happen to know the town myself. A fishing river indeed! With paper mills along the banks! I suppose they'll be making out it's a holiday resort with freshwater bathing next. I'll see it later. Save it for me till I get back.'

She turned away and went quickly down the path to the gate. Usually she let it bang carelessly, not looking to see whether it was shut or not, but this time I heard her lift up the latch, then let it down carefully into its slot behind her, as though to emphasise that though such barriers between human beings might be absurd there was nothing to be done about them, so one might just as well learn to manipulate the various keys and latches and the cunning little iron bolts which had so thoughtfully been provided.

A week or so later she was gone; the summer holidays were over and I was back at school. The duster flouncing out angrily across a density of figures on the blackboard released great clouds of spinning white chalk, silently exploding nebulae through which we stared in the direction of the window and out over the dark chimneys of the town. But all was grey dust now, dust in the air we breathed, dust in the air outside. All illumination had come to an end.

# The Snow Heart

FOLLOWING THE FIRST heavy snowfall of the year, a huge
heart appeared on the bowling-green next to the hospital
grounds. It was deeply marked out in the snow, and for
sheer size – as seen from the height of the new hospital
buildings – it was an eye-opener. It was the biggest shape
that could be put inside the green without running over
onto the surrounding paths; and whoever made it had been
careful not to spoil his line. He had walked narrowly
backwards, foot behind foot, and let his stick swallow up
most of his prints. There was a line of chunky footsteps
leading up to it, a line leading away, and no other marks.

The bowling-green was not connected with the hospital. High hedges made it private. Yet it was visible only
from the hospital windows. All during summer and up
till late autumn, when the green was closed, old men
bent and swung their arms over a lawn smooth as a
billiard table. Patients and visitors to the hospital were
used to the sight of an endless turnover of players. There
were bowlers strong as bulls down there as well as old
men on their last legs. There were bossy bowlers and
browbeaten bowlers. But whatever they were, domineer-
ing or defeated, the place was geared to age. Overnight
the snow and the heart had changed all that. While the
old men had been sleeping or sitting in their clubs or
pubs their place had been smoothed out and engraved. A
rejuvenation had taken place, and they were to know
nothing of it.

The hospital staff were too busy in the morning to do
much more than glance at the bowling-green in passing. It

was left to the afternoon visitors who were always in the
high corridor on Mondays, Wednesdays, Thursdays and at
week-ends, waiting to be beckoned into certain medical
and surgical wards on the stroke of three. The place where
they waited was at the top of the building – a wide corridor
with a staircase and a line of lifts at one end. Opposite were
the swing doors leading through to the wards. On the
window side it was almost entirely glass divided up by
strips of metal and it was here that visitors lined up while
they waited. They varied from day to day but most of them
were long-distance people who had arrived early. Amongst
these were the few who came to visit long-term patients and
who formed a small in-group amongst the random coming
and going of the rest. They were a clique who had their own
private and sometimes silent language. They recognized
one another and formed bonds even though they might
have no clue to the other end of the attachment – the man,
woman or child in the beds beyond.

On this particular afternoon half a dozen or so were
waiting at the windows. They were glad, in a businesslike
way, to see the snow. They were glad to see the heart. Any
new thing at all on the way to the wards was something to
be grateful for and visitors to long-term patients had to be
particularly skilled collectors of news items, no matter how
small or unimportant. Delivery of news was always a
chancy affair. There was no knowing how long their patients might take over the bits they were given. Events
which should have provided talk for an hour could be
brushed aside in a matter of seconds. Patients had been
known to listen lackadaisically to news packets containing a
cease-fire and a new war, and grasp at the tale of a bad egg
in a bowl. Today the early visitors at the window were too
tired to go overboard for this heart. They had seen better
last minute talking-points in their time. All the same they
took it and filed it amongst other items where, with luck, it
might fill a gap. While most of them collected it silently and

turned to other things, one man remarked to the woman
beside him that he would be telling his son about this.

'He'll be amused when I tell him,' he said. 'I mean the
grotesque size of that thing will intrigue him.' It was a grave
mistake indeed to make any pronouncement on what
would or would not amuse or please one's patient. Few
experienced visitors risked it. But there was a desperate
streak in this man. The woman listened pleasantly to him
and said that no doubt she too would be telling her
daughter. But she knew it was a very different matter.
The man's son had been here a long time and he would
not get better. Her daughter, in a surgical ward, was getting
better every day. Occasionally the man talked about his
son, though rarely about his illness.

'He is rather difficult to please,' he had said one afternoon a few weeks earlier. 'He's inclined to find fault.' And
some time after he had said: 'You know, he is very, very
difficult to please. He finds fault with everything and everyone.'

'Poor fellow,' she had replied.

'And I'm afraid I irritate him,' said the father.

'Maybe,' she said. 'But of course it's not really you.'

'I don't know whether it's really me or not me. I just
know I seem to irritate him more and more every day.'

One way or another the woman had got to know a bit
about this man. His wife was dead, and there were not
many other people to share the visits with him. His son,
who had just finished his architect's training, had one good
friend who wrote regularly from his new job in Canada. A
few other friends took turns to visit him. Some had stopped
for good. He'd had a girl friend once but she had disappeared early in his illness. 'Naturally enough – or unnaturally, whichever way you want to look at it,' said the
man. There was this difficulty about hospitals and long-
term visitors felt it most. As they went on it grew harder and
harder to figure out what was natural and what was un-

natural about the set-up. And it was not only the place
which set them problems. They worried about themselves.
Were they becoming less human or more human? And
which was best under the circumstances? They sank and
surfaced again, alternating in mood with those in the wards
who sank and surfaced continually. The boy's father had
been depressed himself for some time. But this afternoon
he seemed cheerful, as though the snow, by levelling cracks
and ridges and smoothing all anomalies of building and
landscape, had made it possible to start again from the
beginning.

The bowling-green was not the only thing visitors could
look down at. The hospital was built round three sides of a
large courtyard, and down there was a new fountain with
two fish mouths which would one day blow water. There
were a few newly-planted saplings, and three small flower
beds sunk in the paving-stones, ready for planting. Triangles and oblongs of red, blue and yellow enamel had been
set in a pattern along the side of the concrete wall which ran
under the hedge on the bowling-green side. But the visitors, like ungrateful children, never looked at these things –
or if they did it was only momentarily before staring above
and beyond at scenes not intended for them. They looked
across at the windows of the west-wing wards. There they
could see distant figures in beds – spry figures sitting bolt
upright, half-reclining figures with knees sharply angled
under red and blue blankets, and flat-out figures. The
corridor people never wearied of this spectacle. It seemed
that the people in the distant beds were more interesting
and more mysterious than their own relatives in the nearby
wards. This afternoon they looked across and saw the scene
transformed. Bits of the outside world had invaded the
inside. Nurses were moving about over there with caps
white as the snowcaps on the chimney-pots. They were
bouncing up pillows which were smaller versions of the fat
snow-pillows below. A few outgoing scarlet capes were

moving along the path towards the gates. It was not only the boy's father who was cheered. The others also felt hope in the air, though it was mixed with ice. They were anxious that it should not melt too quickly.

On the stroke of three the swing doors burst open and were fastened against brass hinges on either side. They were being beckoned in by a familiar, smiling nurse. But the man stayed behind talking with the woman for a few minutes longer. He was telling her something and it was easy enough to guess what was happening. He was no more telling it to her than he was telling it to the fire extinguisher. He was simply rehearsing in detail what he would tell his son.

'Yesterday afternoon,' he was saying, 'I'd no sooner got in than my neighbours came round for a chat, and to tell me about their latest bed-and-breakfast. They do it summer and winter – have done for years. And do you know who this latest man turns out to be? A first-class chef turned preacher. Imagine it. He'd been giving people a great deal of pleasure, no doubt, whipping up the soufflés and concocting recipes à la Robertson or whatever his name is. And now . . .! Not only that, but he can't leave well alone. He's got to go round condemning his former job. Condemning it! Oh, that some of our present preachers would turn Sunday chefs! Would that not give us a more digestible day?'

They had now started to move through the swing doors but his voice came after her. 'And so I see this architect on TV last night is proposing a floating city. I like the idea. Do you like the idea?' Yes, she said, she liked it very much indeed.

'I've forgotten how it would work, but every window would have this magnificent changing view. How about that?'

'Yes, wonderful,' said the woman. But she kept moving on because they had to be rather strict about time here and the hour passed quickly.

'But I'm not so sure,' his voice pursued her, 'about the sort of city that goes a mile up into the sky.' This time she didn't turn round and wasn't meant to. His eyes were already fixed on the passage to the left and on a door at the far end of it. Her own route took her up a flight of stairs and along a corridor on the other side. They parted abruptly as they always did, he to the left and she to the right.

It happened that they met again in the evening at the seven to eight visiting hour. For some time back they had come in on both afternoon and evening visits, though they did the double shift for different reasons – the man because his son was very ill, the woman because her daughter was almost well. It seemed the two extremes demanded most. For the second time that day they stood at the plate glass windows staring across. But the transformation from afternoon to evening was always spectacular. In place of solid buildings were row upon row of incandescent light cubes set in blackness, giving a vision which was almost clairvoyant into the rooms opposite. Here and there among the white cubes were a few dim rooms lit by blue, and visitors tended to stare at these with particular intensity as though the distant blue rooms held the secret of life and death – a secret being unaccountably withheld from themselves. Tonight, however, brightness came from the ground as well as the walls. Even the skimpy trees spiked with snow looked theatrical. On the bowling-green the line of the heart showed up thicker and clearer than before.

As usual, the man and the woman arrived early, and after their first few comments, they fell silent. It was not a vast silence but the woman decided it was too long for comfort. They did not know one another well enough for this. She had also become accustomed to the non-silence policy of the hospital. This was not made too obvious but it could be felt. When necessary a good deal of chatter, not to say clatter, covered certain black pits of feeling. Even the brisk rattle of curtain rails round an emotion was better than nothing. The woman could chatter herself when she had a mind to.

'If the forecast's anything to go by it's to be colder than ever,' she said. 'But no more snow meantime. Well, thank goodness for that. The bus had the worst time ever on that hill tonight. There was one moment I thought we'd all be out on the road pushing. What's your opinion of double-deckers on a hill like that? Last year there were letters to the paper. Do you think double-deckers are dangerous on that particular stretch?' The man nodded but gave no opinion, so she answered for him. 'Yes, they *are* more dangerous and not just in snow – in a wind too. In a high wind they can pitch and swing like a ship at sea.' Again there was silence as they stared ahead. The woman took courage from the brilliant patches of light below. 'What did your son think of the cook?' she asked, smiling. The man unfocused his gaze reluctantly. His eyebrows indicated a complete noncom-prehension. 'The chef turning preacher,' said the woman with still unfaltering brightness.

'Oh *that*.' He waved it impatiently aside. 'Absolutely nothing. It didn't interest him at all. There was nothing to it, of course.' The woman could have stopped there. She was virtually being invited to take no interest in anything herself. But she felt the need to go further. 'The floating city – what does he make of that idea? If it doesn't sound ludicrous to put it that way – isn't it his line of country?'

'He hardly heard it. He thought it scarcely worth while listening.'

The woman looked down quickly and started to rear-range some of the things in her bag, but a moment later she was startled by his tense voice, suddenly much louder. 'There *was* one thing he took up. *One* thing he listened to. He took great exception to my mention of the heart.' The woman stopped rustling in her bag and took a quick look down at it. She had almost forgotten it was there.

'Never again!' said the man. 'What a mistake to talk about outside things. How stupid I've become. How thick!'

'But what happened?'

'Nothing – except he worked himself into a fury. And don't think,' said the man as though picking her up, 'don't think he'll forget it. I know my son. He's going to lie there and meditate on hearts and the people who draw hearts.'

Sometimes the doors would be opened for early visitors. It happened this evening. At least fifteen minutes before time the friendly nurse came through and wedged them back. She noticed that this pair were tired and that the cold glass where they leaned had taken colour from their cheeks. They looked deserving of comfort, of some privilege for themselves. But whatever it was they didn't take it. They acknowledged the open door but remained where they were.

'Who are they then?' said the woman. 'Who are these people who draw hearts?'

'Vandals!' the man cried. 'And no different from any other kind. So he says. Secret vandals!' They both stared at the bowling-green, the woman in some surprise, the man with bitterness. 'Oh yes,' he said, 'harmless *this* time. That he admits. But whoever could do that could do it in much worse and lasting ways. It's the brand-new hearts chiselled on standing stones he's thinking of, hearts dug out of trees and slashed across pillars. He's seen himself a hideous double heart complete with dates and arrows branded on a temple wall. Can you blame him? Buildings are his job. Oh, it's not only hearts! He is thinking of every effacement he ever set eyes on. And I set him off!'

'It will melt,' said the woman who could think of nothing better to say.

'But not from his mind,' said the man. 'I know my son.' He turned and walked quickly away through the open door. The woman waited on for a bit. She felt she was getting to know the young man too. And she had to admit that with the best will in the world she didn't absolutely care for the sound of him. Had never in fact cared. On the whole her opinion was that illness made neither devils nor angels. She took the view that it brought out and perhaps exaggerated what was already there. From what she had heard, there was and always had been a born complainer there. Long before his illness he had complained. She had never seen him and she was exceedingly sorry for him. She was sorry for any obsessions he might have. But she was not, she was thankful to say, obliged to like him.

She didn't see the father next day. But on the following afternoon they met in the corridor. It was colder than ever – colder if possible than on the last few days. Not a scrap of snow had melted or shifted. On the trees the snow blossoms had set like icing sugar. The heart on the bowling-green had not altered its shape by a single ice crystal. It was clear when the man spoke that his son had not altered his views either. He was preoccupied with vandalism. It had been no good trying to change the subject. The boy had kept an irritable silence before bursting out in the same vein. They had not mentioned the heart again, but it was the basis of the business. And the vandalism had broadened to include all spoilings in country as well as city, past damage and damage to come.

'Is it so strange?' said the father. 'He's an architect, isn't he? As far as he's concerned nothing in its final shape comes up to what was planned. Everything falls short. Just now he exaggerates. Yes. But he was always like that. His expectations are high.'

'I'm sure,' said the woman quickly.

'A perfectionist.'

'Yes, of course he is!'

'And such people can be reminded, can be irritated by things which the rest of us . . .'

'Oh, I know that!' she exclaimed. The man looked exhausted with the effort of explanation. He took a deep breath before saying:

'But I've a feeling this evening will be different. We'll get off the subject. Why not? It was an accident that it ever got into the picture at all. He *will* forget.' He dropped his eyes to the bowling-green. They both stared at the heart. Engraved as it was out of a substance which might vanish at any instant, it had kept its shape. It seemed innocent and at the same time bold – a peaceful, yet a childishly stubborn shape. In the absence of initials, arrows, prints of any kind, there was no message to be read. But emptiness gave it power. It was no longer strange. Already it was part of the surroundings. It was a harmonious shape, and the woman decided it was benign. But she wondered how the man saw it now. As a deliberate disfigurement? A shape, meaningless and gross, perhaps, set there to try the endurance of his son and himself.

It had begun to snow slightly again at the evening visiting hour, but the corridor was crowded as usual for Saturday was a popular day for family visits. There were plenty of new faces and tonight even the regulars were in good form. The snow had put fight into them. They were not prepared to make a mystery out of this building. It was something to get in from the cold, and they expressed some envy for the patients in their snug beds. There came a point when even illness must be kept in its place. There was a big difference between being alive and being dead and it had better not be forgotten. At any rate, ribaldry, in place of awe, was long overdue in the place. It was a night for comparing fat and thin sisters, for stripping doctors of the laundered coat. Surgeons were scrutinized as either wilder than the wildest maniac or staid as councillors, and the immaculate matron in her virgin pie-ruff must be sacrificed to one or other of them before the night was out. There were few doctors around just now. It was not the time for doctors. But when one did appear as though by accident, going slowly past looking neither to right nor left, the relatives stared boldly after him. They were controlling the desire to spring forward and wrench an answer out of him – an explanation, a diagnosis, or even a plain yes or no. The stray doctor was aware of this. He kept his eyes fixed on a distant mark at the end of the corridor in an effort to maintain dignity and keep his footing on the spotless floor when on every side the endlessly questioning eyes threatened to topple him up.

The young man's father was not among the earliest arrivals tonight. He came on the dot of seven and disappeared immediately in the direction of the wards. This time the woman was ahead of him but she looked back once and got a quick response. He waved. His smile was cheerful, as though he'd quickly caught the mood of the evening and had no intention of being odd man out. The woman waited for him in the corridor when the hour was up. It was not an evening for formalities or reserve.

'And how was he?' she asked at once as he came up. 'Did you manage to get off that subject?'

'No,' he said, 'I did not. And we are back to square one.'

'The bowling-green?'

'Oh, I thought *that* at any rate was over and done with. But he'd thought of something else. How am I to put it to you?'

'Tell me then.'

'He was upset, to put it mildly, brooding now on the fact that the heart down there has nothing inside it, none of the usual appendages. No words or signs. Not a mark. If it's to be properly denounced it must conform, and this one has not come up to expectation. It says nothing. It gives nothing. It is not even a lasting blot on the landscape. This empty heart is not enough for him it seems!' The man had forgotten to subdue his voice to the required hospital mildness. It got louder as he went on and ended on a note of pain. One or two people glanced sympathetically at him in passing. One or two looked annoyed. He had become a threat to the hard-won mood of cheer.

The woman didn't move or speak for a long time. She

was looking straight in front of her out of the window. It was still snowing and there was a slight wind. It was hard to see how the fine flakes would ever touch ground. At one moment they formed spirals in the air and at another, slanting lines which shifted, or on sudden gusts blew upward higher and higher until the widely separating flakes disappeared into darkness overhead. All the same, the thin layer of snow had already altered things below. The two lines of footsteps on the bowling-green were almost obliterated. The centre of the heart, shining in the light from the hospital windows, was softly padded out with new white snow. It still proclaimed itself, but gently. Now that even the footsteps were gone, this smoothing and rounding had given it a feeling of completeness and an absolute calm.

'Do you know,' said the woman, rousing herself at last to speak. 'I think I shall put it to my daughter – your son's problem, I mean. Just as a matter of interest I'd like her opinion. How would that be?'

'Certainly. Please tell her anything you like,' said the man politely.

'In my opinion she's got insight as well as common sense.'

'I'm sure,' said the man, keeping himself from moving off with an effort.

'And then, of course, she is young herself.'

The man answered by making a weary obeisance in the direction of the wards. It was done without irony. He acknowledged youth while admitting that he himself was absolutely played out. Finished. Right now there was only one thing he wanted and that was to get home. He had talked so much about his son, however, and asked so little about her daughter it was up to him to stay on the spot. But the woman was moving off herself. 'Then I'll see you tomorrow,' she said.

Their meeting next day came at the end of the afternoon visit. It seemed casual, almost accidental. The woman was standing at the window with her back to the light, studying herself in a small handbag mirror. The absorbed, disapproving regard of the middle-aged woman for her own face disappeared as he came up. But she turned back for one more caustic glance at her left cheek.

'Well, I've seen my daughter,' she said, forcing the mirror back into her handbag's jungle. 'She thought about it for a long time. And I may say she has the greatest sympathy for your son's point of view. Indeed she shares it. She understood perfectly his irritation, his frustration . . . But as for the heart – well, she takes a more straightforward view of that. Why worry? Why fuss about what is or isn't inside it? It was never meant, she says, to have letters, words, signs, or anything else. That is not the style of the thing. On the other hand, it is not an *empty* heart.'

'No?' said the man.

'I'm simply repeating her words,' the woman said, looking at him impatiently for the first time. '*Not* an empty heart, but an open one. For anyone and everyone. One can take it or leave it, but there it is. It is fabulous, she says. It is fantastic. It is an outsize super-heart. And there is absolutely nothing more to be said about it.'

The man said nothing more about it, but he thought for a long time. 'I shall pass on the message,' he said at last, bowing his head, '. . . and how on earth I will manage . . .'

'You'll make nothing of it, I hope.'

'I'll certainly try to make it nothing. I am tempted to scoff a bit at your daughter's view.'

'Oh, she's tough enough to take it! In that way – your son and my daughter – aren't they both tough enough? And that they've never met and never will meet has absolutely nothing to do with it. They stand together.'

'Indeed I hope so,' said the man. He turned quickly away and went on past her towards the stair.

Next day the woman was occupied with other visitors to her daughter. He saw her only in passing. But they met briefly the following day at the end of the evening visit. It was hot in the corridor. The woman was complaining about the tightness of her snowboots on the thick rubber floor. The radiators at the window were scorching, and visitors emerging from lemonade-filled wards complained of thirst. Beyond the swing doors one or two women patients were already wandering about in open, flowery dressing-gowns. The nurses looked warm and pink as sun-bathers. Tonight the hospital was like a huge, hot ocean liner, stranded in ice.

'So our promised thaw has not come after all,' said the woman.

'I can't say it worries me one way or the other,' the man replied. The woman looked at him quickly and was encouraged by something in his expression. She waited for a bit and getting no further response said:

'And your son. Is *he* reconciled . . . to the snow?'

'Reconciled? Never! That is not his way. He reconciles himself to nothing. He takes his own view and always will. If he does change his mind he must think it all out for himself – through it and round and over it.'

'Of course, of course,' said the woman. 'But what is his view – of that?'

The man looked in the direction of the bowling-green and away again. Yet the woman was still encouraged by something about him. She was now reduced to pointing directly down at the heart. The man consented to look at it again but said nothing. He was stubborn like his son.

'Oh well then,' said the woman. 'What is *your* view of it?'

The man shrugged his shoulders and glanced down. He considered it as though measuring it, as though matching it up against all other possible shapes.

'Oh – the size of that thing!' he exclaimed at last. 'The extravagance! Isn't it a regular pantomime piece . . . ?'

'Yes, yes,' agreed the woman, and waited.

The man shook his head as though finished with what he had to say. Nevertheless he put down the bag he was carrying and opened his arms wide, bringing them slowly together again into a circle with only the tips of his fingers joined. For an instant he enfolded the empty space in front of him. He demonstrated an almost imperceptible capture, an embrace.

'It is a not unfriendly shape,' the man said, dropping his arms and picking up his bag again.

But the woman seemed perfectly satisfied with these words. At once she began to move away from the window, taking care to do it with the least possible fuss or disturbance to the man looking down on the bowling-green. As she was a large woman and rather clumsy, it was not easy. It was a case of drawing on her gloves without moving her elbows, of sorting out a complication of handbag and carrier-bag straps while pulling down her helmet shaped cap over her ears. She managed not to open her mouth again. She didn't look in his direction. Padded with clothes, strapped and helmeted, like a diver she moved, silently, in rubber boots over the rubber floor. Slowly, cautiously – yet with some hint of deep-sea buoyancy in her gait – she drifted off.

# The Colour

MR GARRAD HAD rung rather late in the day – some time after tea when the disorder had shown itself. But it wasn't as late as all that, and anyway they'd had it in writing that in an emergency someone could always come right away. It was urgent all right – not something to be cured at home by a bit of tinkering and on-the-spot treatment. It was not the first time it had happened either. Garrad looked pained when he came back from the phone. His wife sat on the sofa nursing a pillow for comfort. She knew instinctively it would be a comfortless evening. The son and daughter had emerged from their bedrooms and hung limply on the banister to hear the diagnosis.

'They will come this evening,' said Garrad sitting down at the other end of the sofa, 'and they will do something about it, if possible.' That was the devil of it – the 'if possible' which sounded the dirge on hope. How many 'if possibles' had these two not heard – and yet weren't used to it yet.

'If possible?' muttered his wife as though testing out a foreign phrase in her mouth.

'That's it. I'm giving you their word for word.' They sat in silence. 'What will you do then? Will you go out?' said the wife after a bit.

'I'll wait till they come. *If* they come. Then I'll go out.'

They waited fifty minutes until, as by a miracle, two young men turned up. The family watched them as they knelt and tested and talked together. Nothing came of it. All the others could see was the odd red streak that made the heart jump till they saw it was only the reflection of the bus-stop sign on the other side of the street. The men answered Garrad's questions. They were very young. But it wasn't their age that bothered him. It was their politeness, their gentleness. They had the cheerful gentleness of stretcher-bearers on a serious case as they lifted the set in their arms and carried it out. This same pair had actually put in the colour. Now, for the second time, they were taking it away. 'How long this time?' Garrad asked as they went past him, carefully manoeuvring it round the corner of the passage and shielding it from the sharp edge of the hall table. They shook their heads and smiled. He watched them go through the front door, careful not to jolt or trip. He watched the colour being carried further and further away until it finally disappeared into the waiting van.

'Well, that's that!' he cried coming back, falsely cheerful, into the living-room.

'Nobody minds a couple of nights without,' said his wife. 'But there's Friday. It's Friday I'm thinking about.'

'And Sunday,' he added. On Friday there was a thriller serial two episodes from the end. There was also a cookery demonstration which they all watched hungrily week by week, never mind whether they'd had their meal or not. They were hungry for the colour of this food – the familiar yellow yolks of eggs being broken into scarlet bowls, white cream poured into chocolate sauce, and all stirred with a blue spoon. In the background tomatoes were piled against aubergines, polished to ebony – on the side, platters of apples, grapes and oranges. Now and then the demon-strator would wipe her hands on an apron striped green and blue. Garrad's wife was a good cook herself. She used milk and eggs. She could have got a scarlet bowl if she'd wanted it. She'd have been the first to admit that her milk was whiter, the eggs yellower than the screen ones. But that was not the point. Where was the comfort in it? For Garrad, who liked the country, there was a regular Sunday series of different landscapes filmed hour by hour from dawn to moonrise, showing the changing colours of sky, field and river throughout one day. The colour was not bad, in Garrad's estimation. It was as real as you could get unless you actually had the thing behind you in the window. Yes, they'd done a good job on colour and the chances were it would get better as time went on.

'You're going out then?' said his wife.

'Might just as well.' He stepped out into the street, into a warm autumn evening. His own street was made up of small modern houses with long gardens, well-known in the district for their new-planted trees. Most people were tending a sapling. Garrad was proud of this himself but this evening he had no eyes for the spindly branches beside him. In spite of himself he kept looking up at the TV aerials growing overhead, frail-looking yet tough enough to withstand the most ferocious blast. Not a house without these magic roof-twigs. All the same he was the only man for a long way round these parts who had colour. The first man. A kind of Adam of the new vision. Very soon – perhaps in a year or so, possibly in a few months, they'd all have it. But he was the first. He strode along quickly at first, then gradually more and more slowly as the first fury of his frustration spent itself. He was able to smile at the few persons he knew who were sitting at windows or working in their gardens along the street. At one or two he stopped. A married couple he knew rather better than the rest were out staring at a bed of roses and Garrad stopped and stared too.

'You're out early,' the man remarked, stepping across the bed towards him.

'Yes. Good to get a breath of air after the office.'

'And the wife?'

'Fine. Or not bad is more like it. She gets easily put out, thrown off her stroke . . .'

'But she's well?'

'She worries.'

'Like the rest of us. And yourself?'

'All right. Rather dull, as you see.'

'Sorry to hear your wife has worries,' said the woman. 'Not serious ones, I hope.'

'Nothing much. It's the colour trouble again. Have you thought about colour yourself?'

They immediately stripped themselves of all frivolity, let go of the roses. 'Colour? I may say we read and listen to everything that's being said on that particular issue,' the man said. 'I think you know my views on the colour question.'

'It wasn't that though. It's colour TV I'm talking about.'

'Oh, I see. No, I've no views on that, I'm afraid. Not yet. Haven't got the money to have any views on that at the moment. Now, this colour question. As I said before – I think you know my views on that.'

'Certainly I know them. I share them.'

'I hope you do.'

'That's a queer way to put it, and not particularly complimentary to Mr Garrad here,' said his wife coming nearer. 'You're implying he may have prejudices of one kind or another or that he's afraid to come out with them.'

'That's utter nonsense! But there *is* a queer thing. Here we all are airing our views about colour, with lowered voices. Some day, looking back, the world will think it's unbelievably ludicrous. We'll be all colours and thankful to be. It'll be a disgrace to be pure white, pure black, brown or yellow. That's how it'll be in the world to come.'

'In a future world you mean,' said his wife.

'The same.'

'Because "world to come" usually means "next life". Which is a very different matter.'

'I have no views about a next life, none whatever. Except there's said to be no marriage or giving in marriage and that's all that interests me.'

'So you can see where your colour views get us,' said his wife to Garrad. 'I hope your wife doesn't get what I have to put up with. And by the way, what about a bunch of roses to take back?'

'Lovely,' said Garrad quickly. 'Lovely. But I'll get them on the way back if it's all the same . . .'

He moved on past other gardens competing in brightness and neatness, past doors painted blue, white and green, down to the busy corner and round it and on towards that part which grew more and more congested near the crossing of main roads but where, miraculously, on clear days, in a minute closed-in wedge between a pub and a church, you could just see the blue line of distant sea. When he was a young man Garrad had cherished this almost invisible wedge of the town. There was some fractional romance about it which he occasionally remembered nowadays when he was struggling through the rush-hour crowds or waiting in longer and longer queues. There was sometimes a pin-pointing of clouds over this sea, now and then the fleck of a ship. Sometimes it was no more than the narrow dazzle of light between black brick. He seldom looked for it now. When he looked he seldom saw it. Twenty more years of traffic had nearly obscured it. A smart addition to the church and a new signboard on the pub had pared it to an even smaller piece of sea and sky. He went further and further in towards the centre and slowly out again on the other side where most of the town's public buildings stood – banks, town hall, libraries and Technical College – all with a sizeable bit of green in front. He came to the main modern school with its huge glass frontage where you could look right into empty classrooms and corridors and see flowers blazing along the sills, and maps, mobiles, posters on the opposite walls. A late janitor strolled up to the gates as he went past. 'Ah . . . the young devils . . . they're in luck, aren't they?' Garrad said. 'They're never done looking. They can see the whole world go past as they do their sums. When I think how we had to fix our eyes on a two feet by three block of blackboard. There wasn't anywhere else to look. What wouldn't we have given to see all this!'

'But would you say it was a *good* thing?' said the janitor, leaning his elbow on a spike of railing.

'I was just coming to that. Is it?' said Garrad. 'Does it help them concentrate? Does it help them choose what things to look at out of all the stuff going past the window? Does it make them selective? Selective!' Garrad rolled and relished the word on his tongue. The janitor took his elbows off the spike. 'And these are going too.'

'What's that?'

'The spikes are going.'

'Well that's good I suppose. No spikes, eh? All this and spikeless too. Makes you wonder how *we* came through at all at their age.' He walked on gravely, passing one or two acquaintances on his way. He made this distinction with middle-age. Real friends got fewer and fewer while acquaintances grew and multiplied. These days he used the word 'real' a lot. Real. He hung on grimly to reality like an acrobat with a metal plug between the teeth hanging over a void. Real friends, real food, real entertainment, real service, real flavour, real bread, real leather, real hair, real love, real money, real women. They were all whizzing away from him. Some things he'd missed out. Real colour. It was not yet added to his list.

It was cooler now and the street quieter. At another crossing of streets a miniature market was packing up its stalls. Men and women, untying aprons blotched with juice, were getting ready to heave up piles of empty crates onto lorries or into their own shops behind, while round about a few left-over baskets of battered fruit were being fingered by late-comers. A few stalls were still intact. One was slung round like an Arabian tent with purple and crimson cloth, overhung by long red and blue nylon dresses with flowered sashes. Rows of boots, dangling from their laces round the top of the stall, kicked half-heartedly in the breeze as though engaged in some mild, disembodied game of football.

A couple who were hurrying past stopped suddenly beside Garrad. They were coming from their shop where, over a long time-span of changing fashions, every single object there had changed from junk to antique and back to junk again. They kept their spirits up. 'Hullo Mr Garrad. Very thoughtful you look. Are you contemplating the skating boots up there or what?' asked the husband.

'Well I might yet. Right now I'm only out for a stroll.'

'Good. But don't forget to be back for seven, will you?'

'Seven. What's that?'

'What's seven! Don't tell me you were thinking of giving a miss to the last of the Great Gardens?'

'I've no choice. It's broken down on us.' Garrad told the tale again. Of how colour was brought and taken back, and brought and taken back again. He didn't fuss – simply told it with a wry smile while they exclaimed in sympathy. But they were still leaning at a steep angle towards home. 'So we'd have been better to stay with plain black and white for a while,' Garrad went on. 'That way we'd never have known what we were missing.'

'Do you think so?' Their faces lost a little sympathy. They had no colour. Garrad knew he'd been tactless.

'It's just,' he said, 'that it doesn't take long to get used to colour.'

'I suppose so,' said the wife. 'Do you find it true?'

'True?'

'Yes, I believe it varies a lot. Some say they'll never get it true to life.'

'Well it's different of course.'

'They're never going to get it absolutely true. That's what I heard.'

'I wouldn't say never. It depends what you mean by true. It's going to get better and better.'

'Does anything?' said the man. 'I'm afraid I'm a pessimist. And I'm rather odd about colour. I don't believe I'd like it unless it was absolutely true. I suppose it's because you could call me a bit of an artist. Isn't that right, Cath?'

'That's right,' said his wife without enthusiasm.

'Not in anything I do, of course. But in how I look at things.'

'And everyone sees things differently,' said Garrad.

'But not as differently as colour TV sees them,' said the other with a laugh. Garrad said nothing. He pretended to look around him at the world. He didn't tell this couple that he'd come to like the blue-tinged eggs, the etherialized pink of TV flesh. He'd had half a mind to tell them, if only they had been more sympathetic, that these days he found the world painfully hard-edged, almost too real, too steadily bright for comfort.

'And anyway,' the husband was saying. 'Do I *want* it all in colour? Why not save something I can discover for myself.'

'Such as . . . ?' his wife asked.

'Well, let's say the foothills of the Himalayas.'

'You've left that pretty late,' she said. 'I don't think you're going to make it. And anyway I'm not worrying about what *you* might or might not discover. What about all the invalids who can't get around at all? Don't you want them to get the benefit of seeing the world in colour?'

'Listen! That's the first time she's ever mentioned invalids and TV. It's all a ruse to make me sound selfish. And talking of invalids, I may say it's the operations she'll go for first if ever we get the colour. I mean the open heart and the bisected brain are going to look quite something, don't you think?' They moved swiftly on their way towards home.

Garrad remained looking around him for a while, then wandered slowly back along the way he'd come. The colour was beginning to go out of the streets and into the sky. Alleys, archways, back-courts were all a deeper grey, but the upper air was glowing. The open heart. He repeated it to himself. Now there was a phrase – a suggestive phrase if ever there was one. It had a life apart from the operating table. And there were some more prone to speak of hearts than others. Open hearts or broken hearts, warm hearts or cold ones – such words were easy for some people. But not to him. He never mentioned this heart to anyone, not even to himself. Yet it was real all right. In the world where he longed to put his hand on all real things – heart still had meaning. He slowed down. His heart was beating steadily as it had done for the last sixty years, as it would do for the next – how many more? 'Well, I'm not so crazy about a long life,' he had murmured out loud. In the doorway of his shop, near closing-time, James Byers heard him, heard the murmur 'not so crazy', and murmured very softly in reply:

'Now who would ever call *you* crazy, Mr Garrad?'

Garrad stopped abruptly, turned to the doorway and saw the spread of the evening newspaper, dark with disaster, and above it Byers' impassive face with its spectacled, secretive eyes watching him. The shop had no need of billboards. Here, morning and evening in the doorway Byers spread and read the paper. Passers-by read snippets hungrily and went in for more.

'I said I'm not all that crazy about a long life,' said Garrad. 'Look at old Peterson now, fumigated and isolated in that high-class nursing-home. I dread what I'll become. In his own home, my father – if he's anything to go by – was such a nuisance to himself and everyone else from his eighty-eighth to his ninety-first, poor man, that his funeral went like a regular jamboree. The surprise was there was no cavorting and singing.'

'You might be interested in a longer life when you come to it.'

'I doubt that. Ask me if you're still around.'

'I'll do that. This isn't your usual time for walking, Garrad – on a Wednesday evening.'

'It's not. I'm running from a sort of hole in our house.'

'A plumbing job?'

'No, not plumbing.'

'Hole? If my sister heard it she'd think of mice before you could say "tail". Even rats. There are rats behind those stinking old station sheds and plenty of them.'

'The hole I'm thinking of is a squared off bit of empty space.'

'Ah . . . so we're on the metaphysical plane, are we?'

'Maybe. Our colour's gone. The box is away.'

'And you with it. Are you destroyed?'

'No, but it makes you think.'

Byers folded his paper impatiently and held it together in one hand while he adjusted his glasses the better to see a clock some blocks further up the street. He was a reader. In the evenings, after listening for a certain self-specified time to the complaints of customers who rang him about his paperboys, he would go off to the library – the phone still buzzing behind him. Once there, he would go through a further set of papers and magazines and return near closing-time with a pile of books under his arm. Garrad sensed the impatience of this man, but he went doggedly on: 'It makes you wonder about what's real and what isn't. Or whether it's all one. A TV tree and one outside the window, for instance. Would it matter if you never saw the outside one again? Or is it better?'

'So we're on morals now,' said Byers. 'Good, bad and better has nothing to do with it.'

'Maybe not. But I want to make sure I *feel* the difference between them.'

'Pleasure's the only thing that matters. The thing that gives you most – that's the one to go for.' There was a silence. Byers held his paper up again and they were joined by an old woman who scanned the headlines for a moment, decided against the full version, and shuffled off.

'Women have this way of skimming the cream off everything,' said Byers. 'It seems to satisfy them and at the same time they get it for nothing. But you were saying . . ?'

'Real and unreal. One day at lunchtime, a while back, coming out of a restaurant I bent down to a table near the door and tried to smell a vase of those small, red artificial roses. Oh, very real they were! As I sniffed several people sitting near saw me, and guffawed.'

'But did you get no pleasure?'

'None. It was a very unpleasant sensation. What next? Maybe next time I'll be asking the way of a scarecrow. I was afraid it would grow on me – mixing up real and unreal. I didn't feel one hundred per cent human.'

'Well who is? Don't worry. And concentrate on pleasure.'

Garrad stared at him, at his melancholy mouth, downturned, as though by the continual drag of the dark headlines he held beneath his chin. 'So you've no colour,' Byers said suddenly as Garrad was moving quietly away. 'Better try walking westwards.'

In the west it was smouldering up into a sunset, not yet in full blaze. There was already a glow around him, but Garrad's thoughts were grey. He felt some loneliness walking back by himself in the pale pink. Even his own talk of real and unreal had unnerved him a bit. He'd been lucky to meet a few people, but he needed more than that. He was turning in now to a long street of identical houses whose front-room windows were so close to the pavement you could have almost touched the glass by stretching over one strip of grass, narrow as a doormat. The difference between one place and the next lay mainly in these green doormats – some were well-groomed and plushy, others were threadbare or dotted with daisies. Now the pink light, growing deeper, illumined housefronts, stained smooth doorsteps and glinted overhead from a thick bristling of aerials. Most curtains were still not drawn and he had a full view into front rooms. He went more slowly. Most people had already switched on. In some rooms there were families, in others single persons – all bathed in a mixture of pink, and ghostly TV light. At one house the box flickered over an empty room. Garrad stood staring at a fisherman until a woman appeared in the doorway, stood watching the fisherman for a time, and went out again. Again she came back, switched from fisherman to skyscrapers to a shampooed head and back to the fisherman. She went out again and Garrad moved on. The fisherman was now on most screens and on one in four he was in colour. It made a fine colour-picture. The fisherman was knee-deep in a river on a summer evening and it was an evening which seemed to keep step with the actual evening outside. The river was flowing red just as the pavement where Garrad walked was beginning to glow. He went more and more slowly. Where groups sat he saw only profiles and backs of heads and at one or two windows heard snatches of screen commentary. Here whole families were sitting, spellbound or bound by boredom. He had the feeling that if he stepped over and tapped at these windows not a head would turn. If a head *did* turn and he beckoned – who would exert the strongest pull? He with his fires behind him or the fisherman with his? He felt unfairly matched for he was now tired. He imagined he made a rather poor picture compared with the rapt riverman. Not even switched on. To all intents and purposes, though with the red behind, an invisible man.

Garrad was three-quarters down this long street when he met his match. A dozen houses or so from the end he turned his head towards one wide window and saw – himself. He was set up like all the rest of them, handsomely framed and mounted – the same for size, the same for clarity. His background glowed out stronger and redder even than the fisherman's. He was looking into a mirror which stood squarely in that place where in all other rooms he had looked for the TV set. It was an old-fashioned mirror set up on a stand, like a picture on a short easel, and placed on a side-table well away from the wall. The room itself was identical to all the other rooms of the street. Yet in

atmosphere it was different. It lacked the sealed-off, all
absorbed look of the others. There was no spellbinder here
– only two young women who, backs to the window, were
bending over the end of a long table. It wasn't easy to see
what they were doing. They might be wrapping and tying a
dumpy parcel from the look of it, or pressing and persuading a yeasty lump of dough. They stood aside for a moment
and he saw a baby being zipped into a nightsack. Its head
rolled on the tabletop. Its furious feet made the corners of
the bag squirm like a flame-curled envelope. Garrad
watched the performance. For more than half the street
he'd been an invisible screen-watcher, familiar only with
the backs of heads. But now one of the women, catching
sight of his head in the mirror, twisted round to face him.
This double look fascinated Garrad. At one blow he was
twice hailed, twice identified as a living man. Now the other
woman had turned. As though aware of some oddness in
their background, lacking a TV, they did more than turn
their heads. They seemed amused at the man gaping in at
them. One of them swung the baby in its bag up off the
table and both came to the window and pushed it wider
open. Garrad leaned on the gate. The baby was placed on
the window-ledge, its white woollen bag absorbing sunset
like a sponge.

'Talk about fire!' exclaimed the young mother leaning
out. 'That sky is quite something!'

'The best I've seen for years,' Garrad replied.

'He's never seen one yet,' she said, hitching the baby
further up. 'It's his first, I believe. This *is* his first.' Garrad
felt that only with reluctance had the baby let his fury
subside. At any moment it might burst again. Meanwhile it
continued to stare out.

'It's not the sky that interests him,' said the other, who
was obviously a sister. 'I don't believe he'd so much as blink
if the sky turned suddenly green or black or whatever.
*People* interest him.'

'He loves *colour*. And I believe he even looks at distance,' said the mother. Stern and impassive, the baby hung between them while they bickered gently behind his back. There was some jealousy around. Even Garrad felt jealous for himself. He had alerted them to colour. He *was* colour. His shoulders and back were saturated with it, his hair pronged with pink. Between their shoulders he got a glimpse of himself in the mirror with great streaks of fire behind his head.

'Yes, it was seeing you in *that*,' said the sister following his glance. 'If you hadn't stopped just where you are we wouldn't have noticed until too late. It's past its best already, isn't it?' Garrad was appeased. He was about to move on when there was a flash of lightning and some moments later a distant rumble of thunder.

'Oh I knew that was coming!' said the girl holding the baby. There was another flash behind Garrad's left shoulder followed directly by a much louder boom. The women at the window were now staring at him transfixed. He was something now all right with his flaming sky and lightning springing between his shoulders. For a moment all three were satisfied to stare – the women at the sudden drama outside, the man at the scene indoors. But the baby, peeved by the momentary withdrawal of attention, began to girn and twist in its bag.

'You'll excuse us if we shut the window now,' said its mother. 'But thanks – thanks for drawing our attention . . .'

Garrad waved. He saw his own hand move in their mirror and again got the double response, as they faced him and as they turned inwards and saw his image. He moved away, past more family groups, past couples and single viewers. The fisherman had long ago packed up and a dozen soldiers were galloping with spears poised through a narrow gorge between mountains. Thunder was rumbling very far off. Garrad walked slowly though he was still a long way from his own part of the town. The fiery sky was

already half extinguished, yet for a short time the colour
down in the streets seemed deeper than ever, as if trapped
and richly mixed with dark stone or floating through the
dust and soot in the air. By the time Garrad reached his
district the whole upper sky had faded to a yellow-green,
but here and there between the distant cranes and spires on
the town's horizon there were still some streaks of orange
light. He turned another corner, walked up a long street of
empty offices and shops and out into the part where the
double villas and careful gardens began. He was near
home. A few steps further and he was looking into his
own front room. The place was lit but deserted and the
square of emptiness where the TV had stood seemed more
conspicuous than ever. Yet as soon as he was in the door he
knew the heavy atmosphere had fractionally lifted. A moment later his wife came through from the back of the
house.

'The colour's coming back!' she said.

'It's what?'

'They phoned soon after you left. And there's not all that
much wrong. We'll have the colour back first thing tomorrow.'

'Well, thank God for that.' His gratitude for the returning colour-box sounded thin to his own ears. The very
flatness of his tone gave the lie to it. Yet when it did come
tomorrow wouldn't he welcome colour back with open
arms? He didn't doubt it. At this moment, however, he was
loaded with the stuff himself. The new substance. The real
thing. His clothes were soaked in it to the skin. The whole
gamut of reds had penetrated to his bone marrow and was
now thickening his blood. But he was not, as far as he could
see, radiating any of this spectacular colour himself. His
wife looked blank. The hall was dim and getting dimmer.
On the right hung a large mirror and on the opposite side a
smaller one reflecting into infinity a square of biscuit-toned
wall. Between these Garrad moved forward carefully but

stopped at the foot of the stairs. His wife was watching him closely.

'What are you thinking about?' she said.

'Colour, of course.'

'Are you thinking about the missing colour?'

'No, just colour.'

'*Not* the missing colour?'

'No. Colour.'

'What, to be exact?'

'The usual. Starting with that odd tree that sticks out into the road. Never noticed before but it's got half its bark peeled off. Every boy that passes tears a strip. It's dead white on the pavement side, black on the other. It's a cartoon tree now.'

'Black and white? Are you still talking about colour?'

'I went past the market. Rails and rails of red, blue and yellow dresses. Who buys them?'

'What's so *new*?'

'Nothing. I went as far as the school with the glass. There's actually a palm-tree in the corridor. Imagine it! There'll not be much stripped off *that* one. And back again. The stalls were packing up. People fingering huge piles of bashed plums and split tomatoes.' He paused.

'What else?'

Garrad had his foot on the stairs. 'The sky.' He drew his breath with a slight hiss. 'There's still a patch.'

'A patch?'

'Of red. Of pink now. You might still see something from the back room. One patch left, and getting smaller every minute.' He started to go up. His wife who had been staring at him as though expecting the knobs of his backbone to light up, now stood reluctantly pondering the pale pink patch, her foot on the bottom stair. Slowly she went up after him.

# Waiting for the Sun

'I DON'T KNOW whether you've seen this one before,' Mr Shering would say, passing the photo round a company at his fireside. 'A fellow at my hotel took that – never seen the man in my life. He bobbed up in front of me one day – and that was it! Not so much as "by your leave".' Walking across to the lamp he would study another one for a long time, murmuring to himself: 'I haven't an idea where this one was taken. Wait a minute though. Wasn't I just stepping off the boat at Marseilles? It must have been the mother of that child who took such a fancy to me for some unknown reason. And here's another. Believe it or not, this time I simply haven't a clue. As likely as not some complete stranger took it when I wasn't looking. These things happen to me!' But his sideways glance as he passed between two handsome mirrors which hung on opposite walls clearly showed that he saw every reason why such things should happen to him. In these glasses he was reflected, diminished but shining, within an infinite number of gilded frames – a tall, heavily-built man in his sixties who carried himself as though he had, in the past, held his chin up over a series of stiff collars and was now keeping it that way, no longer supported by the formal neckwear but simply by the memory of these people who had once turned to stare at him as he went by and wondered who he was. An actor, a visiting conductor, some distinguished man of letters? Once he had kept them guessing. Nowadays he thrived only on a few upturned faces staring at him from his own fireside, or the brief turning of heads as he laboriously boarded the trains and buses of out-of-the-way towns. He had to make the most of these rarer and rarer occasions when he believed himself recognized for what he was.

This need was greater now. All the same, he was hard put to know what he was himself. He occasionally referred to his 'full life', but somehow he had missed doing anything which gave him the right to display a label or put out a sign. Moreover, since he was a young man there had grown up a much greater demand for exact self-description and the clear listing of virtues and vices in black and white. Confident 'yes' or 'no' answers to quick-firing questions were now expected as a matter of course. In the days when he had money it had been different. It was enough then to set out a tray of ornaments before his visitors and to keep a silk polishing cloth and a magnifying glass at hand for studying details and inscriptions. In no time he would find himself described by at least one of the company as an antiquarian. He had only to unhook one or two dark brown oil paintings from the walls and study them under the light, or thumb reverently through a worn leather-bound book – and he was unlucky if two or three did not refer to him as a connoisseur of painting or collector of rare books. It was a matter of picking the right company and keeping them at a certain distance so that there could be no question of disillusionment on either side. He respected other people's feelings and was extremely tender with his own. He deplored the growing tendency to probe and question. Born sceptics were nothing more or less than bores to his way of thinking, and he had a particular dislike for those who, in season and out, were avid for the truth. He looked on them as selfish people, greedy for a special form of nourishment which had always been hard to procure, and was in any case a luxury which he himself had been able to do without for years on end.

Some loss in income made a difference to his way of living for a time. His health was affected, but only enough to keep him mooning about the convalescent wings of nursing-homes and from there to the back gardens and spare bedrooms of various acquaintances during the summer. When after a few years he took up his interests again, he discovered the world was changing out of all recognition. Speed and absolute efficiency were demanded, even for the forming of relationships. On every side there was a gathering in of facts and information, while the tools and mechanical devices for detecting flaws in machines and human beings were working overtime. He suspected that they were contained, when not in use, in the shiny plastic bags and steel-hinged cases which were everywhere being carried about in place of the crushable, bulging ones he had known.

He began to move about in a world of his own, politely ignoring the people who asked him what he did, staring intently over the heads of those who tried to tell him what they did themselves. Long ago he had discovered it was not necessary to listen to every word spoken. Only a few words were needed in order to place the speaker. The rest had been a matter of patience – unending, unquestioning patience. But now, like it or not, he was moving into the sink-or-swim era of experts. Mr Shering realized he would sink without trace unless he found a new and effortless way to assert himself.

It was the necessity to combine being somebody with doing nothing which led him to his new interest. In no time it amounted to an obsession. In place of the prints and paintings and glittering trays of little knick-knacks, fat albums of photos began to pile up on top of his bookcase. When his finances improved and he began to move about again and see the world the interest came into full force. The time came when he could hand round photos dating back over years and point out the details which had a topical interest at the time.

'This was that town where there was all the rumpus – nine years ago – over the leading councillor. If you look closely I think you might just see his name chalked up in white on that wall there. The abuse was in red underneath – bigger letters in fact, but you'd have to have good eyes to see it. It's the red against the dark wall does it. And here's one in Sicily. It's supposed to be a photo of the volcano of course, but here's the tail-end of a bus come in the way. Incidentally that same bus was in the news a day or two later – overturned into a ravine with a load of tourists. It's rather a horrid photo, I'm afraid – the more so when you remember the volcano started erupting six months or so later!'

People looking through these photos were more surprised, however, to see their extraordinary variety. There were all types here from small, blurred, amateur snaps to the studies whose light and clarity approached professional standard. Sometimes at first glance they made the mistake of imagining that Shering was himself the photographer. Nothing could be further from the truth and their mistake was quickly corrected on a closer inspection. While Mr Shering was pointing out the palm-trees, flags, ruins and mountains which marked his travels, his guests were studying the figure, dignified and solitary, standing sometimes in the middle distance but more often in the foreground of each photo. Though his appearance in these pictures changed over the years, though his clothes varied with the summer or winter backgrounds against which he stood – like those animals whose brown coats turn white against the snow – he was always easy to spot. Shering never had to point himself out. He simply referred to the many friends he made as he went about, travellers like himself who'd taken him up on the spot as though they'd known him all their lives. He was lucky, he supposed, to have met the people who took him as they found him.

But the real reason was that though the world had changed he'd no intention of being left out of the picture. The desire to be photographed had grown from the need to be in contact again with persons who could admire him from a distance. This distance, lengthening with each disillusionment, gradually became the space between himself and the person with a camera. There was a fascination about such a contact. It was intimate yet impersonal. It was with people who, except for one sunlit encounter, would remain strangers to him for the rest of his life.

It was not others who took him as they found him. It was he who found and captured all those with cameras in their hands, recognizing them even from a great distance by their surroundings and gestures, as a birdwatcher spots his special birds. He would then come running heavily down some cliff path or down the worn steps of a cathedral, breathlessly descending to the beach or crowded square where someone was balancing their black box against a rock or the rim of a fountain. 'Hullo there!' he would shout while still some distance off. 'Wait a minute! Have you got that quite right? You're going to spoil a magnificent picture if you're not careful. Hold on. I'll be right with you!'

Occasionally he made mistakes in the people he approached. Any other man might have been struck to the ground by the looks certain photographers directed towards him as he came waving and running. He had withstood some terrible abuse in his time. But such incidents were rare. In any case the skin which appeared to be drawn so finely over Shering's well-cut features was surprisingly thick. And years of practice had enabled him to spot the amateur almost without fail. When this happened it was no time till he'd struck up a conversation with someone behind an out-of-date camera, not long either before he was standing, his head turned away, his profile white as marble against some dingy ruin or black as basalt against a sun-whitened archway – waiting for the click which would release him from a casual, dreaming posture. 'Is that how you want me? Tell me when you've got it,' he would murmur, scarcely opening his lips or lowering his eyelids.

'Well, if you can really be bothered,' he would say in parting, drawing out a visiting card with his home address. 'It would be a memento of a very happy meeting, of a most interesting talk.' It was in this way that his collection of photos grew.

In great cities the poses Shering took up were sculpturesque. His look could be stern and sorrowful like the expression on statues in public squares. Occasionally his face, which showed the mildness of a sheltered life, could take on the look of a man of violent action – an expression he'd caught sight of on some nearby helmeted figure mounted on a bronze war-horse. On the other hand photos taken in the country showed him as natural and pliable as his backgrounds. He was snapped leaning on gates or bending down to study a flower in the grass – always looking up at the right moment to flash a smile. He had no attractive wife to steal the picture, no restless children to smudge the effect in the foreground. He was suspicious of all tricks in photography – gadgets which made a raindrop on a cabbage leaf bulge like a crown jewel. People who used these devices tended to be more complicated than the others and might show less patience for taking straightforward pictures of himself. In spite of everything he maintained he had more friends all over the world than he could ever keep up with. The friends he spoke of were simply those people with whom he had sat and waited for the sun.

The hours he had sat waiting for the sun took up the greater part of Mr Shering's waking life. He had sat waiting with people amongst ruins, on the edge of piers, on mountains, in boats and in buses. Infinitely adaptable, he could wait calmly with a solitary and tongue-tied tourist winding the first reel into his camera as with the seasoned traveller already halfway round the world. Long habits of posing had given him an expression of concentration which never wavered, whether he was listening to the endless comparisons of hotel bedrooms or to the peculiar history of certain engraved stones set in a nearby arch. He was not attending. The brightening gleam in his eyes was not evidence of the climax to a thrilling tale but of the long-awaited appearance of the sun at the edge of a bank of black cloud.

It was the sun which held all things together in Mr Shering's disconnected life. His casual encounters were made only in its light, and faded when the light faded. Under heavy skies he lived from hour to hour, dulled and diminished in his own eyes, making few contacts, seeing and hearing little of what was going on around him. But he knew when the sun rose and when it set on every day of the year. Elusive as its shining was, the sun was the only dependable in a monstrously unreliable life.

One fine morning in summer, Shering, who was coming to the end of a fortnight's holiday near the south-west coast, decided that for his final outing he would climb as high as he could to get a last view of the sea and the surrounding country. The small hotel where he had been staying had become inexplicably crowded the evening before, and he'd decided to move on as soon as possible. Crowds were not for him. He needed a great deal of time and space for himself and he had resented this inrush of young men and women who overnight had transformed the quiet hotel into a place as busy and noisy as a city office. The irritation vanished, however, as soon as he'd left the village and taken the path which led up through a group of young birch trees onto the slope above. This was the only hill in the district and it counted as high. But the climb was easy. The air was clear. As he went up, the blue spaces of the sky widened out and the mist rolled off the fields until at last he was able to look down at the sea sparkling in full sunshine below. He took the last part of the climb slowly, scarcely looking up till he reached the boulders which marked the top. When he did raise his head and stop for breath he saw a young man already seated there. Shering marked with approval the camera slung on his shoulder. But he also saw as he came closer that the man belonged to the party which had arrived at the hotel the evening before.

Shering remembered him all too clearly – this business-like fellow packed with information of one kind or another who'd made it perfectly plain to the rest of the company, as he spread out maps and plans and diagrams, that he and his friends were not on holiday like the rest of them, but were involved in some project of the utmost interest to the entire world. Shering had got well out of earshot long before the nature of this research could be explained. Being on perpetual holiday himself, he had an instinctive suspicion of people who discussed work enthusiastically in public and a particular dislike of those who, groaning at the swift passing of time, insisted on counting up the few days of freedom left to them. Freedom lay heavily on Shering from one year's end to the next – limitless and all-enveloping. Long ago the word had lost its meaning. When he heard it discussed he felt as much resentment as if words from an unknown language had been suddenly thrust into the conversation. It had seemed to him possible, as he watched the earnest young men and women, that at any minute there might burst on his ears the question of time wasted and made up, a discussion of extra efforts to be made, of timetables, calendars and the hour-by-hour recording of important events. He had gone early to bed.

The young man on top of the hill, however, showed no particular emotion on seeing Shering. His face was thin and stern and his dark eyes stared confidently out from behind horn-rimmed spectacles. To the older man who was climbing laboriously up towards him he gave the impression, even though slight and rigid in build, that at this moment he owned the hill, the sky, the sea, and the whole surrounding countryside. He was absolute master of the situation, whatever it was, and this time Shering himself had not an inkling how the land lay. The young man gave no clue and threw out no communication line. But Shering, secretive himself, knew he was bursting with some purpose of his own. He was not here for the view. Not a muscle of his body was relaxed.

'We are far too early of course,' he remarked as Shering came up, and he gave a short laugh as though scorning himself, 'but I prefer to take up my position before the others arrive.' He seemed relieved that the necessity of speech was over and done with. He turned away at once and examined the sea with exaggerated curiosity. Shering sat down on the smoothest boulder and looked around him.

'It *is* early.' He spoke politely to the rigid shoulders. 'But not an unnatural time for me to be out and about, I can assure you. I think it's safe to say there won't be anyone else around for some time – unless of course you're expecting friends.'

The young man turned his head slightly to one side, but said nothing. It now became clear that the set of his face was due to extreme nervousness. He sat straight, his arms tightly folded across his chest as though rigidly controlling himself. Shering, who prided himself on putting all kinds of people at their ease, felt instinctively that this would be as hard a case as he had yet tackled.

'I somehow imagine – I may be quite out – I imagine from certain things you said last night that you are a teacher,' he began in the hesitating voice which overlaid an inexhaustible persistence.

'Science,' the young man muttered through his teeth.

'A teacher of Science,' said Shering with an edge of disapproval to his voice. 'Then in many ways I think I envy you. To be able to convey something of the mystery . . . something of the miracle . . .' But the young man was staring at the sky where a long strip of cloud was drifting across the sun. His face grew more than ever pinched and severe, and when at last the sun was completely covered he jumped to his feet with a groan. Shering saw what he could only describe as a tearing of hair, and he was amazed. Nothing in his opinion could account for such emotion, unless the relation between cloud and camera. But though he had stood by and watched the disappointment of hundreds of photographers – never had he witnessed a disappointment like this. By this time he also was on his feet and now stood with folded arms, his head flung back watching the sky. He had seen all this before. A whole continent of cloud might move across to blot out the sun. He could be patient.

'If I'm not mistaken it will all pass over in about twenty minutes or so,' he said quietly. 'You'll have your picture, if that's what's worrying you. Indeed, if I'm any judge of cameras, that one there will take a very fine picture in just this light.' But as he spoke these words he knew they were worse than useless – he even judged them downright dangerous. For the young man had turned abruptly. Shering found himself looking into a pair of glaring eyes, eyebrows raised in outrage above the hornrims. It was a fanatic's face. At any minute he could be expected to raise his fists in the air and curse Shering for ever having set foot on the same hill as himself.

'I have as much right . . .' began Shering, taking a step back and glancing behind as he did so. But what he saw below him cut short all stating of rights.

A great crowd of people were slowly making their way up onto this hill where, in the last fortnight, not a soul had set foot. They came from all sides – men, women and children, winding their way purposefully along the grassy paths at the foot and looking up now and then with an air of expectancy towards the top where the two men stood. Further out in the lanes below Shering saw that cars were drawing up. Beyond that again and for as far as he could see, cars, vans and caravans were coming in, one behind the other, all along the criss-crossed roads of the surrounding district.

Twisting through them and wobbling behind were long, glittering lines of bicycles, with the odd motorbike coming up, jolting and bursting, from the rear. Every now and then those on foot who'd been pressed back into the hedges by passing traffic, widened out again in pairs or groups across the road and were passed in their turn by some solitary figure with a knapsack who had been plodding along since early morning. There was a continual movement going on – a knotting, a fanning out, a stepping back and forward. But there was no chaos on the roads. A single purpose drove them forward towards the foot of the hill where the first arrivals were climbing out of their cars and had started to move up behind the rest onto the lower slopes. In a few minutes solid ranks of people, close enough to hide the green, were climbing from all sides over rocks and through bushes, coming on with the silent determination of an army on the move. There was something strange to Shering in that determination. Were they converging on *him*? In one panic second his innocent life flashed by. For what crime was he to be punished on the hill? To placate what gods?

The panic passed. Looking closer he could make out specific groups among the crowd. Small family parties emerged with rugs and raincoats over their arms. Some carried thermos flasks, lemonade bottles and wads of sandwiches in brown paper. Shades of navy blue marked the circles of pupils from surrounding schools, accompanied by their teachers. Here and there official uniforms stood out. A driver and his conductor were coming up with a bus load of passengers. A couple of off-duty policewomen were going along with them, while down at the foot five nuns were paying off a taxi, chattering excitedly, their black habits blowing behind them as they turned to climb. Most prominent amongst the crowd was the large group of young men recognized by Shering as the group who had arrived at the hotel the evening before. It was at once clear to him that they, along with his companion in the hornrims, were the natural leaders of this gathering. They did not spread themselves like the others and their heavy, angular equipment had nothing to do with picnics. They were serious if not actually grim as they climbed up silently together to join the young man at the top.

Most of the crowd had now gathered on the highest part of the hill and soon the grass was patched with raincoats where the families were sitting down, already surreptitiously unscrewing thermos flasks. But there was something different here from the usual picnicking crowd. These people were focused outwards. It was more than a normal interest in the view. Their eyes remained mesmerically fixed even while they poured the tea and put their hands in and out of paper bags. Shering saw a few miss their mark and more than one stream of tea flowed down the side of a mug into the grass. Meanwhile those solitary persons who had come up to roam restlessly about on their own, now met and passed one another without a glance, only dropping their eyes from the distance once in a while to stare at watches.

Surrounded as he was on all sides, Shering felt increasingly ill at ease, like the solitary unbeliever in a crowd of visionaries. If he was conspicuous it was because he lacked the expectancy which marked all other faces, and feeling safer unobserved, he sat down cautiously on the ground. All the signs now persuaded him that he was part of a great open-air organization – a political or religious sect grown strong and drawing followers from a vast area. At any moment an orator would spring to his feet. There would be answering shouts and chants and a raising of banners with secret slogans. Shering had watched such things before, but always from a distance. His spirits sank. It was too late to make his escape. There was now an unmistakable rounding-up going on. Teachers were gathering in the pupils who had strayed too far and here and there a parent was running after a child who'd broken away to other family groups. The bus driver had placed himself in front of his passengers in order to count them, his lips moving, his eyes going from face to face. The nuns stood quietly together, their tilted, white-bound brows towards the sky, arms on their skirts. While all around the groups drew closer and closer together, a hush had gradually fallen on the crowd. Shering noticed it first in the nearby families who had stopped talking and seemed to be taking care to fold up their paper with as little sound as possible. Nobody hurried. There was almost stealth in the movement about him and those who had got to their feet did it as though fearful of disturbing the earth they stood on. More and more people were staring at their watches and with an intentness uncanny to Mr Shering to whom time meant nothing. And now the silence which had deepened with every second was broken suddenly by a rustling whisper which swept over the crowd as they bent towards one another like reeds over which an unnatural wind had passed. Shering listened intently to the curious sound which came again and again from those nearest him. 'The sun!' It was this word he managed to sift from all the rest. It grew steadily in volume until it seemed his own secret sun obsession was being declaimed from all sides.

'So that's it,' he said to calm himself, unaware that he was whispering like the rest. 'Well, what of it?' He saw only a bright, mottled sky with one darker strip of cloud hiding the sun. He saw nothing strange. It was the same sky he had always stared at, the same cloud hiding the longed-for sun.

'Are you waiting for the sun to come out?' he said, throwing his words with enormous effort into a silence. No one answered, but several faces turned momentarily in his direction – shocked faces staring at a blasphemer. Swiftly they turned away again towards the sky.

Shering had gradually become aware that for the last few minutes a peculiar gloom had been falling through the air. He noticed it first upon his blanching hands. Then he saw the grass. It had faded as though a sudden blight had eaten up its green. Now sea and sky turned grey. If a great storm was impending it was not from the few clouds overhead – but rather from some black cloud rolling up to cover the whole earth. Shering's only thought was for shelter. But there was no shelter for him on the hill. He saw the sky change to the north and the ground, as far as the eye could see, turned grey as though sprinkled with ash. All over the hill, as the darkness deepened, there was a soft surge of movement as people inside the groups pressed closer and closer together while those on the outside swung in nearer to the others. Shering felt more than unsheltered. He was alone, unprepared for whatever disaster was about to break. For suddenly a single gust of cold wind passed over him, pricking up the hairs of his head. At the same instant, like a great net flung rifling into the sky, a flock of starlings went up behind him and took flight to the west. Shering raised both hands to his head and in the silence heard his own voice whisper: 'No! Not yet . . .!' But this time the sun was no longer a partner in the game. He knew that in less than one minute he was to be witness to its eclipse.

The smoky yellow clouds covering the sun now turned dark red, changing as the darkness grew to a deep violet which Shering had never seen before, even in the most spectacular sunset. But the rest of the earth darkened and withered rapidly. The faces around him turned livid. Clothes, rocks, grass and blazing gorse bushes had faded to ghosts of themselves. Shering, like the survivor of some dying planet, was appalled to see a few stars shining in the clear patches of the sky. The last light faded and he covered his eyes. Stooping, his knees and shoulders limp as if even the red blood ran grey, he gave himself up to the darkest moment of the eclipse.

Half a minute later Shering found himself on the ground staring at the same landscape from which a heavy veil was being swiftly lifted. Colour was coming back over ground and sky with such speed that it seemed a thick membrane covering his eye had split to let in this astounding light. But in seconds this brilliance had faded again into the ordinary light of day. Over the whole hillside there was now an air of recovery and relief and from all sides there came a murmuring which grew gradually louder. Shouts and laughter broke out, and amongst certain groups violent discussions started up. The young men and women from the hotel were putting instruments back into their cases and tucking wedges of smoked glass into the pockets of haversacks between maps and charts. The eclipse had not been perfect. Shering could see the earnest young man standing apart from the others, still staring at the clouded sky, pale with disappointment. But the others had recovered from their frustration and were now rapidly making notes in small black exercise books. On all sides people were gathering themselves together, briskly brushing off the astounding along with the earth and grass from their coats.

Soon, over the round top of the hill, patches of green appeared again as groups started to move down the slopes – slowly at first, still dazed and chilled, then more quickly as they came further down where the grass was smooth. In a few minutes the whole hillside of people seemed to be taking part in a great race to see who could reach the level ground first. Where he sat Shering could feel the urgent beating of the earth under him. Flaps of coats and rugs brushed past his knees in a steady wind of movement, and once a swinging handbag tilted his hat over his eyes. Still he sat on, motionless, his eyes on the ground, feeling the racing current around him grow gradually less and less, until it was no more than a gentle fanning of the air as the last and slowest on the hill went past. Far down below, those who had reached the road were already starting up cars and pulling bicycles out of the hedges. The bus driver was in his seat patiently watching his passengers file in. The nuns, all folded and sober as birds after a flight, were

waiting inside their taxi. The hikers were moving purposefully off down the lanes. Determined now to weld themselves to solid earth, nobody looked back and nobody
looked up.

The last to leave the hill had been a group of schoolboys
who'd waited for the lecture on what they had not, but
might have seen. Their spirits were still high. As Shering
had watched them race off he saw, halfway down, one of the
group break away from the rest and come pounding up
again towards the spot where he was sitting. As he came
near the boy started to swing about in circles close to the
ground. Now and then he pounced and raked the long
grass with his toe. Nothing came of the search. His circles
grew wider and dizzier, and he was already moving back
downhill when there was a shout from above. 'I have it!'
Shering was pointing to something red a few yards away in
the grass. By the time he reached him the boy had fastened
the red pen into his pocket and now flung himself, gasping,
down beside Shering. 'A piece of luck!' he exclaimed when
he could speak. 'I thought I'd never see it again!'

'It was lucky *I* saw it,' said Shering. He was not in the
mood to speak of luck. Something about the boy's red face
and the way he rolled himself exultantly on the ground
reminded him that he himself had sat on the same spot,
cold and motionless, for a very long time. His gloom and
silence made itself felt.

'Why are you still here?' asked the boy, suddenly
straightening up and staring at Shering with interest. 'Are
you waiting for something more to happen? Because it
won't. You've had it – probably for the rest of the century.'

Shering's eyes swept the horizon coldly. 'Nobody told
me,' he said, speaking to the sky.

'We've known about it for months in our school,' said
the boy. He took out a square of smoked glass, spat on it
and polished it regretfully on his sleeve. 'A lot of use this
was!' he said staring through it at the clouds. 'I could tell

you all the eclipses for years back – totals and annulars. Of course you won't see a total till August 1999. Well honestly, I don't think you'll be around by that time, will you? But of course you might come in for a few lunars. By the way, did you ever hear of Bailey's Beads?'

'Never!' said Shering curtly. He took a quick look into the thick grass.

'Lots of people haven't,' said the boy with satisfaction. He was silent for some time, looking out over the country-side and relishing the widespread ignorance. Then he said: 'All the same, I wouldn't have missed that blackout. Did you know that one of the kids from Lower School nearly fainted? Our Maths man, Baker, laid him on his back and produced a bottle of whisky. That would have been a botch-up for a start. Even beginners First Aid know that. Anyway, you should have seen this infant's face! We thought he'd died. Imagine what a morning that would have been. Eclipse and corpse at one swoop! Well, he wasn't dead, but he was terribly sick afterwards. All the rest of us looked grey and white at the time. But do you know what colour *his* face was? It was blue – pale blue with purple shadows. Of course we'll be getting an essay on this, and I shall put in someone lying dead in an eclipse – and no one looking at him. If you saw it in a newspaper you wouldn't believe it, would you? You could be lying dead right here in the grass where we are now, and no one taking any notice – just staring at the sky.'

'It's too cold to sit,' said Shering getting up from the ground. 'As a matter of fact I only came up for fifteen minutes, and I've been over an hour. I don't care to catch a chill on the last day of my holiday.'

'But the sun's coming out,' said the boy. He drew a small flat camera from his gaberdine pocket. 'I've got one photo to get before I go.'

'What kind of thing do you want?' asked Shering, auto-matically taking his pose a few steps back.

'Well, as a matter of fact, I wouldn't mind a snap of myself,' said the boy. 'That is, if *you* don't mind. There's nothing else to take, is there? I'd like it right here on the spot where we saw it happen. It'll be unique. And maybe I won't have the same interest even if it does happen again. I mean you hadn't been all that interested yourself in eclipses, had you? It goes to show you can't go on and on feeling excited about things forever.'

'And I thought boys of your age weren't all that excited about having their photos taken,' replied Shering sharply. 'Did you mean that *I* would take it?'

'Of course I would have asked one of the others,' said the boy. 'But they were all off like a shot. Anyway there's nothing in it. It's the simplest camera out. You simply press that – when I tell you. That's all there is to it. Wait a second!' He ran to a flat rock. 'What about this?' he called. 'Am I all right?' Shering didn't answer. He held the camera gingerly, bending his head only an inch or so as though over an unexploded bomb.

'Am I all right?' came the shout again. 'Can you see me?'

'Of course I can see you!' Shering lifted his head and glared before him. The boy was sitting on the rock with his knees drawn up, his hands clasped around them, and on his face the serious obliquely-focused look of one born to be photographed. Shering experienced a sudden crippling spasm of jealousy.

'I'll send you a copy if it comes out!' called the boy. 'Press now!' His lips, Shering noted, scarcely moved.

'What are we waiting for?' called the boy again. 'The light's all right, isn't it. Have you got the sun behind you?'

Shering turned and stared in the direction of the sun. It was there where it should be, shining serenely over a quiet hillside. Except for the flattened squares of grass and a few empty paper bags there was no sign that anything unusual had taken place. But the face which Shering turned to the sun was utterly changed. It was no longer that of a trusting man, but rather of someone who can now believe anything of his accomplice – even that day might become night or night day before he can turn his head.

Among the photos which Shering showed to visitors there appeared, from time to time, one on which he made little or no comment. At first sight it was naturally supposed to be a rather dim photo of Shering himself, taken in his schoolboy days. He was, after all, there in every other photo they had seen, and there was even something reminiscent of him in this small figure who sat with averted profile and firmly posed hands and feet. But Shering was quick to correct the mistake. 'This – of the schoolboy – is the one I took myself,' he would say in a voice more restrained than usual, and in the silence which followed he would add in a low tone, still more sternly controlled: '. . . The sun disappeared for a time.' Nothing more was said, and no question ever asked, though during the swift appearance and disappearance of this photo it occasionally occurred to imaginative visitors that the man might even be hiding the fact that he had a son. But Shering, putting it back carefully into the middle of a pack of photos like a man hiding an unlucky card, gave them to understand that this was one snapshot on which, dim as it was, he had no intention of throwing any further light.

# *Allergy*

THE NEW LODGER glanced down briefly at the plate which had just been put in front of him and turned towards the window with a faint smile, as though acknowledging that the day was fair enough outside, even if there was something foul within.

'I can't take egg. Sorry.'

'Can't take?' Mrs Ella MacLean still kept her thumb on the oozy edge of a heap of scrambled yellow.

'No. It's an allergy.'

'It doesn't agree?'

'No. It's an allergy.'

'Oh, one of those. That's interesting! But you could take a lightly-boiled egg, couldn't you?'

'No, it's an allergy to egg.'

'You mean *any* egg?'

'Any and every egg, Mrs MacLean. In all forms. Egg is poison to me.' Harry Veitch did not raise his voice at all, but this time his landlady withdrew the plate rather quickly. She put it on one side and sat down at the other end of the table.

'Yes, that *is* interesting,' she said. 'I've known the strawberries and the shellfish and the cat's fur. And of course I've heard of the egg, though I've never met it.' Veitch said nothing. He broke a piece of toast. 'No, I've never met it. Though I've met eggs disagreeing. I mean really disagreeing!'

Veitch was pressing his lips with a napkin. 'Not the same thing,' he said. 'When I say poison I mean poison. Pains. Vomiting. And I wouldn't like to say what else. Violent! Not many people understand just *how* violent!'

Flickers of curiosity alternated with prim blankness in Mrs MacLean's eyes. 'And aren't there dusts and pollens – horse's hair and that sort of thing?'

'All kinds. I don't even know the lot. But they're not all as *violent.*'

There was a silence while Mrs MacLean with a soft white napkin gently, gently brushed away the scratchy toast-crumbs which lay between them in the centre of the table.

'Do you find people sympathetic then?' she enquired at last.

Veitch gave a short laugh. 'Mrs MacLean – when, may I ask, have people ever been sympathetic to anything out of the ordinary?'

'I suppose that's true.'

They both turned their heads to look out onto the Edinburgh street, already crowded with people going to work. There was a stiffish breeze – visitors from the south, like Veitch, used the word 'gale' – and those going east-wards had their teeth bared against it and their eyes screwed up in a grimace which made them appear very unsympathetic indeed. On the pavement below their window, a well-dressed man stooped in the swirling dust to unwind a strip of paper which had wrapped itself round his ankle like a dirty bandage. They heard his curse even with the window shut. This sudden glimpse of the cruelly grimacing human beings, separated from them only by glass, gave them a stronger sense of the warmth within. Human sympathy too. Mrs MacLean was a widow. It was a street of widows – some of them old and grim, living at street level between lace curtains and brown pots of creep-ing plants, some of them young and gay behind high window boxes where the hardiest flowers survived the Scottish summer. Mrs MacLean was neither of these. She was an amiable woman in her middle years, and lately she had begun to wonder whether sympathy was not her strongest point.

In the weeks that followed Veitch's status changed from lodger to paying guest, from paying guest, by a more subtle transformation shown only in Mrs MacLean's softer expression and tone of voice, to a guest who, in the long run, paid. They talked together in the mornings and evenings. Sometimes they talked about his work which was in the refrigerating business. But as often as not the conversation veered round to eggs. As a subject the egg had everything. It was brilliantly self-contained and clean, light but meaty, delicate yet full of complex far-reaching associations – psychological, sexual, physiological, philosophical. There was almost nothing on earth that did not start off with an egg in some shape or form. And when they had discussed eggs in the abstract Veitch would tell her about all those persons who had tried their best to poison him, coming after him with their great home-made cakes rich with egg, boggy egg puddings nourishing to the death, or the stiff drifts of meringue topping custards yellow as cowslip. It was all meant kindly, no doubt, yet how could one be sure? After all, he'd never made any secret of it. But people who called themselves human were continually dropping eggs here and there into his life as deliberately as anarchists depositing eggs of explosive into unsuspecting communities.

'You'd be amazed,' he said. 'Even persons who profess to love one aren't above mixing in the odd egg – just to test, just to make absolutely certain one isn't trying it on.'

'Oh heavens – Oh no!' cried Mrs MacLean. 'Love! Love in one hand and poison in the other!'

'That's just about it,' Veitch agreed. 'With my chemical make-up you get to know a lot about human nature, and sometimes the things you learn you'd far, far rather never have known.'

By early spring Mrs MacLean and her lodger were going out together in his car on a Saturday, sometimes to a quiet tea-room on the outskirts of the city or further out into the

country where they would stretch their legs for a bit before
having a leisurely high tea in some small hotel where, as
often as not, Mrs MacLean would inform waitresses and
sometimes waiters about Harry Veitch's egg allergy. Then
Veitch would sit back and watch the dishes beckoned or
waved away, would hear with an impassive face the detailed
discussions of what had gone into the make-up of certain
pies and rissoles, and would occasionally see Mrs MacLean
reject a bare-faced egg outright. He never entered into such
discussions. It almost seemed as though he had let her take
over the entire poisonous side of his life. On the whole, he
seemed to enjoy the dining-room dramas when all heads
would turn and silence fall at the sound of Mrs MacLean's
voice rising above the rest: 'No, no, it's poison to him! Not
at all – boiled, scrambled, poached – it's all the same.
Poison!' But once in a while the merest shadow of irritation
would cross his face, and on some evenings he drove home
almost in silence, a petulant droop to his lips.

'But you did enjoy your supper, didn't you?'

'Quite.'

'And you didn't mind me saying that about the egg?'

'Why should I?'

'You see, I actually saw them through the door – whipping it up – even after I'd warned them. Even after I'd told
them it was actual poison to you. They were whipping it up
in a bowl – with a fork.'

'Exactly.'

'What do you mean – "exactly"?'

'I mean your description is obviously correct.'

'How stilted you make it sound. Why don't you relax –
make yourself comfy?'

'While I'm driving? You want me to relax into this ditch
for instance?' Very touchy he could be, almost disagreeable
at times. But then he was allergic, wasn't he? A sensitive
type.

Before long Mrs MacLean had given up eating eggs

herself. She wouldn't actually say they disagreed with her nowadays. That would be carrying it too far. But how could what was poison to him be nourishment to her? She hardly noticed when the usual invitations to suppers with neighbours began to dwindle under her too vivid descriptions of eggs and their wicked ways. She was too busy devising new, eggless dishes for Veitch. By early summer she and her guest had explored the surrounding countryside and every out-of-the-way restaurant in the city. Mrs MacLean gave him a great deal. It was not only his stomach she tended. She gave him bit by bit, but steadily and systematically, the history of Edinburgh as they went about. 'You're standing on History!' she would exclaim, nudging him off a piece of paving-stone. Or, as he stood wedged momentarily in the archway of a close on a wild afternoon, her voice would rise triumphantly above the howlings and whistlings around him: 'You're breathing in History! Look at that inscription above your head!' He would step up cautiously onto slabs of wintry stone from which famous clerics had declaimed, sit in deep seats where queens had sat, while Mrs MacLean held forth herself. All the teaching experience of her younger days came back to her as she talked, and often when tourists were around a small crowd would gather and ask questions. One or two Americans might jot down her answers in notebooks and occasionally a photo was taken of her standing in the doorway of St Giles or with one elbow laid nonchalantly on the parapet of the Castle Esplanade. Sometimes Veitch got lost. He got lost for hours and hours, and after much searching Mrs MacLean would have to return home alone. It took a lot out of her. At times History really hurt.

By late autumn Veitch had got his job well in hand. It was expanding, he said. Really bursting its bounds. Mrs MacLean knew little about his job, but she identified with it and she was not one to stand in the way of his work. When he spoke of expansion and bursting bounds, however, refrigeration was the last thing she had in mind, but rather some mature and still seductive woman bursting through all the freezing restrictions into a boundless new life. But she felt a difference. He was not so available now. He worked late and had little appetite for the original eggless dishes she set before him at supper. Worst of all, when a few days of unexpected Indian Summer began, a sudden spate of work took him away from her for longer and longer sessions. He began to be busy on Saturday afternoons, and even on Sundays he found he must use the car to make certain contacts he'd had no time for during the week. Reluctantly, Mrs MacLean decided that until the pressure of work slackened she would simply take a few bus trips on her own while the weather lasted. She set off, good-naturedly enough, on solitary sprees at the weekends – as often as not ending up with tea alone in some country hotel or seaside café where they had been earlier in the year. She still had supper and breakfast talks with her lodger, but mostly it was herself talking to keep her spirits up. She never mentioned History now. Egg-talk was also out. In the bleak evenings she secretly yearned for the buttery omelettes and feathery soufflés she had whipped up in the old days.

One Saturday afternoon she took the bus right out into the country to an old farmhouse where they had been a couple of months ago. It stood well back from the road amongst low, gorse-covered hills, and winding through these were deep paths where you could walk for miles in a wide circle, eventually coming out again near the house. Mrs MacLean decided to take her walk after tea. There was nobody in the place but her spirits were rather higher than usual. She ate haddocks in egg sauce, pancakes, scones and plum jam and as she ate she talked on and off to the friendly girl who served it. She even managed to bring in a reference to a great friend of hers who was unable to eat egg in any shape or form, and for a while they discussed the peculiarities of people and their eating habits. Then she set off for her walk.

It was one of the last warm days of the year – so warm that after half an hour or so she had to remove her coat, and a mile further on uphill she was glad to lean on a gate and look down to where, far off, she could just see the line of the Crags and Arthur's Seat with the blue haze of the city beneath. Near at hand the weeds of the fields and ditches were a bright yellow, yet creamed here and there in the hollows with low swathes of ground-mist. But something jerked her from her trance. She realized with a shock that she was not the only person enjoying the surroundings. Unseen, yet close to her behind the hedge, there were human rustlings and murmurings. She bent further over the gate and craned her head sideways to look. Seated on a tartan rug which came from the back of her own drawing-room sofa was Harry Veitch, his arm round the waist of a young woman whose hair was yellow as egg yolk. Their legs lay together, the toes of their shoes pointed towards one another, and Mrs MacLean noted that under a dusting of seeds and straws Veitch's shoes still bore traces of the very shine she had put there the night before. For a few seconds longer she stood staring. From the distance of a field or two away it would have seemed to any onlooker that these three persons were peacefully enjoying the last moments of an idyllic afternoon together. Then, Mrs MacLean suddenly lifted her hands from the top of the gate as though it had been electrically wired, turned swiftly and silently down the way she had come and made for the bus route back to the city.

Sunday breakfast had always been a more prolonged affair than on other days, and the next morning Harry Veitch came downstairs late in green and white striped pyjamas under a maroon dressing-gown. He looked at ease, and on his forehead was a faint glow which was nothing more nor less than the beginning and end of a Scottish sunburn. For the weather had broken. Mrs MacLean greeted him, seated sideways at the table as usual to show that she had already eaten. But now Veitch was showing a strange hesitation in lowering himself into his seat. For some moments he seemed to find extraordinary difficulty in removing his gaze from the circumference of the plate before him, as though its rim were magnetic to the eyes which, try as they might to burst aside, were kept painfully riveted down dead on its centre. But at last, with tremendous effort, he managed to remove them. Casually, smiling, he looked round the room at curtains, pot-plant, firescreen, sideboard – greeting them first before he spoke. And when he spoke it was in an equable voice, polite and low-pitched.

'Mrs MacLean, I can't take egg. Sorry.'

'Can't take?' There was a cold surprise in her voice. Veitch allowed himself one darting glance at the smooth boiled egg on his plate and another at the mottled oval of his landlady's face, and again let his eyes roam easily about the room.

'No, it's an allergy,' he said.

Mrs MacLean now got up with the teapot in her hand and poured out a cup for her lodger. 'I don't quite catch your meaning, Mr Veitch,' she said, coming round and standing with the spout cocked at his ear as though she would pour the brown brew into his skull.

'An allergy, Mrs MacLean,' said Veitch, speaking with the distinct enunciation and glassy gaze of one practising his vocabulary in a foreign tongue. 'I have an allergy to egg.'

'Do you mean you want special treatment here, Mr Veitch?'

'Mrs MacLean, I am allergic to egg. Egg is poison to me. Deadly poison!'

Mrs MacLean's face was blank, her voice flat as she answered:

'Then why should you stay here? In an egg-house.'

'An egg-house!' The vision of a monstrous six-compartment egg-box had flashed before Veitch's eyes.

'Yes, I love eggs,' she replied simply. 'Eggs are my favourite. I shall order two dozen eggs tomorrow. There will be eggs, fresh eggs, for breakfast, for lunch, for supper. Did you know there are ways of drinking eggs? One can even break an egg into the soup for extra nourishment. I have books crammed with recipes specifically for the egg. There are a thousand and one ways . . .'

'Poison!' cried Harry Veitch on a fainter note.

'Yes, indeed . . . if you stay. A thousand and one ways . . .' she agreed. And for a start – with the expression of an irate conjurer – she produced a second boiled egg out of a bowl and nimbly bowled it across the table towards her shrinking lodger.

# The High Tide Talker

'I'VE NOTHING TO take me back! I could stay for hours if
I wanted to, or if the weather was anything. All the same,
once he starts to talk it's likely to be the same thing as
yesterday and the day before.' The woman at the first
drops of rain had pushed through to the front of the crowd
and now stood close to the balustrade of the promenade,
looking down onto the beach. 'You wouldn't call him a
good-looker, would you?' she said to the young man
beside her. 'But then, he doesn't need to be. Look at
his background. Waves and clouds and ships, and sometimes even a sail or two. And no surprise to me if he got a
whale spouting before he's through with the place. That's
the kind he is. He's lucky. You can say anything as long as
the setting's right. Now if there were brass rails and a
pulpit round him or maybe an ugly black cloth behind –
would you have stopped to hear?' The young man said
nothing. 'Or come to that – if he'd black boots on instead
of bare feet – would anyone look twice?' Watson, the
young man, kept his eyes fixed on the beach. A man on his
other side spoke across him to the woman: 'But have you
thought of the snags of open-air talking? Gulls can tear the
words to bits. Waves can gulp them up. And now he's got
the weather to contend with.' But the big, warm splashes
of summer rain had come to nothing. The woman who
had stepped aside with her umbrella half-open, closed it
again. 'Will you come often?' she asked. Watson muttered
something and shook his head. But whenever possible
these last ten days, he'd been here. He would come
tomorrow if he could get away, and the next day and

for every day after that, as long as the man below had breath to talk.

The man on the beach was called Carruthers. He was a large man, tall and burly, wearing today a blue cotton jacket and striped grey and brown trousers rolled up at the ankles. On warmer days his shirts were brilliantly flowered and checked, and always, whether it was warm or cool, he had on a large tropic-style straw hat, red-banded, and cut into fronds round the brim's edge. His head when he removed the hat was square and strong with stiff, straw-coloured hair which showed grey at the roots as the wind lifted it. Sometimes he would swing his arms up as he talked and his eyes would follow the green glint of a ring on his finger as it stabbed the air. Very often there was this contrast between the movements of his body and the watchful person who studied himself with interest or listened attentively to the ups and downs of his own voice. He was not always shouting. He would begin every afternoon or evening when the tide was still a good way out and all was quiet on the shore. Each time he would be cut short in full swing by the crash of waves as the tide came up. There was a beginning but never an end to his harangue.

This evening there were not many left on the shore. A few children who had been splashing about in pools far down on the rocks were slowly beginning to move up the beach, but they could still be clearly heard against the soft, rhythmic splashing of the advancing sea. As usual Carruthers began quietly. He hardly needed to raise his voice. It was more like a casual, one-sided conversation as he looked up, smiling, to the group gathered above him on the promenade.

'You're enjoying your holiday, I hope, as much as I'm enjoying mine. You *seem* to be enjoying it. I look up and think: "They haven't a care in the world, that lot", and you look down at me and think: "Look at him. He's strong. He's in good health, isn't he? He's lucky. He's not the worrying kind." But, friends, that's not so. We've all got our worries. Maybe we feel good now. It's still day. But what about the night? It's still fair – but what about the storm? You can still hear birds and children and the cars going along up there on the road. But come down here at midnight as I do sometimes – no, no, not often I admit – but when the tide's full in and it's black, I'm not thinking day thoughts then. I'm thinking night thoughts. They're different, aren't they? I have them and you have them too, even if it's only for two minutes as you're turning over in bed, or just for the time it takes to get to the kitchen and back for a drink of water. But that's enough. It's plenty of time for one or two night thoughts – and heaven help us all, you may say, if we give ourselves much longer than that! All right then. What are these thoughts?' Carruthers drew his hands out of his pockets and the casual air was gone in a flash. His voice dropped. 'We're alone. That's the first thing that comes to mind. But utterly alone. Oh yes, you've got your families. You've got your friends. So have I. Maybe you're lucky enough to have a best friend who comes running when you're in real trouble. But there's some trouble no one can help with. We've all got to die one day and who's to help us then? It doesn't matter if a bishop holds your hand. It doesn't matter if a cardinal's your brother . . .'

'This is where he loses me,' said the woman with the umbrella. 'If I've got to strain my ears it had better be cheery. I never stay for the death bit – not in films, not even in books – certainly not on my holiday.' She moved off, pausing further along at a red collection box fixed to the balustrade and inscribed simply with the two words: FOR LIGHT painted in bold white letters.

The man on the beach spoke on for another twenty minutes at least, before he had to start gradually raising his voice above the tide. During that time he varied his performance. Sometimes he waited while a few more joined the group and he drew in the uncertain ones with extravagant, knee-bending beckonings, as though scooping them up from outer space towards his chest. Or he would turn and watch while a gang of jeering rowdies went by below him on the sand. Then he would make as though to sweep up after them by running and driving the sand before him with an invisible broom, brandishing it in the air and finally hurling it after them. When there was nothing better to do he stopped and studied himself from head to foot with interest. Without a word he would move to the promenade wall, roll up a sleeve or a trouser-leg and unbutton his shirt down to the waist. Pointing, twisting, giving himself a pinch or a slap or two, he'd show them the odd scar, a brown burn-mark, a blue bruise here and there. They were nothing at all. Most of his audience had far better marks themselves. Nevertheless the pointing and the pinching got them. They stared, fascinated, over one another's shoulders.

Not so far down the beach the tops of the first line of sandcastles were dissolving, their deep moats swirling. Just above them was a deep ledge of pebbles and as soon as the sea touched this the sound seemed to increase ten-fold. Carruthers was not speaking against a mere rise and fall of water but against a grinding rattle of stones growing steadily stronger as the waves drove up into their midst. He looked behind him once or twice to measure his distance. The tide was coming in fast.

'But we've got to die the same as we've got to live!' he called up, circling his mouth with his hands. 'And who or what's to help us? It's a fearsome thought all right. But we *can* escape that fear!' Again Carruthers looked behind and gestured to the sea. 'For instance, you may wonder how I'll escape a wetting if that tide comes in too fast. There are no steps at this bit. But I've got a way up. Not everyone knows about it but I know it's there so I don't worry. We're all going to need an escape, friends. Not for the body, but for the soul. But where will we find this escape? How will we make sure of it?' Carruthers waited for a long time examining the blank wall in front of him. He was not forced to answer. There was a roaring behind and a huge wave came lashing up yards further than the rest and broke over the top of the promenade. Spray covered the group right to the back line. In a moment they were gone. The preacher himself had disappeared along the wall to his secret escape route. Watson was carried off with the rest.

He was carried off with the rest, but as soon as he was free of the group he slowed down. He was no holiday-maker. He had the resident's half-scorn for the September crowd, while at the same time working all out to meet its appetite. The place where he worked was the best butcher shop in town – one which for half a century had supplied the ever-increasing demand of hotels and boarding-houses in the district. It was a large establishment, stretching far back to where the loaded tables stood, their white, scrubbed wood sagging in voluptuous waves under decades of chopping. But the meat had its class and blood distinctions. In the forefront of the shop the better cuts were arranged on frills of paper and thick backgrounds of artificial parsley. Sheets of tissue, fine as chiffon, divided ribs from kidneys, kidneys from livers, livers from tongues, and double thick parcelling made certain that no drop of blood was ever seen in the place. On the other hand the necklets of pink and cream sausages which filled the platters on either side of the counter were treated with a certain disdain. The butchers whipped them up on the points of their knives and held them in the air, waiting impatiently to slit the chain while the customer pondered his order. The main distinction of the place was that unlike other butcher shops whole animals were in evidence. On trestles in an inner room lay sheep, legs stiff in air, while on certain mornings great pink pigs, rippling with wrinkles, were swung head downward from van to shop, their smooth, debristled ears veined with scarlet like leaves of flesh. The pigs were met and escorted in by men in white coats and hats. Such sights as these gave the shop its standing. It was also, for those inside, a viewing point, standing as it did at a busy corner, with its long windows facing out on all sides. Watson had a mixture of pride and hatred for the place. All during the last fortnight he had thought about Carruthers. He had kept a look out for him as he chopped and sawed and knotted. Occasionally he caught a glimpse of him between the hooks of swinging joints, tramping past, head down, alone – and once he followed him for a bit on his way to the beach.

It was difficult to follow Carruthers. His message depended on the sea. Without some knowledge of tides it was easy to miss him. There was even a rumour that he would be gone in a week. But early or late and as often as his work allowed Watson was on the promenade. He was not put off by repeat performances, nor that the final message or answer was always terminated by the tide. To Watson repetition was part of the attraction. What was left unsaid might one day give him his opening. 'Which way should we look for help?' Carruthers kept yelling before the waves crashed. 'Is it here?' – thumping his stomach, 'or out there? Is there anything behind the dust and stars? Any power or reason there? Is this possible?' Watson silently noted the questions and came back for more. He was there to catch Carruthers' eye if need be, to stay hidden or to stand out. All he asked was to be recognized as a follower. There was as yet no sign of recognition.

On Saturday Watson had a free afternoon and as soon as possible he set off for the promenade. But long before he reached it a heavy shower had started and as he approached he met Carruthers' crowd already making for the nearby cafés or hurrying back for entertainment at the town's centre. One or two were still looking expectantly over the balustrade but Carruthers had not waited till they disappeared. He was sitting with his back to the shelter

of the wall drawing a pair of rubber boots over thick white
socks. His straw hat, protected by a sheet of newspaper, and
a light knapsack lay beside him. Watson stood at a distance
watching closely until the rain let up a bit, until he saw the
man below stand up and put on his hat, button the collar of
his jacket and slowly start off along the beach – going
eastward to where the distant cliffs began. Only when
Carruthers was already some way in front did Watson
follow him.

The tide was still fairly far out and it was quiet on the
shore. As they walked further and further along, the sand
became smoother and deeper. The castles and trenches,
the huge, spade-written letters, the stone circles and shell
heaps gradually became sparse until at last – far out – they
passed one solitary sandpile stuck round with gulls' feathers. It was a lonely fort, defended by a complex system of
walls and ditches, yet doomed like all the rest. Carruthers
turned his head and gave it a sidelong look as he passed.
Behind him Watson plodded on looking neither to right
nor left. The footsteps he followed were sunk deep and
widely spaced and sometimes he sank his own feet into
them. He was disappointed with the boots. He would have
preferred to follow bare feet. But as he went on he became
reconciled to them. He thought of all the people who had
ever followed behind – who had trekked for years after
explorers, hacked their way westward, plodded north into
ice on the heels of pioneers. He thought of soldiers following leaders, and of all the people beckoned on by guns and
torches, crosses and flaming swords. He thought of the
single, lonely followers who accompanied hermits at a
distance, seconds-in-command who took over from gen-
erals, and the patient understudies who stood in at a
moment's notice for actors and preachers, taking on fans
and followers and paying off the hangers-on. Sometimes
Watson stood still and looked back to the complex trail of
double footsteps behind, and forward to the single track he

followed. And he thought of the appalling complexities and conflicts of followers compared to the single dedication of leaders.

The man in front stopped suddenly, glanced back for a moment and went on again. The beach had begun to curve round and cut off sight of the town. The main shopping street had long since disappeared, and then the big, south-facing hotels. One by one the spaced-out villas went and finally the furthest caravan. In front was a long stretch of black stones and a great gash in the nearest cliff where they had been torn out. Once or twice Watson found his foot jammed between rocks and once he stopped to put on a shoe which had been ripped off. It took longer than he'd bargained for. He had to balance himself at a slant while he tipped out the sand and knotted up the wet laces. When he set off again he had to stop himself breaking into a run on the smoother stretches. This would have looked like pursuit. He was not a pursuer but a follower. Carruthers stopped again, shouted something unintelligible and went on. Watson was used to words being swamped. For all he knew it might have been 'Come on!' or 'Get moving!' He hurried on.

They had now come a long way and again the character of the shore had changed. Instead of black rocks there was now an open stretch of sand in front, covered with grey pebbles. Driftwood was piled under the cliff, stripped trees and bleached green ropes, baskets, and fish boxes with Scandinavian names. And bones. White birdbones, white skulls and the bones of sheep. Everything was blanched here. Momentarily Watson felt himself stripped and blood-less, walking like a ghost amongst cast-offs. He forgot the chunks of red flesh where he worked, the meaty bones and lumps of opaque fat – these were far behind him. He was entering a dimension made transparent by endless wind and sea. He could also see with peculiar clarity what was in front. A long strip of low cloud was lifting and he saw familiar green meadows against black sky – a glassy green today, like the green of thick sea-bottles through which an illusion of great distance can be seen. Watson wasn't looking at the ground now. But the man in front had slowed down and every now and then he stopped to shift something with his foot. Sometimes he picked up a stone or a piece of wood. Watson was close enough now to hear his breathing. Suddenly Carruthers stopped dead and turned round. 'GO . . . AWAY!' he shouted, putting slow and blistering emphasis onto both words. Watson stopped, looked wildly round for guidance, and came on. Again the man in front swerved, again he shouted while still moving on and making pushing gestures back with his arms as he walked. Watson saw the fields more transparent than ever through a shimmer of water. He hesitated for an instant, staring at his feet, then plodded on. Carruthers lengthened his stride until there was again a fair distance between them, but after some time he slowed down, finally came to a halt. Grimly, but on a more resigned note, he called back: 'What do you want?' Slowly Watson made up on him. He didn't, however, come right up but approached to within some yards and stopped.

'What do you want?' Carruthers said again. He looked, close-up, unexpectedly tall.

'I have questions,' said Watson. The voice was deferential.

'I can't hear you,' said Carruthers. Watson turned to repudiate this, for the tide was still a good way out. The water was making no more than a gentle splashing on the stones.

'And I don't *want* to hear,' said Carruthers, watching the direction of his eyes. 'If it's the walk you want I can't stop you, can I? But if it's company – I'm not your man. You'd better go back.'

'Dozens of questions,' said Watson, his voice still soft but at the same time stubborn.

Carruthers gave a great shrug of his shoulders and turned. Not far in front was a hollowed out part of the cliff – hardly a cave but deep enough with its overhanging bluff to give shelter. Carruthers made for this. It was obviously known to him. Already he had wedged himself and his stuff into a ledge of rock and was sitting easing off one of his boots when Watson came up and stood discreetly at the opening.

'So this is your place!' he said at last, looking about him with suspicious reverence. Carruthers had taken off his jacket and was rummaging in his bag. 'What do you mean – my place? I'm not a cave-dweller. It's some sort of shelter from the wind when I want to eat.'

'When you want to think,' Watson corrected him. Carruthers sighed. He unwrapped a packet which contained three rolls, a few rings of raw onion, a lump of cheese, tomatoes, and some slices of boiled egg which he put on one side. 'You'd better help yourself,' he said, pointing to the rolls.

'I don't want anything,' said Watson. 'I didn't come for food.'

'Is that so? Then you can watch me eat.' Carruthers brought back the egg slices and started to fill a roll.

'I can go off if you like,' said Watson. 'I can come back when you're finished.'

Carruthers blew sand from the roll's crust. 'Oh, sit down! You worry me standing out there. You'll only shuffle up more sand. Do you think I'm a member of some tribe who's forbidden to eat in public? As a matter of fact I'm perfectly used to eating with dozens, maybe hundreds, staring at me.' He took a bite of the roll and after some time added thoughtfully: 'Under a spotlight too.'

'Spotlight,' Watson repeated. He thought of a sunshaft. Perhaps even moonlight.

'I'm talking, of course, about eating on stage. And the food was real food. Don't have any misconceptions about

that. I could have made a meal of it if I'd wanted to.'
Carruthers was reluctantly resigning himself to the young
man, but he spoke and ate as though solely for himself.
Occasionally he stopped chewing and his eyes warmed as
some memory struck him. Watson was staring blankly
ahead and Carruthers turned his head for a moment and
looked at him. 'You work in that big butcher's shop in
town, don't you? I caught sight of you the other day
throwing double links of sausages from the end of a knife.'
He opened up another roll, packed it with cheese and
pressed it down.

'Are you going to say I shouldn't work with meat?' said
Watson.

'God – what now! Why should I do that? I was about to
congratulate you on a remarkable act.'

'All right. I thought maybe you were a vegetarian, along
with everything else.'

'Along with everything else! Look, eat up, for God's sake,
and stop staring.'

'I'm not hungry,' said Watson. 'I told you what I'd come
for.'

'Oh, yes – questions, of course. What questions? If it's
questions about *me* . . .'

'No – more than that . . .!'

'If it's about me,' Carruthers went on, ignoring this,
'that's easy. There's only one thing to tell. I've already
mentioned it. I'm a theatre man, first and always – and very
proud of it too,' he added as he watched Watson's face.
'That is, of course whenever the job's there. When the job's
*not* there, when the curtain's down too long, that is, in the
spare time – amongst other things – I'm a preacher. For the
fun of it.'

'Fun!' Watson turned at last a bleak and harrowed face.

'Or for the hell of it, if you'd rather.' Carruthers watched
the movement of Watson's mouth and eyebrows with
professional interest. 'I'd hesitate,' he said, 'to call myself

an actor pure and simple. And I have my pantomime parts of course – not unlike that sausage act of yours. You've got the basis there, I may say, for one or two passable turns.'

Now the silence between them lasted a long time – so long that in the interval the sea had come a few yards further up the beach. It had taken back the heaped-up seaweed and was advancing upon the lowest line of driftwood before Carruthers spoke again. He'd taken some cake from an outside pocket of his bag and was settling down to eat it, his legs stretched out comfortably, his eyes on the horizon. 'Think of it,' he said, waving one hand at the water, 'all those layers upon layers of creatures out there, munching for their lives – nibbling, sucking, sieving through the water for sustenance. Eating and being eaten. And not a speck wasted!'

'I know all that,' said Watson in a stifled voice, 'and I don't want to hear. Your job . . .'

'Right. What *is* my job, in your opinion?'

'Your job's to say what's in it all for *us*! Who cares what's in the sea? It's what goes on above . . .' Watson signalled to the sky. Carruthers slapped his hand down on a rock. 'Will you listen to him!' he exclaimed softly to the invisible shoals.

'I'm the listening one! You saw me. Every free minute, I was down. Every day for the last fortnight . . .'

'I didn't ask you. You came of your own accord, and you're as free to go.'

Carruthers had produced a can of beer and through the hiss and bubble of its opening he remarked with satisfaction: 'There's only one of these. You'll have to watch this time. You see, I wasn't prepared for a picnic.' Watson watched him drink. He drank extravagantly, the knob in his throat frisking. 'You may well ask "what goes on above?" ' he said at last setting the can down. 'Unbelievable things go on. Fantastic blow-outs, spinnings and explosions – wholesale drop-outs, stars, groups of galaxies, groups of groups

. . . you want me to go on? We're still as ignorant of it all as cheese mites about chess, but look – we're getting *some-where*, aren't we? You might say, and without stretching a point, the curiosity is whetted!' Carruthers glanced at Watson. 'Or again you might not.' He fell silent, but after a time he took the ring off his finger and held it up. 'I've another like this,' he said watching Watson out of the corner of his eye. 'Both of them gifts. I've also a gold watch – another gift – which I don't always care to wear. This cheap one does well enough on trips. Time, on seaside shows, counts for nothing. In the theatre, on the other hand, it's everything.' He took another drink and leaned back with the bag propping his shoulders. A strange sound came from Watson's throat as he watched.

'Who was I listening to – up there?' he cried suddenly in an anguished voice.

'Who? Up there on the prom? Why me, of course. Charles Quentin Carruthers.'

'Player or preacher?'

'Both, both! What's the matter with the mixture?' Carruthers sat forward and studied himself. 'I can turn my hand to most things,' he said. 'In the early days I've even taken on conjuring, sandwiched between the usual roles – detective, maniac, grandee, and the like. I've actually stood in for a singer, and no one was any the wiser in that town. Go on. Look hard. Look as long as you like! You may have met, for once in your life, the genuine all-round, all-purpose man.' Watson needed no telling. He had his head turned over his shoulder, grimacing as though his neck hurt him. 'But are you a believer?' he said.

'Oh, I'm a believer all right. Don't worry. I'll believe in anything you care to name – as long as it works. Do you want a list of beliefs?'

'Are you a believer?' Watson said again, without turning his head. Even so his neck seemed to pain him, for his face grew pale. For a long time there was no sound in the cave.

Then Carruthers got slowly to his feet, turned in towards the cliff face and stretched up so that his fingertips just touched the bulge of rock above him. He seemed to enjoy the sensation so much so that it was prolonged and the stretch became an effort to put the palms of both hands on the rock. Now he straddled his legs and swung forward, easing his back down and down until his knuckles scraped the stones between his feet. Watson darted a look behind and saw through Carruthers' shirt the knobbed line of his spine and the fringe of grey hair flopping behind his hands.

'I believe,' Carruthers was muttering to himself as he came up, 'in a bit of exercise – the smallest thing is better than nothing at all. How else could I have mastered all the movements I've had to make on stage – including falling, fainting, dying?' Watson glanced behind him once again and shuddered. Carruthers had flopped to the ground and was rolling in a boneless bundle on the sharp stones, knees drawn up, hands clasping head. 'Unhurt!' he said, looking up with a grin. Watson turned away quickly as he got to his feet. Carruthers began to stuff his things back into his bag, picking up the odd scraps and wrapping them in newspaper. He went after the beercan which had rolled to the opening. 'I believe in keeping the place decent,' he remarked as he went past Watson, 'whether it's a house or a cave – every last scrap. You'll not find a trace of me wherever I've been. And clothes. Yes, I know how to keep my clothes looking good, and what's more, how to wear them. I've never been a one to be part of the props or the background. Never.'

Watson was breathing fast and sitting tight as ever. 'Have you finished then?' he asked, '– All the things you can do?' Leaning against the rock-face Carruthers studied Watson – from his decent lacing shoes to the hard knot of the throttling tie at his throat. There was a squeamish mixture of modesty and pride about the man. 'I like a bit of glitter in my own get-up, I must say,' said Carruthers, 'even if it's only the odd button. People like a show and I believe in showing off. There's no place for modesty or hanging back in my trade.' He waited for a reply and getting none went on: 'People like a fright now and then. I believe in giving it to them. Sometimes when they're properly scared they'll cheer and clap. Make it easy and you'll get chased. I believe in keeping on the move. Never the same place twice if you can help it. Never the same crowd.'

Watson was beginning to recover himself. There was something lighter and smoother about him now, as though to allow as much of Carruthers' talk to slide off him as possible. He had slicked down his hair and buttoned his jacket to the neck. He sat with his legs drawn up under him, his hands tucked in his sleeves. 'You have a box,' he said. 'A collecting box.'

'Which I'm not ashamed of,' said Carruthers quickly. 'I believe in making the odd pound or two any way I can – talking or standing on my head if need be. But for all that I *believe* in what I'm saying. I'm not a hoaxer or a swindler.' He was preparing to leave. He rolled down his sleeves, adjusting the cuffs carefully, put on his jacket and pulled a red and black spotted scarf from the pocket. Lastly he picked up the straw hat and put it on. 'I believe in myself,' he said. He went past the small figure at the cave's opening and out onto the beach.

Carruthers began striding back purposefully in the direction he had come. He didn't look round, for Watson was behind, limping a bit now in his thin shoes and going cautiously. But when Carruthers stopped he stopped, when Carruthers moved on he moved on. The distance he kept between them was always the same, exact enough to be measured with a rule. They'd gone a hundred yards or so when Watson climbed on a rock and shouted: 'I've found your weakness!'

Carruthers stopped and turned. He walked back a little way. 'Don't follow me,' he called out. 'Walk in front or beside if you must. I won't be followed.'

'I can't do that,' Watson called back. 'I'm coming after you, whatever you are.' Again Carruthers strode ahead, quickening the pace, and Watson quickened his steps and kept his distance.

'I've found your weakness!' he shouted again after a few minutes. Carruthers turned and waited for him to come up. 'And I'm not the only one,' said Watson when he was within a yard or two. He was breathing quickly as though he'd been running along behind. 'Others have noticed. Weakness is the wrong word!' Carruthers shrugged his shoulders and walked on, but behind Watson was shouting: 'It's a trick, isn't it? You've been on it for weeks, maybe months. Have you been playing it for years?' Again Carruthers waited for him to come within speaking distance. 'Right – you tell me,' he said, 'tell me about this trick, this weakness you've discovered.' Watson was still breathing fast. There was a twist to the upper part of his body, as though he could as easily run back as come on. 'You've worked out your tide-times cleverly,' he said, 'for I've come at all ungodly hours to hear you – morning, afternoon and evening. Oh, yes, you put the questions all right, but there's never an answer. You make sure of that. Do you ever reach the end of that sermon of yours? No, because long before you've reached the point the waves come up.'

'What point?' said Carruthers.

'You know what point.'

'I'm asking you. What point?' said Carruthers.

'The God bit.'

'Is that all?' The smile accompanying these words goaded Watson to a frenzy. There was good nature in it, plus a hint of scorn.

'All! We don't get God. We don't get heaven, never mind hell. You leave a gap. You leave a blank. You're off, of course, before the trouble starts. Where are your pamphlets, by the way? There's not one placard in the town. Why not? Well I can tell you why not. Question marks are all you could chalk up. And you can laugh!'

With one hand Carruthers slowly wiped the smile from his face and flipped it behind him. 'Anything more?'

'Yes.'

'You want to prove something?'

'Yes.'

'To test something?'

'You.'

'Try it then.'

'Give your talk tomorrow.'

'I mean to. With no encouragement from you, thanks all the same.'

'Give it when the tide's out! Give it when it's so far out you can neither see nor hear it from the prom.'

Carruthers' face didn't change. 'So you're to give me my cues? Dictating times and places.'

'Will you or won't you?'

'Will I what?'

'Preach on the beach when the tide's out?'

For a split second Carruthers hesitated. 'If that's what you want, it's all the same to me. I can do it anywhere and at anytime. You can have me hanging from the edge of the cliff, if you like it that way.'

'Low tide tomorrow!' shouted Watson.

'Low tide. 6.48 p.m. I'll be there.' Carruthers' eyes narrowed and fixed Watson against his background of slippery stones. 'But seeing we're bargaining – you dare to follow after me just one more step on this beach, and I'll make it bad for you, Watson. Stay by your rock. Don't lift that foot! One move from you before I'm off this beach . . .!' Carruthers made off, his head sideways towards the cliff so that without turning round he could still note Watson's smallest move.

Watson stayed where he was. His legs felt weak and after a bit he sat down, still with his gaze fixed on Carruthers as he moved further and further along the shore. Each step he marked, as though, reduced to following him faithfully only with his eyes, he made these eyes as far-reaching, as vindictive and demanding as human eyes could be.

The following day was cold, but the haze was gone. Every near object stood in the sun with a sharp shadow. Even the waves had a flashing, cutting edge. It was a day corresponding exactly to Watson's mood. He had recovered his spirits, and from early morning he felt the scourging, purging strength in him grow. It was a busy day. All morning, with gift-wrapping care, he folded and tied up slices of pork and beef. Between cuts he sharpened the long knives and deftly trimmed the fat from the rims of steaks, as though cutting off the last superfluous scraps of sloth from his own day. He grew quicker and surer as the time wore on. At four-thirty he was scouring the tables in the back room as though washing blood from marble. By six he was washed and dressed and sitting by himself in one of the small cafés along the front. He ate little but he watched everyone who passed the window, and when there was a gap in the passers-by he watched the sea. The tide was a very long way out. Below the seaweed line a great expanse of beach shelved down – dangerously steep in places – criss-crossed with rivulets. All along the foreshore lay large black pools which gradually diminished in the distance till they were mere discs of light. It was his own shore, yet for all that, almost unknown. He had never studied it at low tide. The jagged tops and miniature chasms of unfamiliar rocks took his eye. From where he sat he could see, on the dry band of sand under the promenade, a few figures diminished and darkened against the shining slopes behind. Watson bent forward and glanced along the length of the promenade to the semicircular balustrade which overlooked the beach. There was always a small crowd gathered here staring at the posters advertising evening cruises or queuing at the ice-cream and hot-dog vans. At twenty past six he fixed his eyes on this spot and remained rigid, his forehead touching the window, his feet uncomfortably trapped between wainscot

and tilted chair. At six-thirty, as though twitched by a
distant cord, his head jerked back, the chairlegs stabbed
the floor and he was on his feet. Above the aimless shift of
heads he had caught a glimpse of a red-banded straw hat
moving slowly towards the balustrade.

Carruthers had taken up his stance on the beach by
the time Watson arrived. He had his arms crossed, his
feet were planted wide apart with his hat between them
and he waited, smiling, for the crowd to form along the
balustrade above. They were not long in gathering for
any evening show. Already there were a fair number
when Watson came up and he had to wedge himself in
near the back. He was not sorry to be hidden. The
unaccustomed silence of low tide was stunning, in spite
of a cutting little breeze coming off the sea. Watson
noted with surprise and satisfaction how small Carruthers looked against the space behind. The man had
lost half his stature even before opening his mouth.
When he did begin to speak his voice was conversational
as usual. And Watson smiled. For so it would remain.
This time the sea could never save the day. Drama had
been killed for the man. He edged in to listen.

'I hope you're enjoying your holiday,' said Carruthers
taking in the group with a glance. 'I know I'm enjoying
mine.' There was a slight murmuring amongst the crowd
and a brief titter. The day had been cold from the start and
gradually, throughout late afternoon, all brightness had
been overcast. Nylons were being changed for wool. For
the first time that season the long-term forecast was poor.

'And you're right,' said Carruthers, quick to take his cue.
'One minute it's fair, the next it's dark. We don't know
what's to come.'

'But you'll tell us!' called a voice from the back. There
was a sudden parting in the group and heads turned round
towards Watson who was dodging down again behind the
shoulders. He was known to many as a faithful listener. His

words might be no more than simple statement of fact. There were some who had their doubts.

'Certainly I'll tell you,' said Carruthers easily and with a cool glance in Watson's direction. 'Some questions, of course, aren't answered as easily as all that. Some take a while. Some take a bit of looking into. We'll be coming to those in a minute.'

Watson was heard to laugh. 'And some never get answered at all,' he murmured to those nearest him.

'We've all chosen this fantastic place!' Carruthers swung round, gesticulating towards the eastern cliffs, then to the west with its series of sandy bays, and pointing above him to the winding streets which climbed up steeply behind the crowd. 'We all know why we're here in this town. That's one thing we're clear about. You decided to come and I decided – weeks, maybe months ago. We made up our minds. Right?'

'Not me, chum. It's my missis makes up *my* mind,' said a stout man near the front who was holding a bulging carrier bag.

'We all know why we're here,' Carruthers went on. 'Do we ever ask how we came to be on this globe? Why we're in the universe at all?'

'No. It's you who's to tell us!' called the angry voice from behind. The conviction had now grown strong that Watson must have reason for his change of heart. There was an impatient fidgeting round the edges of the group.

'Who, or what force put us here, and why?' said Carruthers. He paused for a moment to put up the collar of his jacket. 'It may be we're still young with plenty of gumption, or maybe we're on our last legs – but whatever the way of it, we'll always ask questions. One day we're going to need a few answers.'

'Get on with it then!' someone shouted.

'Ay, better buck up. You're getting gey long in the tooth yourself,' said an old man. Carruthers' lips were set in a

smile unlike his usual flash of teeth. He now doubled over
and gave himself a sharp thrashing around the ribs under
pretext of warming up. There was a hiss from somewhere in
the crowd, soft and poisonous as escaping gas.

'He doesn't know how to go on,' murmured a woman
holiday-maker who'd been watching with narrowed eyes.
'Give him another ten minutes and I reckon he'll dry up.'
The man beside her held up a finger to his lips: 'Sh . . .
we're getting answers soon, don't you worry. He'll tie it all
up tonight. Right now he's working up to it. Take a look at
his face.'

'Who cares?' said a young man who was simply passing
through the crowd on his way to a block of boarding-houses
at the other end of the town. 'Don't give me answers! No
one opens his mouth these days but he's got an answer
inside, all smooth and pat as a new-laid egg at the wrong
end.' He elbowed his way through and carried on purposefully between a long line of seats which had quickly emptied
as the air grew cold.

The man on the beach was still speaking in his normal
voice, for apart from the occasional plop in the pools and
the squawk of a seagull swooping down to study the shore,
there was almost no sound at all. Once in a while Carruthers looked over his shoulder as though expecting some
crashing backstage cue to help. None came. There was
emptiness behind. 'Look,' said Carruthers. 'Here we are
gathered together from every corner of the land. And I've
got questions to put to you.'

'Hell . . . no . . .' murmured the fat man with the carrier,
though in a genial voice. 'You got it wrong! It's you telling
*us.*'

'The fact is,' said Watson, edging in from the back and
turning his head about to catch the attention on every side,
'the man's just a high tide talker. He can't do his thing now.
He's flummoxed. I think we've had it. I think we can all go
home.' A sudden bluster of icy wind gave point to his

words. There was a buttoning up followed by a resolute jangling as a woman held up a bangled hand. 'No, I'm not leaving till I get one or two straight answers!'

'Thank you madam.' Carruthers bowed. 'And I mean to give them. Though don't count on them being dead straight.' There was a reproving shuffling above him, some hoots and a thin burst of clapping. 'I'll bet,' murmured the fat man, still genial.

'Let's look at it,' said Carruthers. 'Straight? You can't get it that way. Show me one straight thing. Not a cell in the body. Not an atom in the air or in the sea. In the entire universe – just give me one straight thing!'

'Never mind all that. What I asked for was a straight answer.' The woman was hammering the air with her arm. 'It's about time God was brought into it!'

'Ay . . . high time,' her husband agreed.

'I'm coming to that!' Carruthers was shouting now. He split his legs wide apart, reached for the largest pebble beside his foot and hurled it back between his thighs. It ricocheted from one rock, smashed onto another and fell into a pool. They heard the far-off splash in silence.

'He's got to get to the God bit now,' murmured Watson looking about him with a smile. 'Watch it. He can't get round it. No amount of tricks, acrobatics or anything else is going to help. He's in trouble. If you want my opinion, I don't believe he's got the smallest clue.'

It was now so cold that even the couple in the hot-dog van had closed down the hatch and could be seen through the rear window lighting up over newspapers in the back. High up on the miniature fairfield above the town red and yellow flags were fluttering and a procession of small round clouds moved in very low, like navy blue balloons, above the bunting.

Down on the beach Carruthers had his hat on and was trying to hold its frondy brim down on both sides. His eyes when he raised his chin again looked belligerent. His face was red. There was a feeling that next time a stone might fly either way. 'I'm here,' he said, 'ready to pronounce on any bloody, mortal thing you care to name! But at my own time! It's still my show – remember?'

'Oh . . . ay. Any *mortal* thing,' said the fat man, smiling round in a friendly fashion. 'That's easy. No trouble. I'd be glad enough to speak on any *mortal* thing myself. Though that wasn't what was called for, was it?'

Carruthers was looking through the fat man as though willing him to transparency. 'I'm all ready,' he said again, 'to talk of powers, of forces if you like, natural or super-natural, atom-smashing forces, star-blasting, seed-burst-ing. Forces behind man – and woman . . .' as a bangled arm shot up, 'behind viruses, superstars and space dust. Call it what you want.'

'No, *you* call it,' cried the woman raising her arm again.

'Go on. Name it, Carruthers,' called Watson dodging in from the back.

'The name!' roared the fat man suddenly, leaning right down over the balustrade and making an ugly, upward movement of his thumb. 'Give the name!'

'Maybe I will,' said Carruthers.

'No maybe's!'

'I will!' yelled Carruthers.

The group on the promenade waited for the next word. At the front the fat man waited, poising himself as though to bear down instantly with all his weight if the answer was not to his liking. Watson, on his toes at the back, waited, staring between motionless heads. The woman had mo-mentarily gripped and silenced her bangles with her left hand. Around these three the rest of the group gradually grew still and as the minutes passed an absolute silence fell. Carruthers gathered himself to speak. From the waist up he stretched and twisted, shaking his shoulders to free himself for the impossible feat, while his stubborn legs stayed fixed. It was just as he raised his head and before he could utter that the wind struck from the north. As the force of it emptied lungs, a sharp, collective gasp went up, followed by an explosive acceleration of sounds. The deck chairs, which had showed only a gentle swell of canvas, began to crack like whips, and a row of billboards against the balustrade clattered onto their faces and went shunting past amongst a mass of flying debris sucked from the tops of litter bins. Across the way the proprietor was slamming down the café windows facing the sea, while above him in his awning a continuous low drumming had started up. There was a snarling swirl of sand and the group at the balustrade turned sideways to a man. Another stinging squall and they had turned their backs to the beach.

For a few seconds the wind dropped. It was quiet except for the sound of one abandoned pail far down the beach, rolling desultorily between two rocks. Then the blast struck again – and with a sharper stuff than sand. Horizontal hail flew past. Balls of ice the size of marbles stotted off the pavement, slid in brilliant pebbled sheets down roofs and ran melting through gutters, piled so thickly they could be heard clashing softly past like crushed metal. At the same time it grew dark, for the harmless little cloud balloons had drifted together into one great mass overhead. One or two, staring through their eyelashes, were now convinced they saw hailstones coming down the size of pingpong balls. Umbrellas, opening up here and there, were quickly snapped in the pelting and a spiky confusion grew as the group started to shove outwards.

· 'It's stopped!' someone shouted. Everyone paused at that, long enough to look up, long enough to catch a glimpse of blue and observe a three second silence before hail fell again. This time there was no wind. It fell vertically. By now the crowd was moving forward in one body, yet there was an excess of caution which made the attempt look strange. Half-skating, half-shuffling they went, hanging on to one another like beginners testing the rink. Two persons alone showed independence. The fat man was going lightly along on the tips of his toes by the balustrade rail, touching it here and there to steady himself. Watson was far behind the rest. He had turned once to stare back at the beach where Carruthers was still standing. And he yelled to the retreating crowd:

'Hi – wait a minute! You've been swindled – you've been hoaxed! He never said it. Back to the rails, the lot of you, and let him have it! He's given you the slip. He's never going to say it. He's dodged the word! He's dodged God!' No one heard him through the hiss of ice.

Down on the beach Carruthers had let go of his hat and was now squatting in the sand with his arms out like a supplicant, grinning with relief, and letting the hailstones bounce from the open palms of his hands. His hat had blown some distance along the shore, transforming itself as it went. For a while it lay squashed upside down between two rocks, its pulpy, battered crown gummed to the ground, its fronds stirring indolently like a great red and white sea anemone. From there, by a change of wind, it was driven up again and, gaining speed and freedom, went on, now like a bedraggled, reviving bird – half-scuttling, half-flying, towards the sea.

# The Bookstall

EARLY ONE WINTER evening, a man called Molson was leaning against the bookstall of a crowded platform waiting for the home-bound train. He was a busy man, proud to account for every instant of a prominent official's day. It was even his boast that these moments in the station, and the half-hour's journey following, were the only times he was completely free. Yet he was an optimist. Years of commuting had not absolutely killed his feelings for the place – a belief, though he'd never lived up to it, that at every railway junction came the promise of escape from routine. He saw the glass rather than the iron in his surroundings. But there was a pessimist's view of stations. Its outlook was all iron – unbending and uncompromisingly black. Molson acknowledged it – he even felt slight twinges of it in his bones as he waited tonight – but he could never agree with it.

A full train had just drawn out. It was some time before the next was due. 'That was a heavy one,' said the girl behind the bookstall, leaning out towards him over ranks of paperbacks. Her job made her well-known to everyone – though being looked at was another matter, competing as she was with her customers' constant anxiety with time. But even more than with the clock, she had to compete with the faces and figures on book-covers. A swirling pattern of girls lay before her – nurses, witches and schoolgirls, nuns, queens, spies and housewives, some holding knives and guns to men's heads, and some – raped by gorillas, bitten by vampires, worried by werewolves – were swooning back upon beds and hammocks, upon operating-tables and altars, and some into pits and graves or into whirlpools, strangled by their own hair.

'I said – a heavy *train* tonight,' the girl repeated, leaning still further out as though she would grasp Molson by the lapel. Glossy, butter-blonde hair swung across the books as she turned her head this way and that to attend to paper-grabbers on either side of her. Her expression was not sympathetic.

'Yes, indeed – a very busy train.' Molson automatically looked behind her to see if the other woman was around. He imagined her as the motherly type.

'Mrs Woodlock is not back from her tea,' said the girl following his glance. Something sardonic in her tone made him turn to the platform again. It had suddenly grown quiet – that rare interval when officials can be heard chatting in the booking-office and even, tonight, the swish of an out-size platform brush cleaning up dust and old tickets on the other side of the line.

'Where in the world can they be rushing to – morning, noon and night?' said the girl standing back with her arms folded. Startled, Molson turned round. 'Where can who . . . ?'

'All those people – as though their lives depended on it, for heaven's sake!'

It crossed Molson's mind that talk along such lines could lead to difficulty. 'Well, probably their lives *do* depend on it,' he said. 'For one thing they are going back and forth to their work.'

'And for another?'

'What did you say?'

'What are the other things?'

Molson silently folded his papers and put them under his arm as though he must very soon be moving off himself. He held the view that the business of bookstall women, in the racket of stations, was to be both static and silent. But the girl, as though instantly snatching this thought, said: 'Oh, *we* stay put of course. There's plenty of chance to watch. But I was asking – what are all the other things people do in your opinion?'

'The other things? Well, that's putting it wide enough, isn't it? People visit their friends and relatives, I suppose. But mainly there's all the business in and around the jobs – organizing, contacting, interviewing . . . well, the thing is endless. To put it simply – people go to meetings.'

'People like yourself?'

'I admit I *am* a very busy man.'

'Important?'

Oh, the nerve of the round, blue eyes. 'No, busy,' he said sharply. 'I have commitments – responsibilities.' In the heavy silence that followed he actually heard birds twittering and flapping around the arches of the roof.

'They come in through the broken panes this time every evening, regular as clockwork,' said the girl.

'Well, they certainly don't follow the clockwork in *this* station. There's that clock stopped – and that, and that!' He jabbed an umbrella in their direction.

'Mrs Woodlock says that sometimes, just before a train's due, every one of them stops whistling.'

'Mrs Woodlock?'

'We do have names. My name's Estelle. Mrs Woodlock's no fool. She's been all over the world of course. But not in the usual way.'

'Not in the usual way?' asked Molson. Did the woman have wings?

'Oh no. Years ago she got in with this top trombonist. She followed him in bands up and down the country and across Europe more times than she can count. And for more years. He could put his hand to anything – that one. Bright wasn't the word.'

Molson stared about him as though vainly searching for something to take the shine off the man. Only one wan thing occurred to him. 'And did he ever marry her?' he said at last.

And now, as though conjured up from the shadowy depths of the stall, Mrs Woodlock herself appeared behind Estelle's shoulder. A pair of black eyes in a heavy white face studied him. Dense, wavy hair held up by jewelled combs made her head seem massive, and now and then, as she pushed one further in, there came a glitter as though an icicle had been crushed, unmelted, to her scalp.

'We've been talking about how busy everybody is these days,' said Estelle.

'Well, we've certainly an opportunity to see it here,' said Mrs Woodlock, 'but of course I don't equate rushing around with work. We're busy enough ourselves. But we simply stand all day.'

'As you know by your legs,' said the girl.

'As I certainly know by my legs,' Mrs Woodlock agreed. The dark eyes and the blue watched him.

'I suppose someone has to organize the world's affairs – someone must try to keep things straight,' said Molson, his glance falling on dishevelled figures fleeing from vampires.

'This gentleman tells me he's busy enough anyway,' said Estelle. 'He has these endless meetings.'

'Whom does he meet?' asked Mrs Woodlock with a smile. 'A meeting can be a very pleasant thing. I see endless meetings here on this very platform. Some of them look as if they might turn out to be very agreeable indeed.'

'This is the other kind – around tables,' said the girl.

'Tables are all right,' said Mrs Woodlock.

'These are those polished tabletops. No food,' said Estelle.

'Oh those! Well, there's not much pleasure to be had in that. Just paper, pencils and glasses of water. Oh yes, I've had a sight of those meetings and it's a very dismal business indeed!'

Molson had begun to show little relish for this discussion

of himself as a busy man. Oh, to get onto some other tack –
present himself as an adventurer, a reckless wanderer such
as the trombonist must have been! Instead, by cruel force of
habit, he found himself taking the diary from his inside
pocket. With his back to the bookstall he flicked quickly
through it. These pages were black with engagements.
There were names, addresses, times, underlinings in black
and red, arrows pointing down to future dates and back to
past ones. Certain places and persons stood out where the
ballpoint had instinctively thickened itself upon them.
Fainter lines marked dates of less importance. Even the
crossings-out varied from the bold, impatient stroke to the
narrow line. There appeared to be a sign-language here
decipherable only by the dedicated diarist. 'Not many
blanks *there*!' came Mrs Woodlock's voice from behind
him. Whatever the language was, it interested the two
women. They were bending forward over the stall. Both
were smiling. But he had the feeling it was their own secrets
which amused them. Their faces, as they leaned towards
him, came into shadow, but the stall lights shone down
directly and theatrically on top of the blonde and the black
head. This was their stage. Molson had no inkling what the
entertainment was about.

   'No, there are *not* many blanks,' he said. 'Year after year
my diaries get filled up. There's not much I can do about
that, I'm afraid.'

   'A diary!' exclaimed Estelle. 'Of course we sell plenty of
diaries ourselves at New Year. It's always struck me as a
very funny name to give them. I'd always thought of a diary
as a day-to-day account of exciting events. Did it strike you
like that, Mrs Woodlock?'

   'Yes,' said Mrs Woodlock. 'A daily write-up of happenings is my idea of a diary. As a matter of fact Johnson kept a
diary for many years – a real diary, you understand. But
then of course he did have something to record. There
weren't many countries he hadn't set foot in. He knew the

lot. As for people – he met all sorts and he was a match for all sorts. Of course trombones weren't the whole of it, by any means. He was a first-rate chess player, an excellent cook, and I'd say he was a bit of a magician too. More than a bit. A hypnotist. You could almost say he made them see white where there was black.'

In the pause following Molson felt an unpleasant frisson of nerves. 'But not white to black, I hope,' he said.

'Oh no. Johnson was a good man. He didn't play malicious tricks – even when people deserved them. But he was clever all right. Once he found this gigantic advert on the hoarding outside a hall he was to play in. Cigarettes it was – cigarettes and the fantastic joy and peace of lighting up beside a river with nothing but a pack of hounds to keep you company. Well, Johnson took exception to it, a love to hatred turned you might say. He'd been a wheezy man once, you see, a very wheezy man before he broke the habit. It very nearly cost him his job. Anyway, there he was staring at this thing till quite a crowd came up to see for themselves. "Why must they always keep this great blank placard on the wall," he kept saying, "when so many good things could do with a bit of advertising? Me, for a start. Doesn't that waste of space offend you? Doesn't that great white glare hurt your eyes?' And, believe it or not, there were always two or three who saw a blank and nothing but a blank. I'm telling you God's truth. He had the power and some fell under. Didn't I say he could make black white?'

Molson put up a hand to loosen his collar, but he managed to smile, murmuring: 'There must be some gullible people around.'

'Oh, very likely,' replied Mrs Woodlock with ominous restraint. A red spot had appeared on one cheek and her eyes flashed.

'Gullible!' exclaimed Estelle. 'Bamboozled by a cigarette the size of a tree-trunk and a puff of smoke like a mushroom cloud! There's "gullible" if you like!'

'At any rate he taught me a thing or two that's helped me no end in a tough, ungrateful life,' said Mrs Woodlock, still speaking with straight lips. 'Call them tricks if you like.'

'No, no, of course not,' Molson said quickly. Very high up, somewhere amongst the broken panes and the birds, he heard rain falling, and a wind was finding its way under old, bolted doors and up abandoned stairways. Lights only emphasized the darkness of pillars and girders. The whole place lay under a coating of black. Why couldn't they scrub off this gloom as they did with other buildings?

Estelle, who'd been silent for some time watching Molson, leant forward: 'No amount of cleaning would help,' she said. 'Everything's iron here. Painting might do it. But who'd spend money?'

This time Molson took care that his nerves should not be visible in his face, but his limbs looked eager to be away. Even his arms made ineffectual gestures towards the end of the platform as though signalling his train to emerge suddenly from the tunnel and deliver him. But this was not to be.

'I don't think it's coming yet. I think it will be very late tonight.' Even as Mrs Woodlock uttered these words the booming announcement of its lateness filled the station. 'How unpleasant – having to hang around here,' she said with biting amiability. There was nothing to keep him, yet Molson still leaned against the bookstall as though pasted on by his pocket.

'Have you got all the papers you want?' Mrs Woodlock went on. 'A busy man has to keep up with things, hasn't he? Periodicals?' Molson stretched over and picked up a couple of weeklies.

'Books?' Mrs Woodlock persisted.

'They are not exactly my kind.'

'Oh, you'd be surprised,' said Mrs Woodlock with a smile, not explaining if the surprise was in the books or the people who bought them.

Molson had an armful of newsprint now – enough for the longest journey. It made him no more popular at the bookstall. He had long come to the conclusion that this pair had an ingrained hatred of the papers they were handing out.

'You've got a nice pile to get through before the night's out,' said Estelle. 'Yes, a man *does* need to keep himself informed.'

'Not every man,' said Mrs Woodlock. 'I must say Johnson was different. That's to say he was well-informed all right. Prodigiously. But he didn't rely *only* on the print. Oh goodness no! Most of his information he got by moving round the world. Using his wits. Wits, Estelle – that's what we miss these days. Information to the eyeballs, facts at the fingertips – oh dear, yes – but where are the wits?'

Molson was silent, his head bent over the papers on the stall, as if intent on drawing the very heart and guts from the world's news.

'But don't let us disturb you,' said Mrs Woodlock. 'For us it's different. Any chance for a chat in a long day. But we're used to looking at tops of heads; I am quite an expert myself. Believe me, it would never occur to us to try and compete with print.'

The platform was now filling up again and Molson felt some return of optimism – only a scrap, but enough to get him on the move again.

'. . . Signalled at last,' he said firmly.

'Have a good journey,' said Estelle. 'Anyway, good or not, you've got plenty to occupy you.'

'Yes, that'll keep you going,' echoed Mrs Woodlock. 'Never a dull moment – and I hope you've good eyes.' Estelle and Mrs Woodlock smiled and smiled at him, but only with their mouths. The black and the blue eyes were boring into his with remarkable intensity.

'Goodnight, Mrs Woodlock . . . goodnight, Estelle,' said Molson, careful to get the names across and to pronounce them well.

'Goodnight,' said Mrs Woodlock, 'but I don't think we've had the pleasure . . .' There was a grimness about this familiar phrase – something almost approaching a threat. Molson was about to give his own name when he was engulfed by a group who had emerged from the buffet and were hurling themselves at the bookstall for last-minute buying. He had the sensation of falling back as he started to speak. From a distance he tried to utter his name again, and again shouts drowned the sound. There was no knowing whether it came out as cry or whisper, or whether he had perhaps not opened his mouth at all. Molson suffered a momentary and appalling loss of identity. But with the arrival of his train his attention turned to finding a seat. It was only when he was seated and had time to wipe the steam from his window that he looked towards the bookstall. He had a flashing glimpse of Mrs Woodlock and Estelle between the heads and shoulders of bystanders. To say they were laughing was an understatement. Molson marvelled that the jokes of late commuters could produce such mirth.

The train was full, but it was fast with one stop only where, twenty minutes later, his compartment emptied, leaving one other man. Usually at this point in the journey Molson would start on his papers. But not tonight. Tonight he sat with one hand on them, waiting for his mind to settle. As black fields, lines of street-lights, factories, bridges and rivers flashed past, so his imagination flew from one scene to another over the past week. He saw small committee-rooms fitted like Chinese puzzles inside large committee-rooms, and the long, windowless corridors which stretched ahead through a series of revolving doors. He saw his trays of letters, trays of rubber stamps, trays of coffee-cups. He saw halls of typewriters, silent under their night covers. In the dark landscape, between sheep and cows, telephones gleamed, and filing-cabinets. Huge, black-lettered office calendars slid by across clumps of trees. In front of all these, brighter and more ravaged, floated his own face. Molson turned his head away quickly and nodded to the man in the opposite corner – known to him by sight though not by name. They were travelling companions, meeting occasionally on platforms and in waiting-rooms. They shared grievances.

'Later every day!' the man exclaimed. He stared at his watch, sighed, and fixed his eyes on the space above Molson's head. 'Ideal holiday, is it?' he said at last. '. . . Acres of bog and a crumbling castle! No thanks – not for me.' Molson sat tight as though chary of a crick in the neck. The man's eyes wandered to a space on the other side. 'Now *that*'s more like it. If you can rely on that golden sand and the purple sky. And in my experience of adverts it's a very big "if".'

Still Molson made no attempt to verify the colours. Instead, he quickly picked up the top paper on his pile and looked down the front page pictures. Statesmen stared out at him, honest-eyed to an alarming degree. He turned over to the back and read the fortunes of footballers and found himself going methodically down the list of names chosen for some unknown swimming team. After some minutes, Molson turned to the middle pages – and his heart jerked in his chest as though shaken by derailment. He turned to others. Between back and front every page was empty – blank and dingy as unprinted cotton. Molson raised the paper to hide his face. Once in a while, he told himself, it was bound to happen. Some freak paper amongst hundreds of thousands would get through. Stealthily, scarcely rustling it, he folded it and laid it down. He picked another – an evening paper – and held it for a time, still folded, in both hands, as though reassuring himself of its proper weight of black print, then swiftly opened it in the middle. These pages – blank from top to bottom – brought ice patches to his cheeks. This time he'd not been careful to hide his face.

'Look here, you're not cold, are you?' came the voice from the other corner. 'Just a minute. I believe there's a window open.' He got to his feet and Molson heard him some way along the corridor pushing a window up, saw him come in again, careful to slide the compartment door tightly behind him. Molson thanked him briefly, folded his paper again and placed it on top of the other. The man was still watching. 'There *is* flu about,' he said, 'and then of course it does none of us any good – all that hanging about on the platform.'

Molson agreed it had done him no good at all. He sat back again and tried to take a grip on himself. What had happened? Nothing had happened – nothing except that the bookstall women between the two of them had managed to give him a set of dud papers. That was the beginning and end of it. A poor trick. Why, then, this appalling loss of nerve?

The train was making up for lost time. Small stations flashed past in a single chain of blue and yellow light. Tunnels were reduced to the momentary lowered note. Molson was glad of the speed. For a time the sensation seemed to smooth out thought. Yet in spite of this, an increasing unease came over him as he saw in the distance the lights of one of the larger stations. He sat forward on the edge of his seat and looked out. The train was almost at the station and reducing speed slightly as it approached. And now, for a few seconds, Molson was staring into the empty station, staring with such anxiety in his eyes that a solitary porter on the platform craned his neck to get a further sight inside the carriage as it went past. Molson himself had the flashing impression of familiar lights and stairways, walls and sign-boards – then they were out again into the countryside. But he was still sitting forward. All was not right with the station back there. It was not something he cared to name. What else, he decided, but an illusion from speed and darkness – the flicker of white spaces where the

posters should be, that great, blank signboard without a
name? It was far behind him now. Molson settled back into
his corner, but before three minutes had gone by, cautiously, as though lifting a baited trap, he took up one of the
weekly journals. Its cover had the familiar, cheerful layout
in black and red. One hand pressed to his lips, he flicked
the page over. There was empty paper inside. Molson
dropped it on his knee and grabbed up the second weekly
– cheerful again in black and green. Every square inch
between front page and back – hopelessly blank! Molson let
them slide down onto the pile beside him.

'. . . Only if you're absolutely finished with them . . .'
the voice came from the other corner.

'Take them – take them!' Getting to his feet Molson
lifted the wad of papers in both hands and let them drop
with a thud on the seat opposite. The other's good nature
faded a little. 'Thanks,' he said, 'but I'll hardly get through
that lot, will I? Not unless we've more than the usual hold-
ups.' He got no answer. Molson was staring through the
window on his own side as though life depended on it. Yet
nothing outside held him rigid. He was staring at the
reflection of the man in the opposite corner. Molson
watched as he took up the evening paper, saw him run
his eye down the front page, and waited an age while he
turned it. His expression didn't change. He spent a long
time on this page and on the one after it. Certain bits he
read more intently, holding the sheet close to his face.

'A very peculiar paper tonight, I think you'll admit,' said
Molson. His rigid face cracked in a smile.

'No different from any other night to my mind,' said the
other, 'except for that chap drowning himself on his first
soak in his solid gold bathtub. Then of course there's the
woman helping the police with the hand and the three ears
in the laundry bag. Three! That certainly makes you think.'
Another age passed before he picked up the second paper.
'The odd thing is,' he said at last, 'the daily doesn't say a

word about either of them. I've been through it from end to end – not a word! No gold bathtub. No ears. Whether or not the pound's had a good day – oh yes. There's always plenty on that subject. Do they ever worry about what kind of day we've had. *You're* not looking any too great. Anyway, thanks . . .' He was about to hand back the papers when Molson leant over and pushed his arm back.

'Wait!' he said. 'Did you look at those weeklies?' His peremptory tone made the other man gape. 'I gave you the lot, didn't I? Read the lot!'

The other's annoyance increased dramatically. 'Here – take them! Did I ask to have the whole damn load dumped on me?' He took the pile of papers, delivered them with a thump to the other seat and retired into his corner. After some minutes he took an engagement diary from his pocket and absorbed himself in it.

Molson stared across at him, struck by a chilling thought. He began searching for his own diary – through every pocket of his overcoat, in the zipped side-flaps of his briefcase. The search was pointless. The book, he knew, was where it always was and always would be, year after year – in the left-hand inner pocket of his jacket. He dreaded finding it. Amongst the remembered voices of that day one rose clear above the rest: 'Not many blanks *there*!' Mrs Woodlock had exclaimed on sight of the diary. With what venomous sarcasm she had uttered it!

Molson drew out the flat, green book and laid it on his knee. For a long time he stared at it, willing its contents to be intact. The diary was still warm from being close to his chest. It was a heart of a kind – reliable and exact. No matter if each year there was a change of heart. In essence it was always the same. Molson opened the first page, and his heart leapt. His name, his address, his phone number, his car number – all there, thank God! On the second page and third – Driving Licence, TV Licence, Credit Card and Passport Number, Bank Book and Blood Group, Date of

Birth and Glove Size. He was not totally annihilated. Still, with fearful caution he turned other pages. It was as it had always been – the names in black and red, underlinings and circlings, scribbled letters and block letters. Page after page he turned. He found no gap. His timetable stood firm and clear on all its lines between the red dates.

'Not a blank in the whole book – see for yourself!' cried Molson to the man in the corner and he waved the diary in the air. 'Crammed to the covers. Not a space, not a gap, not a chink!'

But the other was still smarting from their last exchange. 'And what about it?' he replied. 'Couldn't I say exactly the same myself? Amn't I up to the neck in it this year, next year and well on into the next again? If it comes to that I could fill up a three-year diary any day you wanted it. No trouble at all. Oh no, don't talk to me about blanks!'

Molson wasn't listening. He was trying to crush a massive wad of papers into the narrow space under the seat. He was not absolutely successful. A corner of one paper still protruded, but he put his heel on it. Unbelievable vacancies haunted his mind, but his own cosmos was safe. He took out his pen and double-lined certain dates in his diary. His stroke was tremulous to begin with but it gained firmness as he went on. Once in a while he paused to sharpen up an asterisk star, and here and there where the nebulous circles had grown faint, thickened them with a darker line.

# The Night of the Funny Hats

THE BUS – THREE days out from Perth in Western Australia and *en route* for Adelaide – was now crossing the great empty expanse which skirts the Nullarbor Plain. There was one more overnight stop and a full day's travelling still to go. 'You asked for a wilderness – you've got it!' the driver called back defiantly to his passengers as they penetrated further and further along one of the longest and loneliest stretches of the Australian continent. He was an excessively conscientious man and he had need to be, for his responsibilities were heavy. The passengers behind him were a mixed crowd. Many of the Australians were tourists crossing by bus for the first time, others were the ordinary travellers from the west and north-west of the country visiting relatives on the eastern side. There were married couples amongst them, pairs of friends and people travelling on their own, a few elderly persons and one child. Amongst the visitors there was a young woman teacher from Yorkshire, two German tourists and an American geologist. The road they were now on, the Eyre Highway, had been sealed three or four years back and its surface was good, though there were still stretches of deep dust and a few cracked, warped patches where flood and heat had got the better of it and repair work had been going on. There were some on the bus who had covered hundreds of miles of dirt road in their time, or had set foot in the red deserts and tropic places of this land. Even now they thought of themselves as explorers of a kind. And there were some, on the other hand, who'd taken one long look through the window and withdrawn their eyes. Briskly they had begun to discuss the well-kept gardens of their home towns and the difficulties of keeping a green lawn. It had been a time of long, fierce drought. They talked of the regulations on watering, of hoses efficient and inefficient. For in this country from its beginnings, water had been the constant common topic down the years. Water – the struggle to find it and preserve it, water for animals and crops, water for hundreds of thousands of acres of land. As if to keep them always in mind of this, a great pipeline had accompanied them on the earlier part of their journey from Perth for some hundreds of miles, sometimes running parallel to the road, sometimes snaking its way around outcrops of rock or disappearing off into the far distance. Occasionally it would dive underground for a time, only to reappear suddenly a few yards away.

The horizon at which they stared with dread or longing grew no less strange as hour after hour went by. Where land met sky there was a dark blue line, dead straight and endless, giving the illusion of a distant sea. Yet water had once been here and the immense limestone plateau they were crossing had been built up by an ancient sea. This landscape, though flat, was a subtly changing one. During the last hours they had covered regions which were almost desert, and others where a low scrub grew, or where sparse, reddish grass alternated with great tracts of saltbush and bluebush whose colour varied from soft grey-green to blues and dark greens against the cream-pink earth. There were areas covered with white stones as far as the eye could see, and growing here and there along the ground by the roadside, a few low-spreading blue flowers. The perspective of this landscape and its light was such that every object in it appeared to exist by itself in total separateness from the rest. Each bush, tree, stone and flower lived in the naked light with its own black shadow sharply defined – a shadow which would grow longer and sharper as the sun went down. Certain passengers could not get enough of the silent singleness of these things. They stared out beyond the verge of the road as though they had never looked at a stone or at a bush before. Only when light began to leave the landscape would they draw back again into the warm, lit world of the bus.

It was their last full day on the plain. Late tomorrow, after their overnight stop, they would be back to civilization. At intervals throughout this day the bus had stopped to let them stretch their legs, and then it was not only space that stunned them. It was silence. The thing was palpable. It was not a silence they had ever known before. It beat upon the ears. At their second stop on the road one or two travellers walked off some short distance on their own in order to see the full circle of the horizon. Others, amid a steady clicking of cameras, drew closer together and attempted to crack the silence. There was a lively discussion on the making of roads, on the date and construction of the giant water-pipe. There were shouts and laughter when an unwary one, wandering a few yards off the road, put his hand upon a rounded, cushion-shaped bush and snatched it off with a shriek as lethal spikes stabbed him. Others, to bring the unknown into focus, tried to describe in sober detail what they were looking at. Their determined voices died a little. Each human description seemed at once deflected from its object. The place existed for itself. Soon silence closed in again.

The driver allowed them all to have their full fifteen-minute break, but on the wanderers especially he kept a wary eye. They were all tired; their legs were still cramped as they finally climbed back into the bus again. When it moved off, their driver's face – or what they could see of it in the mirror – looked more than ever strained. Nevertheless, on and off throughout the day he had reminded them of some festivity that had been planned for their last night. Now he reminded them again. Each time there was a flatness about his voice as he spoke of it. He was a serious, even a rather melancholy man. Very early on in the journey he had told his passengers that he was first and foremost a good driver, not an entertainer nor a clown. It seemed that he was comparing himself with certain younger, jokier drivers and that he felt some resentment at what might be expected of him. For it was obvious that long ago, during his training, he had been warned that not only jokes would be needed on the road, but that fun and games would be expected at the last meal of any long, outlandish journey. He had been told that a Funny Hat Night would always go down well – it was a painless thing and very easy to plan. Many times he had managed it before. Wearily he brought it up again.

The passengers had listened to the first announcement of this event in silence. They had never needed to be reminded that this man was no clown. From the start they had known him only as a painfully conscientious driver – and one with other unenviable duties on his shoulders. Every morning he loaded the heavy luggage underneath the bus, shifting the stuff again to make room for last-minute bags and boxes, or carting the unwieldier items round to the other side. He sorted out arguments over seats, listened to grievances about beds. At stops throughout the day, he saw to it that his charges never wandered far into the unknown bush – counted them, consoled them, gave them the facts about certain rocks, certain plants, and at night pointed out the kangaroos that pounded away on either side from the headlights of the bus or the occasional dingo dog loping off into the darkness. He made sure of their overnight stops, told them about weather, about water – the water that could be drunk, the water that could not be drunk, mentioned their distance from hospitals, the difficulties of radio doctors, stopped the bus for those who in spite of warning had drunk the water, thanked those who praised him, warned the boorish amongst the men, warded off persistent charmers amongst the women. And now

again in his serious, conscientious voice, he mentioned
hats.

'Hats?' shouted one woman from the back. 'What hats?
We've got no hats!'

'No, of course you've got no hats.' The driver spoke
patiently into the mouthpiece which enabled him to be
heard to the very end of the long coach. 'That's the point.
You make your hats out of anything you can lay hands on –
scarves, ribbons, ties, stockings. Decorate them with twigs
if you want, or leaves – anything you can find out there. Or
drinking straws and paper napkins – whatever you can pick
up at the next café stop. And don't forget the men are in it
too!' Having done his duty, the driver was silent for a while.
But at intervals he spoke of the coming night.

As the time came up to midday, the passengers had
looked at one another's heads and thought of hats. There
was an unreality about this thought as there had been about
everything else on the journey. They could not conjure up a
hat made out of ribbons or ties, far less from anything that
might be found in the impenetrable landscape outside the
bus window. The region they were now passing through
was sparse and sandy, with a scattering of small pink-and-
white stones. The line of distance was still a deep sea-blue.
For a long time they had seen neither animal nor bird.
There was no breath of wind. There was no cloud in the sky
and there never had been a cloud for months on end. At
one o'clock they stopped at a small place on the roadside –
not much more than a drive-in café beside some lorry repair
shacks and a petrol pump. There was little time to eat, for
the driver had a schedule to keep to and there was a long
way to go before their last stop that night. In less than an
hour some of the passengers were already making their way
towards the bus, or standing outside for a few moments to
draw in an oven-breath of air before starting off again.

There were only three passengers travelling on their own
– a mining engineer who'd come to this country from

Bristol over fifteen years ago, the young exchange teacher from Yorkshire, and an elderly woman who made the journey from Perth to Adelaide every other year to visit her son, his wife and her two grandchildren. These three tended to come together more by chance than by choice, or occasionally because it was convenient to sit at tables with one another rather than intrude on the tighter groups. This afternoon they came separately from the café and each walked a short way out into the wilderness beyond the road. They seemed at the same time totally isolated and yet connected, for each threw a sharp, dark shadow on the ground, a shadow linking them with one another and with the nearby stones and bushes – though not in the human way. This was a beautiful and fearful place for human beings to stand alone in. Once it had been a place for pioneers, adventurers and explorers of crazy, unimaginable courage. Even now desperate people might come here, longers after loneliness, addicts of silence and of the receding horizon, and the three persons in the midst of it now drew instinctively together as though suddenly aware of this.

'Well, have you started to get busy on your funny hats?' said the engineer, turning to the two women. It was a harmless enough question, yet by breaking so profound a silence it had taken on a mocking tone.

'I doubt if I've ever worn a hat in my life, funny or not,' said the younger woman quickly. 'And anyway – what about your own?'

'Never thought about it and don't intend to,' he said. His expression, far from being satirical, was sombre. As for his body, it gave the uncomfortable impression of fineness and thickness mixed. He was tall, heavy in build, with a large, round head of black hair set upon narrow shoulders. His arms were ponderous, his hands thin. There was a thickness about his cheeks and jaw and puffy purple circles about his eyes. These eyes were blue – startlingly protuberant and bright, as though by-passing all the heaviness of the rest.

'I suppose,' said the grandmother, 'at my age they'll be waiting for me to turn up in some sort of fancy Victorian bonnet. Well, they can wait. One reason being that I've no intention of covering my head if I can help it. I happen to be deaf in one ear. The left one. People who know me tend to speak on my right.'

Behind her the young woman moved over unobtrusively to the right side. The man stood where he was.

'Do you have to travel a lot in your work?' said this woman, who'd heard something of the engineer's job.

'A good deal.'

'And of course this must be one of your longest journeys?'

'Yes, but I'm not here for the work this time.'

'Well, that's good, then,' she said.

'A complete break away from it all,' added the older woman knowingly.

'It's the silence I'm after,' said the man. There was complete silence for a moment.

'Stupidly I'd imagined we'd be off the bus for much longer periods,' said the older woman. 'Well, we could certainly do with more time to stretch our legs. I know I could. I get cramp here in my calf if I sit too long. And you can't stand up in the bus on these roads. If you stood for a second you'd be hurled around like a ragdoll.'

'It's the silence I'm after,' said the engineer again. 'Total and utter silence. I'd like to go right out and stay out.'

And now there was total silence. No breath from the great plain. No human breath, for his companions did not care to speak. Nevertheless, after some time the older of the two said in a very low voice to the other: 'Of course I have *some* idea what I could make it from. For instance, I've a long, nylon scarf in my case and a couple of brooches. I suppose I could make do with that if I had to. But of course I *don't* have to, so I certainly won't do it.'

'The only thing I can think of is my bathcap with some kind of made-up bow,' said the other. Her description was of a pantomime cap, but she did not smile. Indeed her face was very serious, like that of someone contemplating not the clown in herself but the phantom.

Some of the passengers were still in the café, some had disappeared into the lavatories on either side. A few were already on the bus. The driver now sounded the horn three times – a long, warning bray. He was not an aggressive man and had seldom had to shout, but the pressure of time had grown tighter and tighter around him as the miles went by. Most of the passengers came quickly to the summons.

'Are we all here?' The driver stared round at them as they took their seats. His eyes were red through staring at night and day, and at the bright and dark of the road. 'All here! All aboard, skipper! All set! Ready for the road!' the voices answered him. But the driver took nothing on chance. He walked slowly up and down the bus, his lips moving as he made the count. The two women who were on their own had sat together throughout the journey, changing seats now and then to get the window side. And now the younger one looked round quickly. 'Is *he* in?'

'Of course he's in.'

'He went to the lavatory last thing.'

'Well he's here now. Right there at the back.'

'The stories you hear of someone left behind!'

'Not on this line you don't. Not with this driver.'

'Do you know what he was getting at out there?'

'No, I didn't hear the half. He was on my deaf side, remember? Silence – he was on about that. Well, he's from Sydney. Maybe those in the cities can do with a bit of silence. Now where I live, I'm far, far out. Most of the time it's quiet as the grave. I could do with some noise. Everyone needs something different of course, depending on what they've got.'

On long hauls there were always some passengers who

presented more problems for the driver than others. The engineer was one of these. During the day he made himself felt by a certain cool detachment from the rest of the company, while at the same time he linked himself with the driver by means of a persistent and unprovoked hostility. It was not clear how or why the hostility had started, unless it was his instinct that the driver was a whole person in a way that he himself was not. He alone might make this comparison, but what was plain to every passenger was the driver's feeling for completeness in everything he undertook. They trusted him. Whatever shocks or discomforts it might hold, the day would come full circle. The machine would not break down. The passengers would not break down. Each night's destination was sure. And finally he would get them home. It made no difference that he was an anxious man and not the gayest character they had ever seen at a wheel. They relied on him to know their needs, and even their unspoken demands had been made clear. He was to give them their freedom without letting them get lost, to keep the peace without losing his temper. Above all, he was to go on liking them when they became unlikeable.

The man at the wheel did not make out to be a specialist in anything except driving. But from the first day, it became clear he knew what he was talking about when he described certain plants or pointed out rare birds. Even the geologist held his peace, listening with polite attention when the driver explained the origin of certain rock formations. It was only the back seat passenger who contradicted him at every turn and always with a devious insult. When the driver reported the mileage between stopping-places, named a tree, noted an explorer's route or gave a date, the engineer would wait for a minute until the information had been taken in – then he would clearly pronounce to those around him another mileage, a different tree. The route taken by the explorer had been wrongly given. The date was out. He simply stated, and in a level voice, each different fact. The driver heard some of the corrections but not all. Any he failed to hear were passed on down the bus and usually reached him in some garbled version. But garbled or not, he could not fail to sense the hostility from behind.

There were more serious contradictions from that quarter. From time to time, in something the driver said or in the way he said it, there could be detected a profound pride in the country to which his forebears had come and where his parents and grandparents had worked all their lives. An almost painful emotion would come through as he related the struggles of its beginning. When he described the speed of this progress his voice changed. He breathed more deeply, as though to give himself enough air, enough space inside the chest to explain this spectacular expansion. Occasionally it was with the same deep breath that he described some peculiarity of the region they were travelling through – this wilderness, for instance, and its instantaneous flowering after rain. The man at the back was not slow to sense these things. Besides, he had felt such emotion himself. For the engineer knew a lot about this country and he had travelled widely in it. He gave the impression that he had loved it once to an excessive degree, that he had even had a wild, extravagant love affair with this land. This had gone sour on him. Now he stared at every person born and bred in the place and at every tree long-rooted here as though they were totally alien and in some cases hateful to him. He knew too that such emotion as the driver had allowed himself could not be countered only by facts and figures or by straight denials.

So the engineer laughed when the driver praised openly any part of his own country. It was not a loud laugh, but usually it reached the driving seat and every Australian between heard it too. He was asked to explain this laugh. Well, of course it was a long time since he'd lived in Britain, he said, or anywhere else for that matter. And God knew there was a lot wrong with that place. But if it was the new they were talking about – then over there it was the same as here. Every week in every city new buildings went up, in every part of the country – new roads, machinery, new bridges, new dams. But the most important thing was the mixture of new *and* old. History. That was the point he was after. The engineer talked at length about History – how at every step, and cheek by jowl with skyscrapers, you came across the mediaeval church, the Norman castle, the Gothic cathedral, the Elizabethan palace. He mentioned Roman baths. He spoke as if he had supervised their plumbing, stone by stone, with his own two eyes. The engineer talked of the culture of Great Britain, past, present and future. He spoke as though he himself had measured the depth, the height and the breadth of this culture with a measuring-rod and tape – and found it was all there. For, long ago the engineer had closed his ears to all talk of high accomplishment in the new continent, just as nowadays he shut his eyes to the tropical extravagance and splendour of its flowers and trees. He mentioned, finally, that he came from a country where all the trees were green – a true, deep green. And that went for the grass as well.

The Australians could have made it tough for this man. But they were inclined to hold their hand, for it was not clear exactly what was bugging him. They knew it was not lack of palaces or castles or green trees. They did not absolutely dislike him either, if only because he could do this very much better for himself. It was said, from what little could be gathered from his talk, that he was still outstanding at his job. It was said too that his former wife, his present girl friend, his son and daughter were now as far away from him as they could get – one in England, the other in northern Australia, his son and daughter in America. All day, under the watchful eye of the driver, he was as sober as a judge. His clothes were sober too, and formal, compared to the casual gear of all the rest. In the evenings, when they'd reached their stopping-point, the engineer would drink as much as he could take while still standing on his legs. Then, swivelling from the counter upon his heel in one smooth movement and moving away along a straight line like an artificially propelled puppet, he would walk to his bed, where he would continue to drink until he passed out. And just as in drinking and sleeping the aim was to knock himself out, so too his ears came in for a lambasting. Whenever he came in from the silent road, he wanted noise – the loudest voices and the loudest laughs, though he himself spoke little. He seemed to welcome the crash of glass and dish slammed down on counters, the impatient tramp of travellers' feet moving from room to room. Very occasionally with certain hard-luck stories over drinks he could be sympathetic. The story that contained one breath of success or hinted at a boast he crushed with absolute indifference. He was not approached often, but he was not excluded. Sometimes, by chance, he was the centre of the indoor, night-time racket, and made no move to get away. Yet he spoke of silence, utter silence as being of heaven.

All through the afternoon the bus had been coming nearer to what, for most passengers, was the most astounding sight of the whole journey. For they were gradually approaching that part of the limestone plateau which broke down onto a point where, for the first time, a limitless east-west view could be seen – part of the five-hundred mile stretch of cliffs above the Great Australian Bight. they reached this point late in the afternoon when the bus turned down a chalky sidetrack and they came suddenly upon the expanse of blinding white sand marking the vicinity of the great cliffs.

'Twenty minutes *please*!' called the driver. 'Read the warnings and mind your step. We can do a lot. What we *can't* do is haul you up if you fall over!'

There was a rapid exodus from the bus, a slow walk across the sandy area with its warning notice, then a cautious and finally a crab-like approach to the crumbling cliff-edge. On either side – as far as the eye could see – a sheer white wall stretched, undulating, into the distance. At its foot the dark unbroken waves advanced, churned to a violent storm of foam where they met the rock and swirling on through white limestone crevasses, to narrow and divide in thin, clear streams of cobalt blue. But at certain deeper undercuttings, water raced up in long points and drew back again, raced in and drew back like the continuous thrust of a cruelly sharpened sword of dark green glass. Directly beneath the cliffs, the waves struck in a series of massive thunderclaps followed by a roar which resounded along mile upon mile of the great wall and could be heard in the farthest distance as a heavy muffled boom. From underfoot came sharper sounds – explosive gulps of water down giant potholes, and a continuous sucking, knocking, hissing as the waves scoured through hidden caves deep inside the rock.

There was little chance here for the human voice. But few words could be said, for the place fitted no familiar concept of sea, sand and cliff. Some were glad enough to turn back to the haven of the bus before the time was up, and there were others – incomers never likely to see the place again – who stood as long as possible on this edge. But time was getting short. One by one those on the cliff drew back to find another place to view the sea or to take the final photo. The young men, each with one arm round his girl and the other round the metal warning-post, were being snapped by a fellow-passenger. The two unaccompanied women, a few steps apart, were making their way up towards the bus. The younger stopped suddenly, looked back, and for the second time that afternoon exclaimed: 'Where is he?'

'Still at the cliff-edge.'

'I'm going back.'

'To do what?'

'Just to be there.'

'Oh, go back then, go back!' The older woman walked on briskly, impatiently, while the other turned, and went slowly back to where the engineer stood looking down on the hanging cliff's edge curled back in a white stone wave from his feet. The woman waited until he saw her, then she came near and touched his wrist. A quick, warning touch.

'What?' shouted the engineer above the turmoil and raising his hand into the air. There was now some wind driving the spray sideways – hard as hail – but mixing with it soft balls and puffs of foam which rolled along the face of the cliff in smoke-rings, or piled up, clot upon clot, in quivering snow-white heaps upon ledges or inside black cracks of rock. The man and woman turned, and moved back some distance from the edge to a spot where there was a slight hollowing of the ground. Here it was quieter and the ferment at the cliff's base was not visible, though the ground under their feet shook with a huge, rhythmic thud of water.

'What is it?' said the engineer, loudly again.

'Nothing. Wondering what your impressions were, that's all.'

'My *what*? Impressions? Oh my God!' Because of his white, protuberant eyeballs, the engineer – when once he began to take notice – could look either wildly expectant or very angry. He looked angry. The young woman screwed up her eyes as if rejecting her stilted words. 'No,' she said, 'it was simply to show I'm around.'

The man bent his head and listened carefully to these words, as though making sense of something in a foreign tongue. 'So you're around? Yes, but what did you want to *say* – supposing you could have been heard at all, I mean?'

'Nothing. "I'm here." That was the whole of it.'

Again the man listened to these words as though to their last echo, his arms folded, his eyes roving around the piece of ground where they were standing.

'Did you think I was on the brink? Oh, I was there all right, like all the rest of our joy-riders. What *other* brink, though? That's what you want to know, isn't it?'

'All right then – yes. Yes, for one single second I imagined you thinking – *thinking* how it would be. Common on edges. I did *not* imagine you doing it. Never!'

The engineer, still with folded arms and tracing patterns in the sand with the toe of his shoe, said: 'And yet you can't bring yourself to say what.'

'It's easy. Stepping over.'

'It's easy?'

'Saying it's easy.'

'Now that the unreal danger's past, you mean? As though simply because I haven't thrown myself down I'm not on any brink at all.'

The woman was now looking back in the direction of the bus, willing it to sound the warning hoot though there were still eight minutes to go. Long ago the older passengers had climbed in and were peering impatiently from the windows.

'I've known, I may say, quite a few agreeable women like yourself in the last few years,' he went on, 'not counting the other kind of course. And many more at a time when I was better-looking and a good deal more agreeable myself. They all had this restraining hand when they thought they sensed a drama. Every one of them. But with lesser brinks or dramas, pettier hells – they showed less interest. Most of them, in fact, took off.'

'Dramas . . . ? I don't see you like that.'

'How then?'

'Always in empty space – your own deserts and plains. Nobody gets near. Sooner or later everyone gets the push.'

Turning instantly, his hand gesturing from the wide horizon to herself, he exclaimed derisively: 'These in-comers! You! Always the same. Eight thousand miles from home – so now the sky's the limit! Every spot can be explored, every person explained. They see the mirage, of course – the distant water, companions in empty places. Then they go back – and none the wiser for it. Wild enthusiasts or sour critics of the place – what does it matter? All of them – absolute beginners in this land! *You* will go back to your own small country one day soon no doubt, and no doubt thankfully too. The rest of us – those who've been here for years and years – know better. We'll hate this place and love it for the rest of our lives!'

The woman turned abruptly and started up towards the distant bus, quickening her steps as she saw the last passengers climbing in and the driver standing on the steps with his left hand on his wrist-watch as though feeling an erratic pulse. The woman now took her place beside her travelling companion, the driver got into the driving seat and stared morosely out towards the cliffs. 'We're going to have to hoot for him,' he warned the others over his shoulder. At the first blare of the horn, the engineer again folded his arms and took a long survey of the sea's horizon from end to end, and from the sky's zenith to some point on the water directly below. At the second blare, he was seen moving slowly in the direction of the bus, stopping to shift the crumbled stones with his foot, now and then picking one up, examining it and putting it down again.

'Well, there's always got to be *one* like that!' said the driver. 'They won't hear, they won't move, they won't play. You just have to carry them along.' He said nothing when the engineer finally got in, but for the first and only time the bus started with a jerk that nearly threw him off his feet as he went up the middle aisle.

Gradually they moved away from the vicinity of the cliffs until there was little evidence of them, except for the distant flash of white where sand, through aeons, had been flung and hardened on the headlands, and soon only the appearance of the sky far behind gave indication they had been near water. Again, mile after mile, the focus of their eye shifted from sandy scrub to landscapes of low bushes, to grass, to stones, to scrub again. Once, they got out and walked some distance to see a great hole which had formed under the limestone crust. 'The whole place riddled with them!' said the driver, as he let a few of them peer down into the black opening. The largest holes and vents, he told them, could blow out such great gasps of breath that anything above would be suspended, whirling, in mid-air, or sometimes instead of blowing they would breathe in and suck down to the very depths anything – wing, leaf or flying fur – that passed across. The passengers themselves blew out and drew in their breath as they looked, for this sudden cavity in the silent, endless plain appalled them. They got back into the bus again, some in a subdued and even melancholy mood, so much so that the driver, after a few silent miles, felt it his duty to bring them round again to a more normal outlook.

'You're not forgetting your hats, are you?' he said with a weary attempt at enthusiasm, for talk at that hour was beginning to be an effort. 'I want a funny hat,' he said again, 'on every single one of you tonight. Remember?'

Two or three of them had not only remembered – they were actually constructing hats. The attractive widowed sisters sitting together near the front had been twisting up pink and blue paper napkins which they'd found at the last store ninety miles back. They were making rosettes sewn together with thread and a few safety pins. 'I don't know if they're *funny*,' one of them murmured, 'but they're going to be pretty.' Behind them two husbands were discussing, across the aisle, the possibility of elastic straps stuck with bird feathers.

'Birds? What birds are you expecting to catch before nightfall?' said a wife.

'Anyway, what's the prize?' somebody called out.

'I don't know yet. I'll have to think about it,' said the driver. 'But there'll be a prize all right – don't you worry about that.'

He himself was worried about the time. There had been some unexpected stops; one to help a car in trouble on the road, another to let the youngest passenger off to be sick and to lie for a moment longer, chalk-faced, under a prickly bush. At one point, he'd got out to explore the origin of a rattling under the bus, and had had to unpack and repack several items of stuff, having found nothing more than a tin lid loose in the luggage hold. He'd also stopped for fifteen minutes to let the last half-dozen photos of the day be taken while the light was still good, and to let a few others get out at the same time to stretch their legs. Warmth was still rising from the ground but there was a slight coolness in the air. The sun was low, and so silent was it that the first click of a camera sounded like the whirr and tick of the first gigantic insect on the earth. One woman whispered to another that she would take the chance, before it was too late, to find something, anything at all in the landscape that might do for a hat. She made off at a run into the scrub, dodging spikes and stones and prickly grass to reach the taller bushes. 'What the *hell* . . . ?' exclaimed the driver, bending over his wheel in desperation, closing his eyes, and opening them again to see her break a hard stalk of bristly green out of a bush with the aid of her foot, and come running back, running and throwing up her hand with its thorns against the enormous sky, just as though she were coming up to a bus-stop in a city street.

'Please, please, do not *do* it!' he implored her as she climbed in. 'I have told you not to go in so far.' He now told them, as they waited for the others, the stories of disappearances – of people running away just like that, running after God knew what, after some flower or stone, after mirages of trees and water. He had heard of some who went after a non-existent sea to wet their tongues, after fruits that never were, after boon companions that had never been. In the end, after the terrible sun itself. 'Oh, you would never believe the stories – I could be all night. Only, please do not do that again!' Even the sober ones with cameras came quickly now, seeing the driver with his hands already gripping the wheel, his head already thrusting towards the endless road ahead.

He did not accelerate. He was too careful a driver for that. But already the stones and the prickly bushes were throwing their sharper, blacker shadows. He had planned to reach the motel long before dark, but he warned them their dinner would be late tonight. Yes, it would be late, but it would be good. He had phoned some hundred miles back and made absolutely certain of it. It would be the best meal and the best bed they had seen since being on the road.

The evening light was still brilliant, but in half an hour the passengers looked back to see a fiery red sky such as they had never seen before, and minutes later the huge sun was plunging to the horizon through blue and purple bands like a glaring metal ball plunging through strips of silk. Suddenly it was dark. Eyes glittered here and there along the edges of the road – but all day the driver had been pointing out the dingo dogs and kangaroos. Now he had come to the end of what he would say. The leaping, luminous eyes were left to silence.

It was another hour before the low, grey buildings appeared suddenly in the headlights of the bus, set incongruously in space and darkness like sea-shell fragments in a desert. In addition to the motel, there were a small shop, a garage, various sheds where provisions were stacked, and some distance away a tank for storing water. Two huge trucks were drawn up outside and the bus came in behind them. As at every stop on their journey, the stunning silence struck like a knife the instant the engines of the bus cut out. It took the passengers several moments to recover from this blow. Then they stretched and reached for the racks. They started to clamber out, demanding their luggage.

In many ways this was the worst time of day for the

driver. He had to drag out the heavy bags and cases from the dark innards of the bus, heave them to the ground and line them up for the waiting passengers. He had to dive and search again and again for the lost bag, while reassuring its owner that nothing was ever lost, few things were even dented, handles were seldom frayed. After the baggage, he had to supervise the search for rooms, making sure that the married would be safely tucked up, dealing discreetly with dedicated wife-swappers and generously with anxious lovers. Tact was also needed for those persons travelling alone. Would the girls very kindly share? For girls they must ever be, whether sixteen or sixty. Yes, they had better share, he might have added – three or sometimes four to a room – as there was nothing else for them to do. He had to enquire again about the meal, making sure that what was promised far back on the road was forthcoming now in all its details and that there was plenty of it. His passengers were dead beat. It was the one comfort of their hard day. He had to see, moreover, that their aversions had been catered for. The vegetarians were to be served no hulking steak, no tinned shrimp was to lurk amongst the lettuce leaves of shellfish allergics. Last but not least, the driver had to make certain they knew the time of departure in the morning. 8 a.m. with their luggage on the dot. Yes, and very kindly not one minute later, please! It was the last lap of the journey, but it would be a long one.

Tonight was no different from any other. The driver was praised extravagantly and harangued by turns – praised when he returned from the kitchen to announce that beef was on and chicken too, with matching gravies and green vegetables, deep apple pie and cream. He was harangued by some when it was discovered that certain unexpectedly cramped bedrooms were a long way from the main building, and that someone's hot and cold had let out nothing but an empty gurgling. A young man with his girl came up to him and thanked him for extracting their lost map, which had got wedged between a seat and a window. He pointed out the part of the road they had missed and showed them the distance they would go tomorrow. The engineer went by and said a few low words to the driver in passing. Someone, catching a word at a distance, said it was something about the day's journey, and for a wonder might have been amiable – seeing the man was smiling. But a closer listener said it was a scathing remark on the driving, a comment about the slowness, the roughness and the late arrival. One of the women spoke to the driver about hats, said what a good idea – one last get-together before the parting tomorrow night. Every journey had an end. For her part she would be sad, really sad to see it come. A German approached to say he had been inspired by sights remarkably impressive and instructive that day. Tomorrow he hoped his experience would be as equally rewarding as today's.

The driver stood up energetically to all these things, though certain changes in his colour were noticed by some: an unpredictable paleness, a strange smoothness of the cheek at the praise, a spreading, blotchy redness across the forehead at the blame, so that the man who found the handle of his bag had been crushed kept quiet about it. The couple who had been led to expect pork as well as mutton and beef swallowed their disappointment in silence. What no one could swallow in silence was the announcement five minutes later that supper would not be half an hour ahead, but one whole hour. 'Yes, yes,' called the driver, throwing up his hands for silence, 'but it will give you all time to sort yourselves out and have a proper rest before your meal. And then what about those hats? I want to see some prize hats, ladies. Ladies *and* gentlemen!' He swung round in the direction of his own room – almost, it could be said, clawing and plunging his way towards his place as though making a last desperate lurch towards rest. They let him go.

The two single women had been put together in one room as they knew they would. They were resigned to it, and in fact counted themselves lucky that another two were not in with them. The older woman unpacked her small case. She hung a wide, blue nightdress on the end of the bed, hung a skirt and blouse in the wardrobe and a spongebag on the basin tap. Sitting on the bed, she began to unlace her large canvas shoes and to knock off the heavy sand that had thickened between heel and sole. From the eyeholes she unpicked a few green spikes. Then she washed her hands and face, brushed her hair and lay down on her bed with a magazine which dealt with chickens – how to rear them and house them and feed them, how to market eggs, how to preserve them and pack them.

'It's my back and neck,' she said, looking up after a while. 'And even my eyes. Squinting sideways for hours. *I'm* not sorry we've to wait an hour. Right now I couldn't get food down     my throat's so dry.'

'Well, don't drink from those taps,' said the other. 'Remember he warned us. You'll have to wait till supper.'

'Don't worry, I've got my own,' said the older woman, leaning over to rummage in her carrier bag and bringing out two small cartons of orangeade. 'More than enough. Have some.' They swallowed slowly, seriously, as though mindful of the preciousness of any liquid in this land. For a time they read in silence, one with her magazine, the other with a newspaper two days old.

'Will you join in this hat business?' said the younger woman, looking at her watch.

'Not likely. If I have to – and of course I don't have to and won't – I've got, as I told you, the long, brown headscarf. As if anyone could be bothered at this time of night!'

'Some have bothered already. Those two widow-sisters at the back have made things from napkins that look like bridal wreaths.'

'Trust widows!' said the other.

'Then there's the other who went running after spikes. Looks like hers would be a crown of thorns.'

'I don't doubt it, poor thing. Did you get a good look at the husband?'

'Some of the men are all for it. Back there on the road I heard them discussing elastic bands and feathers.'

'Yes – children, most of them. Any chance to play cowboys and Indians.'

'What will *he* do, I wonder.'

'The engineer?'

'Yes. *He's* no child.'

'Maybe not. But he's a bully. Are you interested in bullies? Some women are, of course.'

'He's alone. He has nobody. Anyone he ever loved is at the ends of the earth.'

'Anyone he ever *what*? So he's drinking himself to death?'

'No. But worse.'

'Is there worse?'

'I'm afraid what he might do to himself one day.'

The older woman read fiercely and intently about chickens for a few minutes. From either side of them in the adjoining chalets – except for the first sounds of unpacking and of heavy shoes being kicked off – there had been a profound silence for half an hour, as though all the couples had thrown themselves exhausted upon their beds. But now gradually the sounds began again, taps flowing, the creak of cheap wardrobes swinging back and stiff drawers opening. Voices could be heard, irritable or placating after sleep, voices hungry and demanding. The grandmother turned a page and carefully examined one by one the separate coloured photographs of first-prize cocks and hens. Then she said: 'I expect we'd better be getting ready. These table arrangements can be tricky. Three minutes late and you'll still be waiting for your cold soup while all the rest are on to apple pie.' She got up slowly, took the blouse and skirt off the hanger, and with fierce, life-long modesty sat stretching and buttoning on the edge of the bed with her back turned. The other meanwhile had got into a hot flowered dress and pressed her feet into a pair of light slippers grown tighter and tighter with each day on the road.

They emerged at last into the dark together and walked along by a line of small, lit windows, past striped and flowered curtains, bright squares which cut out suddenly onto total blackness like flimsy posters pasted on the void. Round the corner, figures were emerging from other chalets to be joined by latecomers hurrying up from behind. A long strip of yellow light slanted from the door of the dining room. There was a smell of chicken, roasting beef and hairspray, and the more intermittent hint of apple pie from swing doors opening at the back. Only now, freed from bus and cramped bedroom, came the chance to take a long, hard look at one another under the sudden light.

There were whoops and cheers, murmurs and quiet compliments. At least two-thirds of the travellers had been at work on their hats, but the headgear varied like its makers from the unobtrusive to the wildly flamboyant. Some were made simply from thin ribbons tied round the forehead. Others were exotic creations out of knotted scarfs or gaudy pyjama-legs wound into turbans and crusted with an assortment of beads, clips and brooches. Several tall hats had been cut from newspaper and, drawn by their conical fashion in millinery, a witch, a cardinal and a chef flirted happily together. The vampire of the company – a shy and hatless man who had managed to attach two cardboard teeth inside his upper lip – stood reluctantly beside the open door. One or two full-blooded women approached him and were swiftly redirected. He was a total introvert, avid for books, and inclined to come out of himself only at dead of night. To be a clown was simple. A small inverted wastepaper basket was found the easiest quick-change method. Other wants were more complex. One young

man, grasping a lasting need for female guise, wore a stiff
blue paper coif looped in mediaeval style around long,
straight hair. A dark blue blanket cloak fell from shoulder to
heel. The peculiar seriousness and elegance of his appearance outdid that of the women, and stilled others in the
company for an instant, as though an area of gravity had
been disclosed amongst the bizarre efforts of the rest.

Now the long tables filled up quickly. The soup arrived.
What kind is it? It looks unusual.

It's mushroom – the same as you get at home. It's from a
packet. The same as you get from Timbuktu to the North
Pole. Did you think it was kangaroo?

Do you wish water?

Is it safe?

Yes, of course it's safe. But for heaven's sake not from the
taps. Don't even brush your teeth from the taps. But
everything's safe at table, so we're told. Except yourself,
Mrs Rodger. Oh, I see now what a dangerous woman you
really are – behind all that gauzy stuff on your head. What is
it anyway? A nun's veil? A nun – my word! Well, I must say
you nuns know a thing or two . . . and where's your
husband got to, by the way? Oh there he is, with Betty
Scott. Well, he'd better look out, hadn't he, because what
you women won't get up to once you've tasted blood . . .
And where's *Mr* Scott? Hey Jimmy – your wife's started to
make eyes at me already! Where's your room? We should
get together, Jimmy. Better put the wardrobe against the
door tonight. These women can get through iron bars once
they take a fancy to you!

Plates of chicken, with a choice of beef, were now being
set down. The grandmother sat on the edge of her seat,
inclined towards the table with a back as straight as a
slanted board. She was examining critically the parts of
chicken on her plate as though comparing them with the
plump, proud specimens in her magazine. Though she had
made no concessions to hat-making, she had done her hair

with particular care – combing and twisting the long
strands of black and white into a shape as crisp as a cap.
Not to be outdone, her younger companion had also made
certain slight changes about the head. Her dark hair had
been drawn back more tightly over the ears – a severity
tempered by the use of two sparkly combs stuck into the
knot at the nape of her neck.

And now began the time of waiting. At first it was hardly
noticed. The second course was finished and had been
cleared away some time ago. This allowed the passengers to
lean freely on the empty table, to talk without interruption.
But after a while, and only gradually, the talk faded to a
minimum, increased again and faded again, once more
revived, then slowly died away as though, one by one, every
voice had been withdrawn.

And now the silence fell. It fell between the couples
chatting opposite one another, it fell diagonally between the
self-appointed cheer-leaders at either end of the table,
between adjacent lovers sitting in passionate isolation from
the middle-aged. Even the clatter round the swing doors to
the kitchen was subdued. No sweet was forthcoming, no
smell of coffee. The serving-women quietly laid down the
plates of biscuits on side-tables, laid out the cups and softly
rubbed them round with paper napkins. Space and silence
widened and widened over the tables, until it seemed great
gaps had opened in the crowded room to let in the hot night
outside. One or two, as though recalling something in a
dream, lifted their heads and smelt through open windows
the mysterious whiff of space and darkness. The senses
were confused. They felt not only distance but knew time
moving past – hours and days and years covering them up
as sand had covered rocks. Close by, an unfamiliar bird was
screeching.

And now – and one by one – as though by common
consent, there was a gradual removal of funny hats. First,
and almost stealthily, the witch removed the scroll of

newspaper from her head and released a bundle of grey hair onto her shoulders. Quietly the widow-brides undid the big pink ribbons from the back of their heads, picked off the folded napkins, the glossy roses they had cut from magazines, and laid them down between their plates. Slowly, almost unthinkingly, a turban was unwound, and then a bathcap removed, stalks and feathers, beads, clasps and brooches were picked off. The wearer of the basket lifted it off with both hands like a heavy crown, revealing for the first time a curiously thoughtful man. The youth removed his blue coif, sleeked back his hair and loosened the cloak from his shoulders. Reluctantly he showed himself as man again. The cardinal was the last to remove his high cap. 'This thing is too tight round the forehead – and the heat in here is frightful,' he said, as he laid it on the floor by his chair. 'Anyway, we can all put them on again when it comes to the judgement.'

'He means the judging, of course – that's to say, the prizegiving,' someone murmured.

The grandmother said she was thankful now she had not bothered about hats. But her room-mate had grown increasingly uneasy during the last half-hour.

'He's not here yet,' she said, looking up and down the long table. 'Is he going to turn up at all?'

'The driver? Well, he knows the people who run the place. He'll be having his meal with them. He'll appear all right when it's time for the prize.'

'No, I'm not talking about him.'

'Oh the other one! Well, maybe he's hanging onto the bar for dear life. Or stretched out somewhere with the liquor running out of his ears. I wouldn't worry about him if I were you.'

'I'll be happier when I see him, though.'

'Is he the kind that makes them *happier*?'

'I never told you all he said back there on the road.'

'No? The cliff-edge confession? That was nothing.'

'I never told you the other things. Some day he'll simply disappear.'

'We'll all disappear some day.'

'It could even be his last trip. This one or the next.'

'It could be mine too. All that fearful jolting and those clouds of dust. I'm getting too old for it. Maybe they'll just have to visit *me* after this.'

'You know what I mean. I mean his last trip anywhere. He'll do away with himself, sooner or later.'

'He told you that?'

'And much more. Physically and in every way, he feels he's done for. His life is all in pieces.'

The older woman smoothed out the bit of tablecloth in front of her with a capable hand, examined her pudding spoon carefully and put it back again. 'So what are you supposed to do about it?'

'I am worried about tonight.'

'I don't think you need to be.'

'If he doesn't turn up soon, I'm going to look for him. If I can't find him right away, I shall tell the driver.'

'I think you'll find him in his room the same as every other night. On the bed or on the floor.'

'I don't care where he is as long as he's all right.'

'You know where his room is?'

'I'm going now.'

'Before your apple pie? They won't keep it for you, mind – nor your coffee.'

The younger woman stared hard at her companion, who returned the look with a shrewd glance. 'Let me know if you need me,' she said at last.

'No, I shall tell the driver. I'm not looking for trouble – only to set my mind at rest.'

'To set your mind at rest!' said the grandmother, smiling grimly at the cleared space before her. 'And when was ever a mind at rest?' But she nodded affably enough, calling after her, 'Have you your torch with you?' and following with her eyes as the other moved quickly down the long table and out through the door, which opened momentarily on a black wedge of night.

The quietness was still upon those at table. But some conversations, though subdued, had begun to revive. 'The whole night will be put out of joint,' murmured the man whose forehead still showed the line of a tight elastic band. 'This great gap between courses on top of arriving late. By the time the prizes get going, it'll be nearer eleven. And I'm whacked, I don't mind admitting it. The point is I'm no use for another day in the bus unless I get a good eight hours on my back.'

'Don't talk about it,' said the cardinal's wife. 'I'm terrified of a Morning Head – what with a late meal and all the rest of it. And I don't mean an ordinary headache, mind you. When I say head, I mean a Sick Morning Head. And only those who've had it can know what that means. Yes, my God, if I get *that*, they can just count me out. They could set me down all alone in the middle of a saltpan and leave me there for all I'd care!'

Outside, the woman who had left the dining room was walking along by the side of the building, walking in the darkness and in the total silence of the Australian night, seeing bright eyes from the bush, seeing the star-stream of the Milky Way above – far denser and whiter than in northern skies. The silent land with its white eyes, white sand and salt and dust was part of its vast spiral. But to stand still was to become part of dust, to lose all heart to go on. She began to move more quickly past the windows and the locked bedroom doors, and round the corner to where one lit, curtained pane threw a yellow square on the ground. Outside this window the heavy brown moths were circling, thick in the air, thick on the ground – moths whiffling their way up the pane, dropping on the outside ledge and beating their way silently up again, spinning, dropping and crowding in ceaseless, urgent drive towards the light. The woman knocked at the door, and stood waiting there in a dust unstirred by breath of wind, amongst the hundred wings that made no sound. She knocked again, then turned the handle of the door, found it un-locked and went in.

In the dining room the restlessness had increased. It had not come to a beating of spoons on plates or a stamping of feet, but there was growing impatience at the long wait for the sweet. Soon however, this changed to the more urgent longing to be released from the hard chair to a bed – any kind of bed so long as they could lie flat. They began to discover what the hours on the road had done to their backs, what the dust had done to the throat and eyes. By ten o'clock another wave of expectant chatter had died away. Two couples, encouraged by the rest, had marched boldly through into the kitchen like ambassadors of reconciliation into territory which might, for some unknown reason, have turned suddenly hostile. They found no one there. Only the great, still-steaming pots stood round with the remains of meat, and empty soup tureens with their outsize ladles. A platter piled with red bones lay on the draining-board and dirty dishes filled one sink. In the other, the water was still lukewarm and at the bottom, through foam bubbles which were still fresh, they glimpsed their own knives and forks shining. On a shelf above stood the neat row of untouched tea- and coffee-pots. From the back of a chair two aprons trailed, with their white cords dangling, and a tangle of dishcloths as though hastily flung down in passing. Was this so strange? They admitted themselves it was no more than might be found in any large kitchen at the heaviest end of the day when a sudden rush has hit the house. What was strange, what had made them hold their breath, was the newly-created emptiness of the place, as if – had they started in pursuit – they could even now make up on the owners, who might be running off into the distance as fast as they could go from their guests. For a few minutes they called and whistled, rapped on the table and clattered the saucepan lids. No one answered. At some distant door a dog was howling.

When the four came back to the dining room, they were greeted with a cheer which was quickly suppressed at sight of their doleful faces. There was little sympathy for them, however. Up and down the table the discontent grew. Why had they not penetrated further into the back regions? Had they knocked at every possible door? They could at least have searched harder for pies and puddings. Was it beyond the power of practical persons to start making tea or coffee themselves? Well yes, but there are some people, aren't there, very helpful and willing at the start, but at the end of the day found to be timid, lacking in enterprise, not really serious at all. Yes exactly, we've all met them. It's all smiles at the start and all leading to what? Exactly nothing. All promise and no action. The will isn't there, you see. And after all, the appetite doesn't last forever, does it? The stomach sort of caves in. Like a plastic bag turned inside out. Painful. I don't want it now. Couldn't care less. It's too late, you see. If I had a mouthful of pie now I'd be ill, really ill. Tomorrow morning you could all leave me behind in this God-awful place. And then what? Right now I don't give a damn what. Only don't give me any food *now*.

There were no further volunteers for the kitchen. Soon, even the discontented murmur died down. Through the windows a brilliant scatter of stars could be seen against the blackness, and a visitor from Britain was heard to remark cautiously how strange it was to see Orion upside down from this side of the world. But it was no time for astronomical observations. Long ago the magician had removed his magic cap and with it all interest in the heavenly bodies. There was complete silence over the room. It was the former cheer-leader who had brought about the final drop in spirits. Even as he had whipped up the cheer, so now, by staring at the kitchen door with a face serious as a judge, he established its opposite. Silently they watched with him. Few expected anything else to eat now. What they did expect was not voiced aloud. A strange curiosity mixed with dread had caught them. Had they perhaps been totally deserted? Left in a place of scrub and desert without food. And don't forget, the pessimistic one had said, don't forget we are not to drink from the taps.

Smoothly, noiselessly, while they watched, the swing door like a small whirlwind suddenly spun round. From its still centre stepped the proprietress. It spun again and over her shoulder two other faces peered. All three were white.

'I have an announcement to make,' said the woman, looking up and down the silent table. 'Your driver is dead. Mr Bill Creevy is dead. A doctor will come when he can. The best driver . . . for years and years he has brought the bus across . . . now suddenly the heart . . . the best driver . . . and a friend. Everything will be done to make you comfortable tonight. Another driver will be sent as soon as possible. And you will get off tomorrow . . . naturally it will be later, but you will get off. Thank you. Tea and coffee will be served directly.' The door spun round again, and the three disappeared.

For a few minutes no one spoke, but here and there along the table the one or two who had not yet doffed their hats now took them off. Only one other person moved. The elderly woman had risen to her feet abruptly. Quickly she made her way down the side of the table, looking neither to one side nor the other, but straight ahead towards the door. A streamer from a discarded hat caught her skirt and was nipped off. A paper rose rustled under her foot and she bent to put it back between the plates. Otherwise her back was straight, her brown face impassive. Through the door at the end she went out into the night, and began walking along by the side of the building with its locked doors and drawn curtains – a place neat as a village street set down in the wilderness. She passed on her right a few bushes of large red flowers which the night had made black. Beyond them there was nothing but space and the great, brilliant stars which glittered right down to the rim of the horizon. The woman walked on round the corner of the building, and there for a moment she stopped. At the end of the row, shining between dark doors and windows, she saw the one square of light throwing a yellow patch on the ground beneath. Towards this yellow light she now walked quickly till she came to the door. For a second time she waited. She knocked discreetly. But at once the voice of her travelling companion called: 'Yes, yes. Please come in!'

The older woman, her grey head circled by a spinning veil of moths, opened the door and went in. Her face was grave and seeing this, the other quickly said in a low voice, 'Yes, you were right. He had almost passed out – probably knocked himself out against the edge of the wardrobe. Thank God not what I was afraid of! Only a cut over the eyebrow, but deep enough. He's sleeping it off. We can safely leave him now.'

The woman in the doorway looked down at the man sprawled on the bed. One foot was over the side, with a loosened shoe held dangling on the joint of his big toe. There were bottles and a mug on the floor, clothes on the table. On the back of the door his jacket, loaded with loose change in one pocket, swung crooked from its hanger. The young woman had put a narrow pink towel round his head, winding it at a slant over the cut eyebrow and eye. With his ears flattened down under this turban, the engineer's head looked small, his body larger than before. And now, while the woman beside him had momentarily lifted his head to ease the pillow further underneath, the other – still with her hand on the door – said: 'Our driver is dead.'

The woman by the bed withdrew her arm and let the head fall. She stared first at the sharp brown face in the doorway, and then behind it to the thorny outline of a distant bush, and beyond again to the low-shining, un-familiar stars – her eyes quickly changing focus from the near to the unknown, as though invoking an answer from further and further out. At last she stood up and, still with her eyes on distance, picked up her torch from the table, carefully smoothed back the strands of hair which had come loose with bending in the heat of the room, and slowly walked over to join the woman at the door.

Meanwhile, the man in the crooked turban had raised his head and with his unbandaged eye, wide-open as the Cyclops', he stared across at them. The women had been ready to go, but now for a moment the grandmother looked back. The engineer, supporting himself on his elbow, shoved away the towel from his other eye. Still the women waited. There was something of changed roles in their aspect. It was now the younger who watched the more impatiently, accusingly. The other – as though drawing upon years of waiting, of dryness, of working over wasted ground – was giving him some further chance. Under her scrutiny, with its distant hint of goodwill, the man drew his foot onto the bed and with a casual half-kick attempted to get the loose shoe back onto his foot.

'Never mind the shoe,' said the grandmother. 'It's that thing on your head. All the rest back there have taken off the hats, the funny hats. Why don't you take off yours?'

For a moment the unbelieving eyes held her own. Then his hand groped about his head, fumbling for the fold tucked in over one ear. Slowly he undid the narrow towel, dropping his head from one side to the other as it unwound, and still with his eyes fixed on hers. The towel came loose and fell on one shoulder. The engineer brushed it to the floor, then swivelled himself to the side of the bed and swung both legs cautiously to the ground.

'Yes, that's right,' said the woman, calmly, as to an awkward child – and still waiting. The engineer rose un-steadily to his feet, supporting himself with a hand on the bedside table the better to get a long, clear look at her – a look no woman had got from him for many years. For her part the woman bent her head, as though accepting – not for herself but for the dead – some token of respect, long overdue. 'Goodnight then,' she said. 'I hope you sleep well.'

The man leaned further forward to look. But there was no irony in the face. She was, when all was said, a grandmother. The good, the sore, the punishers, the ill-behaved, all deserved sleep. The women turned away and stepped out again into darkness. The younger, who was behind, didn't wait to secure the door but started to walk quickly off in the direction of the main building. It was the older woman who turned back and discreetly drew the door to – eclipsing at once its pointing yellow shaft and mercifully shutting out the haunting eyes of night.

# Pedestrian

A GREAT PATCH of scoured and gravelly land at either end
marked the approach to the motorway café. Beyond that
were flat fields and a long horizon line broken here and
there by distant clumps of trees. At no point on this line was
there a sign of building. A glass-sided, covered bridge
joined the car park to the café, and people if they wished
could stand in the middle and look down onto the road
below. The four lanes of the motorway carried every sort of
traffic. The long vehicles were the most spectacular and
there was no limit to their loads – lorries carrying sugar and
cement and tanks of petrol went past, carrying building
cranes and wooden planks, barrels of beer, cylinders of gas,
sheep and horses, bulls in boxes, hens, furniture and parts
of aeroplanes. There were lorries carrying cars and lorries
carrying lorries.

The café itself was filled day and night with a periodic
inrush of people and changed its whole appearance from
half-hour to half-hour throughout the twenty-four. It had
its empty time and its time of chaos. Habitual tough
travellers of the road mixed here with couples stopping
for the first time for morning coffee. Here buses disgorged
football fans and concert parties, and stuffed family cars
laboriously unloaded parents, children, grandparents, for
their evening meal. The cars far outnumbered other vehicles. And no pedestrian, as opposed to hitchhiker, was ever
seen here, for it would be nearly impossible to arrive by
foot. Any person unattached to a vehicle was as unlikely as a
being dropped from the skies. There was no place for him
on the motorway.

Nevertheless there were still pedestrians in everyday life. A married couple who were queueing at the counter of this café one evening found themselves standing beside a man who admitted to being one himself. The couple had been discussing car mileage with one another and they kindly brought him into it. 'And how about you?' asked the wife. 'How much have you done?' The other smiled but said nothing. He had obviously missed out on their discussion, and she didn't repeat the question. From his blank look she might have just as easily been asking how much time he had done in jail. Behind the counter a woman with a long-armed trowel was shovelling chips from a shelf, while her companion dredged up sausages from a trough of cooling fat. 'Sorry,' said the man suddenly, 'I didn't pick you up just now. No. I'm not in a car. I'm in the bus out there. Long distance to Liverpool.'

'Good idea,' said the woman's husband. 'Good idea to leave it at home once in a while. No fun on the roads these days. No fun at all!'

'No, I haven't got a car.'

'You don't run one?'

'No, never had one.'

'Then you're probably a lot luckier than the rest of us,' said the man after only the slightest pause, at the same time giving him a quick look up and down. He saw a well-set-up fellow, well-dressed and about his own age. Not a young man. This look, however, cost him an outsize scoopful of thick, unwanted gravy on his plate. He slid cautiously on towards a bucket of bright peas. His wife, who had kept her eye on her plate, now bent forward and asked politely: 'Have you ever thought about it?'

'Thought about . . . ?'

'Getting one.'

'No, I can't say I have.'

The woman nodded wisely, blending in a bit of compassion in case there was some good reason for it – a physical

or even a mental defect. For a moment the hiss of descending orange and lemonade prevented further talk. The three
moved across to a table which had just been vacated by the
window. From this point they had a straight view of the
bridge and a glimpse of the road beneath. Every now and
then, in the momentary silences of noisy places, they could
hear the regular swish of passing traffic. On the far side of
the bridge glittering ranks of cars filled one end of the
parking space with lorries at the other. Long red-and-green
buses were waiting near an exit for their passengers.

'You don't mind if I go ahead?' said the man from the
bus. 'There's only twenty minutes or so to eat.'

'No, go right on. Don't wait for us,' said the woman. The
couple were occupied with some problem about the engine
of their car and the unfamiliar sound it had been making for
ten miles back. They discussed what kind of sound – tick or
rattle or thump – and with almost musicianlike exactitude
queried the type of beat – regular or irregular? There was
the question of whether to look into it themselves, have it
looked into or go straight on. Even now they were careful to
include the other in the talk in case he should feel left out.
They let him into the endless difficulties of parking, of
visiting friends in narrow streets, or of visiting friends in any
street, wide or narrow, because of the meter. They told him
how much for twenty minutes, how much for forty minutes, how much if you were to talk for an hour. They
discussed the price of petrol and of garage repairs and the
horrors of breakdown on the road.

'And the hard shoulder can be a very lonely place on the
motorway,' said the woman. 'All those cars rushing past
you. Have you ever had to pull over yourself?'

'No, I haven't,' the man said, with a hint of apology in his
voice.

'Oh no, no – of course you haven't! I absolutely forgot for
the moment that you haven't got . . . Excuse me. I am
being so stupid.'

The man said no, there was nothing to excuse. It was easy to forget. He added that the hard shoulder did indeed sound a very unsympathetic place to rest on in the night.

The three of them had now finished their first course and had turned towards the door to watch the next group entering. Half a dozen families were coming in, and a carload of men carrying trumpets. Two policemen were moving slowly about among the tables. At the far end of the room a waitress was mopping up the floor where someone had let a plate slide from a tray. The policemen bent and spoke to a man at a table, then sat down, one on either side of him while he put ketchup on a last wedge of steak pie and ate it with seeming relish. The three of them left the café together. 'This is where you find them,' remarked the car-owner to his wife and the passenger from the bus. They had now started on their squares of yellow sponge cake with a custard layer between. The custard too had been sliced into neat and solid squares, and their plates when they had finished were as dry and clean as when they had started. 'One job less for the staff, I suppose,' said the husband examining his dish with distrust.

The other man – seeing they had confided in him – began to tell them what it felt like to walk along the edge of an ordinary country road while the cars went by. The husband looked vaguely aside. It was not a believable thing for a grown man to do and he did not hear it beyond the first sentence. But the woman said: 'You mean hitch-hiking?'

'No, no – just getting about from one place to another, sometimes by bus and train, naturally, and sometimes walking.'

'As a pedestrian?'

'Yes, I suppose so. In cities naturally one walks a good deal.'

'Yes, I see – a pedestrian,' said the woman, looking at him with a vague interest.

Her husband had now brought coffee for the three of them and the man drank his quickly, for the time was up.

'I'm sorry to rush,' he said, 'but the bus leaves in eight minutes, and they don't wait long. Thanks for the coffee – and a very good journey!'

'And the same to you!' They watched him go, weaving between the tables, and a few minutes later saw him hurrying down the glass bridge and starting to run as he reached the far end.

'A pedestrian,' murmured the woman musingly.

'Well, a bus-traveller.'

'But he tells me he walks a lot of the time, in country as well as city.'

After a while her husband looked at his watch. 'Shall we get on then?'

'Might as well. We can take our time.' They wandered slowly away from the windows, looking back to see one of the buses moving off. '*His* bus, I expect,' said the woman. 'Careful and don't slip on that chip,' she added as they passed the spot where the plate had fallen.

The glass bridge over the motorway was the only viewing-point for miles. The man and woman paused in the middle and looked down onto the great streams below. Four or five chains of long vehicles happened to be coming up on one side with a second line going down on the other. Great grey roofs slid beneath them in opposition like extra roads moving along on top of the others. At this time of day the cars too were coming one after the other with scarcely a second between them, and – seen from above – scarcely an inch.

'I can't say I've met many non-drivers in my time,' said the man broodingly, 'but there's usually a perfectly legit-imate reason for it. Certainly not money in his case though.'

'Physical disablement, maybe,' said his wife. 'Remember Harry Ewing. *He* didn't drive. He had one short leg.'

'You'd never have known. Anyway, with all the dashboard gadgets these days, what's a short leg, or arm for that matter?'

'Some people have bad eyes,' suggested the woman.

'Funny thing, but I've seen cross-eyed people driving about and nobody stopped them yet. And as for one eye at the wheel – that's common enough, believe me!'

Watchers on the bridge, or any persons not in a hurry, invariably attracted others. Something about the static bridge, sealed in above the speed, made company acceptable. So, before long, the two who had been standing there found that another couple had joined them – a man in a blue summer jacket and his wife in a cream coat. For a while the four of them stood comfortably together, silently watching. Then the first man said, 'My wife and I were speaking about non-drivers – their reasons, I mean, for not having a car. Most disabilities can be overcome, you know.'

'Maybe it's nerves,' said the man in the blue jacket. 'Or more likely psychological.'

'You mean,' said his wife, 'like that woman who'd never let her boy touch a machine – not even a child's scooter. So he never had a car all his life, not even when she was dead. Well, I suppose he loved his mother.'

'Well, I've heard that story the other way,' said her husband. 'His mother *wants* him to own this super-car since ever he opened his eyes. Nagged him all his life. And he won't do it, not even when she's dead.'

'Sure,' said the other man, 'because he *doesn't* love his mother.'

They turned and sauntered slowly along the bridge together like old acquaintances, looking down at the motorway to the left and right of them as though it was still a long, long way off.

'That man in the café – maybe he just didn't want one,' said the first wife. Her husband looked aside again with his vague and unbelieving smile. The four of them now seemed reluctant to reach the end of the bridge. They began to walk more and more slowly as they neared the opening. In front the great gravelled space was, if anything, more closely packed than ever – some cars edging out, others slowly burrowing in like beetles into hidden corners. The two couples paused and stared intently at this space, searching for their own. 'Well, nice to have met you,' they said to one another, 'very nice indeed to have the pleasure . . .' For one more moment they hesitated on the sloping ramp of the bridge. An overpowering whiff of loneliness reached them from the fumy air beyond. Then they stepped down and out into the narrow lanes between the cars and the glittering maze of metal divided them.

# The Time-Keeper

IT WAS TAKEN as a matter of course that at one time or other during the summer he would be showing people around his city. Renwick was a hospitable man and for certain weeks it was a duty to be available to visitors. The beauty of the place was written on its skyline in a sharp, black script of spires, chimneys and turrets and in the flowing line of a long crag and hill. It was written up in books. He had shelves devoted to its history and its architecture. It was written on anti-litter slogans with the stern injunction that this was a beautiful city and it had better be kept that way.

Sometimes the people he took on were those wished on him for an hour or two, friends of friends, or persons he'd met by chance passing through on their way north. They were all sightseers of a sort and the first sight they wanted to see, particularly if they were foreigners, was himself. Well, he was on the spot, of course. Yes, he had to admit he probably *was* a sight and even worth looking at in a very superficial way. At certain times he put on his advocate's garb – a highly stylized get-up, dark, narrow and formal. A bowler hat went with the suit and an umbrella which – because of the windiness of the city – often remained unrolled. He was never solemn about the business. He was the first to point out that it was traditional wear – a kind of fancy dress or disguise. 'And there are plenty of them about these days,' he would say. 'We ourselves are falling behind in the game. Look at all the people either dressing the part or the opposite of the part!' But there was no need of excuse. Visitors enjoyed him in his dress and were disappointed to discover he seldom wore it when the Court was not sitting. Sometimes however they were lucky. And he had a face that went with the garb – a rather masked face, long and grave with hair well plastered down over a neat skull, as though to show what an extreme of flatness could be achieved in comparison with the dashing wig which he might later put on.

Renwick's hospitality didn't mean that he was always a patient man. There was a good deal of exasperation and sharpness in his character, and he shared with many of his fellow citizens a highly argumentative and sceptical turn of mind. He developed it and was valued for it. That hint of the suspicious Scot in his make-up was well hidden. The impatience was not so well in check. It boiled up silently at dullness. It occasionally exploded at stupidity. As time went on, he had even begun to be impatient with those visitors who insisted on taking a purely romantic view of the city. It was not after all made up only of interesting old stones, nor were the people going about their business on top of these stones particularly romantic. Certainly not. They were a commonsense, very businesslike lot and more to be compared to down-to-earth scene-shifters doing their jobs against a theatrical background.

This was made clear to an American couple one afternoon, as they stood with him in one of the oldest graveyards of the city. There was a great deal to see and a lot to hear about. Renwick had given them something of the turbulent history of the place and listed the succession of famous people who had been buried here. They in their turn exclaimed about the ancient monuments and walls. They touched the moss-covered dates on headstones. It was getting late. The three or four still left in the place were slowly making their way out. In the distance a blonde girl was moving round the dark church between black and white tombstones. But Renwick's couple were all for lingering in the place until the sun went down. Renwick felt a sudden flare of impatience rise inside him. He directed them to look up and out of the place. From where they stood they could see, rising on all sides, the backs of houses and churches, and beyond that a glimpse of the bridge which carried a busy street over a chasm. Cars and buses crossed it. People went striding past. 'But look up there,' he said pointing. 'We are rather an energetic crowd. You can see we're in a hurry. You're not going to find your ordinary citizen of the place sitting around staring at old stones for long. I believe you might find it hard enough to get him to stop and talk for any length of time unless there was very good reason for it. For better or worse – that is our character!'

The Americans didn't deny this. They had already attempted to detain people on the bridge. They had sensed the bracing air. Now, polite but silent, they stared down at an angel whose round and rather sulky face was crowned by a neat green crewcut of moss and backed by frilly wings sprouting behind his ears. Cautiously they mentioned the old ghosts of the place.

'But just behind you,' came the brisk voice, 'there, in that wall, there are still lived-in houses. Look at that window for instance.' It was true that in the actual ancient wall of the place they were looking into the room of a house. Sitting in the open window was an old man being shaved by someone standing behind. At first they saw only a hand holding his chin, the other hand drawing a razor along his cheek. But while they watched the job was done. The head of the old man and his middle-aged daughter emerged from the window. It was close enough to get a clear sight of them – keen, unsmiling, both staring straight down with eyes which were shrewd but without much curiosity as though they had seen decades of tourists standing just below them there on that particular spot in the churchyard.

'You see there are more than just angels around us,' said

Renwick tersely. 'There are also ordinary, busy folk getting on with their own jobs.'

The young couple looked for a moment as though they might question the business and even the ordinariness, but had thought better of it, especially as they had seen Renwick look openly at his wrist.

Renwick counted himself a polite man. Lately, however, he had given in to this habit, common to persons of consequence in the city, of glancing at his watch – and often while people were actually talking to him. He believed that he was indicating in the politest possible way that he was a very busy man, that even in summer his time was limited. But as the habit grew, not only visitors but even friends began to see the wrist shoot out, no longer surreptitiously but very openly. Those who still hung around after that had only themselves to blame. And as well as the watch he was very well up in the tactics of the engagement diary. 'Well, certainly not tomorrow, nor the day after. This week's out in fact. Next week? Full up, I'm afraid. No, I have a space here. I think I can *just* about manage to fit you in.' Acquaintances might sound grateful, but they felt squeezed and sometimes throttled as they watched him writing them into the minimal space between appointments.

Just as Renwick was both proud and yet irritated by the romantic reputation of the city, so he felt about the supernatural history of the place. He was good-natured about disguises, masks of all kinds. He understood the hidden. But the guise of the supernatural he didn't care for. He had lost count of the number of times he was asked about the witches and warlocks of the city, mediaeval apparitions hidden down closes, the eighteenth-century ghosts of the New Town. Grudgingly he pointed to deserted windows where heads had looked out and stairs where persons without their heads had walked down. Reluctantly he led willing visitors to the district where the Major had made his pact, pointed out infamous tenements and doorways blasted with the Devil's curse. 'And now you'll want to see the spot where the gallows stood – and you'll not mind if I leave you there. I have to keep an eye on my time. The fact is I have a good deal of business to attend to between now and supper.'

Friends dated his concern with time back to a year when his post brought new responsibilities. Others pointed out that business was all a matter of choice, and that the time-obsession was common to most middle-aged men once they'd begun to feel it making up on them. 'And worse things can happen to a man than keeping to a tight schedule,' remarked a colleague as they discussed others in the profession. 'We've had a good few suicides by his age, and quite a tearing of the silk. There was McInnes letting it all rip and making off for the South Seas. And Webster? Wasn't it the stage he'd always yearned for, never the Bar? Yes, retired now, white hair to the shoulders – happy enough they say, and no guile in the man at all. Still, meeting him late on summer nights in loopy hats with orange feathers gave some people more of a turn than seeing the Devil himself.' Other names came up. They decided if it was nothing more than a little touchiness about time – Renwick was doing well enough.

By midsummer a stream of holiday-makers were on the streets. Renwick would become impatient – or was it envious? – at the idea of an endless enjoyment of leisure. How could they wander for days and weeks, sometimes for months? From early spring, when the first few aimless visitors arrived, he would begin to take note of the city clocks. Not that he hadn't known them all his life – the clocks under church spires, the clocks on schools and hospitals and hotel towers. He'd seen brand-new time-pieces erected in his day and had attended the unveilings of memorial clocks. But now he counted them as allies in the summer game, to give him backing when the wristwatch

methods had no result. It was his habit, then, to stare about
him for the nearest clock – if it was old, so much the better.
Having alerted visitors to its history, it was an easy step to
exclaim at the time of day, to excuse himself and make off
with all possible speed to the next appointment.

During one summer Renwick had several visitors of his
own for a short time. He enjoyed their stay. They knew the
city well. It was not always necessary to accompany them, but
he had the pleasure of their talk in the evening. Later,
however, he was asked if he would help a friend out with
four visitors who had been staying in the city and, with little
warning, were to land on him for twelve hours. The friend
had to be out of town on the evening of that day. Could
Renwick possibly take them round for half an hour or so?
Yes, he could do that. When the time came, they turned out
to be two middle-aged couples from the south who had not
set foot in the city before this visit. But they had read the
necessary books. They were well primed with history and
they knew legends about every door and windowframe. They
had expected smoky sunsets and they got them. They knew
that on certain nights there might be a moon directly above
the floodlit castle. The moon was in the prescribed spot the
first night they arrived. They did not mind bad weather.
They said that gloom and darkness suited the place. They
liked the mist and even the chill haar that could swirl up out of
the sea after a warm day. They were amiable, and they had an
equal and unqualified love for all the figures in the city's past.

That evening Renwick had taken them down into one of
the closes of the Lawnmarket, and they were now standing
in a large court enclosed by tenement walls. There were a
few people besides themselves in the place; a group of
youths with bottles bulging at their hips, a fair-haired girl
holding a guide-book and three small children who had
raced in after a ball and out again. It was getting late and a
few small yellow lights were appearing high up on the
surrounding walls.

'If only we could get in there and see some of those weird old rooms,' said one of the wives, staring up.

'And speak to one or two of the old folk,' her husband added. 'There'll be ones up there with many a tale to tell of the old days.'

'Many a tale?' Renwick straightened his shoulders. He directed a rather chilly smile over the heads of the group. 'No doubt there might be tales – and ones not so very different from our own. Of course those particular rooms you're looking at have all been re-done. They are expensive places, very well equipped, I should imagine, with all the latest gadgets. You'll find quite young, very well set-up people living there, I believe. You'll get your dank walls, poor drains, black corners in a good many other places if you care to look. But not up there!'

They had been with him now for half an hour. Renwick had begun to check the various times on their watches with his own, and murmuring 'I will just make sure,' had walked down the few steps at the far end of the court and out to where, overlooking street and gardens, he could see the large, lit clock at the east end of the city.

'I must be off in five minutes,' he said, when he came back, '. . . letters to attend to . . . a paper to prepare.' They asked if he could give them an idea what they should look at the following morning. Briefly he outlined a plan and described the things they should see. They asked if they would meet him again. He explained that in a couple of days he might or might not meet them, depending on his work. 'Do you work all through the holidays?' someone innocently asked. Renwick made a noncommittal gesture to the sky. At the same time he noticed that the fair-haired girl, who'd been wandering about for some time between their group and the shadowy end of the court, had come forward and now stood with them directly under the lamp. Stunning. Not nowadays a word he was in the habit of using. But what other word for this particular kind of fairness? Straight white-blonde hair, fair eyebrows against brown skin, and eyes so pale they had scarcely more colour than water. A Scandinavian – the intonation was plain in a few words she spoke to one of the women, but she was also that idealized version which, along with its opposite, each country holds of another part of the world – strikingly tall, strong and fair, and no doubt outspoken. Renwick waited for her to speak. She lifted her arm with the back of her wrist towards him. She tapped her watch.

'You have given us your minutes. Exactly five. Your time is up,' she said. The others laughed. Renwick smiled. So she had seen his clock-watching, heard his work pro-gramme, had simply stopped in passing for a laugh. But attention was now turned her way. They were asking questions. And it appeared that in her country the light was different. The sun, they gathered, was very bright, the darkness more intense. Different, she made it plain, though not of course better. They took it in, unblinking, while they stared. It seemed they got the message on light in a single flash and with no trouble at all. The girl left the place soon afterwards, and to Renwick it seemed that his two couples were slowly merged together again, and he with them – all welded into the state called middle-age. No amount of good sense, no bracing talk of God-sent wisdom or hard-won experience, and least, least of all the beauties of maturity, were ever going to mend this matter. There they were. Some light had left them.

One way or another, this was to occupy him a good deal during the next day. It was not just that at some stage of life the optimistic beam had been replaced by a smaller light, but that from the start even his awareness of actual physical light had been limited. It was hard for him to imagine variations – how some lights sharpened every object and its shadow for miles around, while others made a featureless flatness of the same scene. He tried to imagine those regions of the world made barren to the bone by sun, and others soaked by the same sun to make ground and water prosper from one good year to the next. He thought with relief of white cornfields nearer home and remembered with a shock of hope streams so transparent you could see the fish, leaves and stones shining in their depths.

The phone drilled at his skull. 'Tomorrow evening – would it be possible for half an hour, if you can manage to spare the time?' Both couples were leaving the next morning. Yes, it would be just possible to fit it in. They would meet at the bottom of the street leading from Palace to Castle. They would walk slowly up. Another voice joined the first in thanking him.

'The weather has been disappointing for you today,' said Renwick as he waited for the moment to put the phone down.

'No, this is how we like it,' came the reply. 'Clear, sharp, with a touch of frost.' This might pass, with those who knew him, as a rough description of himself. Or not so rough. Exact perhaps – though some might put the complimentary touch, others a hatching of black lines. Renwick said he was glad to hear it and replaced the receiver thoughtfully.

The next evening was overcast with a slight wind which sent the black and white clouds slowly across the sky. They were waiting for him eagerly. 'A disappointing evening,' he said, as if to test them again. On the contrary they were enthusiastic. This was the city at its best, at its most characteristic. Renwick saved his disappointment for himself. They walked slowly up, going in and out of closes, through doors and arches. They saw the sea through openings and climbed halfway up stairways worn into deep curves. Renwick led the way through the darker wynds. He answered questions. Apart from that he said little. The street grew steep, crossed a main road and went on up until it opened out to the broad space in front of the church of St Giles with the Law Courts behind. It was growing dark, and from this rise where they were standing they could see down almost the whole length of the street illumined by blue street lights. It was a favourite viewing point for tourist buses and their guides, and there were still a few about. People were roaming around the precincts of the Courts and going to and from the church.

Renwick looked round and stared pointedly at the large, lit clock of the Tolbooth, big as a harvest moon. Further down the street were smaller clocks. Automatically following his eyes, the others stared too. They got the message. Time was important even to citizens of an historic city. Things must move on. Turning back again, Renwick saw the blonde girl a few steps away. She had been looking at the church. Now she was making a beeline for his group. So he had been watched again, scrutinized no doubt as an exhibit of the place, one worth remembering perhaps, but remembered with a good deal more amusement than respect. She had reached the group now and stood waiting until the couples wandered off to make the most of their last minutes of sight-seeing. Then she remarked: 'You have very few angels inside. I have seen the churches. Some of them are very beautiful and very bare.'

'You're absolutely right,' said Renwick. He lectured her gently on the reasons for it. 'Any angels we do have are mostly outside,' he added, 'hidden away in cemeteries.'

And if it came to angels, it was true enough the blue light had given her own face a marbly shine, her hair a touch of green. But her eyes had neither the exalted nor the downcast look of churchyard angels. They were too direct, too challenging for an angel's eyes. She was not the kind to be hidden away. He was going on to an explanation of the spot where they were standing when something struck him. He stopped in mid-sentence. 'I am not a guide,' said Renwick.

'Well, I think you are,' said the young woman. 'You keep them all together. You keep the time. That is important – how you keep the time. Clocks are important, very im-

portant indeed. Clocks are – how do you say? – they are
very much up your street.' Saying this, she made a quick
survey of the street from top to bottom as he had done some
minutes before. Her performance managed, miraculously,
to be both amiable and derisive. She made way genially for
the others when they came back, and after some talk with
them, went off again.

There was nothing to take him out the following evening.
Nobody demanded his time. Yet the next night after
supper, he was out trudging up the High Street again.
The place was still crowded and he made his way around
groups at corners and through lines of people who were
spread out across the width of the street. This time he felt
the need to look about him with the eye of a stranger. Many
times he stopped to stare at familiar things, and once in a
while, as if from the corner of his eye, managed to catch
some object by surprise. It was a warm night, Far above
him he saw rows of elbows upon windowsills and shadowy
heads staring down, and above the heads a rocky outline of
roofs and steep, black gable walls blocking the night sky.
Sometimes he turned back for a closer look at the scrolls on
archways, or to search for some small stone head over a
door. He had become a tourist among tourists, staring at
persons and buildings – critical, admiring, sometimes
bored, sometimes amazed at what he saw. He grew tired.
His own feet looked strange to him as he stepped on and off
the kerb or dodged the slippery stones on uneven bits of
pavement. He plodded on. His face confronted him, unawares, in dark shop windows, and different from the
conscious face in the bedroom mirror. This person looked
distraught, looked lonely, battered even, and hardly to be
distinguished from some of the down-and-outs who wandered in and out of nearby pubs.

Renwick had come a long way. The Castle was now in
view and it was giving all of them the full treatment. He had
seen this often enough – illumined stone and black battle-

ments against a sky still red with sunset. To crown all, a
huge, white supermoon breaking through clouds. Renwick
found himself in the midst of a large group, all turned that
way, all staring as if at a high stage. They were a long time
staring. Suddenly, as if at a warning buzz in the brain,
Renwick resumed citizenship. He was proud yet impatient
of the wide eyes around him. He glanced at his watch,
heard his own voice repeat familiar words:

'Yes, that's often how it is – very dramatic, very spectacular. Illumined? Yes, very often. The full moon? Yes,
don't ask me how – it *seems* often to be full and very well
placed, though more romantically speaking than astro-
nomically I would say. You must remember though –
we are not only a romantic city. Far from it. Yes, yes, of
course there's stuff coming down, but have you seen the
new things going up – the business side of things. In other
words, we are a *busy* people. Time moves on, you see. It
moves on here as in every other place.' He looked a man of
some consequence, a very busy man with a full timetable to
get through. They made way for him. He wished them
goodnight, passed on.

He was alone now and walking in a quiet side street. The
moon and the red sky were behind, the illumination
blocked out by high office buildings. He was making for
home. Once he stopped in passing for a word with an
acquaintance, until they reminded one another of the time
and quickly separated. Five persons made up on him and
passed, talking animatedly, and Renwick recognized the
cadence of this tongue. The blonde girl was walking with
three others and a young man. The man was native to the
city. The rest, he noted, were all tall, all fair, all dressed with
a flair and colour that stood out even in the dark street. If
this was the northern myth it was coming over in style. The
girl gave him a wave as they went by. 'A fine night,' said
Renwick.

'Yes,' the girl called back. 'And how about your moon

tonight? Have you looked yet? Has it turned into a clock for
you?' He heard her answering the young man, heard her say
in a voice – low, but audible to touchy ears: 'No, no, not
moonstruck. He is a time-keeper. The man is clock-mad!'
She made some remark to the others in her own language.
They laughed, looked back over their shoulders and gave
him a friendly wave. All five went on their way, noiseless, in
rubber soles, and disappeared round the next corner.

But Renwick's shoes were loud on the paving-stones, the
footsteps rang in his ears like a metronome. But what were
they counting out? Minutes or stones? He stared round
once, then turned his back again. This moon had looked
cold and white as a snowball. Yet his moonlit ears burned
as he walked on.

# Concerto

ABOUT HALF-WAY THROUGH the concerto, some of
those sitting in the organ gallery, facing the rest of the
audience and overlooking the orchestra, become aware of a
disturbance in the body of the hall. The seats in this gallery
face the conductor, who for the last few minutes has been
leaning out over the rostrum whacking down a thicket of
cellos with one hand, and with the other cunningly lifting
the uncertain horns higher and still higher up into a
perilous place above the other instruments. Behind him
the whole auditorium opens out, shell-shaped, its steep and
shallow shelves, boxes and ledges neatly packed with people. The sloping ground floor and overhanging gallery have
few empty seats and the place has a smooth appearance – a
sober mosaic of browns and greys flicked here and there
with scarlet.

At last the horns make it. But there is a quavering on the
long-drawn-out top note which brings a momentary grimace to the conductor's mouth as though he had bitten
through something sour. The horn-players lower their
instruments and stare in front of them with expressionless
faces. At any other time some eyes in this audience might
have studied the faces closely to discover which man had
produced the wavering note – whether there was a corresponding wavering in the eyes of one of them or a slight
wryness about the lips. But not tonight. Tonight all eyes
have been directed to another spot.

The disturbance comes from the middle stalls. Down
there a man has got to his feet and is leaning over the row in
front. He appears to be conducting on his own account. He

too entreats, he exhorts. He too encourages something to rise. Now a small group of people are up on their feet, and just as the horns extricate themselves, this man who is conducting operations down in the stalls manages to persuade the group to lift something up out of the darkness between the narrow seats. It is a tricky business, but at last a man is pulled clear and comes into view in a horizontal position, his long legs and his shoulders supported by several persons who have started to shuffle sideways with their burden along the row. Everyone now seems anxious to support this thin figure. Each leg is held by at least three people and the arms are carried on either side by two men and two women. Someone cups his head. Another handles the feet. Even those who are too far away to be actually supporting any part of his body feel it their duty to stretch out a finger simply to touch him, as a sacred object might be touched in a procession. He moves, propelled by these reverent touches, bouncing a little in the anxious arms. It is almost as if he were bouncing in time to a great pounding of drums. For since the horn-players lowered their instruments the music has grown violent in tempo and volume.

But suddenly, without warning, the violent music stops. There is a second of stunning silence. Then the solo violinist, who has stood patiently for some time letting the waves of sound crash over his bowed head, begins a series of scales which climb very quietly, one after the other, up onto a note so high that the silence can also be heard like a slight hiss directly above his head. This silence and the icy note of the single violin comes as a shock to those whose eyes are riveted on the scene going on down below. For it is no longer merely a mimed scene floating in the middle distance. The silence had shifted it nearer as though the protective membrane which sealed it off has been abruptly ripped. Now there are sounds coming up – ordinary sounds which in the circumstances sound horrible. There is a dull bumping and dragging of feet, a rustling and breathing, low voices arguing. Obviously the thing is beginning to get the upper hand. It is attracting more and more interest. Heads are turning and the people in the organ gallery can see the round, blank listening faces on either side change suddenly to keen, watchful profiles. There are even heads peering from the plush-covered front row of the dress circle – the silver heads and craning necks of elderly ladies, long-trained never to peer and crane.

But there is one head which, shockingly, has not turned at all after the first glance behind. It is the man who is seated at the end of the row immediately in front of that from which the invalid has been lifted. Everyone else in his row is up ready to help. The man must have skin of leather and iron nerves. Eyes which might have scrutinized the horn-players now study his face to see whether he is going to relent, to find out if there is about him the slightest flicker of an uneasy conscience. But no. What kind of man is this? Is this the sort of man who might see his own mother carried past on a stretcher without shifting his legs out of the way? He does not turn his head even when the horizontal figure is moving directly behind his seat. At that moment, however, the man and woman who are holding an arm, suddenly let it go – the better to support the fainting man's back while manoeuvring the awkward turn into the middle aisle of the hall. The arm swings down heavily and deals the man still seated in front a clout over the ear. It is an admonitory blow, as though from his deepest unconscious or perhaps from death itself, the invalid is aware there is still someone around who is not giving him the same tender attention all the others have shown.

There is now a fervent longing for the music to gather its forces again and crush the disturbance before it gets out of hand. But there is no hint of this happening. The violinist is still playing his icy scales, accompanied as though from remotest space by the strings and woodwind. A man of fifty, he is tall and exceedingly thin, with a bony hatchet face and fairish-grey hair brushed back from the brow. This brow gives the impression of being unnaturally exposed, as though his skull, and particularly the bone of his temples, had resisted a continual pressure of music which would have caused most other skulls to cave in. His eyes are deep-set and give him a sightless look while he is playing. Strangely enough, he is not unlike the man who is being carried out up the aisle. One is narrow and vertical with huge hands like an elongated Gothic cathedral figure – grotesque or splendid, depending on how the light might fall from a stained glass window. The other is stiff, horizontal and grey like the stretched-out figure on a tomb. The prostrate man has his own look of dedication, though in his case it is not to music, for by his collapse he has destroyed any possibility of listening.

These two figures, the vertical and the horizontal, in their terrifying absorption, their absolute disregard of everything else, seem somehow related. Both have their supporters, though now it seems that the horizontal has the greater following. The devoted, inner circle round him have made sure of that. Great, ever-widening rings of curiosity ripple out towards him, interlinking with the rings still concentrating on the violinist and causing even there a shimmer of awareness. The conductor of the devotees in the stalls is now walking backwards up the aisle on his tiptoes, well in front of the others. With his right hand he beckons reassuringly to the group coming up after him, and with his powerful left he attempts to quell any sign of interference from those sitting on either side of the aisle. But those nearest the door, paralysed till now, suddenly spring to their feet and fight for first place to heave their weight against it. The doors crash outward and the heaped figures pitch through.

This crash has coincided to a split second with the quietest bars of the concerto – that point where not only the soloist, but all other players have lowered their instruments – all, that is to say, except the flute. This flute has started up as though playing solely for the benefit of the group just outside the door, visible in the brilliant light of the vestibule. As though involved in a ritual dance, they crouch, rise, bend, and kneel beneath the hands of their leader who is now signalling to invisible figures further out. Someone carrying a jug and tumbler appears and kneels, and a chinking of glass comes from the centre of the group. It is a light sound but clear as a bell, and it combines with the flute in a duet which can be heard to the furthest corners of the hall.

At this point several people turn their eyes, in desperation, and stare at the unmoving man sitting now quite isolated at the end of his row. No one could say why it is imperative to turn to him. Isn't he a brute, after all – a stubborn, fat man with a crimson face, conspicuous only in being a figure of monumental unhelpfulness? Yet something about the man suggests that, like some squat, purple-cheeked Atlas, he is supporting the whole weight of the hall on his shoulders. The short, bulging neck holds up the overhanging gallery. The legs are planted like pillars to the floor, and over his paunch the fingers come together in a massive lock. His bottom is sunk into the plush of his seat like a bulbous root into the deep earth. Nothing can budge him now. He is dedicated to absolute immobility, and the whole house knows it.

This man has never taken his eyes off the violinist. He stares ahead, unblinking – his blue, slightly protuberant eyes fixed. It is as though on him, rather than on the conductor, has now fallen the responsibility of holding audience and orchestra together – of pushing back the white heads in the dress circle, checking the obstreperous group outside the door, and by a superhuman effort of will turning the curious eye of the audience back into a listening ear. The soloist lifts his violin and for the first time throws a piercing glance down into the body of the hall. He exchanges one look with the immobile man sitting there. There is no recognizable emotion in this look, nothing that would ordinarily be called human warmth. Yet the man below glows and shines for an instant as though caught in a flare of brilliant light. The violinist raises his bow and begins to play.

In the meantime, one of the group outside in the vestibule has at last remembered about the open doors. He pulls them to violently and the drama outside is shut away, at any rate from the ears – for figures can still be seen moving about behind the obscured glass. All the same there is a feeling of uneasiness – a feeling that the fellow lying behind that door will not allow himself to be shut away and forgotten after swaying the entire audience. This unease is justified. Scarcely have those around the door drawn their first breath of relief before it swings open again, and the leader of the group strides in. His air is even more commanding than before. Now he looks like an ambassador from an important state. He walks along the empty row looking for something, before starting to tip up the seats and feel about on the floor. By this time the music has again gathered volume and nobody can hear the sound of the seats, though he is as skilful and rhythmical in the way he raps them back as the man behind the kettledrums. And now he is finished with that row and goes into the one in front where the stout man is sitting. He works his way along the seats, tipping, patting and groping till he reaches him. Now he is actually feeling around the other's feet. But the man – this rapt Buddha of non-helpfulness – shifts neither his legs nor his eyes. He allows the other to squeeze past him, to glare at him, and even to push his foot aside.

At first there is mounting curiosity as to what the searcher will come up with. Yet the seated man has managed to concentrate most of this curiosity upon himself and then, by not moving a hair or allowing his attention to swerve for an instant, has directed it up towards the orchestra. This is something which almost amounts to an athletic feat. The sheer effort of lifting this crowd on his eyeballs alone is appalling.

The swing doors open again and a woman appears and moves diffidently, apologetically, down the gangway, all the time looking towards the searcher and waiting for a sign. But the man is now working along a row further back and keeps shaking his head. Suddenly he disappears. He has pounced on something down there. It is a long handbag in imitation plum-coloured leather with a zip pocket at the back – useful but not elegant. An advertisement would describe it as a bag which could go anywhere. And it has gone far and been kicked around a lot. Already it has travelled a couple of rows back and sideways ten feet or so. The man and woman join up enthusiastically and are soon on their way out again, the woman meantime peering into the bag to assure herself that, in spite of the hideous confusion of the last ten minutes, everything is intact inside, right down to the fragile mirror in the lid of her compact.

Now some of those in the audience had imagined it might be a pair of spectacles the man was hunting for – spectacles belonging to the fainting man who, added to the horrors of coming to in a strange place, would find himself unable to focus on the strange faces looming over him. A few have never been able to shake off the suspicion that all the time these spectacles have been lying, ground to powder, under the stubborn heels of the man sitting at the end of the row. At sight of the handbag, however, some tie linking them to the group outside the door snaps forever. As the man and woman finally push their way out there is a glimpse of a deserted vestibule. The group, as though sensing a defeat, have disappeared.

The music is sweeping to its climax. One by one each section of the orchestra is gathered up and whirled higher and higher in a struggle to reach the four, slow, separate chords which end the concerto. On this level plateau they at last emerge into safety, and the end is in sight. The fourth and final chord crashes down, submerging all doubts, and a great burst of clapping and stamping follows it. It is some time before the stout man joins in this applause. Rather, it seems that he is quietly receiving part of it for himself, along with the soloist, the conductor, and the rest of the orchestra. But now, for the first time, he lowers the heavy lids of his eyes towards the ground and allows himself a discreet smile. Then he lifts his hands and begins to clap. His applauding heels shuffle the floor.

# The Swans

THE PAINTSHOP WAS deservedly proud of its reputation as one of the best of its kind in the city. For here it was not simply a matter of selling paints and wallpaper. From morning till night the three men behind the counter offered a never-ending service of advice to customers, regardless of whether they made a sale or not. They were patient over the perpetual problem of matt, gloss or eggshell surface, grave and dedicated when consulted about a pattern for the lavatory wall, properly thunderstruck on hearing – for the hundredth time – the tragedy of the kitchen ceiling. It was no wonder the shop was crowded. Nevertheless, there were certain times in the day when they had it to themselves. Then the three of them – Joe Wheeler, Duncan and Jim Paton – would lean their elbows on the counter and look across to the long, black wall of partly-demolished houses on the other side of the street. 'So are they *ever* going to pull the rest of it down?' Joe Wheeler would say. 'Or are we going to stand here and stare at that until kingdom-come?'

These back walls – the only remaining part of the buildings – had a special fascination for the three men and had added a strange dimension to their day. There they saw ancient patches of striped and flowered wallpaper marked with pale oblongs where the pictures had been, chopped-off shelves lined with worn oilcloth, built-in cupboards whose blue and yellow paint had peeled down to the dead wood. Like old wounds opening, the varnish had cracked into deep strips along mantelpieces. Cinders still filled one or two grates, and pieces of half-burnt coal. A single grey curtain hung at a window without glass. Indeed, it was hard to escape the feeling that everyone who had ever looked out of these windows had been old and grey, that their very clothes had been grey as dust.

The men in the paintshop knew every scar on the walls opposite – walls so lashed by rain, stripped and scoured by gales, that sometimes it seemed time was running backwards, making these the skeletons and ghosts of all the brand-new houses which, week in, week out, they heard described by customers. For here in the shop all talk was of the long-lasting, the indestructible nature of things – unscratchable surfaces, walls which would endure through lifetimes. The paint men could deliver strong warnings, but most of their time was spent reassuring their customers. And the customers could be very worried indeed. It seemed they had to believe that their own house would still stand up even if its inmost fabric was attacked with a hatchet.

This afternoon, in the short lull after lunch, the men were behind the counter staring abstractedly across to the other side. This was a city where whole streets of fine old houses had been needlessly torn down, but the half-demolished street had not been one of them. Jim Paton reminded them of this. 'But you'll agree these had to come down?' he said. 'Would you want the old, decayed stuff forever?'

'Of course not,' said Joe. 'No question of it. All I'm asking is – why can't they make a proper job of it when they're at it? Knock the whole thing down at one go! Isn't the city full of these left-overs?' He turned aside from the others to attend to a woman who'd just come in. They heard him say, 'Depends what you want it for – bedroom, bathroom, kitchen? Now kitchens and bathrooms get a lot more wear. You want something tough. But just take your time. Think about it.' She retired again with a handful of information. Joe returned to the counter and again all three brooded on the scene in front. 'The human species!' Joe shook his head. 'Are we a dirty, messy lot, then? I'm beginning to think it! Is there anything worse than the mess human beings can make when they really get down to it? Look at that!'

They had been looking for months. In front of the wall of houses was a huge area of dust and rubble. Old bricks and blocks of cement, rusty pipes and strips of roofing were scattered around. And into this area had been thrown enough rubbish to fill a thousand wastebins – peel, newspaper and sodden carrier bags, tins, rags, strips of carpet and linoleum, milk bottles, whisky bottles, cartons and old vegetables. The chips of broken glass, in every size and colour, would have filled a cathedral window. 'A stupid, messy species!' pronounced Joe darkly again.

The young couple who now entered the paintshop, however, did not appear to belong to this species. Joe hastened towards them, for beauty lightens the spirit and quickly puts strength back into the legs. They wished to see wallpapers and he took them to the shelf where a tome, heavy as the Domesday Book, lay open, displaying every sort of covering for walls. The girl turned the thick pages slowly, stopping at stripes and certain patterns of leaves. 'Be sure it's the right green,' warned the man. 'Remember the ceiling.'

'Greens can be difficult,' Joe murmured from behind. 'Let me take it to the window shelf. You'll maybe get them in a better light.'

At the word 'light', the three of them turned and looked through the windows straight across to the long, black wall of broken houses. 'The odd things that got left behind!' exclaimed Joe. 'Do you see there's still coal and ashes in some of those fireplaces?'

'I see that,' said the young man, peering across.

'And in winter I've seen snow and coal together. Not exactly what you'd expect to find in your own fireside, is it? And now the willowherb growing up those bathroom pipes! If they stand long enough there'll be moss along the mantelpiece and mushrooms on the shelf.'

The man now wandered away to look at colour lists. But

the girl still stood at the window, looking across every now and then as if to match the peeling papers of the walls opposite with those pristine ones in the sample book. Yet Joe, watching her, sensed something else. Every instant her expression changed as though over there she saw first the black walls and then some flash of brilliance, darkness again, and again brightness. Was it a bird? thought Joe. A glint of red glass in the rubble? Or was she imagining the coal and snow together?

'We see some odd things across there,' he said. 'Pigeons in the fireplaces. And I've seen myself – though you'll never believe it – an owl on a cupboard shelf. In broad daylight too. I was stone sober at the time, and it was no pigeon – that's for sure.'

'But I *do* believe it,' said the girl gravely.

Joe studied her face again. 'I believe it wasn't such a bad-looking street in the old days,' he said cautiously. 'It got worse and worse through the years, and then I suppose it had to go. I only wish they'd bash the whole thing down and have done with it. I can't abide this half-and-half business.'

'Do you know something?' said the girl. 'I've actually heard a good deal about those houses – or at any rate one of them – I couldn't say which. One of my mother's aunts lived over there somewhere. Maybe fifty years ago, maybe more.'

'Well, well, – do you tell me that? Now, *that's* interesting!' said Joe, still with some caution. He tried but failed to remember any good thing he'd said about any house in that row in the last twelve months.

'When she was first married she took in lodgers. Short-term lodgers. Well, there were only two my mother ever heard her talk about. And they were swans. Swans from Russia.'

'Swans!'

'A couple of ballet-dancers from the theatre at the back. It was a company on a two-week visit – a well-known company. *Swan Lake* – they danced the whole of *Swan Lake.*'

'Two swans from Russia!' Joe gave a thin, long-drawn-out sound through his teeth, as though whistling them back across the ice-blown Steppes.

'I don't say they came straight from there,' said the girl, 'but they had Russian names. Their grandparents had been born there.'

'Anyway, Russian or not, that explains it,' said Joe.

'Explains what?'

Joe smiled to himself but did not answer. It explained the sudden changes in her expression as though she'd seen white birds fly over demolished chimneys, or sooty fireplaces sprinkled with snow as soft as swan feathers.

'They worked hard enough on all accounts. How those dancers worked! At it from morning till night. The theatre changed hands long ago.'

'A bingo hall,' said Joe. 'Well, you'll find a lot of birds up there all right, though I doubt not many swans like those. Did she ever see them again?'

'My mother says she kept in touch sent a card now and then to the one who married and had a baby.'

'So that was the end of dancing for *her*?'

'I never heard.'

'Ah well,' Joe gently brooded on the loss. 'Still, somebody got a swan for a mother.'

The shop was filling up again. Turning, he was swept into a discussion on sandpaper. 'Coarse ones for the tough jobs, and fine ones for the smooth, clean finish,' he advised. He moved on. Up at the window the man had joined the young woman and they were going slowly again, page by page, through the book of wallpapers. From halfway down the room Joe watched till they'd come to the end of the book and had closed it up. The girl turned, gave him a smile and shook her head. So there was nothing they wanted. Nothing amongst the flowers, the leaves, the stripes or squares. In a way he was glad. He had pictured something different for her – a wall which was plain and so smooth you might well see, sweeping across as though through an indoor sky, the sharp, black bird shadows.

Almost two months later, work started again on the wall of houses. First a vast hoarding went up around the area and for a few weeks became a gigantic scribbling board where the neighbourhood painted and chalked up its politics and religion, its messages of love and hate. Posters were stuck here and there. In no time the red and yellow slogans became stamped the one upon the other like shouts vying in shrillness. The houses behind stayed silent and almost hidden. Only the empty windows of their top floors and a few broken chimneys could be seen above the hoarding, and for a while it seemed that these chalked boards spoke for the present, while the houses spoke only of the past. Again the people in the paintshop lifted their eyes from the ordered patterns in their hands to stare across at the bizarre, criss-crossing patterns on the boards. Their feelings were mixed. Some shut this out and got on with the choice of stripe or square, as though to show that at least some area of the universe could be regulated. Others saw life in the haphazard scrawls – frantic, vulgar, moving, hateful – but life. Yet even the stuff on the boards did not last. The chalk was washed by rain and the paint chipped off by penknives. Wind tore the posters. The paper mouths of candidates for election, the vendors of quick salvation, were stripped of half their smile in one night's gale.

And one day the final demolishers moved in. All morning a great swinging ball of metal battered the wall of the buildings. From behind the hoarding came a slow, steady rumbling of falling bricks, then the thick sigh of heavy dust subsiding. In places, the more stubborn stone took a fierce barrage of beating before it finally let go, but by midday it was all down. A huge powdery cloud hung in the air over that part of the city, making the noon light glow a dusky orange like that of the setting sun.

All during the morning, whenever they had a moment, the men in the paint shop had looked across. One moment they had still seen the skeletal lines of upper windows.

When they looked again, even these ghosts had vanished. There was only the dust-cloud slowly rising. Joe had been called away to advise on paint. It was the same old question. 'Yes, long-lasting of course,' he reassured, 'but not *ever-lasting*. I can't promise that, I'm sorry to say – not for walls or anything else. *I've* had a bit of wear and tear in my time and it's starting to show . . . Bit of the shine gets rubbed away, your brilliant gloss starts to go, chips flaking off here and there. It's all the same – paint, skin, teeth, hair – well, it's got to come sometime, hasn't it?'

'They get me worried,' said Joe, as he returned to the counter, 'those ones who want a signed and dated guarantee of immortality for themselves *and* their houses. We're not gods!'

The others agreed they were not gods, and folded their elbows more comfortably along the counter.

'In the end of the day – what's left of your house anyway?' said Joe. 'Black walls and a heap of rubble. One or two memories *might* go on, though, *might* pass down through the years – happenings in the house, things that came and went.'

'Naturally,' said Duncan, shifting his elbows again.

'Things?' said Jim Paton. 'Like what?'

'All kinds of things,' said Joe. 'Coming and going. Swans – could be swans.' The others, on either side of him, turned their heads to stare. Jim gave a guffaw.

'Well, we've had a mixture coming and going in *our* house over the years – dogs, cats, canaries, even a hamster, God help it, when the kids were small, but swans! Now where do *swans* come in?'

Though Joe was dealing with questions all day long and every day, there were always some – nearer the bone or heart – he was slower or even downright unwilling to answer. Smiling, stubbornly silent, he wandered off again to stare out at the cloud of dust which was now spreading to merge with the smoke from factory chimneys and with the colder fog from the great sea-river further out.

# *Lines*

AS CHILDREN WE were afraid of this woman. Often she was in the park for half the evening, sitting at the bottom of a steep flight of steps leading down into the lake. The park – untended and usually deserted – had once been the small estate of a house fallen to ruin. Long ago it had been pillaged for its stones and lead. Piles of stone blocks and frames of windows filled its courtyard, and in rooms where there was still a wall, tall weeds grew with the birds and trellises of ancient wallpapers.

At that age we had a zest for certain fears. There was the pale young man in red pyjamas who'd stood one night amongst the trees and lamps of the hospital grounds, bent backwards like a hoop to stare at stars behind his head. We feared and admired the strangeness of this pose. It didn't have to be people. It could have been the pit at the unlighted end of town where dead cars had been dumped along with an uneasy heap of tyres that writhed and glistened on windy nights. It could be anything, in fact – anything to spike the blandness that our elders had provided to quell irrational fears. Of course we took their comfort thankfully when we needed it. Often, however, we suspected their version of certain incidents and characters was too smooth, too fluent to be true.

A few years later the woman was still coming to the park from time to time. But it was different now. The end of school was still a good way off, but it was in sight. We were beginning to look ahead and we had a lot on our minds. The ambitious began to brace themselves. Others grew smooth, in their turn, and listless. The restless ones got ready to drop from sight as soon as they left the gates. As to the woman, our fascination in her had been much reduced. And the fear was non-existent, though she looked harder than she did in earlier days – the frown more deeply drawn, the mouth bitter. By this time we had learnt a few facts to add to the scraps and rumours of her life.

Long before she came to this part of the country and while still a young woman she had been for a short time in prison. It was believed there had been a child's death in the case, though probably not her own – and whether it involved negligence, mania or cruelty was not known. For some time afterwards she was held in care. Then she was on her own. This was the trouble. This was her huge grievance for years to come. She believed – whether with truth or not – that everyone now moved away from her as rapidly and in as straight a line as it was possible to go. At one time she had described this particular movement to anyone who would listen – turning on her heel and shooting her arms out in all directions to show the fearful speed with which they had gone, as though she herself were the baleful centre from which all lines fled off.

Sometimes the woman would be away for a while, but she always returned to the lake. It was a secluded spot. Amongst the trees on the slope above the water were two white marble statues. One was a nymph who had glanced aside while stooping to wash her foot in a dried-up bowl. A few yards away was a young huntsman wearing a fillet of bronze laurel leaves which over the years had stained his nose and his chin bright green. It seemed to us that these two beautiful persons looked at one another with anxiety – the girl who tried in vain to wash her greying foot and the youth whose laurels and carefree gesture could never make up for the anguish of green acne. The young boys and girls of our group who came here to meet one another on certain evenings knew all these anxieties themselves, no matter how they were disguised by arguments or scuffings or the

great show of scornful indifference that separated us. Yet
we didn't come only to see one another. For reasons not
clear to us we also came to see the woman. We had mixed
feelings. We came from curiosity, from long-kept habit.
Sometimes we came as if supporting her in her isolation. Or
we came determined to discover, by staring at the straight
back, where exactly the streak of cruelty might be seen.
We'd no doubt that it must be there – though perhaps long-
hidden – there in the strong hands or the sharp elbow bent
back to throw crusts to the water-birds as though aiming
darts. Sometimes the forward jerk of her head would bring
a loop of hair from under her cap onto her shoulder. As
girls who'd never had a covering on our heads we discussed
the significance of a bright red beret always worn slightly
askew. A sign of one-time elegance?

'But you know, don't you, that the slightest tilt of anything on the head means dissipation and a lot more?' said
Clara who, though the youngest of us, already wore a braid
on top of her head smooth as the plaited crust on a white
loaf. 'And when I say anything on the head I mean *anything*.
Do you remember the first History book they ever gave us?
Those tilted crowns on the kings and queens – the wicked
ones, I mean? It was meant to help you remember the Good
from the Bad. And just in case you didn't get the message
they made the worst ones cross-eyed as well.'

'No, I don't remember that,' I said.

'Oh yes, of course you must! And some archbishops were
naturals for crooked mitres, and a pope or two of course.
I'd never trust the slightest tilt now, not even on a halo.'
Poor Clara didn't keep her resolution. She made an unhappy marriage to a man permanently on the tilt with drink
and soon began to let her lovely hair fall uncombed to her
shoulders as though she'd neither will nor energy to keep it
up.

The woman must have known we were all there behind
her amongst the trees but she hardly ever looked round.

Nowadays her main business was with the various birds of the pond. They literally made tracks for her when she appeared – converging from all sides of the lake and leaving the long, criss-crossing V-lines in their wake. I thought it strange to see the scores of lines approach whenever she lifted her arm, having known of the bitter account she'd given of all those other human lines that had moved away from her during her life. Here the order of things was reversed. Of course she also had the birds in the trees behind, waiting to swoop down when the commotion on the water was over. Sometimes a huge crow landed on the steps and stalked furtively about, ready to make a grab for any bits and pieces that fell from her bag. At the far end of the lake there were also two swans that waited for long enough before joining the squabbling ducks on the other side. Then they would swim languidly across, hardly deigning to bend the neck as they came up to the crusts, or even, at the last minute, ignoring them while instead they turned aside to preen their wings.

One evening, however, the distant swans turned at once towards the woman when she came down. They took a long time coming over but the lines they drew on the water were as straight and parallel as a double rule. One boy in our crowd – a powerful trouble-maker – happened to be leaning against the marble girl, one foot on the plinth, an arm around her leg. As the swans swam up the woman suddenly turned and raked him with an unbelievably scornful and vindictive glance, at the same time managing to look triumphant as if asserting that she could draw this living white sculpture towards her simply by lifting her arm. Though we were used to every look and gesture the woman made, this particular one – aimed directly at him – fairly knocked this boy, Johnson, off his perch. There was something about the look that got him on the raw. It made him mad. In any case he was a spiteful youth known for his bullying way with the younger boys and his knowing sneer for any girl who came near. It was a couple of days later, on a Saturday, that he came down, grinning, through the trees with an armful of toy ducks and swans. Who knows where he got them? He was the kind who would have swiped them from the prams and baths of babies if he'd got the chance. He might have picked them from a counter or from a market stall. They were all sizes including one ugly monster of a duck, for it was the time when shops were grabbing on to the idea that Big was Beautiful and highly lucrative. This particular bird, he explained, he'd got from his married sister – a discarded dented duck already supplanted by a bigger.

But there was worse to come. Johnson stepped back amongst the trees to collect a large holdall from which he drew a doll – one of those huge, coquettish dolls with blonde curls that can be made to represent any female image from infant to adult woman. This one, in spite of brilliantly-painted lips and curled black lashes, was wearing a baby jacket and frilled skirt. The boy carried her down carefully to the water's edge, then took her by her leg and hurled her as far as he could throw. She landed amongst a circle of plastic ducks and floated there on her back, her plump elbows bent and her eyes staring at the sky. We would have been hard put to describe our feelings as we watched this object. The girls expressed anger and disgust. Some of the boys round Johnson laughed and cheered. But not for long. It was the sense of shame that came uppermost – the unexpected shame of confronting, out of the blue, the memory of something we'd once excitedly discussed – a cruel killing or a drowning, some violent, unspecified act which had lodged in the mind and which we knew in our heart of hearts we'd be reluctant to give up.

'That'll show her! That'll give her something to think about – bloody, fucking murderess!' yelped Johnson, stamping and swaggering about amongst the trees. He was not a large boy but he suddenly seemed hefty enough to take on a prize-fighter – bulging from his tight trousers as though they'd shrunk to bursting.

Our shame and confusion deepened so much so that when one of the girls murmured: 'Still the fact remains . . .' the rest of us drew near to have our consciences relieved. All except Rachel who at once said, 'What fact?'

'I mean the fact remains that she did – *must* have, whatever it was – done something black.'

'There was never a fact. It was all hearsay from the start.'

'Some of it was hearsay. But prison was a fact. Do women go to jail for nothing? No, it's hard to get into prison if you're a woman. They're only too thankful to let you out again. So the crime must have been bad. A child was in it. A child – what else!' We drew back again, each to her tree – ungainly, guilty dryads, preferring never to be released from wood or leaf into the occupations of grown women – mothers or murderesses.

We were still around this spot when the woman arrived. She came down as usual through the trees looking neither to right nor left, but seeming to show in her face, as she often did, a kind of grim satisfaction in her audience. We watched her as she went on to the bank and down the steps whose bottom ledge at this time of year was lapped by a weedy brown water, scummed with layers of autumn flies. She sat down, gathering her skirts from the damp, and made ready to open her bag of bread. She raised her head and her hand stopped on the clasp. There was stillness all through the trees as the woman glanced around at the plastic ducks among the rest. Then we saw her look further. She looked out to where a pink, precocious child was floating. The coarse yellow curls had collected straws and leaves. Over the forehead was a small white duck feather, curled like a débutante's plume. The woman stood up. She turned and began to climb quickly towards us. Just as quickly we moved back to other trees. We'd no doubt we were in danger. Even the bragging Johnson who stood out in the open looked a lot smaller in our eyes. But the woman never glanced at us. She was absorbed in the ground, searching intently among the stones and rock fragments that lay around. She took her time in picking them up – weighing some in her hand, impatiently discarding others, even giving one or two a little toss to size them up, before dropping them in her bag. All this was done with such relentless concentration we were in two minds whether to stay or run.

'Well, I'm off then! Come on – unless you want your heads bashed in!' said Sylvia who'd nevertheless had the benefit of a full-grown oak while some of us had a sapling.

'Too late for that,' I said. 'Besides she's going back. The rocks aren't meant for *us*.' By this time the woman was indeed moving down to the water. She let the heavy bag fall on the steps – the crash of stone on marble being somewhat softened by the bread. She bent, took out a stone from the bag and hurled it at a plastic duck. She hurled another and another. She went for each target with such hell-bent aim that not a live duck was touched. They swam some little distance towards the centre and waited, gently rocking, their tails to the bank.

The stoning went on faster and harder. Some of the shots came so hard that two or three of the alien ducks disappeared completely under water, coming up again dented and twisted into peculiar shapes more like small coat-hangers than birds. The luckier ducks and swans were floating on their sides. Others had let in water and were tilted head-down as if drinking, or bobbing about with tails down, beaks pecking at the sky. The huge, discarded duck from Johnson's sister had died a second death and lay crushed amongst reeds under the bank. No plastic interloper was left intact.

At last there was an interval. It had turned into one of those silent autumn evenings where nothing moves. The marble statues which at first had seemed the only static objects in the park were now only one part of all carved and sculpted things. A wooden woman stood on the steps and a frieze of frightened figures watched behind the trees. I know now it was not only due to the time of year or day. It had mostly to do with waiting. We had been waiting ever since we knew this woman, for one word or sign to confirm for us – once and for all – her innocence or guilt. Out there, maintained in the space between real and unreal, a plastic child was floating.

The woman bent and took a large stone from her bag and with one arm high above her head she hurled it down. It struck its target with a crack and the doll twirled once on the water. Its arms were stretched to the bank. We shrank at the sight. She struck a second time. The yellow head ducked and reappeared slightly askew on its neck. She struck again and the doll jumped. It floated out a short distance and the calm, incurious ducks made way for it.

I remember how we came together gradually from our trees and made our way up towards a stretch of ground a long way from the water. There, our backs to a strip of rusted railings, we sat down – a dozen of us. We formed a council now or perhaps it was a jury. We believed the trial concerned the possible cruelty of this woman and the question was whether we had seen this or not. 'Are you trying to prove some awful past act out of a petty one today?' said one of the girls. 'And there was never a question of battering a cat or dog or any other creature, let alone a child.'

'There's always been the talk of drowning though, amongst all the rest.'

'This drowned thing happens to be a *doll*.'

'The toughness of the woman!' exclaimed one of the boys. 'That she could go on pitching stones like that – bloody great rocks!'

Johnson had flung himself full-length on the ground,

exhausted by an orgy of vengeance and the race to the top. He had nothing to say.

As for the rest of us, our muted talk went on for a while. Now was the time to write this woman off as human or inhuman – and move on ourselves, as almost adults, our peace of mind intact. It didn't happen like that. For one thing various people had reversed the rôles and opinions that were expected of them. We were changing. We were divided. Some of us came to the conclusion that there had been no strong evidence against her at any time, neither in the past nor since. This evening had proved nothing. There was no cruelty in it. Others believed that she had been guilty of the greatest crime, that she was a cruel person and always would be. Clara, the exponent of tilted headgear, had taken up another position, if it could be called that. She was unable to make up her mind. She was not to be questioned. She was not to be bullied. She sat contemplating the lake and its further bank which was gradually turning a deeper blue. Her face looked drawn and shadowed as though maturing rapidly with the ending of the day, and such was the silent droop of her mouth that it was almost possible to guess how she might look in twenty years or so.

It was the woman who made the last move, so to speak. Perhaps she had the last say too, though she didn't open her mouth. It was late and one by one we got to our feet, brushing the leaves and twigs from our legs. As we got up the woman sat down. We turned and began moving slowly towards the place where the ground levelled off into an overgrown drive leading to the main gate. Two or three of us stopped before we reached this place and looked back through a clearing in the trees. The woman was sitting on the steps with her bag beside her. She had used the stones. Now she took out the bread. Slowly, with long, persuasive gestures she began to throw the bits out onto the water. The light was fading and the sounds with it, but there was a sheen on the surface of the lake and gradually we saw the long V-lines appear as the black and grey ducks came up. We watched these lines cross and re-cross, more coming from behind – and all converging at the spot where a shower of crusts was falling, to disappear like snow around the gobbling beaks.

There must have been plenty of bread still in the bag but after a time, getting nothing more from her, the ducks drifted off. The woman sat motionless, looking in front of her. We studied her back for the last time before moving on. Given our feelings that afternoon I daresay it struck most of us that we wouldn't want to see much more of her. As a matter of fact we'd seldom seen her face and never exchanged a word. It was her back we'd watched and judged. You could say we were analysts of backs and arms.

It was when the water was almost smooth again that the swans came slowly out from the shadows at the other end – their long tracks cutting the lake like curled-back metal upon metal. They calmly passed the toppled, plastic ducks, the swimming ducks and the submerged doll by the bank. The woman rose to greet them, holding up both hands with the choice bread. Her back was straight and proud.

# Security

'AND I'M NOT really supposed to sit down at all,' said the young man. 'Not on this kind of a job.'

'What kind is it?' asked the girl who'd been sitting for some time on a seat in the gallery watching her small son stumping around close to the wall of pictures. Now and then he bent to examine the look of his boots on the parquet pattern of the floor.

'You can see, can't you?' the man extended his arm with the dark blue armlet. 'It's Security. I'm not even supposed to stand still as a matter of fact.'

'Oh – security,' said the young woman turning her head towards him. She glanced from his one shoulder to the other as though measuring them or rather measuring some other massive shoulders which were mysteriously missing. At the same time she took in his head with its light, longish hair, and again her eyes moved just a fraction above it as if his complement – some tall, strapping fellow – might be directly behind. She glanced at the armlet, a plain one without letters.

'It's not the usual band,' he explained, 'but, of course, its being a temporary thing makes no difference. It's official and it's Security.'

'Well, if you're not allowed to sit or stand or talk I suppose you'd better move on. Maybe I'll see you later when you come round again.'

The security man hesitated for a moment, nodded and walked off. The girl studied his shoes as he went past.

Because it was a busy but small town, this building – the largest in the place – had been used to accommodate both

Art Gallery and Museum. Everything here was on a small scale, as well as being arranged haphazardly on the time-scale. From one end of the gallery one could look through into a place of old and new machinery. On Saturdays and Sundays and on school holidays the wheels of these machines would spin and hum. At the push of a button old engine levers and the limbs of miniature cranes clicked into action, while down the length of the room, in semi-darkness, red and blue lights sparked on and off. Leading out of this was a narrow, windowless place where models of three undersized dinosaurs stood in line, jagged jaw touching scaly tail, with a bat-winged creature hovering from wires overhead. Right at the other end of the Room of Pictures an archway led through into the Room of Weapons – a history in words and pictures, with models and objects varying from Stone Age axes to the latest missiles. Further in was a display of Foodstuffs of the World – their growth and preparation. Bundles of cereal and trays of seed were here, coloured photos of fruits, plants, cattle, sheep – men fishing, hunting, building fires, women holding jars, pots, plates, mothers feeding babies, children eating, not eating, pictures of bursting cornucopia and empty food-bowls. Beyond this another archway opened into a bright room where Greece was represented by a dozen or so white marble heads looking with confidence and a marvellous serenity towards the windows. Even from the far end of the gallery it was possible for visitors to see parts of the street and, occasionally, the people who hurried past on a level with the windows. Sometimes an anxious eye outside would meet the marble gaze inside. A puffy red brow might turn momentarily as if to compare itself with the clear brow behind glass. Occasionally large birds were flung by the wind onto these windowsills while the heads remained half-smiling, calm and beautiful at all times.

The place where the young woman sat was brilliantly lit, but it was getting on towards closing-time and in the domed glass roof the afternoon light was fading. There were many blues in the paintings round the walls but the girl kept looking up at the slowly darkening blue overhead. Sometimes she would turn to watch the little boy who was beginning to trail his feet, now and then bumping softly against the wall in his padded coat, for it was nearly bed-time. The whole museum was quiet, almost deserted, but after a while the firm footsteps of the security man came slowly round again.

'I've been thinking about that job of yours,' said the girl.

'My temporary job.'

'Anyway, I've been thinking about it – the security bit. The pictures and things may be safe enough – even the dinosaurs – but I can't say I feel it myself.'

'Oh, so you think I'm no good at it,' said the young man quickly. 'There were dozens in for the job – *dozens*, I don't mind telling you. But they just happened to choose me.'

'But of course, of course! You may not be all that heavy, but it's the reflexes that count. I daresay you're very good on your feet – good at spotting trouble and all that.'

'You're right,' said the man brightening up. 'I *am* very quick on my feet. In fact at one time I was an absolutely first-rate runner.'

'Very good. But then it isn't really you or your job I've been thinking about after all. It's that word. Security. I can't believe in it, can you?'

The young man frowned darkly again. 'Security here, you mean?'

'No, no. Anywhere. I can't believe in it. And – to be honest – yes, it's this gallery and all the other stuff through there that put me in mind of it.'

The security man looked along the walls. Though most of the paintings seemed neither good enough nor bad enough to invite theft or slashing, there were some more striking and enigmatic. In one canvas the great surface of matt black paint tunnelled down into a well of brilliant, glossy darkness at its centre. In another a scarlet top was spinning in vast spaces of blood-flecked white, and further along an all-over pattern of thick black lines was set over rows of white ovals with dark centres. In closer focus the ovals with dots emerged as hundreds of eyes behind bars. The girl, following his glance, said that these interested her – they were better perhaps than the creamy portraits and the feathery flower-pieces. Of course, she said, she could detect a good many bad dreams amongst this lot. And for a start there was no security against bad dreams. 'It's just that word makes you think,' she said. 'Especially with a child. When you've got one of your own you'll feel the same.'

It seemed a long way ahead for the young man to envisage. Nevertheless it brought him back to take another look at the little boy. He had got over his dreamy patch and was running along the wall again, stopping now and then to test the hard toes of his new boots against the ventilation gratings, then running on quicker and quicker to reach the large Still Life with Melons at the top of the room, and after a cursory glance, back again to the far end where he halted sharply at the painting of a black-striped tiger in a forest of pylons. He cautiously touched the tiger's tail with one finger. At the same time he looked round.

'I suppose you could say that's *one* reason why I'm here,' said the security man. 'There's this difficulty about bringing children in. It's O.K. till they begin to get bored. And it's the kids themselves I'm thinking about. Because sooner or later, you see, a vase is going to get bashed or a painting scraped. And then the child – or rather the father or mother – will be in trouble. You'd be surprised the things that can happen here.' The little boy was now softly stroking his finger down the whole length of the painted black tail and again when he came to the tip he looked round. 'They always know when they shouldn't be doing it,' brooded the young man.

The girl beckoned to the child but there was no need to

call him across. He was already walking back, slowly and proudly, the way he'd come. The man stayed where he was beside the girl, but neither spoke. After some time she moved away to make another slow round of the gallery and then, taking her son by the hand, went through the archway into the adjoining room. So for a time they disappeared from the young man's view, but not from his imagination. For the place they were now in was more familiar to him than any other part of the museum. He had a feeling for history. To him there was an order and logic about the Weapons room which was lacking in the others – a steady progression from rough to smooth, from crude to functional – and all underlined by the efficient lay-out of the place. For him even the most ancient and cumbersome weapons and implements had a certain streamlined quality. The Stone Age axeheads had been shaped and used – enough for him to see the skilled hand at work. Through time the polished flints had become sharper, flatter. Later, the spears and pikes progressed from blunt to fine. He could visualize the pair in there studying the bits of armour – a paltry enough collection in his view. But their ponderous metal also held glamour for him – the smooth, hinged plates sliding the one under the other like the joints of giant insects, while the glittering anonymity of the head in its helmet resembled the anonymous heads of astronauts in the photos further on. The clumsy cannonballs, even the slow-swinging guns, had done the job at the time. The shelves of inlaid pistols in their glass case were his special pride. As for the rocket missiles with their pearl-smooth surface – they were as streamlined as the human hand could make. The security man got little satisfaction from the marbles, he enjoyed the ancient reptiles in passing, he was tolerant of the paintings. But for this particular room he had a proprietary feeling. He knew the history and the function of every object it contained.

A bell in the building reminded him of the time. There

was still time to talk. The young man walked slowly through into the other room. The girl was standing against a wall of rifles slung at angles. The boy, he was thankful to see, was not running around but standing on the toes of his boots trying to look over into the high case of pistols.

'I'm afraid they'll be putting out the lights quite soon,' said the man, looking at his watch. 'But you've still got fifteen minutes or so. Is there anything special he'd like to see?'

'Oh no, don't bother,' the woman said.

'The boys all go for that chest of miniatures – the smallest guns in the world, the smallest flags – like toys, like wedding-cake ornaments – miniature bullets, bayonets, rifles, rockets, and most of them in working order. I can open it up.' Bored or angry she might be – he couldn't say which – but the few steps from one room to the other had changed things. She gave him an unfriendly look.

'Or anything you'd like to ask?' he tried again. She didn't look at him or answer. The thing rankled. He was indignant at the aggression. And she was staring round the walls with a dark face. Did she think he'd invented the lot?

The small boy meantime had been quietly walking about on the backs of his heels, laboriously circling the suit of armour and balancing, with arms outstretched, between rows of spears and arrows, across to the far side of the room. The labour was too much. He straightened up suddenly onto the toes of his boots and helping himself along by the smooth side of the model rocket he stomped back into the picture gallery. For a few steps he staggered on his toes, then gave up and broke into a daring clattering gallop down the length of the room. 'There, I knew it!' cried the security man. The boy had tripped at a corner and landed face down on the floor. He was howling like a banshee. The mother flew back up the room after him and the young man followed slowly. But long before he reached them the crying stopped. He watched the scolding and the soothing with a certain distant envy. Already the child was up on his feet. Now he was walking off by himself staring down at a red knee and a scarred boot with the pride of one who has stroked the tails of wild beasts and got away with it.

'Look how quickly they get over it!' exclaimed the security man. 'Really, for all the worrying you do – they get over everything! Our mother was the same with us at that age, and my sister's just the same with hers. But they're tough – really tough. Look at him! Determined nothing's going to hurt him now or ever, that's what he is!'

He didn't look at the girl as he said this but straight ahead into the glass of a picture frame where he watched her winding a long scarf about her neck, ready to move off. A warning buzz came from the entrance hall beyond the marbles.

'We're just going,' she said, moving towards the boy.

'No need to hurry. You've got lots of time.'

He stood watching as the mother took the child by the hand, as they walked down lines of paintings past good dreams and nightmares, then back through the archway again into the Weapons room, moving quickly on by smooth and jagged blades, past flying cylinders and metal globes of war and on through a hundred knife-points, a hundred gun-points . . .

'But they're tough, tough—' murmured the security man staring abstractedly after them. He was confused. He scarcely remembered who or what had been tough. And the two beyond were receding like creatures in a dream – not fragile, yet seeming totally exposed, disarming and unarmed. Now they were moving through the food displays between cornstacks and fruit baskets and heaped plates, through photos of rich farmland and dried up desert, past bulge-eyed famine babies and smiling feasters. He caught a last glimpse of them in the furthest room where for an instant the child hung back, turning a warm, enquiring head towards a reasoning head of stone. Then they were gone.

The security man walked slowly through the building, switching off lights. Certain lights in the entrance hall would be on all night but, far behind, the dinosaurs had withdrawn into the shadows, the colours in the paintings turned to black. The separate details of the food display – crops, seeds and fruit, the figures in the photos and the posters – had merged together. The marbles' outline was blurred and broken. The man's own skin, reflected from the windows as he passed, looked grey. Now there was almost total darkness through the building. What little glare there was remained in the hard, cold surfaces of metal skin inside the Weapons room.

# A Field in Space

'YEARS AGO,' SAID Sullivan, 'I was at a formal gathering of persons who were for the most part almost strangers to one another. Some enormous committee had been formed. I've forgotten now what it was all about. There were at least forty of us and naturally they were going to subdivide it into smaller and smaller committees – you know the kind of thing. Anyway we were all there – teachers, administrators, lecturers, professors, clerics and social workers, representatives from this and that organization. I remember the catering bit came into it too, for there were glasses and coffee cups on the side, and a few cheese wafers – that kind of thing. As I say what it was all about I can't remember now. It may have been about making money for something or other. A very good cause anyway. The thing escapes me.'

'How can the purpose escape you when you remember the cheese wafers?' said his friend Turner.

'It often happens. As I said it's years ago. Sometimes you only remember odd details. For instance, the main thing, in fact the only thing, I particularly remember about this meeting was the field.'

'I see,' said Turner thoughtfully. 'A field, was it? I pictured this meeting in the city. It shows how the mind runs in grooves. Why shouldn't it be in the country after all? Good idea! A picnicking committee.'

'But we *were* in a city,' said Sullivan, 'and in a large boardroom round a huge polished table – you must know the sort of place. They usually have portraits round the walls, going right back to wigs, and often cups and medals in a glass case donated to people for special services. Even now I can visualize right behind me on the sideboard this huge silver platter with dates on it.'

'Why dates specially? Were they all Arabs? It was a meeting about North Sea oil, I suppose.'

'I'm talking about dates engraved in the silver,' said Sullivan, 'giving the month and year it was presented or something.'

'Anyway, you said a field interested you,' said his friend. 'Was it a picture of a field? You'd be unlikely to see one from a city window, I suppose. Though I know there are places even in the centre of town where you can see green grass – and I'm very thankful to live in a city where that's still possible.'

'Wait a bit,' said Sullivan. 'After the main discussion the thing began to relax very slightly – if you can call it that. Professionals hate to be seen relaxing in public in case they're thought to be not absolutely on the ball. Being a mixed crowd, it was in fact rather sticky at first. People slowly began to ask one another what their professions, occupations, interests were. Oh, nothing personal of course. Good heavens, no! Women, wives, children, sex, salaries, job expectancy, life expectancy and all the rest of it were kept strictly in the background. This meeting seemed a most secret society as these things tend to be. The atmosphere was discreet, very cautious, intensely subdued. Afterwards a silence fell and our chairman – a kind and charming fellow – leaned forward and said courteously to someone at the opposite side of the table, "And *your* field, Mr Peterson? Can you tell us something about that?"

'A natural enough question. Most of us had answered up reasonably and promptly to the field question. You remember the kind of thing: "At present I'm working with Dr Sneddon on Demography and Roman Genetics, but I've been asked to take over a rather broader field on my own in the autumn," or I remember a rather melancholy and reserved young woman telling us that she "was engaged in a study of psychometric techniques as applied in tests of intelligence, temperament and personality and the application of psychological methods to problems of human relations." Of course there were more direct answers. I remember one formidable woman barking out brusquely "Waves and Vibrations" – without batting an eyelid – to be as brusquely echoed by the classical scholar beside her who proudly uttered the word "Hexameters!" and left it at that. One very young man from Theology – looking little more than a schoolboy – promptly gave his field as "Christian Ethics as relating to marriage and the family, social and industrial life, war and peace." There was a fairly long pause after that. It seemed that this stripling had pretty much hogged the whole field of life for himself. A pause, then, until someone bravely chipped in that he was attempting to redress the balance between something or other on one side and something else on the other. I can't remember what the things were at this distance, I'm afraid. What I *do* remember was that as luck would have it, poor fellow, we never heard the outcome of the balancing business because as he leaned back rather sharply to demonstrate it one whole leg of the chair split under him. It wasn't enough to throw him or even stop him talking – you'll agree, I think that very little stops talk in our particular fields except, perhaps, a plus 5 on the Richter scale earthquake. But I will admit it was unsettling – particularly the sudden splintering crack of wood. Such things are supposed to break the ice, of course, but I doubt if this chap wanted any ice broken on his behalf, and it wasn't long before he rose to his feet with those familiar words: "my apologies . . . but another meeting to attend . . ." Well, as I've told you, eventually our chairman leaned across the table to this man, Peterson – a solid-looking person with a lined, brown face and those keen very pale blue eyes that are romantically supposed to belong to the seafaring kind, though they are often to be found amongst city business men and just as commonly seen in computer technicians as in birdwatchers. This man – silent up till now – responded enthusiastically to the field question. "I wouldn't say my field has been absolutely successful," he said. "I don't produce a lot from the ground. On the whole it's a silt soil, but with too much sand and not enough clay to be really fertile. As you know, if the soil feels gritty it's a sand. If it's sticky and silky it's a clay, if sticky *and* gritty it's sandy silt or sandy clay loam. Loam grittiness mostly means sand, silkiness means silt and stickiness means clay. But you don't have to take it from me. I'm quoting from a book that happens to mean a lot to me."

'As a matter of fact it was clear the others had no intention of taking it from him. Even the mention of a book quotation cut no ice in this company. It was a book they hadn't read and they didn't want to hear about it.

'"Luckily," Peterson went on, "even though the soil isn't all that productive, I've got a fine strip of birch and pinewood on the north side, and a good stretch of heath to the south. I shouldn't be surprised if I don't take up bee-keeping one day. But of course there are lots of ways of being productive – it doesn't necessarily have to be turnips or grapes or whatever. Stars or bees – that was *my* choice." The company looked dazed. Was he comparing a bee-group with a star-group? And what was the connection? In our various fields most of us dealt continually with con-nections and comparisons. Coincidences, cross purposes and catastrophic happenings weren't exactly our line. And talking of lines, some of us preferred to speak about our "line of country" rather than our "field". Somehow it made for a wider and more impressive bit of landscape.

'"Well, I decided it would be stars," Peterson told us. "In other words, the fields of the sky."

'Now don't imagine that because this was a countryman he was any more modest than the rest of us. Not a bit of it. He too liked the sound of his own voice. He spoke very slowly and deliberately. He made himself heard all right, though I noticed he didn't look directly at anyone but over their heads towards the window. Perhaps it was as well, for there were certain very irritable eyes fixed on him. Some people hadn't yet spoken of their own fields and were willing him to stop talking. All the same, some of the linguistic people – and I count myself amongst them – had been listening rather carefully to his "sand, silt, silky" bit. I think, in spite of themselves, they were impressed with the alliteration.

' "Well, stars it was to be," Peterson informed us again. "I figured bees and honey could wait to sweeten my old age. So I erected a small telescope in one corner of the field. It was mounted of course – the main pillar set in concrete. Not only that – but a shed to contain the instrument and one that could divide clear in two when the viewing was on. I got help with it of course, and a great deal of time and money went into it – a lot more than setting up beehives in a patch of heather, for instance. Oh yes, it all took time. But then – what hours and hours of pleasure I've had with it!"

'I remember there was an uneasy stirring amongst our company,' Sullivan went on. 'Those "hours and hours of pleasure" made them feel embarrassed. Even our chairman – never anything but kindly and encouraging – flinched slightly at the rapturous tones of the man as though he were about to describe some outrageously romantic encounter. Half the room sat in disapproving silence with a nervous tenseness in the rest of us most of whom didn't know a planet from a star or a star from the fairy light on top of a Christmas tree.

' "So I suppose you'll be watching for Halley's Comet coming in one of these nights" ' said a Careers Adviser. Personally I was glad to see Peterson wasn't to be patronized. "Not due for a long time yet," he replied. "I've no intention of sitting out there for a couple of years. And it doesn't whizz past like a firework on Guy Fawkes night, you know." The adviser sat still under the reproof, drawing on her warm gloves as though ready to sit it out herself through all the winter nights as punishment.

' "The first thing that strikes you when you look at the sky through a telescope is the sudden increase in the number of stars in the sky," our fieldman told us. "One moment you're walking across the field in the dark, looking up at a few brilliant stars and constellations with patches of black between or sometimes behind it, all this faint, grey seeding of distant stars, almost invisible. But the moment you put your eye to the telescope you're shot out into the depths of space, so to speak, as though in a rocket. It's an awful moment. Hair-raising! Not a thing you ever get used to – even the astronomers will tell you that. Suddenly – the number and brightness of those stars! Even the dim, grey seeds begin to glitter. Well, I can tell you, some nights I'm almost thankful to be down to earth again and walking back home across the field in the dark."

'It was difficult,' said Sullivan, 'to say whether the rest of the room were envious or scornful of Peterson's particular field of interest. Besides, it was getting late and rather dim in the room, though none of us thought to put on the lights. We weren't even clear to one another. All our sharp outlines had disappeared in the last half hour as though at once dazzled and darkened by the brilliance and blackness of space. We were on our feet ready to go. The curtains weren't drawn and one or two flung a nervous glance at the sky as they drifted off. Yes, they drifted back to their fields.

'For a time I couldn't see their fields,' remarked Sullivan meditatively. 'I couldn't see the field of Economics. I couldn't see the Administrative field. That evening the field of Christian Ethics looked decidedly foggy. The Waves and Vibrations were flat and static as an ironing-board. The psychologist was walking back alone and silently into her field of Human Relationships. Even my own field wasn't absolutely clear as though there were a low ground-mist hanging over it. Peterson went out with us of course. But he appeared to have a field he could walk very freely in, for he was tramping steadily forward – his boots no doubt gritting on the silty, sandy soil with its small lumps of chalk. It didn't seem so late to us. We were hastening towards familiar cafés where we might find food and drink. But round Peterson's head it appeared to be still black night. For like a hollowed Hallowe'en turnip-head with its candle, his brow shone, transparent, as if – straight down through the first lights of the city – the uncanny stellar radiance had pierced inside his skull.'

# Out of Order

A SHORT TIME in any part of the city and a visit to one or
two of its larger stores was enough to bring up the count.
Today it was seven phone boxes, five weighing-machines,
three sets of traffic lights, a couple of stamp-machines,
three escalators, four lifts, one platform ticket appliance, an
automatic hand-dryer and a swing door. Nowadays Collier
had to remind himself fairly often that OUT OF ORDER
signs had become a natural part of every city scene. They
were meant to be read reasonably and coolly like any other
sign and each citizen was to get the message quickly and
pass on to his own business. They were not meant to be
studied and pondered over like a set of hieroglyphics.
There were difficulties of course. Already Collier had made
life awkward enough for himself by being an unashamed
and critical reader of public words. He brooded on words –
loved them, respected and encouraged them – was unnerved, despairing, infuriated by them – never taking them
for granted whether they came in thousands or in threes. So
was it ridiculous for him to imagine that the three words
OUT OF ORDER were expressed in one way or another
more and more often and more and more boldly around
the place? 'You could be right,' said his friend Taylor who,
though not a brooding addict of words, had keen sight and
a critical concern for all the changes of city life. 'These
weighing-machines, for instance, have been out of order for
weeks if not months.' They agreed that this, though hard on
weight-watchers, was not a tragedy. Nevertheless it was
strange how an accumulation of non-tragic things could
lower the spirits. They had come across one of the out-of-

order escalators in a hardware store. It was difficult to describe what was so dispiriting about an unmoving moving staircase. They both had full use of their legs. They weren't so decrepit, were they, that they couldn't walk up in the usual way? 'No, it's the dead look of this metal contraption,' said Collier. 'Now it hardly even looks like a stairway. Its sole purpose was to move. It's simply a useless machine, and obviously useless things turn ugly.'

'Better keep it in proportion,' said his friend. 'For instance, take a good look at that phone box there on your right. That man in there is managing to get through. If you look carefully you'll see he's actually smiling.'

'I'm not too bothered about the smile. Is he *hearing* anything?'

'Not only that. He's talking too. So it's the stunning pleasure of finding something in perfect working order you've got to begin thinking about. That makes life easier for a start, and is something your all-the-year-round optimist knows very little about. Expect nothing and be astounded!'

'So we remain passive pessimists? Nothing easier, it's already, isn't it, our reputation with foreign visitors?' They walked on silently for a while. It was still early in the day. They were going towards the big black-on-white calamities on news-boards and the solid blocks of newspaper on the pavement, held down by stones – for there was a breeze. The neatly-angled appearance of the papers on the ground and the spotless, rustling bouquet in the arms of the newsvendor had a peculiar attraction. There was something good here to feel, touch and see. Most people liked the smell of the tacky, fresh print, said Taylor. Yes, it was this 'new' business, Collier admitted, that he'd always enjoyed – physically new to the senses, with the promise of something new – or so one hoped – for the mind.

He was not alone in this. There was satisfaction on the faces of most people when being handed a folded, pristine paper from the sheaf or while watching the weighted block on the pavement being untied. There was a ritual going on here. It was the beginning of a new day. However, if the ritual was disturbed by strikes, by hold-ups in delivery, breakdowns in machinery, late trains and vans – the loss of papers could be felt physically as though the public body had been deprived of some clean bit of its daily clothing to wrap itself in. 'And people can be very particular about the folds,' said Collier. 'If a page drops out, for instance, or if the whole thing gets out of order before they've read the stuff – they're in a fury. No wonder the servants in the old days would sometimes iron a page or two if by any chance they'd got crumpled before breakfast. Otherwise it would have been as bad as laying out a creased shirt on the master's bed.'

The two friends bought different papers and walked on down the street. There were some objects too high up for out-of-order signs. Five of the city's main clocks had been stopped for weeks – three on church towers, one at a traffic roundabout, and one above a large shop-front. 'No hurry to mend them of course,' remarked Taylor despondently. 'Isn't everyone supposed to carry his own time on his wrist? And those who don't had better start to reckon it by the old sun and shadow method.' For a while they went on silently, and silently Taylor pointed to an out-of-order self-service petrol pump and to a second non-functioning revolving door leading to an Insurance office. 'Never mind Insurance,' said Collier. 'I've been told there's a leading fashion store where one lavatory door in the six is always out of order. Without fail. Is it a law that six functioning doors in a row are too many?'

One or two buildings in the city obviously felt themselves a cut above the others even in their out-of-order signs, and there were places where an actual apology was offered. Towards its closing-time they found themselves in one of the large central banks. While Collier cashed his cheque –

Taylor wandered about examining the metals and marbles of the place. A small area of the floor was barred off to clients and OUT OF COMMISSION was the sign here with, in addition: WE APOLOGIZE FOR ANY INCON-VENIENCE WE MAY HAVE CAUSED OUR CLI-ENTS. In a way the apology, rare as it was and totally lacking on lavatory doors and phone boxes, seemed wasted here. Few persons on their way to the manager's office seemed to care whether they were walking on perfect tiling or cracked tiling. A nearby cashier saw Taylor looking in that direction. 'Yes, it's taking a long time, isn't it? Those tiles cost money. Money's the problem these days. Always money, money, money!' Taylor nodded. He watched, fascinated, as the young man took up a wad of banknotes, thick and soft as a sliced loaf, as he bound up the limp blue fivers with elastic bands and divided the crisp brown ten pound notes, the one from the other with a snapping flick of finger and thumb. Up and down the counter men and women were going through the same actions, deftly lifting the tops from towers of coins or swiftly rebuilding new lines of silver towers along the counter. Occasionally someone might query a figure in his bankbook. One cashier might consult another. It was even possible that somewhere in the building an out-of-order computer would be reeling off wrong figures. But on the whole the counter-work ap-peared to be running smoothly. Whatever invisible break-downs there might be the visible cash itself was in perfect order. They moved on down the street to a post office where, on the pavement, they found a third stamp-machine out of order. 'And has been for the last hundred times I've passed,' said Collier. 'Surely one should put in a polite complaint.' Taylor smiled. More often than not Collier's polite complaints were delivered in a voice rasping with indignation. The girl at the counter said yes, they knew about the machine – everyone knew about it. And there was nothing to be done about it at the moment – a matter of maintenance staff being shorthanded. And above all, of course, a matter of money. 'In any case,' she added, 'people can always buy their stamps *inside*.'

'But what about stamps after hours?'

'After what?' said the girl, leaning across.

'Stamps at night, for instance – people writing letters and wishing to post them late.' The girl glanced up at Collier. There was something about this look that made the posting of night letters seem very unnecessary indeed, even down-right immoral. 'You can rest assured that everyone here is perfectly aware of that stamp-machine,' she repeated and bent again to her task. There was a good deal of guilt hanging about the post office now, but it was a guilt confined solely to the front of the counter like a heavy gas that had drifted and settled there. It was clear, however, that Collier would not rest assured. Perhaps he did not rest at night at all. Even Taylor, in the brooding atmosphere of the place, seemed to see a totally different image of his friend coming up. A nonresting man rising from the midst of his sleeping family and making his way through the dark house to his desk in order to write a shady, night-time letter. Then comes the punishing revelation – not a stamp in the house! Now for the devious walk by unlit buildings and silent streets to the stamp-machine – and the second punishment falls like some heavenly hatchet stroke. OUT OF ORDER.

The two moved on. Once out into the street Collier's image seemed to change again. He complained of his arthritic shoulder. 'Look out,' warned Taylor, 'or you'll find the OUT OF ORDER round your own neck – though of course there'd be plenty of people, young and old, to join you with labels like it.' They agreed there were lots to choose from and more and more as time went on – OUT OF WORK, OUT OF TOUCH, OUT OF PLACE, OUT OF CONDITION, OUT OF LINE, OUT OF DATE – all calling out for repair, a job, a companion, in need of a bolt-hole or a place in the sun. The town would be jammed with suppliants.

'Well there's no lack of committees, societies and the like, to help.'

'It's us I'm talking about – the company of the street. How do we stop ourselves falling apart – seizing up like clocks and escalators?'

It was a fine street they were in. It had been much praised. At this hour there were a fair number of people around. In the evenings, however, apart from the pubs, there was a strange lack of groups about. Except for a few bands of young persons and two or three couples, men and women seldom got together. 'What do you expect?' Taylor demanded. 'Tables on the pavement under striped awnings? Rousing talk as the sun goes down? Passionate argument as the moon comes up? This is the north, isn't it? It's the wind, you understand.'

'Oh certainly – sooner or later this dark wind gets the blame – and for everything lacking in our particular scene and temperament. But open up your newspaper in this much-vaunted hurricane – one look at the letters – as likely as not it's the English, you'll find, who are to get the blame, and sometimes from the sound of it every man and woman across the border.'

'Our history!' cried his friend defiantly, raising a clenched fist.

'Oh it's often a just complaint all right. And sometimes the shout sounds good. But there's another side, and "girning" gives the sound of it.'

They marched on together, noticing a few more non-working machines, a few more persons, dejected but upright. Gradually they slowed down. 'Where does it come from?' demanded Collier, '—the idea of order – this unknown, perfect state of things that makes us feel askew. Can you get some sense of it? In the memory, is it – or where?' They had taken a short cut through a secluded park and now they were walking silently on grass between glittering hedges of dark leaves and borders of sharp-scented herbs, still wet from a stormy night. They crossed the place without a word and, as they neared the gate, looked back. There was a certain completeness about the place. It was sunless, silent. There was no movement of tree or plant. Only the shadows of black storm-clouds moved slowly across the place casting a strange but brilliant darkness through which transparent cups of white and scarlet tulips floated – single, separate, on the air. The two men sat down on a bench, took out their papers and glanced at the headlines for a moment. Then they opened them out, folded them back along the centre line, read again, folded them horizontally and creased them down. All across the city people would be making much the same movements at this hour. 'Well it's an important part of the ritual,' said Collier. 'So here it is – this paper – first, the actual look of the thing – clean, pressed, cool and stylish, and then    the real meat inside.' Today the meat was raw. There was the smell of blood inside. The eye skidded helplessly on and on from the pile-up of guns and bombs to party preparations and the pile-up of presents – from the poisonings and pollutions of sea and river to Babycare and bathtime. There were days when they were appalled by the weird, mesmeric nature of their reading – the veering, flickering movement of the eyes from catastrophe to catastrophe. When and how would they dig their heels in? But the wanton eyes went on their way, giving a never-ending illusion that, by this simple devouring of print, something was being done.

The men were now making for the different suburbs where they lived. They took a long way round to get out of the city, first skirting a housing-scheme and further on a deserted playground. Chaos had set its whirling vortex here. Up-turned litterbins had flung their mouldy food and burst bags around the place. Tins and old vegetables had rolled in the wind as far as the swings. Fat, black sacks had been dragged here from nearby streets to have their throats slit. Dozens of bottles had been smashed against the lavatory wall and a row of others, propped along its base – jagged ends up – had been a target for the stones that littered the place. Friday night's chip-wrappers had been wedged between the railings and paper bags stuck on the spikes. Newspaper had gone wild here in the night as though a page had been taken from every street basket, while long, coloured strips had been torn from the advertisements and theatre posters of the shopping quarter. For good measure the swing chains had been looped about with yards of pink and blue toilet paper. For a time these various decorations prevented the incomers from studying the ground more closely. Now they looked down. A cloud moved from the sun, and the asphalt glittered sharply. Thin spears, needles and pins of broken glass lay here. The larger wedges – thick triangles, oblongs and the circles from the base of bottles – lay like a lethal jigsaw under the slide. Near the edges of the playground, where the asphalt had been worn down, fragments of green and yellow lay embedded in grey gravel as though the better to show off a diamond brightness. The place crunched and cracked underfoot as they walked about. Birds sang, the swings creaked gently and a breeze rustled the paper loops. Collier bent suddenly to pick up a great green splinter, drew a sodden carrier bag from between the railings and dropped the piece of glass into it. Taylor – a conscientious and self-conscious man – crunched uneasily on towards the gates without looking back. It was this hopeless business of Doing Good – and worse – to be seen doing it by every passer-by on the road. Not great good, of course – no – trivial good, infinitesimal – almost meaningless in its smallness. He came from a long line of persons who had done a great deal of good in the community. But not by stealth. With lots of noise in fact. 'Don't start it!' he called, glancing nervously round to where Collier was still quietly working on the glitter round the swings. 'There's no end to that! Leave it, leave it! You'll need a sieve, a shovel and a pair of gloves to get through that lot. Leave it to the authorities!' He watched in embarrassment as Collier continued to pick up splinters and drop them into his bag. Of course it was easier for him with his face, thought Taylor, than if he had himself attempted it. Collier had a face that looked at all times more interested than concerned, more curious than conscientious. He was picking up the stuff systematically – dealing first with large spears and chunks. Now and then he held up a big splinter to the sky and squinted at it intently as though through a prism. In this particular light he looked a cool character, even cold. Taylor wondered – not for the first time – if he was not rather unfeeling. Not ruthless. Certainly not. But did he, at the end of the day, have all that much concern for the bare feet of children? Moreover he gave the impression that he would go out of his way only if some job had a fascination for him. Still he *had* gone out of his way, his friend admitted it. Collier was now working down to the slightly smaller bits of glass. 'And for heaven's sake watch those splinters,' said Taylor. 'Your fingers will be in shreds before you've done the job.' Collier held up a stiletto of emerald glass and studied it with the curiosity of a connoisseur of daggers. Taylor was silent, listening to the creak of swings, the crunch of stone and glass and the occasional ring of broken bottle against bottle. Already a couple of cyclists had dismounted and were leaning against the railings, hoping for a pantomime.

'But of course I happen to believe that this is *not* the way to do it,' said Taylor at last.

'Not the way to pick up splinters? Well, I haven't a pair of forceps with me, you see. No forceps, no tweezers, not even gloves.'

'. . . To set the world in order,' Taylor went on. '*Not* the way – not this chip by chip, splinter by splinter, pin by pin method. To my mind it's self-indulgent, petty and inefficient, dangerous even.'

'At the moment I don't know any other way. Certainly

I'm self-indulgent, inefficient, dangerously lazy as far as the world goes. All the same this does happen to be a playground, not the globe. Until the authorities, as you call them, take over, I can amuse myself as I like.'

'I can't stand around swings and slides all day.'

'Then don't wait for me. I'll see you on Monday.'

Taylor walked on a dozen or so steps and found a large splinter under his foot. He picked it up gingerly between finger and thumb and walked back. Collier got up from his crouching position and held out his bag.

'Oh stop jingling that thing in front of me like a church collection bag! And don't imagine,' said Taylor, about to drop the splinter in, 'that this gives me any particular satisfaction.'

'Of course not. Nevertheless, it's rather an interesting specimen you've picked up. Look at the way it's split along that line.'

'I'm not interested in glass and its properties. And I'm not going to help you in your great task. I shall leave you in your playground.'

'But of course. You're a man of principle!'

'I am simply making a small contribution . . .'

'Not small at all. That's a splendid great bit of glass you've got there . . .'

'A small contribution,' Taylor persisted in an exasperated voice, while with a covert and commending glance he took in the growing bulk of Collier's splinter bag, '. . . a ludicrous, totally useless, pointless, infinitesimal contribution to world order.'

# Bulbs

'I THINK I ought to tell you – moving from place to place as I do in my work – I tend to have great difficulty in getting adequate bulbs,' said Mr Springer to the proprietress of the Brackenbank boarding house not long after he had arrived there – the small hotel having been full up. If she found this remark unexpected Mrs Palmer showed no surprise. Certainly it was unlike the usual things guests brought up in the first half-hour – pleasantries about district and weather, comments on the journey and even mention of the sort of supper they preferred. But she had long ago discovered the importance of taking no notice whatever of quirky remarks or prejudices. Instead she turned at once and opened the cupboard of the sitting-room where they were standing. It was an unusually large, deep cupboard. There was a whiff of old boots, old dogs, old gas and an earthy smell which was soon explained when she gestured to the row of shapes on a shelf above. She emerged with one in each hand – identical bowls filled to the brim with black fibre. 'And not a single failure amongst the lot of them since I started years ago. Hyacinth, iris, narcissus – and if there's any art in putting bulbs in bowls I've certainly got it. Well, I'm sorry you've no luck with *your* bulbs. I suggest you experiment with different kinds.'

'No,' said Springer. 'It's light-bulbs I'm talking about – and in particular, of course, bulbs by the bed.'

Mrs Palmer seemed not to hear the word 'light' and kept poking around the dark stuff murmuring, 'Try different bulbs, buy different *makes*.'

Springer tried again. 'Light-bulbs, Mrs Palmer. Experiment's no good if you happen to be a reader and stuck with a 20 watt.'

'If you're a what?'

'I read in bed. Of course when I was younger I could take the 20s and the 40s but not any longer. The print's got poorer, I've noticed, and the eyes along with it.'

But light had reached Mrs Palmer. 'So you read in bed?' She gave him a look which suggested that beds down the ages had been designed for birth, for death, for marriage and even for single persons sleeping the sleep of the just. But reading was not in this category. Further, she managed to convey that reading in bed was an immoral relationship with a book and merited no light but the dimmest being shed upon it. Nevertheless her guest persisted.

'I've tried removing the shade up there, as I've often had to do in other bedrooms, but without success, I'm afraid.'

'I should hope not indeed! Do you know who made that lampshade and every other lampshade in the house? My husband made it and painted it, just as he made and painted the wastepaper baskets. He was artistic from the tips of his fingers to the very hairs of his head. I treasure every item he has ever made. He would have been heart-broken if he'd known that any visitor would think so little of these things that he might wish to remove or even destroy them.'

Mr Springer was silent. He did not wish to enter into the theology of the thing though he thought it unlikely that Mr Palmer, wherever he was, would have his eyes fixed forever upon the baskets and lampshades of 10, Lime Terrace. He said, 'I suppose it's just that I've got used to the brighter lights in certain hotels.'

'Exactly!' Mrs Palmer agreed triumphantly. 'And this, you see, is not a hotel. It is a home!' She seemed to remember she was still holding the bulb-bowls and she put them back amongst the others in the dark cupboard, saying as she came out, 'These are not properly up yet and the light disturbs them. It hinders growth, you know.' Mr Springer who was fully grown himself and even past the peak was again silent. His landlady waited as though for argument, but getting none took leave of him with the parting words: 'That may be what is wrong with your bulbs, Mr Springer. Perhaps you've been giving them too much light too early.'

For a good many years Springer had travelled as an adviser on strong metal draught excluders for old houses. The house he was in at the moment was not old but it was very cold. Even apart from the light problem there was no possibility of sitting in the bedroom. He was forced, therefore, after an early supper, to sit with his book under the dim, red-shaded standard lamp in the sitting-room. This was no better than his bed light but at least he could get his head so close in under the shade that he appeared to be sporting a scarlet boater. Nevertheless his eyes began to feel the strain. To make things worse he was reading a History of Lighthouses. He read of glittering lenses, of blinding and revolving lights which sent the beam further and further out with each decade. Mr Springer, his eyes itching with imagined glare, at last laid down his book.

It was at this point in the evening that the only other guests in the house joined him – two elderly sisters who had come to the district for a few days to visit their widowed brother who had been ill. They had been out all day, they said, shopping for him, tidying his house, entertaining his visitors and cooking his meals. Now they were only too thankful to rest. But rest of course did not mean passivity. 'I must have something in my hands, no matter what,' said the elder of the two, drawing a hook and a rucked collar of white crochet from her bag and giving a frowning scrutiny to its loops and chains. Her sister silently reached for the newspaper on a side table and moved nearer the lamp. And now there was a belated show of gallantry on Mr Springer's part – an offer of his lamp-lit seat, a useless offer to shift chairs and tilt shades. Very little could come from these moves and in each case they were politely refused. Since Mrs Palmer had retired to the back of the house Springer now went further. 'How about my making a quick tour of the rest of the place to find brighter bulbs?' At first the others maintained there was no need for it, but after a while, the one drew her hook from a line of ravelled loops and the other laid down the paper unread. They turned hopefully toward Mr Springer.

It turned out to be more of a lightning tour than he'd expected. Upstairs there were three empty bedrooms, a bathroom and a drying-cupboard. Downstairs, apart from their sitting-room, there was a bedroom and a dining-room. But from each room, as he switched on, came an ever dimmer circle of light. In the third and best bedroom upstairs Mr Palmer's painted peacocks and fountains had obscured what little light had managed to seep through the shade. The towels and sheets of the drying-cupboard had been allowed the strongest bulb of all, but even so it could only be called the brightest of the dim. The bathroom's unreachable grey light, boxed into an overhanging corner of the ceiling, had been designed only for those who detested their own bodies.

'No good,' he said as he came back quickly to the sitting-room.

'All the upstairs rooms – the drying-cupboard too?' asked the elder sister. Mr. Springer nodded.

'Downstairs? The dining-room?'

'Only that soft pink light above the table. Well, I suppose what more should one want for eating? It is the palate, after all, that differentiates spinach from cabbage – not the eyes.'

'So that's the end of it,' she said. 'We must sit here for the next two days, doing absolutely nothing, reading nothing.'

'We could talk,' said her sister tentatively.

'With nothing in our hands?'

'Well, tomorrow we can rake the streets for bulbs.'

'Had you forgotten it's Sunday? Unless you remove the electric candles from a church.' There was a short silence. Then she turned her head. 'And that cupboard over there?'

'Bulbs,' said Springer. 'Bowls of them. Little chance you'll find your light in there. No harm in making sure.'

They cried out as he touched the switch and a brilliant light struck the cupboard. 'At least 100 watt!' exclaimed Springer, 'perhaps 200!'

The others fluttered towards it like grey moths to a searchlight beam.

'And all wasted,' said the elder sister staring enviously at the bowls under the naked glare. 'But what can you do? Can you unscrew it? Can you reach it even?'

For there was nothing but a soft, low chair to stand on and two rickety stools. Springer tried for some time to reach the bulb by putting stool on chair and stool on stool. But it was no good. 'No, you will have to leave it,' said the sister at last. 'We are wasting our time. Better come out and shut the door. We have seen the light. That has to be enough.'

Though they went back to their seats they had been loath to switch off. A brilliance streamed through the cracks of the cupboard and round the edges of the closed door. Light stared at them through the keyhole.

'But what nonsense this is!' cried the crocheter, rising suddenly to her feet before ten minutes had gone by. 'You do what you like. I, for one, am taking my chair and my work in there. I am not spoiling my eyes to please anyone!' She gathered up her bag and balls of cotton. She refused help with her chair. Soon she was linking white holes under the light.

'What does she mean, "to please anyone"?' murmured her sister. 'I am not pleased she should spoil her eyes any more than I want to ruin my own.' There was a slight pause. 'I will help you in with your chair,' said Springer, rising from his corner. He carried it into the cupboard and she sat down silently beside her sister. Springer returned to his lamp and his lighthouses. It was very quiet in the house. Now and then from his dim, acolyte's seat, he glanced at the cupboard and the two brilliant figures, now exalted like goddesses.

'Mr Springer, please don't hesitate if you wish to join us,' said the kinder voice. 'Either in front or behind – there is plenty of room in here. It would not hinder us in the least.' Mr Springer carried his chair into the cupboard, disturbing the others only to take his place behind. In front he could even stretch his legs. Bowls surrounded them on either side. '. . . only for a short time,' he murmured, though he was not in the habit of talking to plants.

'What's that?' said the older sister sharply.

'I was simply telling them they would not have to take the light for long. We'll all be in bed before midnight.'

'I daresay,' she replied. 'All the same, I think I've as much value as hyacinths or lilies.' The others didn't argue the matter, and the rest of the evening passed peacefully enough until it was time to go upstairs.

Their second evening in the cupboard was less peaceful. Mr Springer, inclined to be pessimistic by nature, had half-expected it, believing that peace, brightness and silence together could not last. It was half past nine. The chair-moving had gone smoothly as before. They had been settled in their places for almost an hour when the door of the sitting-room opened. But it was Mrs Palmer who had the greater shock. She came forward, and stopped aghast at the spectacle of bright people. 'My God – what's this! What's going on? The three of you! Come out of there. You are *hiding*!'

'In a sense – yes,' said Springer, rising with dignity. 'We have taken refuge from the dark and gloom.'

'So – theatricals! And much, much more to it than that, I daresay.' Intent to flush out a séance or even a trio of witches, Mrs Palmer drew near.

'We are saving our eyes,' said Springer.

'Exactly what damage has been done in here?' she said.

'No damage.' The elder sister now rose to her feet. 'But if our eyes have suffered – now that's a different matter. The costs and damages will all be yours. If proper lights are not to be supplied under your roof, Mrs Palmer, we can expect, of course, a very substantial reduction on our bills.'

'A swingeing cut,' added Springer thoughtfully, '– amounting, most likely to a total non-bill – seeing the gap between what's promised and what's given can interest lawyers.'

Mrs Palmer swayed a little where she stood, but her far-seeing eyes swept the cupboard. 'And the bulbs? What about them? Night after night exposed to the light! Of course you have shifted them around. Have you broken any bowls?'

'Certainly not. But your two guests here value themselves as much as crocuses or tulips.'

'And you, Mr Springer? What kind of flower or weed do you rate yourself with? Well, I can't stand here all night. You will certainly not sit there. And what, if I may ask, do you intend to do for the rest of your stay in this house?'

'Why, Mrs Palmer, that is very simple. We'll be doing nothing. We'll be waiting – waiting for different bulbs, different *makes*.'

Just before suppertime the following evening the guests, returning from various outings, met at the corner of the street. All three had an air of expectancy. They were not disappointed. As they approached it the house was gradually switched on. 'She has been watching for us,' said Springer as slits of light appeared between the downstairs curtains. A few minutes later unfamiliar globes shone from the windows above. Through the opaque, bubbled glass of the bathroom a ray appeared like the headlight in a fog. They went upstairs as soon as they got in and emerged from their bedrooms with the same story. Suddenly on every bedside table the bulbs had bloomed extravagantly. Down-stairs it was the same. In the bowl above the dining-room table there was a dazzling white flower. Under the lamp-shade in the sitting-room – a brilliant bud.

'Well it is nothing to write home about,' said the elder one cautiously as the others exclaimed. 'But compared to yesterday I will admit the place has sprouted like a fun garden.'

'I could sit here all night,' said Springer as he took up his book, 'and I believe there is not a single dark corner in the entire house. *We* are flourishing down here at any rate. Who wants to sleep?'

But behind them the cupboard was in darkness. The rows of bulbs – equally determined on flourishing – lay deeply, thankfully asleep.

# Shoe in the Sand

'KATE AND I are going home the long way round,' Paula told the group of young picnickers as she got up with her friend. 'We're going to look for fossils round by the red rocks. This is the shore for them. Great fossil fish were found here once – fins, jaws, tails and all.'

'Yes, that was years and years ago,' said one of the party. 'You'll not find anything now but small grey pebbles with specks and dents in them. If you're very lucky I suppose you *might* find a fraction of a fin.'

'We're going anyway,' said Paula firmly. The two girls were aware that the moment they left the group the place at once appeared darker, colder. Of course the sun was beginning to fade from the shore at the other end, but the real reason was that the company behind them had already started to move away – taking the quick route back. The two girls looked round once. The bright figures of these friends in their summer dresses were vanishing up into the dunes like flowers picked off, one after the other, by a cold wind. There was a premonition of winter in the air. Resolutely the two set off, facing the darker sky.

This eastern shore on the coast of Berwickshire had indeed been a place rich in fossils. Far down that coast the city's museum showed the bony, strong-jawed fishes under glass – showed other fish like splintered flowers, and thick-fleshed plants resembling animals. Cases of shells and pebbles lay there, crusted with the spikes and beaks of ancient sea creatures. People still searched this shore – found badges, belts and buttons, found clips, coins and contraceptives, but seldom the rare fossil. The girls knew they were unlikely to find anything of value on this beach, but they walked slowly, all the same, as if careful not to crush frail shells and skeletons.

First they walked up in the deep, dry sand by the rocks, then down close to the sea where the gluey, wet sand sucked at their feet and left deep, widening holes behind them. It was only when they'd sat down on the rocks at the far side that Kate discovered she'd lost one shoe. But how does one lose a shoe without knowing it? 'Oh, that's easy,' said Kate, 'and it was *you* who wanted to go near the shore where the sand was sticky as clay. So it's *you* who should go back and look for it.' Paula went off willingly enough, running hopefully here and there towards strips of old cloth, half-buried stones and bits of basket washed in by the tides. She came back slowly, empty-handed, and sat down. And now Kate was almost crying. It turned out she'd actually hurt her foot on a sharp rock as they'd come along. 'It seems you don't know anything today,' said Paula sharply. 'You don't know where you lost your shoe. You don't know how you hurt your foot. Do you know how we're going to get home, by any chance?' She didn't continue the scolding, for some distance away she noticed a figure coming along the beach. A man was approaching from the city side of the shore. It wasn't easy to see him against the grey and white ribs of the sea for he was dark and light himself – wearing a voluminous black anorak and a thick pale grey muffler wrapped around his neck. Paula stood up straight with one hand on Kate's shoulder. With her other arm she hailed the man. 'Did you see a shoe in the sand as you came along?' she shouted. The man came nearer, hand cupped to his ear.

'Because if we don't find it,' the girl called again, 'it'll soon go out to sea.'

The man was close. 'No chance of that,' he answered. 'No fear of it, because the tide's turned. It can only be brought further in now. No, I didn't see anything. But I'll go back and have a look.' He turned, treading the sand down in his strong black boots. So thickly wrapped he was, there was little of him visible except the white hands dangling from his jacket cuffs. The girls, still thinking of picnics and sunlit beaches, were surprised at these clothes and Paula turned up her collar and put her hands into the flimsy pockets of her dress as she watched him go. It seemed that summer had finally disappeared with this last man on the beach – summer and daylight too.

'Don't move, will you?' he said, stopping for a moment to look over his shoulder.

'No, of course we'll not move,' said the girl. 'It's getting more and more difficult to move at all. My friend needs that shoe to get home. She's hurt her foot, you see.'

'Well, we can't have that, can we?' said the man. 'Are you far from home then?'

'We're on holiday,' said the girl. 'It's a hostel, not home. Out of the town, but even so there's lots of pavement and steps before you reach it. Are *you* on holiday?'

'Oh – holiday! That's one word for it, I suppose. I'm not working, if that's what you're asking, and haven't been for months. Right you are then – I'll go back.'

'I'll spread this red scarf on the rock so you'll spot us again,' said Paula, pulling it from under her collar.

'Don't worry,' said the man. 'I saw you both miles away. The one so dark and the other fair.'

After he had gone neither girl spoke at all or even moved. Birds flew over them with raucous cries. The grinding battle of the pebbles and the incoming waves began. Suddenly Kate exclaimed: 'I didn't like you hailing him like that!'

'What else could I do, Kate? You've got to get home, haven't you? And I can't leave you here.'

'And I don't like *him*,' Kate went on. 'He's mocking us, you know. Grinning to himself as he went off!'

'Maybe he was,' Paula said. 'We're helpless, you see. Maybe he sees us as a couple of stranded, flapping fish.'

'Do people smile like that at helplessness?' said Kate. 'I

don't know whether he's good or bad. There's not another soul on the beach and won't be till tomorrow.'

'That's childish, Kate. He's neither good nor bad, of course, but just like everyone else. Like you or me, for instance. Like Sara, like Tom, like Paul, Julia and Anna.'

'Oh, how I wish they were all here now!' cried Kate.

'Poor Kate. It's just that you're cold. People get scared when they get cold. Sit down quietly against that rock out of the wind.'

'He'll be ages,' her friend replied. 'What shall we do?'

'We can talk.'

'I'm shivering too much. You'd better begin. Tell me again how your aunt managed to lose weight. I've heard it dozens of times before, of course.'

'She went out one day and bought this grey silk dress,' began Paula. 'A shift dress – slinky – the most expensive thing she'd ever bought in her life.'

'And how ridiculously out of date now,' interrupted Kate, 'and most probably was even then, knowing your aunt.'

'Look, do you want this dress or don't you?' demanded Paula. 'She opened up the box in the sitting-room the moment she got in, and in front of my uncle. Nothing but the rustle of tissue paper for a few minutes. Then she held it up against herself – couldn't even wait to try it on. It was a joke really, for my aunt swelled and bulged around it like a live, fat person round a thin grey ghost.'

'No ghosts please, Paula. Make it cheerful, can't you? Where is he now?'

'More than halfway along.'

'I don't believe he's been looking at all.'

'Yes, of course he's looking. He's been bending and searching all the way. Well, to go on – my uncle was furious of course. Very angry indeed. When exactly would she wear the dress? he asked. She never went to a party, did she? And did she think he was made of money? "That's the point," she said. "And true enough, I never go to a party. I want to be ready for anything now. And I'm going to make myself fit this dress if it kills me." "Well, I suppose you can get buried in it, if nothing else," my uncle said.'

'More cheerful!' called Kate. 'Don't talk about burials.'

'It was just a joke. She took it in good part,' said Paula. 'In two months, by the way, it fitted her. No butter, no cream, no chocolate for weeks. She ate her first chocolate éclair at her first party. That was the funny bit – and went on eating. After that she was the same size as before.'

'Not funny at all,' said Kate. 'It's getting sad again. So don't go on. Can't you think of something else to talk about?'

'It's your turn, Kate.'

'Well, I suppose it has to be that boring old tale of getting into the wrong train and landing up the other end of the Caledonian Canal. Is he coming back? The thing is I don't believe he even knows what he's supposed to be looking for. He hardly glanced at the shoe on my foot. And I keep thinking we're the only people on the whole of this beach. You and me and that man. And I can't even run.'

'Why should you run?' Paula asked.

'There are terrible stories around. And I don't mean the stupid ones we tell one another, of course.'

'I thought he looked rather a decent person myself,' said Paula cautiously.

'That's the whole difficulty!' her friend exclaimed.

All that stuff about what you look like – whether you look good or bad, good-tempered or bad-tempered, soft, hard, patient, impatient, stupid or clever, kind or cruel – all that seems to have gone overboard. Do you remember that photo face I pointed out in a paper months ago? I showed it to you and said, "Look – who would you say that was? Is it a triple murderer, do you think, or is it that man who's giving all his fortune to the relief of pain?" It was the first, but you guessed the second. And you're bright, after all – not easily fooled. So is it all nonsense – this telling character by appearance?'

'I wouldn't say it was all nonsense,' her friend replied.

'Maybe you have to see people in all sorts of situations to know anything about them. I agree a flash look – a snapshot, so to speak, tells you nothing. It's a flash judgment, that's all.'

'Do you remember long ago as children we were taught to trust everyone?' said Kate meditatively. 'And when I say trust I mean right up to the hilt. To bring the good out of them, was the idea. It was all part of the Sunday School equipment of the time. Whatever would it be now?'

'The same probably. I still believe a lot of it myself, I think,' said Paula. Kate looked over her shoulder. 'He's coming back, Paula. He's got an *armful* of old shoes, and what looks like a boot or two. I told you he'd never once looked at my foot.'

The man was coming up now, laughing and laughing at his loot. 'Would you believe the sea could throw up this lot?' he said. 'Where on earth do they all come from, for God's sake – ships, rubbish tips, foreign beaches, shoe factories, back gardens?' He shrugged and looked down doubtfully at his pile. 'Well, I'm very, very sorry,' he said, holding up a weedy boot by the heel. 'I found everything, you see, but your other pink slipper. And I don't mind telling you now that I'd begun to think you were both fooling around with me. So I was just about to give up the search and go up town for a drink and a meal. But then I had another think to myself. At first you'd looked like a pair I could trust. So back I came. And here I am. All the same, I saw you watching me as I came near. Ah – such knowing, frightened eyes! I almost turned back again. Such clever artful girls, I thought!'

'What do you mean – "*knowing*"? We don't know a thing,' said Kate.

'How can we thank you?' said Paula.

'Why should you?' the man replied. 'I haven't even brought the right shoe.'

'I can wear anything', said Kate. 'Any old boot, if I have to.'

'But here's something smaller,' the man said, holding up a wet black shoe. 'How does that feel?'

'Feels O.K.,' said the girl. 'But it looks awful. Do I have to walk through the place looking like a clown or a tramp?'

'Don't worry,' the man said. 'It's wonderful how soon you can get used to it if you have to. Well, this isn't the Cinderella story, is it? No use waiting around. It seems there's no glass slipper coming up, and I'm no prince. Personally, I wouldn't say you're a princess either. I'll never understand what you two girls are doing on the beach by yourselves this time of day. Well, I'm going back now, so I'll say goodbye.' Kate put on the wet black shoe and laced it tight. 'Safe home then,' said the man. 'No – beg your pardon – it's *not* home, is it? A hostel, you said.'

He turned abruptly and went walking back the way he'd come.

'Yes, it's quite a long way home,' said Kate, limping up the shallow slope of a dune and down into a hollow place. 'There. Now *I'm* saying it! Home. I wish it *were* home, though. I don't fancy answering all the questions when we're back to camp, and having to show them this horrible shoe.'

For some time they plodded on, seeming to make little progress away from the incoming sea. The sand squeaked and slid under their feet as they climbed a further slope. 'I think you were probably right,' Kate remarked. 'He did seem quite a sympathetic person after all. I feel terribly ashamed of myself for imagining anything else. And what's more I feel an absolute fool. The rest would laugh at me if they knew. You are much more trusting of persons, Paula – you always were, and I daresay you mightn't even laugh at me now. But I can't forget the kind of things that went through my mind a few minutes ago down there – stupid, childish stuff. I even thought of that man they were looking for months and months ago and miles and miles away. To be here at this moment in time he'd have to have hopped onto a jet-plane, going like the Concorde – infantile, idiotic thought! You can sometimes be tough on me, Paula. But I'm proud of you. I always was. You don't lose your shoes, you don't lose your head, and you never lose your temper.'

The dunes gradually grew steeper as they climbed further from the sea, and they were divided by deeper and deeper hollows. The pale yellow day still remained on the highest crests of these sandhills. Blue night was growing in the hollows. The two girls stopped once or twice for breath. And now for the first time, Paula – moving her head round stiffly as an automaton – looked back. Very far in the distance she saw the man walking away. Suddenly he hesitated and slowly made off in another direction, taking a long, curving backward path somewhat inland.

'What exactly *is* trust?' Kate asked. 'Not just the old Sunday School thing again, is it?'

'No, of course it must be more,' said Paula in a low voice so that her friend had to come close in order to hear. 'Of course it's more. I don't know what it is, but I know what it is not. Feeling the slightest fear of anyone, for no reason at all, is lack of trust.'

'But surely you must *sometimes* have fear Paula! For defence. Adrenalin! I haven't a clue what the stuff's made of, but it's the thing that makes you strong, that makes you run, that lets you climb walls and trees and fences you could never climb before.'

'I'll have to rest,' said Paula, breathing hard. 'They are so steep here. I never knew it would take so long.' Again with the strange, stiff, doll-like movement of the head she looked back. The man, walking very purposefully now, was taking a deep curve in towards the dunes. He was still a good way down and still going slowly – the black track of his footsteps now fading on the beach into mild, shadowy dents, soft and grey as velvet in the twilight. Now, slowly, deliberately, he started to climb the dunes. Paula put her hand to her throat in order to prevent some sound. It seemed to her that any sound would have been outlandish in this place where three persons were moving in total silence – all separated by their own thoughts and feelings – unpredictable feelings and even, perhaps, interchangeable – the fierce and the fearful, the predatory and passive, the tormented and the trustful.

It had seemed for a time that Kate had no other thought in her head but an overwhelming tiredness and her tight shoe. Yet once or twice she raised her head and looked high beyond the fields to where a large expanse of brown land stretched up, studded with white and purple turnips. Mild, fat sheep roamed here. Now from their silent hollow and with the sea far behind, the girls could hear the quavering falsetto voices of these sheep as if they had apprehended their intruders even from a great distance away. And now Kate was sitting down, quietly spreading out her jacket like any summer visitor in the sand. 'We're in the most sheltered place on the beach,' she said. 'If only we'd brought food and found the place sooner we could have had a picnic.' It was true this place was out of the wind for it was fringed with stiff, rustling grasses and so deep they could scarcely see over the top to other dunes. They noticed that the sky above was now streaked with long pink clouds all hurrying over to join the dense mass of blood-red clouds in the west.

'No, don't settle yourself,' said Paula. 'We've got to get on.'

'Are you as cold as all that?' Kate asked. For Paula was pale. She had climbed half-way up the sand-slope and was staring below her. There was no one to be seen either on the beach or on the dunes.

Suddenly Kate gave a shout from the burrow and raised her hand – 'Hi!' Paula looked up quickly. The man in the grey muffler was walking directly above them along the high, hard ridge of the dunes. He looked down at them for a moment and waved casually. Paula tried to wave as well, but her arm was heavy as if she brandished a sword. She could scarcely move it. 'Hi! You two!' the man shouted.

'Don't get cold down there. The sun's gone. You should have been back hours ago!' He walked on, stumbling from time to time on the crumbling ridge and moving gradually away to be hidden amongst other hollows out of sight. 'Do you know,' exclaimed Kate after he'd gone. 'I could have sworn he'd found that slipper and was bringing it back! Did *you* think that, Paula?'

Her friend was silent, looking down. Suddenly she bent and picked something out of the sand at her feet. 'Look, Kate – a fossil – right up here, after searching the whole beach down there! No, of course it's not very exciting – the usual dots and dents.' She held the pebble in her hand for a while. It was a round, light, porous thing. Yet it was dense as the earth. It contained the aeons of time, the fire and the ice, the plant, the fish, the mammal and the man. Fear and ferocity, love, hatred, and brave deeds were here. Here shame and distrust had come to birth.

'Well, at least we've got something to show,' said Kate. 'But my foot is really hurting now. Scorching and chafing worse than before. How I wish I'd chosen the huge, green sea-boot or even that silly red sandal with the broken strap instead of this. He knew I was vain, of course. He knew I was too vain to put the weedy sea-boot on. I'm not blaming him. I think that man was clever. I think he guessed what we were like. Did you feel that too, Paula?'

'I've no idea what I feel now or what I'm like either,' said Paula. 'I'm not even sure what *you're* like, Kate. As for that man – how can I judge him? Yet the fact is I *did* judge him – a dangerous man, I thought him, and our enemy too. The wildness and treachery of that sea, Kate! Shattering the whole earth at every tide, confusing every one of us with every wave!'

'Well, it's flattened every castle on the beach, if that's what you mean,' her friend mildly replied. 'It's washed out all the names along the shore.'

'Dividing us and drowning us!' Paula cried again. But

they were leaving this sea. Above them the sheep's wool – gathering the last light of the sky – was luminous against a growing darkness.

'So you say we're all strangers,' said Kate slowly. 'You say you know nothing about me now – me, your best friend. No, Paula, we *are* friends. Remember? We had a picnic by the sea, walked along the beach, lost a shoe and talked to a stranger. That was the day, not so different from any other.' Kate took her friend gently by the hand and helped her up. 'Come on, Paula. Whatever it did to you – forget the sea! Look, we're almost up to the green fields. And the land has forgiven you.'

'Why on earth should I want that?' said Paula. 'To be forgiven by the grass, the sheep and turnips, do you mean?'

She stared into the distance where, far off, the man was limping along, now almost merged into the dark red sky. 'I wish he would turn round just once again and wave,' she said. 'Just once. I could wave back. Then I'd know *he'd* forgiven me.'

'For what exactly?' Kate asked.

'For being afraid of him of course,' Paula replied.

'Perhaps he never even imagined that,' Kate insisted.

'He guessed everything we were thinking. You said so yourself, Kate.'

'But imagine if he were to come running back, waving or not,' said Kate. 'Then it would all start again.'

'I shall never forget him, never,' said her friend. 'I'll forget Bill like a shot, of course. Almost certainly I'll forget Peter and Charles. And no way I'll ever remember Tom. I might even forget you one day, Kate. I mean one day a long, long time from now when we're both very old. But I shall never forget that man. Never.'

She stood, still watching, with her foot on the path leading up through the fields. The man never turned. Soon he was lost to sight.

# Couchettes

GRADUALLY THE RUMBLE and creak of luggage carts across the platform, the banging and shouting along the corridor, died down. A full trainload of passengers – men, women and children – were looking for their couchettes. Here and there someone who had just smoothed his sheet, spread his blanket and was attempting to make himself comfortable in the cramped space, would be ejected with curses on either side. He would then climb down the ladder, heave down his bags and continue his wanderings through the train, searching for his own berth. This carriage near the end of the train was already full except for one place. Two men occupied the couchettes on one side. Two women and a young girl lay opposite. The racks above were heaped with rucksacks and bedding-rolls. Knotted black sacks were slung between jackets, oilskins, scarves and boots. Coils of climbing-rope had been flung up there with a jangling selection of kettles, pans, mugs, heating and lamp equipment strung together with wire. The women lay with their few belongings beside them – each with her head on a softer bag stuffed with woollens for a pillow.

For a time the carriage was brighter and its occupants slowly settled down – preserving their distance simply by keeping their eyes from one another. Remarkably – for this was not an age of privacy – no glance went across the narrow passage between bunks as the passengers got ready as best they could for the short night. At the last minute a young man came in, climbed the narrow ladder with his bags and threw himself down into the last empty berth. Although the place was far from warm he at once stripped off shirt and sweater before lying face down. No sun had touched him. His eyes moved around, taking in the whole carriage, and this glance made him appear vulnerable as if he had accidentally removed the tough protective layer from himself, for he was white-skinned from the waist up. One long, plump arm hung down, almost touching the berth below. Nevertheless, in this private place where no one spoke, it appeared hardly a human arm, but resembled rather some actor's limb, overwhitened with luminous powder. The woman opposite wondered at the boldness of this boy who had needlessly bared himself to both curiosity and cold.

Suddenly every door along the corridor crashed shut. In the carriage it was now pitch dark with only a dim, blue light along the cracks of the door and in the hole of the lock. A sudden, sick claw of claustrophobia caught the woman for a second as she stared at this blue lock-hole. Then she wrapped her scarf closely about her head and shut her eyes. Along the train a few persons were calling goodnight to one another, but already the night and the dark had distanced them.

In the middle of the night it began to grow cold. The woman, half-awake, imagined the train slowly climbing out of the fertile valleys of Central France where the lowest bunches of the vineyards were almost touching the red earth, alternating on either side with ragged fields of Indian corn – and up into a landscape which was now gradually changing into a higher, rockier country, not yet mountainous, but already swept by a sharp air from the snows. Soon she was rummaging for gloves and another scarf. She sat up to jerk the undersheet about her waist, to wrap the blanket more tightly round her legs. She lay back again and fell into a deep, cold sleep.

Sometime, somewhere, in the early hours the train jerked to a stop with a massive rattling and jolting as if lurching across great lumps of iron. Outside, up and down the platform, voices were shouting. Suddenly the doors of the carriage crashed apart and a bright light came on. One by one the sleepers rolled coldly from their dreams to find a black-coated woman official crouching beside them, demanding tickets, questioning destinations. Startled eyes opened. The bare young man, no longer bold, drew up his arm and searched frantically for a while in the round, corded pouch about his neck. From this he first drew out a handful of grey fluff, bits of chocolate wrapping, last year's bus and train tickets, a thumb-sized photo of a girl, some old newspaper cuttings and a piece of chewing-gum stuck to an envelope. Watched closely by the official, he at last found the ticket carefully folded into a slit of the bag. The woman nodded and knelt to look further down. It was darker in all the lower berths and she flashed her torch about her. There were more sudden awakenings, more desperate searches. For some time she knelt beside the travellers, asking questions, ignoring the stammered excuses in a foreign tongue. Finally all the tickets appeared. One last time she nodded to the bright carriage and left. The place was again in total blackness. The sleeping woman had been lucky enough to find her purse quickly for it was stuck inside the shoe at her side. Again she wrapped herself in the blanket, drew the gloves over her wrists, the scarf about her ears and once more settled herself to sleep.

Nevertheless she could not sleep at once. It seemed to her that during the last few minutes this dark carriage with its blue cracks of light had changed. Like some ghost train it had moved bodily back in time and space. For trains had played an ineradicable part in the memory of this country, carrying with them those stories of day or night-time journeys which would be suddenly interrupted at any time and in no known place, for no known purpose. In seconds there could be a lightning change of clothes – a fearful pantomime ending in life or death, papers would change hands, be shoved inside caps, inside shoes, under dentures. Instantly expressions must change from wild to bland, while beyond the windows still no indication of place – simply that the overcoats of the guards, entering from the dark, would smell of a frosty orchard or the smoky back room of some remote village. These iron faces would never change, but with luck – a luck which afterwards seemed unbelievable – they might step out at last and the doors slam shut. Impossible to imagine the feeling inside the carriage. The woman's imagination didn't go far enough for that. How far then did it go? Did it go to an even earlier time and a different kind of train, no longer, in fact, a train at all? Her imagination from its limited, comfortable life, didn't go to that, wouldn't or couldn't go. Was it not obscene to pretend it could? The train she was forced to think about was no train known to her – a train for animals, yet still with carriages of a kind, packed with death and terror, with degradations, humiliations, she and nobody known to her could properly conceive. Still, she was human, and there was a price to be paid for it – even in having to imagine the unimaginable. And a worse price to be paid for not allowing oneself to imagine anything at all.

It was now really cold inside the carriage. By lying absolutely still the woman tried to preserve a little heat about her. But she knew that sooner or later she would have to climb out of her blanket and go down to the other end of the corridor. In the last days, eager and greedy for sun, fruit and colour, she had bought the warm peaches from baskets on the street, had tried the ripe grapes and the bursting plums. All about her people had been enjoying their own produce. But the bowels of the stiff northerners were easily loosened. She climbed down, drew back the door quietly and went down the train. The lavatory was cramped, ill-lit and not particularly clean. But how unbelievably lucky she was to have such luxuries! There was running water here, supplies of paper, a basin, paper towels and soap, a door

with lock and bolt – a private place where she could relieve
herself alone. Nowadays how lightly, how scornfully people
spoke of privacy as if it were a thing long out-moded, a state
hypocritical and puritanical, with something foolish and
even wrong about the need for it. Togetherness and open-
ness were everything, as though the ghastly togetherness of
trains, trucks and prison camps had been forgotten.

Shivering, she went back along the corridor. From the
windows she saw a few lights pricking the high villages of a
distant landscape, straggling out into remote farms – lonely
places where no doubt people had been sheltered for a
night or two before being sent on their way one morning to
an unlikely escape. She drew back the carriage door as
quietly as she could, but the light from the corridor shone
momentarily on the place. Again there was an uneasy
movement in the couchettes as, one above the other, bodies
rolled over – some on their stomachs, others on their backs.
The faces, pinched and strange, looked up. Here and there
a begging or protesting hand was flung out, the fingers open
like claws. The blinking eyes, with startlingly black pupils,
were turned towards the door as if fear were just below the
surface of all human dreams. The woman, as she wrapped
herself up, saw that the carriage had changed again. It
would not, could not now take on its ordinary rôle – that of
an apartment carrying workers, students, travellers and
holiday-makers like herself. It was not a carriage, not a
truck, but a series of close-set death-bunks. She moved
over towards the wall, turning away from the remembering,
from the imagining, from the believing, not feeling she had
to confront it again. For hadn't endless other horrors
happened since then, would go on happening again and
again? Who could keep up with it all? She drew the blanket
up to her chin, icily separating herself from the idea of this
death. But for this separation there was a price to be paid. It
was necessary for her to become dead herself. And if
becoming dead to degrading death – then dead also to

the living landscape going past, to the sunbaked earth with its people bending amongst vines, dead to this whole land, once lost and given back again by acts of unbelievable courage, and finally dead, totally dead to all those in the nightmare shelves, some of whom had been able, with their last breath, their last gesture, to offer human warmth to the other.

She sat up with a groan and immediately like an echo of her thought, came a voice from above: 'Are you all right? Do you want tea? I've still a mouthful in the thermos. I saw you go out and come in. You looked white in the passage.'

'It's nothing. Only it's freezing cold out there.'

'You're not faint? You want me to call the guard?'

The woman below laughed quietly to herself at the mention of guard. 'No, it was nothing.'

There was a breathing, a rustling, and a woollen cardigan dropped down. 'Take it. I'm wearing two. And there's other stuff in the rack. No, you *must* take that, I'm warm, you see. And better lie back and go to sleep. The best way to survive.'

But no. For the woman below knew how easily she herself could sleep comfortably in the present, could stiffen and die to the past. Everything can be forgotten, *should* be forgotten, some said. Even now, rattling and jolting through the night, she felt she must stay with the last one awake. There was no difficulty about that. But to survive as human was a different matter. To do that she must set forever this compartment – warm enough, comfortable enough – against those other carriages and bunks. It would be necessary to be on the look-out and wide-awake for the rest of her life. 'To keep watch' was how she imagined it. In less than ten minutes she was asleep.

# Thorns and Gifts

WHEN MY FATHER and mother came back from seeing my uncle in hospital I remember they were quieter than usual. I was having my tea – swotting for the first school exams of the year, with a map of the Middle East propped against the teapot.

'Well, how was he then?' I asked. I prided myself on being his favourite nephew. And it was something to be proud of. For he had other nephews of course – my Canadian cousins whom I'd never seen, though he had visited them several times. We ourselves were a family of five. I had one grown-up sister, newly married and living in England; a younger sister and an older brother, the one several classes below me and the other above me in school. And the youngest boy was only six, a delicately darned and patched, disarmingly scruffy child who still had the choice of every bit of cast-off clothing in the house – yet never complaining of his weird mixture of tight shorts and baggy pullovers, even deigning to accept the occasional shiny belt or clip from the girls' wardrobe. I can still see my mother doing him up more and more cautiously in a jacket which would soon be too tight over his plump bottom. Passively he took over my navy blue shirts which hung on him like the voluminous smocks on a diminutive painter. My mother's fingers would move, tentatively, flutteringly over the buttons as if she sensed the day of reckoning was coming very near, the day when the great strip-off rebellion would begin. He knew nothing yet, of course. He was still dumb and mild. His butter-smooth hair and pink cheeks had made him automatically into the Good Boy of the neighbourhood. We didn't resent this. Indeed we were rather proud he'd managed to keep it up for so long, just as we were proud of our little cream cat who'd kept sleek and clean, sweet-tempered and pink-pawed while wandering across jagged tins, around dustbins and through hedges for the same number of years.

'He's better, but different of course,' said my mother in answer to my question.

'How's that?' I asked.

'A slight stroke. He cries when you praise him – shakes with laughter if you scold. Nothing's quite the same. You'll come with us tomorrow and see for yourself.'

'I don't want to,' I said. 'I've got nothing to tell him.' I turned to the map again. It was strange how colour changed everything. They'd made the Middle East look very sinister by putting splodges of queasy yellow and patches of dirty grey across it. The map of Great Britain had always been green as though it were all sweet grass surrounded by an innocent blue sea. No cities, no smoke, no illness there, no shipwreck.

'You're coming with us to see your own uncle,' said my mother firmly. 'You can carry the flowers.'

'I don't want to. Someone might see me.'

'Well, what about it?'

'I'll carry anything else you want. Not flowers.'

Next morning my mother went out into the garden and started snipping off the last of the roses. They were great, showy, red, pink and white blooms with thick stems covered in huge three-dimensional thorns. Very tough as though hanging on as long as possible to life. It had been a long, chill autumn.

'Don't pick them too big,' I said. 'Take the smallest, shortest ones.'

'The best for the hospital,' she replied.

'Yes, but please make it a small bunch,' I begged her. 'I won't even be able to carry that lot properly.' She held up

the great bunch under her chin. A sudden gust of wind
swept the trees and a few white petals fell on her shoulders.
My mother must have been very pretty when she was
young. She was brought up surrounded by brothers and
sisters in another country. In the early photos she was often
in a garden. Even though there were few coloured photos in
those days I had the impression of light and colour, swings,
flowers and gay dresses. You didn't need to see the colour.
Instead a kind of radiance illumined the faces. I never saw it
again outside these snapshots. She was never meant for the
grey, suspicious village life. All the later photos after she
was married – even the new coloured ones – looked flat and
dim as though she'd cramped and clipped herself to suit a
new environment where – speaking the same tongue
though with a different accent – she was thought almost
a foreigner. Now her smiles were duty smiles – nothing gay
or flirtatious. No swings, no songs at the piano, no sisters,
brothers or brothers' friends. My father kept a prosperous
ironmonger's shop in those days, so she never lacked the
'necessities'. What she longed for, however, were the trifles.
He was not a hard man but perhaps there was something
about the drawers of nails, springs, screws and flints, the
saws and hammers swinging from the wall – that had
worked through to his bone. He was an elder in the kirk
and would help to carry the deep velvet collection bag with
its wooden handles up to the altar on Sundays. The religion
was tough there, yet the bag was charitably deep, you might
say, in that people's hands were hidden right up to the wrist
and beyond it – whether they put in a penny or a pound. To
put it mildly, my parents were not suited to one another. In
those days of fewer experiments or trial marriages, less
living together, people could make the most eerily un-
suitable unions. So is it better now? people ask. I've no
answer to that. But to go back to the early days – my mother
only asked to be allowed to charm people and not to harm
them. Not much to ask, you might say. But you can say that

again. Slowly, slowly she learned better and she learned her
part well. Charm was not a thing that was liked or understood much in our part of the world.

Next day, just before two o'clock, we got dressed and my
mother placed the great prickly bunch in my hands. The
flowers were so unwieldy I had to put both arms round
them. Thorns scratched my chin and the insides of my
elbows in the thin jersey sweater. The three of us left – my
father carrying a large cake in a box. 'Let *me* carry the cake,'
I begged again. 'Now hurry up, Charlie,' said my mother.
'Don't let's have any more of that nonsense.'

The hospital was at the other end of the town. As we
neared it we met lots of other persons carrying flowers and
boxes, though there were few children. People were smiling
down at me and my bouquet in the too-sweet, kindly way
that made my stomach sink a bit as though I'd been given
too much creamy fudge. As I said I'd always been fond of
my uncle and he of me, and all the more I resented my
parents for making me do something that seemed unnatural. It was as though they were trying to force me into
the rôle of a good, giving boy – a part suitable to my little
brother but one I myself was not cut out for. It reminded
me of those awful occasions when my mother – never a
particularly happy or devoted church-goer herself – would
notice someone without a hymn-book and would push me
forward in front of the whole congregation to lend one of
our own. Agonized and blushing, like the crimson-faced
angel blowing his own trumpet in the stained-glass inset
above the pulpit, I would step forward to do my priggish-
looking task while one or two persons smiled at one another
and at my mother as though they'd been approached by
some shining acolyte for the first time. These were the
games uneasy grown-ups played simply to divert some
virtue or sympathy toward themselves.

We were now at the hospital and had entered a long,
crowded ward, already rustling with gift-wrappings. People

were coming and going with chairs from the corridor as though assembling for a concert. Those who had no visitors were still anxiously and surreptitiously watching the doors over the tops of newspapers. Fathers, husbands and sons were laboriously slinging their legs over the bed to try on tight, new slippers. Here and there the diabetics were religiously warding away the chocolates, fruit drinks and sticky cakes. My uncle looked rather better than I'd expected. All the same it was true something had happened to him.

'Why, Edward, you're looking much, much better than you were a couple of weeks ago,' said my father. Great tears came into my uncle's eyes. 'Yes, you're looking almost one hundred per cent,' said my mother. 'And *he* has something for you,' she added, prodding me in the back. I placed the thorny bunch beside him on the bed. I knew he'd understand it had absolutely nothing to do with me.

'Sister says we can all go to the lounge today,' my mother remarked. Two kind-looking nurses set themselves one at each side of my uncle, with my parents and myself going behind. We escorted him through the long corridor and down a side passage. 'We can take these along with us to cheer the place up,' one of the nurses had said, catching up the bunch of roses before we left. A few other patients, both old and young, were going along with us – some being pushed in wheel-chairs, others moving, stiff as dolls and glassy-eyed, at funeral pace. The lounge was noisy and full of smoke. People stared into a corner as if they'd never seen TV before. On the screen several couples were shrieking and cavorting, whipped on like dogs by a joky showman, while he handed out the huge presents they'd earned by going through their humiliating paces in public or by answering intimate details of their private lives. I thought how unhappy they looked, stumbling blindly round the stage amongst ovens and organs, waterbeds, motor cycles, record players and fur carpets. One woman had her arms around a refrigerator, tied with pink bows, as though embracing some icy, unyielding lover who would never turn her way no matter how hard she smiled and hugged. Her husband, meantime, was staggering under a great load of high-powered tools, designed for a do-it-yourself addict who would no doubt be building a dreamhouse for the rest of his days. They'd been compelled to adore and demand these things and it was important that millions of viewers should see the humiliation and the gratitude. The thing ended with the newest car of the day – a sleek Supercar – being wheeled on-stage. A honeymoon couple were bouncing and sliding on the shiny roof. The girl was sobbing with joy on the young man's shoulder though the chances were they'd have moments of terror before the night was out, struck suddenly with the thought of being forever locked together inside a fabulous metal container.

Meantime my uncle had been let down carefully into an armchair and my mother beckoned me to place the bouquet on his lap. As I did so my uncle gave a shout and flashed me a sudden sharp look. I knew what had happened. A long thorn had pricked the old man's knee. At this look, however, a thrill of the old sympathy was established between us. I knew he would get well again – so bright was this look, so clear and piercing. The thorn, keen and sharp as love, had pierced right through the mist of smoke, through the noise, and brazen load of telly gifts, even through our roses and sweet cake – to his former self. I knew he was all right.

'He's going to be O.K. now,' I said casually.

'How do you know?' my mother said more doubtfully.

'Because I pricked him and it hurt. No, he didn't mind. He yelled out, of course.' Not long afterwards my uncle, being tired, was put into a wheelchair for the return to the ward. As we went down the corridor all the roses dropped, one by one, from his hands. 'Oh, for heaven's sake – it's all my fault!' my mother exclaimed. 'I should have tied them

up properly. He's going to lose them all.' I looked back.
Here and there down the long, brightly-lit corridor both
visitors and patients were stooping to pick up roses for
themselves. No one stopped them or tried to hustle them
forward to give them back to us. Light gifts they were, and
free as though fallen from the skies. One woman had
already fixed a long stalk through the buttonhole of her
coat. Behind her an old man was stiffly bending to smell
one of the blooms. Warm, velvet petals fell on the cold
linoleum of the passage. I saw some children pick them up,
press them deep, deep into their eyes and hold them there.
It was like watching some kind of cure for sight – a fragrant
eye-balm to press out the memory of the ferocious giving
and taking on the screen we had just left.

Talking of eyes we saw a blind man on the way home.
That was one bit of advice I'd been spared up till now. I
mean no one had yet told me to help blind men across
streets. And why do they always have to be mentioned in
this connection? As a matter of fact, though the others knew
nothing about it, I happened to know one blind man very
well indeed. For the last two years, at around four o'clock,
whenever I took the shortcut home from school between
factory and river, I'd met him. A tall, spare, intelligent-
looking man, very well-dressed. At first sight there was
nothing about him that suggested blindness – no faltering,
no white stick. Nothing. Even his eyes looked curiously
sharp and of a shining blue. He'd certainly no intention of
being helped across anything, not even the narrow overflow
from the river that cut across the lane at one point. He
always jumped over that. But what he did want was to be
spoken to. And so did I. I can say – during all that time – I
never spoke to anyone as often or as freely as I did to him. It
was a mysteriously calming thing for an awkward and
ignorant schoolboy to be invisible – to have nothing between himself and the other except the voices floating out
on the air – no good looks or bad, no sex appeal, scarcely

even youth or age. It was communication cut down to its essence. I noticed lots of girls spoke to him too, and I could see how it pleased him. These were girls who would no more have gone up to a strange man than fly to the moon. For I was just beginning to sense what women might have to put up with in attempting to talk to men. But these girls were lucky for once in their lives. And so was he. After a while he went to work in a factory in another town. I never saw him again. For a time communication lost all its closeness and mystery for me and became the usual smooth and cautious exchange we sharp-eyed ones have grown used to.

On the way home from hospital my mother murmured to herself: 'I wonder if I should go round and have a word with the Rev. MacNair.'

'Why?' She had the usual uneasy and unhappy voice which would seize her when she spoke about religion.

'In case he should die suddenly. People have to be spoken to before they die.'

'What about?'

'About this life and the life to come.' Her voice trembled slightly on the last three words because of the awful uncertainty of it.

'Two very different states,' said my father ponderously. He was not particularly comfortable himself about the turn the talk had taken.

'But he's not going to die,' I said. 'Why didn't the Rev. MacNair speak to him years ago. He was always hard up for people to talk to. He told me so.'

Although we seldom saw eye to eye on things nothing would have pleased me more than to be able to reassure her on the matter of afterlife. She'd married very young, had brought up five of us, and was never done excusing herself for every penny she spent. The only time she took a taxi she apologized to the taxi-driver for not walking two miles in the pouring rain. I silently planned a magnificent afterlife for her full of gallant men, sunny gardens and wonderful holidays, plus nights and nights of unbroken sleep. There would be plenty of children of course. But I'd also made plans for the special nurseries, the crèche, the kibbutz – loving places, of course, and run in a heavenly way. Ours was not a street you were ever likely to miss the morning-till-night, night-till-morning tiredness of women, at a time when they had little choice in their own lives.

As we neared home black clouds with silver rims were coming up over the low roofs. Although my parents were not comfortable together they were always full of optimistic and comfortable sayings. I dreaded to hear from them how every cloud had a silver lining. Yet I had to admit these clouds were obviously crammed to the brim with the stuff. I eyed them suspiciously and they let fall a few drops of rain. By the time we got home it was almost a cloud-burst. The last of the top-heavy roses were looped to the earth and some of them were lying flat under the stormy yellow light.

'What a good thing we picked the best of them earlier,' said my mother who'd obviously forgotten how swiftly the hospital flowers had changed hands. 'Well, you'd better sit down and get on with your revising,' she added.

Upstairs my young sister was howling because she'd forgotten to bring back her Arithmetic exercise book from school. An ink exercise. That made it really bad. She knew she'd not only get the big row first thing on arrival, but double the work for the next night.

'I wish I was dead,' she said when she saw me.

'Don't say that. There are so many dead people around.'

'Are you talking about the hospital?'

'Oh no, they don't keep them lying about there. Every-thing's neat and tidy.'

'How's uncle Edward?' she asked, getting up on her elbow.

'He's fine.'

'There are all those years in front of me,' she said. 'If

there are going to be many nights like this it'll be pretty horrible. And we were going to the cinema tomorrow night too.'

'We can go the night after.'

'Does it all get better or worse?'

'Depends how you choose. It's your own life after all. You're supposed to be free.' I gave her a short, brisk lecture on freedom.

As I went downstairs I heard her begin, mechanically, monotonously, repeating the word. She seemed to like the sound of it, though the solid way she struck the second syllable made it sound heavy as lead.

"The accent on "*free*"!' I shouted up. But the heavy 'dom', 'dom', 'dom', now partly stifled in blankets, went on like a muffled drum from above. It sounded all wrong, of course – still only a parrot cry, simply the distorted echo of a fellow prisoner shouting about freedom. She'd even managed to waken the little boy who shared her room. And yet, in spite of everything, this word sounded so loud, so confident! I believed it just possible she would one day reach the lightness and balance of that precarious state.

# *Accompanists*

THE PROGRAMME NOTES of this recital have attempted to
make everything plain. The theme is there: Songs of Love
and Seeking. They come under three headings: The Search
in the Mountains; The Search at Sea; The Search in the
City. The singer – nearing the end of his search in the
mountains – is giving it all he's got. But the audience also
has its work cut out, for the songs – most of them ancient
and unfamiliar – are all sung in the language of their
country. The French, German, Italian and Spanish are
easy enough for some, of course. All the same there has also
been a brief search in Russia, amongst the snowdrifts of the
Ural mountains. A lake in Finland has been looked into.
Even some high Hungarian villages have come under the
fruitless survey. To complicate the programme, each song
is written down with its translation alongside, and during
the short interval between songs the linguists in the audience have been busy comparing the two columns. A few
scholars are picking great gaps in the translation. The more
serious among them have decided to forego the first coffee-
break and get down to a thorough examination of the text.
Altogether there is a lot of reading to be done. Even on the
platform the accompanists appear to be studying the words,
though by this time after years and years they must surely
know them by heart. There are two of them – a middle-
aged woman at the piano and beside her a young girl who
turns the pages of the song-book.

The first group of songs is nearly ended. A Spaniard, an
Italian, an Icelander – all have been looking for the ideal
beloved in the highest regions. It has been a strange, cold,

melancholy search – a recital of slippery paths, stumbling horses and straying donkeys. The unlucky ones, unable to get hold of a donkey, have fallen down precipices and into waterfalls. The cow-bells, sheep-bells, church-bells that seemed to summon them on have led only to endless glaciers and lonely mountain huts. Their shouts are lost in the hurricane. Strangest of all, a woman would occasionally be glimpsed on a mountain peak before the mists hid her again for ever. At the end of the day the searcher – his songs and sonnets still in their folder – would find himself back in his stuffy tent or in the dismal room of some local inn with only alpine flowers or the small mountain animals to talk to.

Though this is not a large concert hall it is full and the audience are attentive. Polite rather than enthusiastic – most people seem prepared to take a sensible and sensitive interest in the plight of the persons in these songs. There are some, however, who have begun to wonder how on earth these men have been driven to search out such elusive women despite all the hundreds of thousands they must have encountered back home. The women in the audience become particularly restive and begin to peer more closely into their translations to find the reason for it. This is hard to find. Instead they read that one man has followed a star in mistake for a diamond on an unknown woman's breast. Reading of this mistake and of this diamond for some reason makes them feel tired beyond belief as well as deeply unsympathetic.

'Well, I suppose the sea will be better,' said one, leaning across the man beside her, so that she could speak to the woman on his right.

'Better? Better songs, you mean?'

'I mean the sea might be a better place to find these women.'

'You think so, do you? I can't see it myself. A man would have to follow her in a boat. Unless she was actually swimming in the sea or under it, in which case he'd have to go in after her. And these men aren't usually swimmers. They weren't allowed into the sea as children, you see.'

'I don't really know what kind of men we're talking about.'

'Neither do I. I just assume there's been something lacking in the background.'

'You mean they weren't allowed into the mountains either?'

'Probably not.'

'Nor even into the cities?'

'We'll just have to wait and see.'

'So you think the mothers are to blame? For not letting them run around as children. Isn't that fearfully unfair?'

'Everyone *is* unfair to mothers. Always have been down through the ages. Always will be. No way they can win. Don't ask me why. I'm not one myself. Something to do with the Greeks, I should think. Those huge, beautiful, tragic, dangerous women.'

An absolute silence falls and a short burst of clapping as the accompanists unobtrusively take their seats again after the interval. There is some time to study them before the singer himself comes back to the platform. The audience stares fixedly at the two women. The young girl who turns pages is wearing a black blouse and a black silk skirt. She is slim, pale, with straight hair swept back from the forehead. Once she is seated they are aware of her startlingly straight back. She waits, modest yet confident, thin fingers clasped on her lap, her head already slightly inclined towards the piano. The pianist – a more formidable woman – waits, her feet firmly planted, strong hands spread out on her knees and her head bowed. She is in black to the ankles. These two wait patiently, unmoving as images. They have waited like this through the months and the years, for the sound of doors opening, for the sound of steps, for great bursts of clapping or cheering. Through these years they have become welded together unawares like some mediaeval tableau carved out of solid black wood – the girl with high, bare, rounded forehead, smoothly carved cheeks and a grave half-smile, the older woman with her large strong-boned fingers spread on the narrow lines of a pleated skirt.

The singer now enters quickly and takes up his stance near the piano amid a prolonged burst of applause. The woman places her hands on the keys and the girl bends her head close to the score. The second group of songs – the water-search – begins with an old Portuguese song about a sea captain looking for his woman through all the oceans. He skirts around volcanic islands, is becalmed amongst the weeds of the Sargasso Sea and hurled about by the stupendous winds and waves of the Southern ocean. There is nothing clear or straightforward about this business. All is driving spray, whistling wind and tangled weed. The situation is a particularly hopeless one. Neither the captain, the singer, the anonymous writer nor the audience know anything about this woman – whether she is sitting on a beach, floating, or sailing in a ship – whether she is perhaps a mermaid or an ordinary bather out of her depth. She is loved. It is all that is known about her.

But isn't that enough? No, it is not enough. A mixture of feelings in the audience makes for a sort of lassitude. Some men are taken aback by the realization that they ever managed to find a partner as quickly as they did. Wouldn't it have been better, after all, to wander for most of their lives searching the remoter regions of the earth? And how little opportunity for this there is once the quick choice of partner has been made. As before there is a great deal of doubt in the female part of the audience. Would these men – these sea-captains, scholars, priests, princes and poets – be really happy to find this woman? Would they notice her if they passed her in the street, for instance, rather than spotting her on a high peak or at the back of an ocean cave? Would they be prepared to sit down and actually talk to her rather than offering her a life-long devotion? The sea-songs are finished. A fairly thorough search has been made. Men have broken their legs, their necks, their hearts on the business. The second interval is longer than the first. It gives the audience time to imagine some small room backstage where the singer is resting. Are the accompanists with him? Serving his coffee perhaps? Perhaps even praising him on the purity of his top notes? They imagine the girl, still straight-backed, but leaning a little forward – passive, thoughtful, with lowered eyes, pouring milk into his cup, asking if he takes one, two spoonfuls of sugar and apologizing perhaps for not remembering after all these years. The more formidable woman will be sitting squarely and rather clumsily, her legs apart, elbows on knees, her large hands hanging against the black cloth of her gown. Will she have changed her character backstage? Become motherly? Thankfully the women in the audience guess she is not the motherly type. She is not prepared to brush the biscuit crumbs from the singer's jacket, to arrange his collar or tuck a pillow behind his back. As well as imagining things backstage the audience also have time to talk again.

'It will be a lot easier in the cities,' said one woman. 'There are so many of us around. Compared to men, I mean. And as statistics go, for better or worse, we *do* live longer.'

'Well, you could say there are a lot of *older* women around. Older women aren't so much in men's minds of course. Nor in the poetry, except of course when the poets happen to mention those old mothers, aunts and nurses who had such influence on them, but who – let's face it – could be just as much hated and feared as they were loved.'

'All the same I can't help looking forward to the cities. At any rate I'll be on solid ground again.'

'Dangerous ground for meetings, though. Or disappointing, rather. Every excuse for missing people in cities. You can't count on being noticed what with crowds and traffic and police and traffic wardens moving people on and all that.'

'I do still think we'll be easier to spot though. A man has only to use his eyes.'

'Yes, but the ones we're hearing about are obviously the long-sighted ones. It's the very distant things they tend to see and go for – the almost invisible things – really dim women, and the more mist around the better. So naturally they're frightened of anything too near, and really clear, hard-edged types are an absolute menace. No, I'm afraid I can't say I've got all that much hope for the city either.'

The singer appears again followed by the two women. He is certainly not one of those performers who takes much notice of his accompanists. He seldom looks behind him. He does not beckon them forward, far less indicate by word or gesture that through years of song he has been solely sustained by these two. His smiles, bows and kisses are for the audience. The accompanists settle themselves quietly. The older woman sets up her score, adjusts her music-stool and feels for the pedals. Finally she smooths the page in front of her to show that everything is finally clear and ready. The girl leans forward, one hand already angled to flick over the first page. Again they have the appearance of two skilfully modelled beings in perfect accord. There is something almost too perfect, static and agreeable in this composition. In fact it seems scarcely human and belongs rather to the super-human or even to the angelic side of things. For as well as looking good as a fixed pair they have, as individuals, the attraction of total reliability and faithfulness – more suited, perhaps to an altarpiece than to a concert platform.

The audience gradually get their minds round to the third and last section of the recital – the Search in the City. Here are the men who have searched all the cities of the world. They go from street to street and from dawn to midnight, looking for the Woman. There are a good many

women around – young, old, gay, serious, pretty and plain.
Yet the singer misses out the shopping centres where most
of the housewives, at any rate, are to be found in the
mornings. He doesn't linger round child guidance clinics
or public health centres. He gives a wide berth to schools,
offices, factories, police stations, banks and bars. Instead he
concentrates on attics and obscure stairways. He searches
for her on the steps of great cathedrals, looks into cloisters
and convents amongst groups of attractive nuns. He mixes
with gay carnival crowds and funeral processions and goes
– totally uninvited – to great balls and weddings. He does
not know who he is looking for and he does not find her.
The interest of the audience has begun to wander a little
from these men and from the singer himself. Most people
have had their eyes fixed on the accompanists some distance behind him on the right. There is a hypnotic sort of
drill about their movements. Every now and then the girl
leans closer in to the piano and quickly flicks over one page
of music while the older woman completes and acknowl-
edges it with an almost imperceptible lift of her head before
returning her eyes to the top of the new page.

It is in the middle of these last songs that a change comes
over the accompanists – not at once noticed by the audience, for the page-turning, the movement of head and hand
are still perfectly co-ordinated and the poise of both women
is still respectful, still dedicated to the service of the
searching, clueless heroes of the songs. Nevertheless one
or two persons in the front rows are surprised to see the girl
staring intently at her watch as she puts out her arm to turn
a page. She bends her head to the watch and lifts it to her
ear. They wait to see if she will shake it or even wind it up.
Meantime the pianist, while still giving the involuntary
head-lift to the top of the page, manages to bend sideways
to her companion, her eyebrows raised, lips moving. It is an
urgent request for the time.

The last songs are also some of the longest. There is a

moment when a man, after scouring the streets, climbs to the top of the highest tower in the city the better to get a bird's-eye view of the place – its parks, squares and mansions. It is not town-planning that interests him. He is simply trying to spot the Woman amongst the crowd below before it gets too dark to see anything at all. But the singer himself has time to flash one look behind him. He is not so thick after all. Some instinct tells him that the two women there are no longer accompanists. They are accomplices. The girl seems ready as usual to turn over a page. But the woman grips the back of the music-book firmly between finger and thumb, closes it up, and with a confident hand smooths down the front cover – an almost consoling movement, as if explaining a final farewell. Now she leans back more comfortably in her seat – at the same time patting down her hair at the back. Having made herself presentable, as it were, she stands up and stretches both arms above her head, at the same time flexing her fingers. So tall she seems now – away from the piano – like a giantess released from a black box. But now she remembers the main business and begins to rummage about in some hidden pouch at her waist or rather from a long, black-beaded bag swinging from one side of her sash. From this she draws out a strong brown paper bag. She returns to the piano and hands this to her companion who dips her thin fingers inside and draws out several bright red objects which could be large sweets or even polished beads except for the fact that they shine and swing in empty space under her hand.

Only the front rows see it is a loop of cherries. The girl doesn't eat them at once but hands the bag back to the other woman who puts her whole fist inside and comes out with a handful which she eats more greedily, more deliberately than the girl – throwing her head back and biting the cherries from their stalks like some tropical bird nipping off fruit with its strong beak. These gestures, under the bright platform lights, make for something of a centre-stage performance. A few more cherries and more head-flinging has brought a strand or two of the carefully-pinned hair down onto her shoulders. This gives her the air of a versatile actress in a new rôle – one which enables her to make wild, carefree gestures in place of the careful, rhythmical ones of some former part. She is even careless of the cherry-stones which drop from mouth to hand, from hand to beaded slipper. And now she goes back to her piano-stool again. But not to play. The singer himself has given up all hope of this. Now he is wandering all alone in an ancient city, wavering a little on the cobbled pavements like a drunk man. Cautiously, fearfully he hits his top notes, as cautiously, fearfully he raps on doors and windows in his search. Behind him and in front he senses chaos and confusion. For all he knows there may be cherry-trees between himself and the piano, strong trunks and blossoming branches twisting about the great organ pipes at the back of the platform, branches and blossoms between the rows of rigid seats, or amongst the statuary down the side-aisles of the building where dumb, marble women hold up flaming torches and musical instruments. He sees worse things to come. Far in the future he visualizes twigs, branches and blossoms spreading across court-rooms, conference halls and public platforms, around executives' desk-chairs and judges' seats, up pulpits and rostrums. Even the sea-captains who took him here and there around the world on a fruitless quest may be due for a change. And there are fruit-trees planted around the Holy See as well as the public swimming-pool.

The woman on the piano-stool turns sideways to the audience, leans forward meditatively chewing, her heavy arms akimbo, and exchanges friendly, expressive stares with a few women in the front seats. She seems to sense some need, if not an actual appeal. As if rising to this she gets up, shakes out her skirt and goes forward to the edge of the platform. She squats down, giving the bag an encouraging little shake and throws a few loops of cherries into the nearest group of women below. A few hands come up to catch the loops, and there is a slight murmur of acclaim. The accompanist stares intently into the bag, finds half-a-dozen cherries for herself, eats them quickly and drops half-a-dozen stones on the bare boards of the platform. And now even the tight-lipped, listening women further back expand a little. How long – centuries long – they have endured the songs and poems, these hymns of adoration and contempt. This adoration has cost them something; at certain places – stonings and jeers – at certain times – a hand or two cut off or even a head. For once in their lives they forget to fuss about the wet cherry stones dropping round their feet, the bitten stones along the platform's edge.

The paper bag is empty. The woman tosses it carelessly aside and gets up slowly, shaking her head and grinning wryly at her own stiffness. She limps back to the piano where the girl is waiting. Meanwhile the singer, willing himself blind to everything around him, has managed to get through, unaided, to the end of his final song. But the great climactic piano chords that sustain his anguish have been lacking, as also are the wild trills and the long, running series of notes which convey the distance he has had to jog in his search.

The final, bitter discord which means that the search will never be ended but will go on till the end of time – this has totally disappeared. The accompanists have disappeared also. Unobtrusively as ever, but not waiting for him, they have gone out through the side door.

A tentative clapping begins to build up after the singer has left the platform. Nobody would call it wild applause and though it goes on steadily the man does not appear again. He can be glimpsed in the dim doorway, looking out. A few women who have actually got up to their feet to clap are looking through him and beyond him over his shoulder into the shadowy room behind. In spite of this the singer doesn't set foot over the threshold, wouldn't for the world appear. Something tells him these women are not applauding the hardships and sorrows of the search. They are applauding their own escape.

'Well, those two are done for, anyway,' says a man in the audience to his girlfriend. 'Finished! Where on earth will they get a job now? Where will they go?'

'Very likely they'll be off on the world-trip themselves. I'd be surprised if they don't land up in those same mountains, or maybe somewhere far out at sea.'

'Searching for anything?' says the man.

'Not at all. You mean, of course, are they, in their turn, to be running after men.'

'Well, *are* they?' her companion replies.

'They are running,' says the girl, 'because they love running around the same as the men. Some have always escaped like those two. Aeons of passivity and hard labour have made the others stiff – the digging, planting, cooking and gathering, the plodding patiently behind with outsize bundles, huge pots and armfuls of babies. And at the end of the day the seat outside the sacred circle.'

'The older one up there was certainly stiff,' says the man. 'But not the young one. She is rather beautiful, to my mind.'

'Yes, she may soon stiffen inside the walls of her own house,' the girl replies. 'Not the huge pots and bundles for her, no doubt, but the cleaning of floors, beds and tables, the shifting of little objects inside drawers and the filling up of store cupboards. Sometimes she will even look back to that straight-backed piano seat with longing.'

The hall is beginning to empty now. The two get up. Neither is noticeably stiff, and the girl is exhilarated by what she has seen. They walk away arm-in-arm through the noisily wrangling crowds.

# Death of a Doctor

THE DOCTOR'S NURSING assistant comes into the waiting room rather earlier than usual – just before seven o'clock, in order to say a few words to each person sitting there. The room is already half full. It is midwinter, and throats and chest complaints can be expected. Even though the place is warm enough some people are still wearing scarves. The children have on their knitted woollen caps.

The girl standing in the doorway is an extremely pretty person. In spite of her stiff, white cap and the well-laundered blue overall there is nothing starchy about her. She hesitates for a moment on the threshold, looking about her, then begins to go round the room, saying something quietly to each patient. The words, in fact, are so quiet they can scarcely be heard except by the one person she is speaking to. What she says is: 'I am very, very sorry. I have to tell you that Dr Sneddon died last night.' Often she gives a little touch to a shoulder or to a hand as she says this, and occasionally a light tap on a head as if to instil some unbelievable message into the hard skull as gently but firmly as possible.

Snow is beginning to fall, though the flakes are still so few they can hardly be seen except when they fly suddenly sideways and glitter close to the waiting-room window. Sometimes they are blown backwards and up towards the high wall of the houses opposite. This long, black building has lighted windows in it and now and then a dark figure can be seen – a woman at a sink, an old man pulling a sweater over his head, a dim room behind, sometimes a set table, and always from the corner the flickering blue light of the TV.

'Dead?' says an elderly man to the assistant. 'Oh, but I've been here a long, long time, and I've come a very long way too. I had to leave my work early. And that wasn't easy, I can tell you.'

This waiting room is by no means a gloomy place. It could almost be called gay with its brightly coloured posters stuck on every inch of the wall – posters about accidents in the home, about diet, about drink and driving and about exercise – showing swimmers, runners, walkers and people bending and stretching in airy bedrooms. There are posters asking for kidney donors, eye donors and blood donors. There are new posters about AIDS and well-known ones calculated to reduce the fear of cancer. There are posters to encourage cervical check-ups and discourage smoking. There are posters on contraceptives and healthy mother-hood, on pre-natal clinics and post-natal clinics, on child-care, on vaccination and immunization. Some of these posters make a dramatic pictorial impact with their flaming frying pans and dizzy drivers steering towards the crash, with their enormously fat and attractively slim people, their mothers with perfect babies and mothers with sad babies. The frenzied businessmen with bulging eyeballs, heading for the heart attack, are hung beside careless people cutting themselves with sharp instruments, or poisoning them-selves with badly labelled bottles. Yet whatever these poster-people are doing they are still managing to hang on to life, if only by their fingernails. The elderly man scans them all carefully and seems to feel the lack of something. 'Well, I've been here since six,' he says again, as if this fact in itself should awaken the dead. He stares fixedly at the door as though awaiting a resurrection.

'Yes, I know,' says the girl patiently. She had heard often enough what people can utter under shock. 'And another doctor will be coming tomorrow,' she adds. Yet the man doesn't look shocked, simply tired – tired to death, you could say.

'Well, *when* is the other coming?' he calls after her as she
moves on to speak to four people – a young woman in a red
coat with her child, and her father and mother, the child's
grandparents, on either side of her.

'How can that be?' says the young woman almost brightly
when she hears. 'I saw him two days ago. He looked
flourishing. Said he'd been golfing. The best round he'd
ever had, he told me.'

'You've got to expect anything,' says her father. 'I, for
one, am *ready* for anything. That's how I've always gone
through life.'

'Well, that's absolute nonsense,' says his wife. 'You're
not ready for anything – never have been as long as I've
known you. You were never ready when the builders came,
never ready for the plumber, always late with the TV
licence. When were you ever ready for visitors, even your
own grandchildren? How can you be ready for death?'

'It's all beyond her, poor thing,' says the old man,
appealing to the nurse with a friendly smile. 'She's speaking
of death as a person, isn't she? She's not into the big ideas
yet, you see, not into abstractions.'

But the young nursing assistant goes on quickly to take
her message round the room. Two pregnant women sitting
together take it very badly indeed. Both weep when they
hear it, knowing very well how birth and death can be
spoken about in the same breath. For a moment the nurse
sits between them and puts an arm around their shoulders,
praises their hair, their eyes, their complexion, speaks of the
happiness of new life, compares their choice of babies'
names, asks after their other children and reassures them
about the other doctor who will be coming in tomorrow.
'But is he as good, as kind?' they ask anxiously, their hands
laid protectively on their bellies as though around precious,
easily damaged jars.

There is now a feeling in the room, even amongst those
who haven't heard, that something has gone wrong with

this place tonight. Several people get up and slowly approach the table where daily and weekly papers are laid out along with certain magazines – romance, beauty, housekeeping for women, with gardening, fishing, engineering and do-it-yourself for men. People are taking a long time to choose. There is a great deal of fussing, rustling and whispering round the table. The women leaf impatiently through those pages devoted to polishes and perfumes for the face and body, polishes and perfumes for the house. Some of the magazines are fearfully old and limp, rough-skinned and dingy. Yet some glamour still remains. Unlike the recent dailies, no tragedy has touched them. Both men and women pick up these newspapers very cautiously to-night, glancing back and forth from the pages to the white-flecked blackness beyond the window as if forcing themselves to relate the innocent white-on-black outside to the sombre, headlined black-on-white within.

The young assistant leaves the pregnant women and continues on her round. Those who suspect nothing out of the ordinary gratefully watch her coming. She is indeed young and pretty, unlike a harbinger of death. On the other hand it seems just possible that she is coming to tell them some comforting news she has picked up about their ailment. Unlikely but possible. In this building all possible and impossible things have been heard and spoken. 'Well, when *is* the other coming?' shouts the elderly man from the other end of the room. In the silence following a man holding a fishing magazine is heard to remark that fishing has saved him.

'Not drugs,' he says, 'not doctors, not diet, not exercise.'

'What was wrong with you then?' says the man beside him. 'What was wrong, that only fishing helped?'

'Nothing wrong with the body,' says the other. 'Not unless you can talk of a body as strung with nerves as a hung-up puppet. Nerves were what was wrong. Nerves and nothing else.'

'Sounds bad,' says the one beside him. 'I've never had that. But what have fish got to do with it?'

'Casting a rod over a deep pool is what it is. Flicking the fly over a flowing stream. Not a sound from the bushes on a still day and not a ripple on the pool. The one and only thing that's cured a bad bout of nerves. No, don't talk to me about the medicine men, don't give me the psychiatrists. This is Nature, you understand. Or maybe you don't. Not many do these days.'

'But there's the tooth-and-claw bit, of course,' says the one beside him. 'How do you square that?'

'I don't. I've seen creatures gobbling one another up while I sat peacefully on the bank, insects biting, tangling to the death with other insects, great bugs chewing up small bugs. I've seen cats purring and pawing over mice, grown men forcing poison down rabbit holes. Screams and agony all around on a summer's day.'

'Funny that doesn't get on your nerves,' says the other.

'Well. I count myself one of these animals, of course. Maybe that's the reason. I've got used to my own cruel breed, for better or worse. I'm pretty tough, I daresay. Though I admit I came round here this evening because I didn't feel so good.'

Having got through papers and magazines there is little for the patients to do except watch the girl making the round of the room. Everyone stares at her – the women even more than the men. Their feelings are mixed. Some who have been flicking through romantic stories ask themselves whether the doctor has ever been in love with her. They wonder what the lonely, ageing wives make of such girls – the beautiful attendants of doctors and dentists, the glamorous private secretaries of business executives and politicians, the gorgeous guardian angels of every clergyman, spiritual director and bishop, the comely companions of all-night petrol-pump attendants, the stunning policewomen and the teacher's pretty helpmate. Tonight the thought of this weakens their resistance more than the flu or the sore throat, more even than the asthma. The awful injustice of it all grabs them in the pit of the stomach like the start of labour pains. True enough, somebody said, the wife is everything at the end of the day. A faithful wife is more precious than rubies. Rubies, was it, or was it emeralds? Emeralds or diamonds or just plain pearls? It is always terribly hard to get these jewel qualities of wives properly sorted out.

'And when is the *other* coming?' shouts the old man again from the end of the room.

'Just hold your tongue, you, and show some respect!' a woman exclaims.

Some of the children are getting bored now. There are a few toys near the table but they are for the younger ones. The older group ignore the scarlet wagon on wheels, the drum, the yellow truck carrying bricks, the moth-eaten teddy bear. The tired babies, their eyelids a faint blue with sleepiness, have started to wail and are being bounced on their mothers' knees. The girl in the blue overall watches the older children for a while, then holding a small boy and girl by the hand she takes them to the window and lets them kneel, each on a chair, to watch the flakes blowing outside. Now more people can be seen peering from kitchens across the street. Some there have almost forgotten they are looking into a waiting room. They have stayed so long staring out from darkening, empty rooms it seems they are envying the carefree closeness of the crowd opposite – the lively talk, the table covered with papers and coloured journals, the toys, the children playing, and in their midst this amiable young woman who is exceedingly attentive, who bends and speaks intimately to each person in turn like the good hostess at a party. The food is lacking, certainly, but no doubt there is a laden table somewhere behind the scenes.

By this time the nursing assistant has reached a very old

man sitting close to the gas fire. He is holding a small sporting paper and his hand shakes so wildly the sound of paper is out of all proportion to the size of page. It resembles some gale-swept poster tearing itself off the sea wall. His head is shaking too. To those who watch, it looks as if he is not at all startled by the girl's message, but rather affirming every word she says with a violent nodding of the head as if – unlike the others – he is agreeing silently but energetically that death is inevitable, not surprising at all and must be continually accepted without question. The girl braces his shoulders firmly for a second and passes on to a youngish couple sitting together by the window. 'Will he be long over the patients tonight, do you think?' says the woman glancing over her shoulder. 'We've such a distance to get home. If this goes on we might even be stuck out there. This time last year the car scarcely got through the last two miles on the hill. Of course, I know he can't help it. But will he be long? My husband's in pain. It actually took him an age to get down into this chair. He can neither sit down nor stand up, you see. And as for lying! Even a few pills for the night would help. Of course the doctor can't help it. He's no say over his time when the surgery's full. That's the worst of practices these days.'

The young assistant is thoughtful for a moment as if considering carefully this question of time. She raises her eyes and looks into a mirror between two posters on the opposite wall – one persuading people to stop smoking, the other discreetly mentioning kidney donation.

'No, they'll never get a kidney out of me,' says the grandfather of the child as he follows the direction of the girl's eyes. 'Not a kidney, not an eye! I'm keeping every bit of myself to the grave, and every drop of blood to the last. It's hard enough keeping myself together as it is, and getting harder every day!'

In the mirror the girl's face looks smooth and youthful. To the old people it seems she could never be thinking of

the passing of time, far less about death. Still she con-
scientiously gives her news to the once snow-bound couple
who lean forward attentively to listen, then grab one
another's hands. This young husband who is supposed
to be unable either to sit down or to stand up, gets to his
feet in one straight, sudden movement like a dancer who
raises his partner with him by force of an unexpected
discord in the musical score. The three of them stand
together for a moment – the young couple with the nurse.
Slowly she presses them down into their chairs again. She
takes great care doing this – putting one hand on the
woman's shoulder, supporting the man's back with the
other and making sure their feet are firmly set on the floor –
planting them, so it seems, like fragile plants into deep
earth before she turns away.

Beside them are two men discussing the repair of an old
car. The older has his arm encased in plaster from wrist to
elbow and he holds it out stiffly in a half-salute towards the
middle of the room. Once in a while children come up and
tap it curiously with a fingernail. Unlike the drum on the
table it makes a dull, heavy sound. These men have already
heard what has been said to the couple on their right. The
nurse stops beside them only for a moment. 'Well, that's
the saddest thing,' says the youngest man, 'and he can't
have been much older than me. I always liked that doctor –
loved isn't too strong a word. He came once in the middle
of the night – when I could hardly breathe, when I was in
such a panic I thought it was the finish of me. Believe it or
not, I started to breathe again the minute that man came
through the door. And when he started to talk to me things
were O.K. as if nothing had happened. What did he talk
about? I remember something about his mother's hens.
Anyway the sheer stupidity of those hens, clucking and
scraping through that night, brought me round. And then
the smooth, harmless eggs lying there in the morning straw.
Well, the whole thing calmed me. Whenever I have another

attack I think of hens. What else he did for me I *can't* remember. The poor young man. To tell you the truth I'm terrified to hear that news. I feel bereft. I'm sorry I sound so heartless – talking about myself,' he says to the nurse.

'Not heartless at all,' she replies, noticing that he is pale and beginning to gasp a little like a man forcing his head suddenly out of a strong wave. She takes his hand and draws a deep breath. When his colour returns and they are both breathing slowly and regularly together, she moves on. Once again from the far corner of the room the old man shouts louder than ever: 'When is the other *coming?*'

It is snowing heavily now, and with their fingers the children follow the criss-crossing tracks down the window-pane or make sudden, swooping movements with their hands as the flakes blow upwards on a gust of wind. In the windows of the houses opposite several people are still staring across. Some have even left the TV screen to watch. The ghostly blue light still flickers behind them as they peer enviously down into this real, lit room full of flesh-and-blood men, women and children with their genuine fire, their real toys, papers and pictures and all presided over by a friendly girl, prettier than a TV star. This girl has made the full circle of the room and now she reaches the door where she stands in silence. Everyone waits for her to speak, even the children loading the yellow truck with the last brick and the kneeling snowflake-tracers who have now climbed down and are rubbing their red knees. The watchers in the windows opposite, seeing nothing but her moving lips, wonder if she is welcoming the company, promising something better to come, or already on the point of saying goodbye. 'I am so sorry I had to give you this news tonight,' says the girl. 'It's a terrible shock for all of us. You've waited here too long, I know. But I thought it better to tell each one of you.' She puts her hand on the door and tells them that another doctor will be here early the next day and that meantime any emergency can be seen around the corner in the next street. She gives a name, a street number, a telephone number. And now she waits for the patients to leave. Slowly they get up, one by one, and come across. Some touch her quickly on the arm, in passing, or on the shoulder, as she has done to them. One or two give the crown of her head a quick, light stroke. These are all cautious touches as if to discover if she is truly flesh, blood and bone, to make sure she will still be there for them tomorrow and the day after and all the weeks to come, if need be. Yet all these discreet touches have done something to the girl. Her hard shore-substance is being gradually dissolved by this sea of need. The determination is wavering slightly. The last people to leave see that she is in tears.

In spite of the movement through the door the waiting room is not yet empty. An old woman, sitting where she has sat for the last half-hour, is still there, knitting. Opposite, on the other side of the table, a serious middle-aged man is still engrossed in his book. Long ago the nurse has spoken to them, but it is as if they had never heard. She approaches the woman. 'The others are going now,' she says. 'I'm afraid you'll have to go off as well. You see, I have to close the place in a few minutes.' For a while the knitting needles click on more rapidly than ever. Then the old woman drops the red, woollen scarf for an instant to remark:

'I am waiting to see my doctor! No, not *any* doctor. My *own* doctor! Even if I have to wait all night!'

'Will you help me?' says the girl, moving across to the reading man. 'She doesn't seem to know what's happened, though I tried to tell her. Perhaps you can help. I'm sure you understand.'

'Yes, I understand all right, but I can't help,' says the man. 'Of course I'd *like* to help. But I can never get this death business into my head straight off. I don't just mean the doctor's death. Any death. It's stupid, isn't it? At my age. Utterly stupid and childish. But do you mind if I sit

here for a while longer till I get the hang of it? Then I'll
certainly try to persuade the old girl to leave with me. Do
you mind?'

'No, I don't mind at all,' says the girl, 'and I'll sit myself
for a bit. There's not all that hurry.' The three of them sit
silently and apart with only the sound of needles clicking
and the surreptitious turning of the pages of a book. After a
while the girl goes through a door leading to a cupboard
and comes out five minutes later with a tray, a pot of tea,
three cups and saucers, sugar, milk, three biscuits on a
plate. She pours the tea and hands it round.

Opposite, the lonely TV watchers, peering from dark
rooms through flurries of snow, can scarcely believe their
eyes. Oh, the luck of some people! This easy get-together,
the comfortable tea-talk and the friendly warmth on a
freezing night. How they have missed all this, not just this
night but every night! Yes, every night of their lives this very
thing has managed to go past them without their knowing
it.

The man with the book makes the first move. He goes
across to the old woman and takes her ball of wool between
his hands. 'What's this you're knitting?' he asks.

'A scarf for my third grandchild,' she replies. 'Two years
old next month.'

The man presses the soft, scarlet ball against his cheek
and stares at her. 'Will you let me take you home in my car?'
he says. 'I'm going to take the young lady home too. So
you'll be perfectly safe,' he adds.

'Yes, I'll go,' she replies. 'Though I'd always feel perfectly safe here, of course, even if I was the last one left. As a
matter of fact I always feel safe when I'm waiting to see the
doctor, though I do happen to know there are certain folk
who feel they've never been nearer danger or even death
when they set foot inside this waiting room. But there's
really no need for that, is there?'

'None at all,' says the man. 'Come along now before it

gets worse out there.' He takes her one arm, the girl takes the other, and they leave the room.

The snow is driving down so thickly against the windows that, fortunately, no watcher from the opposite side can now see this desolate, vacant room, its empty chairs arranged as in some séance which – deserted by all its members – still hopefully awaits the return of one punctual and devoted spirit.

# The Man Who Wanted to Smell Books

THIS WAS THE time when every book in the world had been put on tape, when long ago every catalogue in every library could be read from hundreds of flickering screens which quickly settled down into a steady blue and green twilight shade, or at times a purple, violet and pink the colour of rainbows. The library which had once been a murky, mysterious place was fun at last. It was a place of games, movement and excitement. The change not only made the whole thing as colourful as a film show – it was also a tremendous help to everyone. No reader had to get his hands dirty searching along dusty shelves. There was no need to question and pester the librarian from morning till night. All twisting stairs and dank corners where intruders could lurk unseen had been demolished. Gone also were those dark cellars where people had eaten their sandwiches, made love, written their own books, meditated, slept and even occasionally died. Nowadays it was no longer necessary to lug awkward holdalls, briefcases and carrier bags. The heavy books were gone. The age of the Easy Reader was in. So also of the Happy Librarian.

Naturally there must always be someone who wants to spoil everything, who begins to look backwards instead of forwards. His head is forever twisted the wrong way round like the odd man out in a well-drilled regiment. Such persons have to be brought to heel in one way or another. For those with happy memories, or any memories at all, for that matter, are enemies of progress. Such a man was Charlie Syson who – while standing in an immaculate and streamlined library, strung with glittering tubes and wires, shining boxes and rainbow-coloured screens – remarked that he wanted to smell books again. He politely voiced this wish to a young girl standing by a table. She looked frightened at first, then agitated, then, as he hung about, moved nearer to her colleague and replied:

'I'm sorry, but you've come to the wrong place. You will never smell a book again here. I doubt if you'll smell one in any decent library now. All that sort of thing was done away with years ago. I've heard them talked about, of course – those smelly books. I believe you had to wash your hands after touching them in case you caught something. Most of them had those dark grey, brown and black covers so you could never really tell what was inside. Oh yes, my grandparents remember them. Sometimes they used to prop them up at mealtimes against a milk jug, poor old souls. Hygiene was scarcely thought of in those days. So I'm sorry, I can't help you about smelling books. But we still do have talks about them from time to time in this library, though people aren't very interested in the subject, I'm afraid. So there are always lots of tickets left over for these meetings if you care to apply for them.'

'But it wasn't *only* the smell,' said Syson, going back to his opening bid. 'I liked to feel them too. Some of them were rough, hard, even lumpy on the outside. Others were plump, padded and soft. And there was something thrilling too about the difference between the outside and the inside. The pages were either thick and grainy or smooth and silky. They could be yellow-brown or pale brown, pure white or creamy-white.' The two librarians exchanged a glance and looked around to see whether the head of the place was near. They realized whom they were speaking to now. They were speaking to the Sensual Reader and, what was worse, an elderly sensualist at that. 'But it's true,' said the man. 'You couldn't tell what they were really like. Well, what is anything *really* like – man, woman or book? Yes, they were often black, brown and grey, but even that dingy disguise appealed to me, if only for the surprise when you opened them up. I liked to stroke my fingers down the centre of a book before I started to read. It is best with two fingers – the third and the index, for example. Though naturally you can do it any way you want.'

'Nobody does that sort of thing in here,' said the first girl quickly. 'We deal with corners, edges, and flat, clean surfaces. And everything is absolutely open and above board. You are perfectly free to look around if you care to.'

'Thanks, but I can see everything at a glance,' said the old reader. 'That's the amazing thing – this seeing everything at a glance, yet actually seeing nothing at all, nothing but flashes and reflections, moving lights and blinking coloured dots. It's mesmerizing. It's a brilliant idea!' He was thoughtful for a moment and went on: 'But don't think I was remembering only the old black and brown books. Not at all. When I knew it, this library occasionally got the brand new books as well. They were so new that when you opened them for the first time they gave a strange creak, a cry of pain – or perhaps it was pleasure – at being discovered by an ardent reader. In this way I established a kind of relationship with the writer.' Their visitor looked about him. 'Obviously you are very far from your writers in here, and a great deal better too, I daresay – uneasy, touchy creatures that they are! Vain, shy, irritable, inarticulate, unpredictable and uncompanionable. Yes indeed. How much better to file them away in boxes and on screens.'

'Oh I see you know a good deal about writers,' said one of the girls more cordially. 'What was your own job then?'

'I've been an addict of print as long as I can remember. I was a compositor in the old days. I suppose that gave me a head start. Naturally I miss the books. I miss the shelves. Even half-empty shelves were moving to me – those where the books stood alone and apart after the others had gone, like separated friends communicating only through empty space.'

'And I was told there were others,' said the librarian, 'so tightly packed you could hardly draw one out without breaking a finger joint.'

'Yes, and I liked to give those grimy old books an occasional airing,' the visitor replied. 'Those ancient histories of dentistry, yellowing like old teeth, the musty clerical biographies and the volumes of hell-fire sermons, surveys of streets and houses long since demolished. How close yet isolated they were!'

One of the girls whom Syson had first approached stepped forward now.

'You don't find the screens rather exciting?' she asked. He looked around him. It was true the eerie screens seemed related to the space and movement of a universe rather than to a city library. The man had to admit that this was their attraction. The flickering green and white lines against an unearthly blue were like no known writing. With this script one was meant to speak and write to dead friends, consult oracles or angels, make one's pact with the devil or with God, as well as learning languages, taking advice from the doctor and dictating the details of the funeral. These screens had the mesmeric quality of all glass, thick and thin – the glass of telescopes, microscopes and crystals. The magic of hieroglyphics was here, and of undiscovered numbers and letters. Perhaps, the old reader thought, the whole world would soon become a gigantic screen on which one might decipher stories and histories of the cosmos – a huge white blank like those monstrous drive-in TV screens on which limousines, skyscrapers and gigantic, mouthing faces loom out suddenly from a lonely American background of forests, mountains and prairies.

But the girl was speaking again. 'Don't think we don't understand you. As I said, most of us had parents and grandparents who were great readers in their time. I personally had grandparents who had a load of books they carted from place to place, lugged reverently from house to house. No, I haven't smelled one myself but I have an old photo of my grandmother holding a book very close to her face. No doubt she was doing just that: Or was she hiding?'

'Yes, yes,' the visitor admitted, 'it was possible to hide the face or even the whole head in a book. For complete privacy one simply shifted the book sideways or up and down. Every reader knew the trick, and no-one held it against the other. Not many places around here to hide, are there?'

The girl looked rather uneasily around the place. She was slim, but it was true there were few places to hide face or body. Here all things had been arranged in space as economically as possible. Most objects were sharply rectangular. Amongst them were flat containers holding hundreds of flat slides and round containers holding stacks of thin, round discs.

'I've no need to hide,' said the girl. 'And anyway I still can't understand what you have against cleanness, against neatness. The world's getting smaller every day, more crowded, and the time shorter. Think of the new space created here, the extra time. Can't you understand the miracle of the new techniques?'

'Talking about miracles,' said Charlie Syson, 'have you ever been round a paper-mill?'

'Never,' said the girl, closing her lips about the word as if paper was not and never had been a concern of her profession.

'Luckily,' said her visitor, 'I once had a friend who worked in such a mill when he was young. And very thankful I am I saw it before all those places disappeared for ever. This was one of the last to go. I saw the paper being made – the best paper, I'm talking about, not the fibrous newspaper stuff, the woody end of the trade. No, this was the best. I've seen the rags come down in lorryloads from factories and shops. White cuts and strips from shirts, blouses, sheets and tablecloths, some coloureds amongst them, all sorted into piles. Then every snip had to be beaten, pulped with water, pressed and squeezed dry.'

'And then?' said the girl.

'Beaten again,' said the man. 'Beaten. Then squeezed again, squeezed and squeezed dry.'

The girl sat down on the one chair near the counter. She murmured that she had been standing for a long time in the hot library, and that paper, as compared with light, colour and speed, was not something she could ever become excited about.

'I simply wanted you to feel how people laboured over the centuries to make this finer and finer paper,' said Syson, 'how they polished and refined it till it had the gloss of ivory or silk. They were proud of the stuff. Paper had always a royal history. It was a fit present for a king, emperor or pope. It was in monastery libraries, in palaces, even in ancient tombs. I myself when I left this paper-mill, was given a wad of fresh-cut paper, fit for a king.'

'What kind was it?' the girl asked.

'Writing paper. A great packet of the first-class stuff.'

'So you write endless letters?'

'None at all if I can help it. A postcard's all I've ever managed for years.'

'There, you see!' she exclaimed. 'All this praise for paper. Yet you've no use for it yourself.'

'Certainly not for letters. But it's not writing I'm talking about. It's reading. And by the way, what did you do with all the books? You must have been in the pulping business yourself. Or maybe you burned them.'

'A mixture of both,' the girl replied. 'But please don't imagine that we haven't saved a few. Of course we have. And people are perfectly welcome to look at them whenever they wish to.'

'You mean you can take me to them right now?' said the reader.

'Just wait for a moment. I'll come back in five minutes and take you down.'

Syson wandered about for a while, hands in pockets, in case he should disturb the zigzagging script on the screens. Yet he knew nothing could be disturbed here. The pattern was set, frenzied yet rigid. It was he himself who was madly disturbed by the brilliant predictability of the place, the cleanness, the smoothness, the demented mathematical order of every machine. Once in a while he raised his eyes to the window and saw – almost with disbelief – a cloud go past, expanding, dissolving, saw a bird, a leaf fly up, wayward and restless on the wind. The girl came back five minutes later. 'I'm ready now,' she said, 'if you'd like to come down to the basement where we keep some of the old books.'

The old reader went slowly down with her. Now he almost dreaded to see the old loves of his youth. Indeed, he dreaded to see how much they might have changed, how he might have changed himself. The girl herself seemed nervous, talking in a whisper as if careful not to awaken some dangerous creature from its lair. She opened the door a crack and he looked in, sweating a little in the warm, burial atmosphere of the place. He was aware he was peering into a Tutankhamen's tomb of buried books. 'You can smell them now, if that's what you want,' said the girl over her shoulder as she went in. She bent down to a shelf where there were some large volumes. Syson lifted the heaviest in both hands and studied its hard, dark grey cover with the black lettering.

'Do you know what this is?' he asked.

'No, as a matter of fact I've never known,' she replied. 'Never wanted to know either. Is it an art treasure?' She opened it up gingerly. 'It doesn't look like one, does it? No colour, and the writing's nothing special, neither the writing nor the paper.'

'It's ordinary print and paper,' said the visitor. 'And it's a book on insects – every insect in the world from A to Z.'

'Oh, what a disappointment for you!' cried the girl with genuine pity.

'No,' said Syson. 'It's a privilege to hold one of the surviving books – and very well preserved it is too, no mark or tear.'

'Just how it managed to survive, I've no idea,' said the girl. 'I daresay the cover was stronger than most, or maybe it's the dry atmosphere down here. All the same, I'm still sorry the first thing you laid hands on should be a book on insects, of all things.'

'What better thing to find,' said the reader. 'Aren't insects themselves the great survivors?'

'We haven't much time to worry about survival here,' said the girl. 'And the smallest flea could hardly survive upstairs. There's not a speck of dust to hide behind. But tell me about your insects.'

'To put it plainly,' her visitor replied, 'if we blow ourselves off the planet along with every living creature, those wiry insects will keep going. Perhaps a few to start with, then more and more as time goes on, till they take over the entire globe – a buzzing, hissing, crawling globe.'

'Could we go up soon?' said the girl. 'It's stuffy down here and there isn't a lot more to see.'

'No more treasures?' Syson asked.

'Very few. Some old pens, I believe. A typewriter, a curious reading-lamp that can bend its head any way you want, a magnifying glass, an ancient pair of spectacles, some rather sinister little bottles of white poison – the kind of thing the ancient scribes tipped their arrows with – Tipp-Ex it was called.'

Syson drew out a few other books. There was a small pencil-written diary of some early polar expedition. He pressed the thin book against his chest until the warmth of his body penetrated the pages. Through the cover he felt his heart knocking against his hand. 'Feel that,' he said to the girl. 'No book was made simply from sheets of paper. There's blood and a beating heart in there.'

She laid her hand cautiously on the cover, saying again, 'Could we go up now?'

Upstairs the other girl at the counter was waiting. 'Has the gentleman seen what he wanted to see?' she asked. 'Did he look at the books? Did he have time to study the old writing-desk with the ink stains, the revolving desk-chair, the bookcases with the shelves? If you're making a private museum,' she said to the reader, 'we'd be very pleased to consider selling them.'

'No, no, they're safe enough here,' said Charlie Syson. 'You must keep them. I'm getting old. If I took them, who knows what might happen to them when I die. I have no children, you understand.'

'But take something,' said the librarian. 'Take something – seeing you're so interested. What about an unusual pen? A Biro it was called. Or I believe we could find a real old pen with ink in a bottle if we looked in the basement cupboards.' A pen and ink arrived for Syson and he opened the visitors' book. There were other signings on this page. Amongst a list of names he noticed many symbols – flowers, birds, beetles, animals and trees. These were the signs of the oldest visitors who had almost forgotten how to write their names.

Charlie Syson turned over a leaf and signed boldly on a smooth, new page. Something told him this was the last time he would write his name on a good piece of paper again.

'And if you don't mind putting your occupation too,' said the librarian politely. Beside his name Syson wrote: READER (ext.).

'What does ext. stand for?' asked the librarian. 'Is it a foreign degree or an honorary term?'

'Not a degree,' Syson replied, 'and certainly no honour. Ext. stands for extinct.'

'Why, Mr Syson, we are all readers here!' she exclaimed. All around her, as if to confirm this, the green and blue lines flickered from every screen, while pulsing red and green dots and a rainbow of reflections streamed from distant corners of the room. There was a throbbing, a ticking, a humming of smooth-running instruments.

'I can add "a reader of the paper pages of books", if the meaning isn't clear,' the visitor said, 'or even "the good-smelling pages of books".'

'No, that's all right,' said the librarian quickly. 'We understand perfectly what you mean.'

At the same time, when Charlie Syson took his eyes from the machines he realized that the handling of paper and ancient books here had created a warmer feeling towards himself. It was not that they were hard on him, not critical. He was to be treated as a child, regressed beyond cure. But a child – even one with a total lack of adjustment – must still be cherished, set right and kept going for years and years in the better world.

It was nearly closing time and the two young assistants opened the heavy, outer door. As their visitor stepped into the street a strong wind struck him. While he was momentarily sent staggering it came to him as a pleasant shock that nobody so far had managed to tidy and control this particular part of the planet. A few old scraps of paper flew towards his feet like birds towards a bird-lover. He picked one up as it brushed his ankle. It appeared to be torn from an ancient 'thank you' letter, but the paper was tough, good quality stuff such as he'd described not long before. Moreover, it was inscribed in very clear pen and ink. 'It may be some time, but I will come again,' the scrap of sentence confidently predicted. Charlie Syson held it up and waved.

From the doorway the neat librarians waved back, before fastening the door firmly upon the dust and grit, the peel and paper, the petals, fluff and feathers of the runaway natural world.

# Choirmaster

ONE DAY, OUT of the blue, it came to Sam, the choirmaster, that God must be very tired of people constantly flopping to the ground and begging for this and that. Rows of men, women and children on their knees – whispering, imploring, pleading, whether in song or prayer. What way was that to ask for anything? God, it was said, was all-powerful and could do anything on earth or in heaven. Heaven was an unknown quantity, of course. But, looking around the earth, people could see things had gone badly, drastically wrong. Drought and famine had ravished some lands more ferociously than others. The sickening stench of death rose from the hot earth, and from the baked mud of the riverbanks. Birth and death arrived suddenly together. Scarcely was there time to dispose of the afterbirth than the burial cloths were unwound. Gone were the days when any choir could sing cheerfully of the good seed being sown and scattered regularly by men and watered just as punctually by God. The eyes of all those in this land dried up in their sockets while staring at the terrible, brazen sky. At each dawn all the vessels in the place were brought out – the jugs, the pitchers, basins and baths in order to catch every drop of the miraculous, God-given liquid when it fell. No water fell. No water had fallen for weeks and months. Obviously, as the old choirmaster now believed, God must be weary of the bent knee and the humble, bowed head. Perhaps it was bold, abusive songs and outraged shouts He was hoping for, not the quiet, muttered prayer and the thanks which would make the lesser gods shrivel with shame. Was it not possible that God wished to be commanded for a change, not cajoled at all?

Sam had always been a lusty shouter himself. He had formed his choir as he travelled, and as he travelled continually, he gathered together a huge company of men, women and children from the remoter parts of the world. He picked his singers from the desperate and hungry, from the ill and even the dying, from people too weak to work and from some who had been almost beaten to the ground by servitude. He therefore knew that wherever they went in the world, his choir would be singing to companions in suffering; and so, whatever else it sounded like, whatever words or music were used – the song must ring true. His singers understood this, and if they were forced to compete with tornadoes, the pounding of huge waves, claps of thunder, the last rumblings of earthquake – the more they tried to rise to Sam's demands. It was true they had their own demands, but never for anything petty. Depending on what piece of land they were passing through, the men asked for what they imagined were the simple rights of every man. They demanded work, water, bread, decent huts and medicine. Occasionally they might pray to God for death. The women asked for all these as well as care and comfort for their children. Occasionally they might ask for fewer babies and sometimes even for more, as long as they still had milk to give them.

As time went on some desperate people asked if it were possible that God might be a little deaf on account of His great age. Perhaps He was no music-lover, in spite of some talk of angelic choirs. Then the choirmaster saw that he would have his work cut out, teaching, explaining, reprimanding and generally dealing with the strong emotions of his singers.

'Look,' he said one day to his hungry and unhappy crowd. 'Please, if you can possibly help it, don't cry when you're begging for anything. Begging's bad enough, but begging *and* crying must make God feel really mean. Do you want Him to feel mean?'

'Yes, I do,' said a blind old man with fly-encrusted sores around his eyes and down his legs. His feet were bound in grey bandages and he leant on a stick. It was true he was on his last legs, yet might still live for a day or so.

'No, I don't think *I* do,' said a gaunt-faced, middle-aged woman with four small children behind her, two others clutching at her cloak, and a bulge-eyed baby in her arms. 'They are all beautiful,' she said, indicating each child with a nod of her head, 'but will I have the strength to love and feed them all?'

It was true that hundreds of people in the huge choir had hardly enough strength to raise their voices. A few could do nothing but lie on the ground and wait for death for themselves and their children. This would often come quickly. But a decent burial took strength from the living and many died in the doing of it.

Not everyone in the choir agreed with Sam's method of singing loudly all the time with scarcely a break.

'Hadn't we better stop and listen once in a while?' asked one old-fashioned believer. 'Wasn't there something about a still, small voice?'

'Yes, I've heard that, but I've always been against the idea,' said the choirmaster. 'As long as we've got the strength, we're here to sing, not to listen. Sure, people want to join my choir for all kinds of reasons. They tell me they've got great voices, clear voices, that they can reach the highest notes and the lowest. And, naturally, people like that have ambitions to be the star singer. Or maybe they've no voice at all, but just want to get away from a plaguing family back home. Whatever they've come for, what help are they to a company like ours, especially if they're interested in small voices? Isn't it hard enough to get people to stand up straight and open their mouths?'

Yet for a time the old choirmaster did think of adding to his singers. And it was not only here that he looked. There were plenty of good voices back in his own country to which he returned for a short time. Many there had joined in processions and stood on platforms, for one cause or another. Groups with banners gathered outside hospitals, colleges and churches. Some he brought back to his choir, whether they had fine voices or not. He needed to make up for all he had lost through sickness or death. But he himself changed a great deal as he grew older. He had seen so much of horror, pain and misery in the land that the idea of singing songs of love or thanks for anything on earth seemed out of the question. Nowadays, outrage towards heaven was what he looked for in his singers – anything that gave force and fury to the human voice, his only rule being that they sing with chests out and heads flung back. Always they must be defiant, never suppliant.

Sam would have liked the suffering creatures of the earth to be heard in his choir – birds and animals as well as men. For he believed that many creatures might find more protection there than those outside who suffered the cruelty of human beings – the trap-setters, the cage-builders and the money-makers behind the bleeding hell of the slaughterhouses. Yet, on second thoughts, he decided to stick only to humans and allowed them to sing exactly as they pleased, whether in fear, pain, fury or sorrow. As long as they made a loud enough noise they might curse or weep as much as they liked. There was, he told them, no one God to cry to – or, if only one, he had obviously been created by all races of men, in all ages of Time, and out of every belief that had ever been attempted on earth. The choirmaster again reminded his singers that thanksgiving must sometimes be very tough on God. No doubt He might rather be bullied a bit, scolded, and even openly threatened for a change.

The choirmaster was growing old and tired. These days he was often hard put to vary the singing to every catastrophe. They came so thick and fast there was hardly time to draw breath before the next shattered the community; the flood and famine, dust and drought, disease and death, and all followed by endless questions: 'Why, why, why?' Then the hopeless non-answers. Finally silence.

But the old man kept on with his training. Above all, it was essential to teach his choir the loud and soft notes in the human voice. They had to sing as loud as possible to be heard through the landslides and earthquakes, or simply to alert the desperate inhabitants of lonely places that help was on the way. It also took great skill to teach them to change from the loudest possible crescendo to a sound so quiet that the cry of an infant or even the whisper of a dying child might be located under some mountain of rubble.

By this time the outrage choir was pretty well established, but one day the choirmaster – ever on the look out for likely singers – picked up another possible member. His company was passing a forest one evening when a young man appeared out of the darkness between two trees. The trees were tall, their broad jungle-leaves casting great shadows around the newcomer, giving the impression that he was delicate. This was an illusion. He was thin but sturdy with strong, muscular legs and large, workman's hands. He had the unusual attraction of a darkish brown skin and clear, blue eyes. It was hard to tell whether he came from the north, the south, the east or the west.

'I heard you coming a long way off,' he said. 'What sort of procession is it?'

'No procession at all,' Sam answered. 'This is a choir, and monstrously hard work it is too, dealing with an unruly crowd like this. But I'm not grumbling because that's exactly what I want them to be – unruly and complaining!'

'What are they complaining about?' the young man asked.

'Complaining's a poor word. I was wrong to use it,' replied the choirmaster. 'They're not girning or whingeing about some paltry thing, some petty grudge. Those who still have strength are shouting to high heaven about the hopelessness of this earth – the thirst, the hunger, the pain, the misery. Some are still singing quite sweetly, of course. Most are cursing.'

'Lord, but it must be a tough job leading a choir like that!' exclaimed the stranger.

'It certainly is. But one day I might get them to sing properly as well as shout. I confess it was I who worked them up. But still, it *is* supposed to be a choir, not only a furious rabble.'

'May I join your choir?' the young man asked.

'It all depends on the voice,' said the choirmaster.

'A tenor,' the other replied.

'Then I doubt if I can take you on,' said Sam. 'Tenors tend to sing about sweetness, peace, love, harmony and the rest of it. All the things this world is almost totally lacking in. Myself, I believed in all that once. Not now, of course.'

'And I can sing solos,' the young man went on, as if not having heard the last remark.

'Sorry, but I never allow solo singing,' said the choir-master firmly. 'Soloists always become vain, no matter how modest they seem to be at the start. They tend to be temperamental too, and before you know where you are, they're acting like spoilt children. There is this terrific silence whenever a tenor solo gets up to sing – you must have noticed that yourself – as if he were a prince or god or some such being. People can even fall in love with tenors before the last note's out. It all plays havoc with a well-trained choir, and this *is* a well-trained choir! Once they've settled down you'll hear them sing. And I've worked so hard with them. A good choir is my one real aim in life. As in every art it's a case of balance and gravity, if you like. We can't afford too much emotion.'

'Nevertheless, you need a hell of a lot of emotion to sing well,' said the young man. 'To put anything across at all – that's a lifetime's work. Anyway, you're certainly putting it over. There's no doubt it will reach this Almighty Person you're singing to.'

'You mean He has huge, listening ears as well as everything else?'

'Possibly,' said the other. 'I've never thought about His different parts.'

'Wherever He is, I seldom think about Him nowadays,' said the old choirmaster. 'He has allowed such fearful things to happen here. I can hardly bring myself to look up at all, far less utter a respectful word. I think I'd choke if I did. Yet I can still manage to train a good choir. Imagine that!'

'You're probably best to choke and have done with it,' the newcomer replied. 'And I like people who speak their minds. Myself, I'm not so fond of the meek as I was sometimes thought to be when I was young.'

'You certainly still look young enough to me!' exclaimed the choirmaster.

'No, no, I can scarcely remember what that was like. I think I never was really young at all.'

'Well, I'll let you join us for a bit,' said the older man, 'and we can judge what kind of voice you have. Naturally, I can't promise anything right now. A great many people have wanted to join, but the moment they find it's not a church outing with picnic included, they fall away at once.'

'I've no interest in church choirs myself, nor Sunday School picnics, for that matter,' the young man assured him.

So it turned out that this newcomer was allowed to practise with the rest. But the choirmaster knew he was taking a big risk. The choir itself was never too pleased with his rare, haphazard choice of new members. Moreover, it was no longer as straightforward as in the old days when the choirmaster had been full of optimism and simple belief. Nowadays any new recruits he chose for his choir were strangely mixed. Either they would show too little anger in their voices – falling back into the old, placating tone, or else they allowed out-of-hand fury to spoil the rhythm and tempo of the song.

Yet the old choirmaster didn't hurry his new member into song. He allowed him to find his feet before he even opened his mouth. The young man was simply encouraged to walk along with the choir for a while, not singing, but just chatting with them, finding out how much strength they could still summon up for practice, hearing how they could still manage to sing in harmony even while often hating one another's guts. Some would confess how deeply they resented what they'd heard of other choirs in the cities of the world – choirs used to all the perks of wealthy companies – applause that went on for hours with endless flower-throwing, plus banquets and bouquets and beautiful women. Many, in fact, were bitter that they'd ever met up with the old choirmaster who, for reasons of his own, had, early on, gathered them into this company where they now suffered the humiliation of becoming a crowd of travelling beggars under a one-time raving idealist who could offer no food, no water, no medicine and no comfort of any kind, while gradually letting his own hopes and beliefs peter out as the arid, blazing days went on. Sometimes he appeared unsteady on his feet as the starving inhabitants of each village pressed around him, trying to claw pity from his heart. Often, at night, he would wonder what would become of him if pity ever deserted him.

As for the choir, the reasons for their present suffering gradually became clear. Long ago, when Sam took over, he had forced them to sing – no, not merely to sing but to shout – loud and triumphantly about the Love of God. Love! The scorn, the fury, the disappointment and bitterness in their singing gradually grew to a raucous crescendo as they realized what they had walked into, unawares. And now, even the old choirmaster was disintegrating before their eyes.

'So he's seen no more of this enormous love than we

have!' they cried. 'This old man's taken us through deadly heat and freezing cold with nowhere to camp – through forests and deserts, all of us hungry and filthy as pariah dogs. He thinks we'll follow for the rest of our lives, like fools. Let's sing something different, so furiously blasphemous it will frighten the life out of him. Then we can run back to our homes, if there's still a home to run to. But where will our children be now? Will our husbands and wives have left long ago? They will curse us for leaving, then curse us for coming back! What a fix the old one has got us into! May he be damned!'

The new singer held up his hand. 'Wait!' he shouted. 'Don't forget your God gave you freedom – the freedom to come or to go, to turn good into bad and bad into good. But have you taken your freedom?'

Again the air was filled with furious muttering. More fierce cries and curses went up into the sky. 'There must be silence!' the young leading singer reminded them, 'or else the God will not hear that He is loved and forgiven!'

'Never! How we have suffered!' came shouts from every side. 'Where is this love? He had no love. Now we have none ourselves!'

The great trees whistled and creaked in accord. Hissing came through the dripping leaves. At least a quarter of the choir left immediately and ran back as fast as they could down the way they had come. The new singer watched them go sympathetically, while the rest hesitated, in two minds whether to follow or to stay. Many were still pondering on this unknown Love of God.

'What kind of love is this?' they demanded, 'this love that allows terror and torture to innocent men and beasts?' There had been loving parents in some lucky lives, of course: a few loving friends, a loving teacher or two, loving cats and dogs. A few admitted that, not clearly knowing what love meant, they had recklessly given it to all sorts of undeserving persons, and been let down, dropped, deserted, and swiftly passed over or replaced. So did this God-love have infinite meanings then – all different from anything known on earth? If so, what was the use of talking about it?

'Time to talk or sing if we ever get to heaven!' came a shout. 'Right now, let's keep our mouths shut!'

There was complete silence, so much so that the old choirmaster came back to see what had happened. 'Are you working them up about something?' he asked the new member. 'If so I'll have to ask you to leave at once. I've put a life's work into training them, and I can't afford to hear it all go for nothing. What's more, I'm afraid I've changed my mind about the love-singing and even the love-talk. I'm into *Justice* now. *Justice* is the greatest thing on earth!'

'But will you let me stay and sing with your choir a little longer?' the young man asked.

'That's fair enough, of course. And I will stand and listen as hard as I can,' said Sam, stepping from the fringe of the forest into the sunlight.

The sound he heard was like light itself – sometimes flashing up through the trees and descending again into blackness through thick leaves, and once more climbing up a scale of brilliance till it reached a sunburst of sound. Bells, flutes and cymbals like those that herald the appearance of a new king were heard, and then a second descent into the dark evening shadow moving swiftly along the ground.

'Have they fallen on their knees to pray and praise then?' Sam asked incredulously, peering at the men and women on the ground.

'Not yet,' said the new singer. 'How on earth could they sing with tongues parched dry with thirst, with stomachs blown tight as drums with hunger?'

'But have they sung up forgiveness to God yet?' the old man asked.

'No, no,' the other answered again. 'He will not be

forgiven for a long, long time. Only when the desert is green as an orchard, when the dying children get their milk and lose the look of wizened age. Only then.'

The old choirmaster stepped forward defiantly. 'Of course the *singing* sounded good,' he said. 'But I'm not sure what you're trying to do. Are you trying to be different from all other singers?'

'Yes, I suppose I am,' the other conceded.

'Then what exactly are you aiming at?' the old choirmaster went on. He had known all along that this particular singer was proud, if not actually arrogant. He had met all types in his profession – the cringing and the confident, loud-voiced braggarts and soft-voiced hypocrites, bullying voices and begging ones. Yet it was difficult to know where this particular voice fitted in. All he could vouch for was that it was a totally new and beautiful one. And so powerful it was that the man was automatically taken as leader.

The young man was silent for a while before answering Sam's question. 'You ask what I'm aiming at. I am helping people to forgive the Almighty One for all the terrible things He has allowed on earth – the unbelievable wretchedness and frightful pain. He has forgiven them for many things. Now they can forgive Him. *He* can never be human. *They* can never be gods, but at least they can show they are human and be proud of it.'

'Don't try to change my singers,' said the old choirmaster. 'It has taken me long enough to prevent the bending knee and that horrible, begging note.'

'There'll be none of that if I have anything to do with it,' the new member assured him. 'They must go on shouting and cursing for as long as they wish. First the God must be shown fearlessly all they have endured. Then He might be forgiven. You will let me stay a short time with your singers, then?'

Again the old choirmaster could only agree. He waited, rather jealously, to hear what other sound this newcomer would bring from his choir. The old man believed that he had heard all sounds produced by animal and human throat. But this was something else. Fearful sounds and words evoking frightful images; young men, women and children of every race sliced to the bone by guns, beheaded by bombs; the frightened breath of children waiting for doors to open in the night; the roar of the wounded lion, the scream of the trapped hare, the terrified bellow of beasts with rolling eyes, slung up for slaughter; the rumbling of earthquakes spurting from unknown depths. These were not sounds only from throat or ground. These were the sounds of Hell on earth.

The young leader lifted up his arms, urging the choir to louder and louder shouts of outrage. Then he raised his hand for silence. 'That was excellent!' he called. 'You have shown a magnificent fury for the things allowed by God. Now you can show forgiveness to match!'

Again the air was filled with furious mutterings and cries of complaint.

'You see, they are not stupid,' the old choirmaster explained. 'Most of the things we heard are the fault of Man. They have nothing to do with God. Anyway, He is above thanks or blame. To think anything else would be blasphemy.'

Old Sam had once hoped to be a popular preacher in a large city church with a decent stipend and a gathering of well-dressed ladies and gentlemen who would listen to him with unquestioning respect. How he longed, after all these years in the wilderness, to arrive at a cool, Christian building where there was no cursing, no obscenity, no endless questions and no striving on his part to offer quickfire explanations for every single horror that had ever happened upon earth!

He sidetracked a good deal of the argument nowadays. Yet he was still left with the humiliating desire to keep on with his own nagging questions, whether directed to an

angel or devil in his own mind or even to some interloper
who might happen, in passing, to step out of a dark wood.
He turned again to the young singer for reassurance. 'It *is*
the fault of human beings, isn't it?' he asked anxiously.
'The old barbaric gods would have allowed these horrors,
of course, but not the great, good God of Love we have
prayed and sung to day after day, year in year out.'

'I can promise great changes will come one day,' the
younger man replied.

'One day, one year, one eternity,' added the old choirmaster, shaking his head dolefully.

The young man smiled. He had always foreseen more
doubt than hope. One had to wait aeons and aeons of time
for hope. Suddenly he left the path. He entered the forest
again. Black darkness hid him.

'Is that young man gone for good?' asked one of the
singers. 'I liked him. His standards were far too high, of
course. He will never be popular.'

'He may well come again,' the choirmaster replied. 'He
was simply here to see the damage and the pain for himself.'

'But who brought it on us?' the singer asked again.

'No doubt we brought it on ourselves,' said the old man.

'That is an easy answer,' said the other.

'Yes, I believe you're right,' the choirmaster agreed. 'It
would take some superhuman power to bring all the
catastrophe that has occurred on earth.'

'So that is the only answer you can find?'

'Well, I am only human,' said the old man. 'And I am
tired. What more can I say? For the whole of my life I have
been dumbfounded.'

Hearing this, the rest of the choir circled protectively
around him. They were no longer angry. Doubt was more
lovable than an iron faith, they decided. This looser circle
they had formed let in both light and shadow. People felt
free to break away from it and to come back again, to stand
still, argue or be silent, to sing in tune or discord, to listen

or to stop their ears. It was no sacred circle. Those who left were not followed or persuaded by love, the binding ties of friendship or the community spirit – to come back.

Over the centuries came changing groups of singers with their choirmasters. Rules changed. Tunes changed. Hopes rose and fell. Only music itself remained and the great forest of ancient trees. But every choirmaster taught his group not only how to sing, but to listen intently and to count the beat. Sometimes the songs were strident with bitterness, sometimes mellow with hope. Often for endless time there was no singing at all in the forest. But always an ardent listening for the return of a young leader hacking down branches to let in light – and for the terrible and confident crackle of His approaching footsteps over aeon upon aeon of fallen twigs.

# Through the Forest

HE LIVED ON the outskirts of a huge, ancient forest, but as he grew older Martin began to be disenchanted with his walks there. That was the difficulty with fairy tales and why, he supposed, some parents and teachers advocated more down-to-earth reading for children. The forest tales had told of entering the great woods and remaining for years or perhaps for ever. After walking for ten miles or so an ugly but exceedingly wise dwarf would disclose the secret and the strangeness of one's birth and upbringing. Some years later and many miles further on one would meet the beautiful and ideal companion for life. Great happiness began and that was the end of it.

But there was something missing in the forest these days and something menacing. It was not in the fear of meeting wild animals. Most of the animals, wild or tame, had been shot. It was not in fear of darkness, because the gaps between the trees had become wider and wider in recent months and soon there was so much daylight to be seen that there was no possibility of losing oneself.

The fairy stories quickly faded in the light of day. In fact, as time went on, they began to seem foolish. Where were the lonely cottages where some old woman would emerge with bowls of soup for the cold and hungry? Where were the kindly old woodchoppers who pointed the way home to lost travellers? Often he felt a spurt of anger towards his parents who had brought him up on such tales when all the time they had known the true, hard facts and had hidden them from him.

However, one day – not far from the path – he did come

on a cottage and, glancing through the window, saw a room full of people. Three or four girls caught sight of him and came out, led by a young woman in clean, blue dungarees. Her chest was firmly flattened by a clipboard from which hung a Biro on a chain. She looked him over through horn-rimmed spectacles. 'Did you bring anything to eat?' she asked. Martin looked puzzled. 'Anything to *eat*?' she repeated briskly. 'If you're joining us even for a day I'm afraid you have to bring your own food. We'll probably be here till evening.' She held out her board for him to inspect. 'As you know, we're collecting names,' she said, pointing to three columns already filled. 'We're fairly near the road here, so we get people coming from the city and also coming through the forest from the other side. We want to be completely unbiased ourselves, of course, though obviously we do know where we stand.' To Martin she looked exceedingly tough and biased, but as yet he didn't know on what side. He was intrigued. For a moment the old fairy tales came back – the good spells and the bad. Name collecting, name speaking could be a matter of witchcraft just as surely as the taking of photos, the painting of portraits could be to primitive tribes. Certainly this brisk young woman was not his idea of a witch, but his parents had misled him on so many things. They could have misled him on this one too.

The young woman held the board steady. 'If you could simply sign your name here,' she said, pointing to a clear space and handing him the pen on the chain. 'Just your full name and address, your age and phone number too, if you don't mind; and there's a space for anything else you might wish to say about yourself – married, single, divorced. Any brothers or sisters? Illnesses in the family. Your job, special interests, hobbies and that kind of thing. The name of your bank and your account number would be helpful. Are your parents still alive? Did you ask what we're here for?' She raised her head momentarily. 'We are speaking for the right of people to have houses built where they please, the right to have more and more freedom to spread, to build schools, churches, shops and offices with garages and transport nearby. Maybe a couple of cinemas, a dancehall and a skating rink.'

'Did they tell you?' said Martin.

'Naturally, I don't know them myself personally. The city tells us what they want. The city speaks for all of us – for you, for me, for everyone. Perhaps you think you are alone in liking trees. As a matter of fact, I like trees as much as anyone else. But there's no use being romantic at the expense of others. Now they are making room for houses.'

'But there isn't room.'

'There's plenty of room!' She circled with her arm the sky, the ground, the leafy distances of trunk and twig. 'It's waste ground,' she said.

'No, it's a forest,' Martin replied, wishing that the leaves at least would rustle and snap in protest, that branches would sway and crack in violent gestures of grief and fury. But no wind sprang up to move them. They had no voice.

'You know I do believe you've got the wrong idea of me,' said the girl, smiling. 'Don't imagine I don't love nature.' The young man who was called Martin stared at her. She was a well-groomed girl. Her shoes were very new – neither dirty nor down-at-heel. Her fingernails were immaculate. Her face was calm and well made up. Her hair would be trim and smooth until the wind got at it. She had walked through sun and rain without being torn or spat upon by pouncing trees, without getting lost, being frightened by darkness, startled by strange sounds, clawed by hateful thorns or brought down by hidden roots. God knows she would never be fool enough to eat the poison berries brought by an evil witch. She had come by way of a superstore and bought the morning-fresh sandwiches wrapped in Clingfilm.

'It's just,' she explained, 'that people are more important

than trees.' Martin glanced at the busy, unprepossessing group behind her. There was no room for sentimentality here. He saw at once that they were not more important than trees. They might, at a pinch, be more important than certain kinds of prickly bush. They were undoubtedly more important than the overpruned trees on either side of a new thoroughfare, but they did not appear, at this moment, half as important as the great trees of the old forest. Nevertheless he realized he was on dangerous territory. Might he not be felled to the ground for such thoughts?

'Well, I see I've been mistaken,' said the girl, briskly pressing her clipboard more firmly against her chest. 'I see you are not *one of us*. Perhaps you'll come to a different, more human view when you've had time to think about it. The trouble with you,' she said as a parting shot, 'is that you're so immature. In fact, if you don't mind me saying so, you're what we all call *green*.'

'Yes. Well, naturally I am. I've just joined it.'

'Joined what?'

'I've joined the Green Party.'

They stared at him pityingly. 'Fair enough,' said one, 'but it's got little to do with real day-to-day politics. Nothing to do with helping The People. Anyway we'll give you one or two forms to read, and you can contact us when you change your mind.' Martin noticed she said 'when' not 'if'. There were no 'ifs' amongst the pioneers of progress.

There was an assenting murmur amongst the group as they parted to let him through. Martin walked on. There was no wind and overhead there was silence. Under his feet it was quiet too with the silence of moss and herb, fed by centuries of sun and dew. Only the snap of a pine cone came to his ears and the sound of a bird tapping at snail shells in the leaves. He was a good deal shaken by the clipboard girl and by his own childish naïvety in thinking that any growing thing could now remain untouched.

Again he was astounded that his careful guardians, teachers and elderly relations could have shown him endless pictures of flowers and green forests without pointing out the huge, smiling bill-boards on the outskirts, advertising toothpaste, cigarettes and Coca Cola. Why, in their stories of fairies, elves and angels had there been no warning of wild, screaming streets, the blocks of black factories, the smell and glitter of thousands of cars along the highway?

Now, as he walked on, he noticed that the path was gradually growing harder underfoot. The moss changed into smaller and smaller stones until he found himself walking along a newly gravelled path. Suddenly an electric saw started up in front of him, beginning as a thin whine and rising to a steady, skull-shattering scream. There were wood-cutters here – not at all like the wood-choppers of his early stories, ever ready to tell a gormless traveller some unlikely tale of the woods. No, this lot were getting on with it as quickly as possible, ready to talk when the job on hand was finished. The sound of the screaming saw stopped suddenly and total silence beat about the spot. The men stood watching Martin in amiable amusement. 'You've not heard that sound before?' Martin shook his head.

'Where have you been living all this time then?' Martin indicated vaguely some distant place on the other side of the forest. He was loath to confess his ignorance of what went on in any other part.

'Well give it a year or two or even less, and you're going to see a few tidy rows of bungalows going up along here and a broad main road, of course. We'll see a beauty once the concrete's down, with lamps and all to come. Obviously it's going to take longer than the plan. Pedestrian crossings. Stop and Go. Ladies and Gents. Bins. Shelters. Telephones. The lot. Nobody knows where the money comes from or even who wants the things. But they always come in the end, no matter if the talk goes on for months.'

'But I never thought you'd gone so far already,' said

Martin. 'There's a crowd back amongst the trees who are still collecting names.'

'There's always funny folk among the trees,' said the woodman. 'What names?'

'People who agree and disagree. It's all been agreement as far as I can see.'

'Makes not a bit of difference,' said the other. 'The whole thing's settled and done with long ago. Years and years ago.' He gave a crack of laughter. 'Surely you didn't think a huge job like this was going to wait for *agreement*!' he exclaimed scornfully. The saws screamed behind him and two great dinosaur cranes lowered their necks, opened their jaws, gulped greedily at a hole in the earth and creaked on. The workman looked sympathetically at the young man's face. 'Real brutes, aren't they?' He stared at the wood-strewn ground. 'Don't worry,' he said, 'all the bits of good wood round here won't be wasted. Most of the better stuff will be shifted to factories. They'll be used for making wooden spoons, toys, chests, tables and what have you. Some of the better chunks go to the monastery up there, so I've heard. I believe the monks like making wooden bowls. A good relaxing thing to do between prayers and keeps them out of mischief, I suppose. Though where the mischief comes from on that cold, windswept hill beats me, it really does. It must come from inside, mustn't it? Well, everyone's got their own ideas. But there's something about wood they go for, I believe. It's natural, you see. Good, clean and natural. But the funny thing about being natural too long – it begins to get *un*natural. Yes, all good people are supposed to like wood. The rest of us go for the flashy stuff – the brass, tin, steel and aluminium, and gold and silver, naturally, if you can get your hands on it. Well, I never meddle with things that aren't my line. Everyone's got their own ideas. Leave them to get on with it is what I say. I believe they get up in the middle of the night to pray. I couldn't do that myself though sometimes when I've been

out with the boys I get up once or even twice, though
certainly not to pray. Talking about being unnatural, you
look a bit out of this world yourself. Where do you come
from?'

'From the other side of the forest.'

'So you've never been properly out?'

'Oh yes. I had to, of course,' said Martin. 'I went off to
school like everyone else. Then I came back.'

'No good,' said the other. 'Once you've got out, never go
back. And you're still too young to be shocked at changes
like the ones around here. Don't think I don't detest some
things myself. But then I'm far too old to shout and kick
about it.'

'I'm going to shout and kick all my life about ugly things,'
said Martin. He added that his father had once taught
woodwork in a small school on the far side of the city.

'There, you see!' exclaimed the woodman. 'Your father's
a *good* man. He's a lover of wood like our friends the monks
up there.'

'I don't believe he ever made bowls,' said Martin. 'He
made a wheelbarrow once. Mostly it was chests he made.
Tables and chests. Years ago he used to make bookcases.
But it's all different now. You've got to make them for
ornaments, not books – for crinolined ladies, fat cupids and
what have you, standing on shallow shelves. Still, he always
used good wood. He's old-fashioned of course, but I think
he *is* a good man.' He stood for a moment looking into the
half-sawed branches above them. Already the tallest tree
was lying on the ground with the woodchips and sawdust
on top of a tangled heap of shattered twigs and a frenzy of
leaves.

'Now you'll be asking about birds,' said the woodman,
following his eyes. 'They'll just have to find other places,
won't they? Just like everything else, like the moths, the bats
and butterflies, the hedgehogs, the hares and the foxes. I
hope you're not the sort who thinks it helps to take one bird

or bat home out of its misery, while driving your mother round the bend.'

'I'm not an idiot,' Martin replied.

'I never said so. I believe I'd join you if I could,' said the man, picking up a great barrow of red earth. 'Anyway, I'll see you around.'

Martin walked slowly back through the forest to his home. He said nothing to his parents of what he'd seen that day or whom he'd talked to. He didn't often cross the forest after that, and the days passed slowly as usual. Occasionally he wrote a few mediocre verses. His father and mother were delighted. They said that nothing would please them better than that he should become a poet – a good or even a great one. Lots of other parents, they added, would hate this idea. But they would love it. From that moment he wrote no more verse.

Martin's father was now in his late sixties and he was glad enough to retire from teaching. It had taken a long time to reach the school by the roundabout bus that circled the forest. The new houses going up on the other side had meant that his classes had become larger and larger. As for his mother, she saw few people. She was becoming frail and rather querulous. She said that trees were her only friends, but it seemed that wood itself was not included. She complained of her husband's job. He brought in sawdust on his shoes and scattered woodchips around the place. There were, of course, no shops near, but a few large vans were now moving about the place. Because of the growing housing schemes on the far side they carried everything that anyone could possibly wish for in a forest including romantic paperbacks, insect repellent, shoe polish, high-class writing paper and denture cream. Martin dropped all poetry and began to paint a little – studies of trees gesticulating against luminous puffball clouds. Again his parents were overjoyed. There had been painters as well as poets in the family. They took pains to buy him a box of the most expensive paints and a fistful of genuine horsehair brushes. His mother was just about to buy him a voluminous linen smock with pleats down the back and front when he said he had changed his mind. What did he want to do then? He wanted, at this moment, to do nothing. His mother, on the whole, was a patient person. It was her one great virtue, but she made the mistake of showing it day and night. Such patience made her son angry. Two winters later Martin's mother died of a dangerous flu, and bad conscience was added to his other feelings. The father now confessed to his son that he'd had a quiet but rather a disappointing life. He didn't enlarge on this, but Martin decided that, though his own life was quiet – quieter than that of any other young man he'd ever known – yet it must never end in patience and disappointment. His father was now over eighty and did not have long to live.

'If it will cheer you, father,' said Martin one day, 'I'd like you to know that I'm going to take up painting after all.' His father was overjoyed. 'Oh, if only your poor mother were alive to hear it. Your uncle Joe was a painter, and your second cousin – the one in America – *called* himself a painter, though, in my poor judgement, not a good one. Plates. Teapots and fruit. He tried to be a Cubist, but far too late. That was his mistake, of course. Square apples and grapes like those strange oblong green beads your mother wore. I suppose he was clever. He even managed to get indecency into his painting of pillows. Hard to believe, but there it was, art or no art. I'm afraid it was no art with him. But you – I know you've got the right stuff in you to make a painter!' There was silence for some moments.

'But I won't be painting *pictures*, father, so don't worry,' said Martin. 'I mean to be a housepainter. That's what I've wanted to be for years.'

Martin saw that this was another disappointment, but his father was used to these as he'd said, and his life was now short. He said nothing against his son's ambition – simply

gave the whole idea his blessing and only asked that the
young man should use only the very best brushes, pails and
paints for his trade, that his planks and ladders should be
safe and strong and that he should get the highest pay for
the job. There had been quite a bit of money in the family,
he said, and now it was all his. The father did not live long
after this. Martin was surprised and pleased that, so soon
after death, his face seemed to change. The expression of
quiet patience and disappointment gradually sharpened
into a look of strange, peering alertness and expectancy.
His son wondered if this might indeed be the sight of
heaven in the far distance between close-set trees.

Martin now tidied up the house ready to sell it. Most
people who came into the forest passed it without interest.
One day, however, a romantic, middle-aged widow came
round to view it. She didn't care for the cramped, untidy
house, but she took an immediate fancy to the young man.
This alarmed him. He saw that it was the extraordinary
convenience and economy of the arrangement that had
struck her. A pleasant middle-aged bachelor living alone
could be thrown in with some useful items of furniture – all
going dirt cheap. She asked him if he was lonely. He replied
that he was not. She asked him if he had always been a lover
of trees and forests. He replied that he was now beginning
to hope for other things in his life. He was careful not to
specify what these things might be in case she would offer
them on the spot. She asked what he was going to do now
that he was quite alone. He said he was going to paint. The
woman said it was one of the most romantic things she had
ever heard – a man alone on the edge of a great forest who
was setting out to be a great painter. He replied that his
painting was probably not the sort she had in mind. When
he had learnt the trade he was going to paint the interiors
and exteriors of the houses on the other side of the forest. In
fact, he intended to buy one himself and start from there.

Eventually Martin sold his house to a botanist and his

wife. He took an immediate liking to them both. He noticed how, after a cursory examination of the place, they kept moving towards the windows and stayed there looking out for a long time. The wife made no mention of measuring the rooms at once for curtains or carpets, and her husband, though he mentioned the creakings and crackings of the place, took no steps to see if all the floorboards were sound. They seemed, in fact, more interested in the scene outside. There was still a great strip of trees beyond the house, but Martin warned them that the scene would soon look very different. Many more houses would certainly go up on the other side. The strips of sunlight between the trees they were looking at now would eventually be cut by paths and even busy roads. They might be staring at an illusion, he added. One day the forest would not exist.

'Well, isn't everything an illusion?' said the botanist. 'We're looking down, up and sideways into a universe that doesn't exist in any way we can possibly conceive. But at least we can remember and enjoy the illusion. I'd remember these trees, for instance, even if they disappeared tomorrow – even if they turned overnight into masts and telegraph poles.' He added that long ago he'd given up the idea of anything in heaven or earth being lasting. The whole thing was totally mysterious, a mind-blowing process of metamorphosis.

This was a great relief and comfort to Martin. It was as if he could hand over to these benevolent strangers everything that the forest meant to him – the blessing and burden of ancient trees, their strength and fragility in the modern world, the tragedy of their disappearance, and even the unexpected friendliness of those who had put axe and saw to them. Now all these emotions could be left to the incomers. As a duty he mentioned all the things that could be made with the spare wood – cooking spoons, breadboards, stools, toys, bookends, trays and boxes. 'I daresay there will soon be a shop over on the other side that would take and sell all of them,' he added.

'We're not really interested in what can be made from bits of wood,' said the woman. 'My husband simply likes to study trees and everything that grows under them. I'm writing a book myself. This place is ideal for that.' She mentioned fairy tales.

'I never cared for those,' said Martin cautiously. 'I heard them all as a child. Rather cruel and sad they seemed. Nobody ever met the kind and beautiful people passing by in the distance.'

In a few weeks he had moved out. But the clearing of the house had taken him a long time. He discovered that his parents had been more interesting and even more secretive people than he'd imagined. His mother had kept old letters in a shoe box – letters from some young man written to her when she was a girl. They were unusually personal letters, expressing thoughts and feelings, but never mentioning love. Obviously for her, however, their long sojourn inside a box and hidden, like bulbs, in a dark cupboard, had turned them into love letters – precious things ready for a future flowering that had not materialized. His father had collected only things connected with his work – the tools of his woodwork days along with the designs for things that had never been made. There were also a few bowls that had not come up to the mark and had been scrapped. Either they had not been perfectly round or there was some almost invisible flaw on their surface. Along with these there was one photo of his father. This photo – very spry, very bright-eyed and hopeful – made Martin feel sad. He had only seen a different side. So was there no way the young were ever going to know their hidden parents except as tired and rather desperate people, long past their best, if there had ever been a best?

One day he abruptly stopped his search into the past. He swept up the place one last time, then sat down and waited for the van that was to take him and his possessions to his new bungalow on the other side. He never turned his head

as it drove off and his cottage disappeared like a small ship
going down in a green sea.

It was some time before he got to work on his next place,
but meanwhile he put up a prominent sign inviting orders
for painting and decorating the neighbouring houses. Their
owners were not slow to answer. There had been many
changeovers even in the last ten years or so. Martin soon
found himself inside rooms where, before painting, he
would have to strip and scrape down into the recent past
like an archaeologist of wallpaper. He found himself un-
covering bizarre ambitions and longings. Carefully and
tenderly he peeled away old fears and desires. Sometimes
someone's longing to get away was suddenly revealed by a
paper covered with ships, aeroplanes and sleek motorcars.
Certain kitchens and dining rooms boasted old wallpapers
covered with wine bottles and glasses, tropical fruits hanging in branches, and criss-crossing designs of knives, forks
and spoons. Nurseries had wallpapers of bears and dolls,
drums and pink bows overlaid by other designs as the
children grew older. In some bedrooms he stripped off
naked dancing girls with pumpkin breasts. Occasionally he
came on a tree paper vainly trying to echo the vanishing
forest. He uncovered clouds, stars, moons and flowers.
Soon he began to repaper every room. Before long he was
ready to paint the outside of certain houses – their doors,
windows, railings and garages. He offered a restricted
choice of colours to his clients. He told them he used only
soft shades of green and blue. He also used purple, brown
and black. 'These are the forest colours,' he would say to all
objections and queries.

'But the forest will soon not exist,' the bungalow people
insisted. 'And these are houses, not trees. We can't go back
to the monkey stage, can we?' They had lived a long time
beside a dark forest, they said, and now they wanted to take
bright yellow to the doors, to outline the railings in brilliant
scarlet.

'Do you want your great-grandchildren to remember you when they dig up ugly planks of shiny yellow, when they trip over lethal splinters of scarlet railing?' said Martin.

'Anyway, nothing matters now,' said the old pessimist of the district, 'whether our houses are red, yellow or black. Soon concrete will cover everything. Concrete's the strongest stuff in the world,' he added as he watched a huge machine rolling out the stuff in the distance.

'Don't you believe it!' exclaimed Martin. 'Living trees are stronger than dead concrete, stronger even than all the lifeless metal in the world. Tree roots can pass through cracks as thin as threads. They can burst through steel vaults. No. You'll never get rid of the trees. Never.'

'We'll see,' said the neighbour. 'Meanwhile we'd better stop theorizing and get on with the painting. I'm not too keen on nature talk. It begins sensibly enough, but ends with cranks knocking their heads together.'

'By the way,' Martin remarked after a while, 'are the monks still around? It was said they were keen on wood. Wooden bowls, to be exact.'

'Begging bowls, you mean?' the other asked suspiciously.

'No, just plain, round wooden bowls. You can get them from the craft shop down there. Natural circles, you understand. Something to do with perfection. It all appeals to the religious outlook, I daresay.'

'Oh, I don't know about that,' said the householder. 'My wife's got a thing about bowls too. Bowls on every shelf and table, in every corner. Wooden, china, metal, glass – you name it. She collects them wherever she goes. And I can tell you straight off it's nothing to do with perfection. She's very far from perfect as she'd be the first to admit. I wouldn't know about the monks, of course, but I *do* happen to know my own wife.'

The road was becoming more used to Martin's forest colours by the time he came to paint the outside of the bungalows. Even from an aeroplane the houses, on the edge of ground where trees had once grown, looked more at home. They now appeared to grow out of the landscape instead of being stuck on like separate, bright bricks. The saws still screamed amongst the few trees left. The concrete was gradually going down and in some months the road might be ready for heavy traffic. But Martin was thought of as some sort of mediator between city and forest. His large brushes stroked the walls, gates, railings of houses steadily, confidently. Yet people would still stand round to watch and question: 'Why do you use that dark blue?'

'I'm bringing the evening sky down into it,' he would reply. 'I'm trying to bring back those deep forest pools that have all dried up.'

'Is that not too dark a brown, Martin?' they would say, pointing to certain parts of the outside woodwork.

'Well, it's not as dark as the earth after that great thunderstorm, if you remember,' he would say.

'And what about that green on the garages? That could be more cheerful, couldn't it? It's a real gloomy green.'

'Yes. Late summer is always dark in the forest.'

Once in a while Martin would cross over to visit the botanist and his wife. They now looked out on to a very different scene. The new road across the ancient forest was coming nearer. They knew the sound of saws, of crashing trees, and finally the noise of traffic would one day burst through.

'I never knew it would be as bad as that when I sold the place,' said Martin.

'Well, how could you?' said the botanist's wife. 'It was up to us to find out.'

'The first idea was to leave a wide strip of forest on this side,' Martin went on. 'I saw the plans, in fact.'

'Plans go for nothing when money comes into it,' she said. 'We saw plans too. A very nice man pointed it all out on the map. Of course I see now he thought we were a pair of dear old sentimental things who'd be happy with a flower patch and a garden gnome. He told us he loved trees himself. It really seemed as if he couldn't bear to see a twig fall off, let alone a tree lying on the ground. When we saw him off he murmured: "Life must go on, you know." But we've enjoyed living here and we'll stay as long as we can. I'm still writing a book, but I'm finished with fairies and forests. It'll have to be water now. We've always been travellers so we'll move off while we can to some great lake or river. My husband's an expert on water plants too, so that will suit him. Surely nothing will happen to dry up the water unless it's a nuclear disaster.'

'Will you be moving away soon?' Martin asked.

'No, luckily they're not going to knock us down just yet. They're just going to surround us with new houses. And we're to be "landscaped" to keep us quiet. A few trees and bushes and a patch of grass, I suppose. When the road reaches us we'll move to some lake or other as I've told you. Meantime I'm going to start up a small woodland tearoom or something of the kind. I've no conscience, I'm afraid. We need a lot of money if we're to move away, and I can make it. The tearoom will try its best to be twee, olde-worlde and horrible, but I hope to nip that in the bud. The place will become more and more expensive, even fashionable. People will drive out from the city and from all the new housing estates, and I shall slave for hours. I shall make an unusual jam from berries. It will be called Forest Conserve. Conserve, not jam, because we can give talks on conservation at the same time and encourage discussion. My husband obviously knows the eatable from the poisonous berries, so that should be all right. I shall have to learn to cook and bake at last, and he can talk about plants and trees till the cows come home. The tearoom will probably be called "The Botanist's Bothy". It will be very exclusive and will be a tremendous draw even to those who have hardly seen a leaf.'

'I've never met such an optimist!' Martin exclaimed.

'I might as well be. Jack is the pessimist. The mixture's explosive, stimulating, or whatever word you want to call it. At any rate, we're too old for marriage guidance. Years and years ago we went, but I fell madly for one of the guiders and botched the whole thing up. But to go back to jam. Eventually this special conserve of mine may reach the city shops. The jars should bear a special tree label designed by a proper artist. You *are* an artist, aren't you?'

'No, I'm told I'm not – not the kind you're talking about. I paint houses, doors, walls and windows. I'm a house-painter. By the way, I expect you'll be needing lots of wooden plates and bowls for your Bothy. Probably chairs, stools and tables too. You can get them all from the craft shop on the other side.'

'I'm not a crafty person, as a matter of fact,' said the botanist's wife. 'Are you trying to bring us all together? I'll look over sometime, of course.'

'Then there are the monks up there,' Martin went on. 'When you've made enough, why don't you try some of your jam with them? Everything good and natural would be welcome there.'

'I haven't even made the stuff yet, and I very much doubt if I'm good and natural myself,' she replied. 'But I'll think it over.'

A year or so later, climbing down from the window of a house where he'd been painting, Martin caught a glimpse of pale green on the path below. He bent down and saw a single seedling pushing up between the flagstones. This excited him like the sudden sight of a new comet to an astronomer, or like the feathers and leaves blown towards an early ship of discovery – signs that some huge, unknown continent was near. He didn't dare touch the fragile green thing, but was across within the hour to his friend, the botanist. Quickly they came back together to study every detail of this new life – its straight, determined stem and the infinitesimal green leaves.

'Yes, there you've got it!' exclaimed the botanist, rising triumphantly and dusting his knees. 'Your first oak tree and, if you're lucky, the beginning of a forest!'

'You mean if we live for four or five hundred years?'

'Well then, let your heirs and all their distant offspring have it. In no time the trees will be strong. They'll push down the houses, topple the poles and cover the concrete. In some hundreds of years' time people may have learned something. Stupidity can't go on forever. They may long for wood rather than iron, for strong roots to strangle the steel. Have you *seen* the roots of trees? Ferocious, tenacious, and so strong centuries of gales won't move them.'

'Yet this seedling could be crushed in seconds,' said Martin.

'Of course,' replied the botanist, 'but jungles have covered civilizations with a green so powerful you could hardly drag it off the stone.'

'But you can't stop progress on the earth,' said Martin.

'What progress?' asked the botanist.

'New machines, new rockets, new satellites, new robots, new bombs, new space-probes to the great Computer God in the sky. I only paint houses but I've tried to paint in forest colours. But do people *want* green? No, they want yellow, scarlet, electric-blue, orange and pink inside and out. Green's supposed to be unlucky and always has been. Ask your wife. Ask in any shop. Who wants to wear green?'

'Well, I don't know anything about superstition,' said the botanist. 'I just know the earth always wants to wear green and always has done. Leave it alone for a few years and look again. Everything has gradually disappeared except green. What's lucky for the earth can't be unlucky for people, can it?'

They now hurried back to fetch the botanist's wife who agreed that green was supposed to be unlucky, but in nothing else she could think of but clothes. She herself, however, donned an apple-green skirt to show she was no party to superstition. She accompanied the men to the gardens at the other side of the forest to look at the seedling. Quite a few neighbours from adjoining gardens now gathered when they saw two men and a woman staring fixedly at the crack between the paving stones. Most stayed away, suspecting something horrible. One man, in fact, shouted across his fence: 'Is it a *snake*?'

'There, you see,' said the housepainter. 'People expect a *snake* in the grass, never the grass itself. Very soon they'll see only snakes and no grass. Can you blame them?'

Nevertheless, when the people of the road discovered what the three were staring at they searched their own paths and gardens. Suddenly there were shouts from one side and the other or even from upper windows where people were looking down. Yet they were peculiarly mixed shouts – mostly shadowy and doubtful, yet gradually lit here and there with a glimmer of hope. It seemed as if those who'd lived on the edge of great trees at first could hardly recognize a green seedling. But soon more and more people were looking for them. They went running here and there into one another's gardens, bumping together in their search as if enacting a clumsy fallback into Eden – that magnificent memory of green trees. Soon there would be no more discussion about forest colours in a house. It was the forest itself they longed for. Naturally there were those who mocked at the fuss over this colour green. Weren't lots of awkward things green? Mould was green. Phlegm was green. And so was immaturity. Above all they laughed at the idea of green ever covering the engines of destruction. How could greenness ever get a grip on the smooth, round bombs, or take root on the slippery satellites of war? But the botanist himself knew how childish the idea of greenness could become if it meant only grass and plants covering the surface of the earth like a comfortable, plushy carpet. He spoke up now about the destruction – as weapons and poison took over – of all fruits and crops, the disappearance

of all peoples and animals, the poisoning of air, sea and soil
to unknown, enormous depths. He stopped all talk of
seedlings. Instead he lectured them on science. 'What will
the earth become if we carry on as we've been doing?' he
asked at the end of his talk one night. There was silence and
he answered himself: 'A small, stinking poisoned pill in
space.' A few successful businessmen who'd continually
and comfortably travelled the earth took affront at the name
'poisoned pill'. They asked the botanist to illustrate his
ideas to an audience. He complied and showed them great
parts of the sky on screen. It was just possible – though not
very likely – that man was unique, he said, while pointing to
swirling blue veils of nebulae, infinitely distant in time and
space.

But the botanist's lifespan was not infinite. The old man
caught a chill one evening as he sat outside his cottage and
not many weeks later he died. He was buried on the far side
of the forest where, months afterwards, it was observed that
many small, green seedlings were growing up around the
mound of his grave. Though no doubt the seeds had come
on the wind, others assumed they had been carefully
planted by the gardeners of the road. Up at the monastery
it was put down without question as a true miracle of God.
Whichever way it was, he lay – after many years had passed
– in a grove of tall, green trees.

The botanist's wife lived on alone, keeping her house and
tearoom going at the edge of the forest. The visitors to the
tearoom increased and even her jam, Forest Conserve, was
beginning to make its name in distant city stores. She made
an arrangement with the craft shop at the other side which
still took wood from the forest to make small tables, bowls,
stools and wooden spoons. The botanist's wife helped to
advertise all these at her own tables and got a substantial
cut of the gains. Every summer she took several pots of her
jam up to the monks. Luckily, the head of the monastery
loved Forest Conserve. It was an indulgence which at first

he had only grudgingly allowed himself. Now, as he grew older, he positively craved it. Often they chatted together and on one visit she enquired if he would care for some beautiful, hand-turned wooden bowls as well as jam. She went on to ask discreetly about the unbroken circle as a sign of perfection. Shortly afterwards the monastery acquired a set of bowls at bargain price, and the shop with its holy back-up became known far and wide. Again the botanist's widow made a good thing out of it and at the same time was praised by the head of the order for bringing a steady stream of sweetness on to the long tables of the refectory. They had many talks together on religion, on love, death, heaven and hell, good and evil. She congratulated him warmly on the curious fact that he – a confirmed bachelor living in a wood without apple trees or women – should have such a deep and detailed knowledge of the sin of Eve, and advised him that the average woman like herself had little time or opportunity for the more interesting sins. Over the years they became close friends.

The housepainter lived on, but as he grew older he was a little more careful about climbing ladders. Though he was in and out of many houses he was still an outsider and a lonely man. He was not so fussy now about his colours, though still drawing the line at scarlet and shocking pink for doors and windows. Often as he painted he sang and whistled like a bird in a high tree. He rejoiced that after some hundreds of years no roof that he had painted, no window, wall or chimney pot would be seen for green.

# The Morning Mare

FOR SOME TIME back the best break in the whole year for
Kate had been the short visit to Ireland on her own. No
study of the map or talk of any other place could change her
mind about this ideal holiday. The town she visited was
Dingle in the south-west, where her cousins lived with their
parents. It was fun to be with a large family. On her latest
stay, however, she found the two oldest boys had just left
school and gone to jobs in Dublin. The rest were still at
home. Brenda, at sixteen, the oldest girl, was her own age.
Two little boys, twin girls in junior school and a ten-month-
old baby made up the rest of the family. Kate envied and
admired them all. She envied them their black hair, their
blue eyes and their casual, colourful clothes. She enjoyed
the songs and music of their country, and most of all their
stories – admiring the soft or brilliantly cutting edge they
could give to the meanest phrase. Mockery and tenderness
were here combined, and the sudden, thorny prick of
malice. It was useless to try to tell such stories afterwards.
They lost their shine and sound, like pebbles carried far
inland from a turbulent beach.

The house she visited was an old one, very beautiful, very
distinguished – a wreck of a house, needing paint and
plaster, needing nails, new pipes, new drains and long,
loving care, but getting none. Occasionally someone might
make a start on the garden, but after a month or two of rain
mixed with the salt wind from the sea, it would become a
wilderness again. When the wind was really high a mass of
frenzied ivy darkened the graceful frontage of the house and
two great twisted thorn bushes would scratch backwards

and forwards over the glass of the austere windows. Mosquitoes floated on the sludgy pool where a few perfect waterlilies opened, almost unnoticed, grew brown, and wilted away again. Once, perhaps, the iron gates had creaked open to welcome strangers. In recent years only a few persons had walked, with velvet feet, on paths green with thick moss. Kate liked this place exactly because of the total contrast to her own neat home and its circumspect street with the well-kept gardens. But here, in the land she visited, startling contrasts were near the surface. It was a place of dream and nightmare, cruelty and compassion. Black water could suddenly well up from clear ditches. Huge, ancient rocks jutted from smooth, green fields and blocked the progress of the plough. It was a land where people walked devoutly from church, talking with love and gusto of a pagan past. It was no use trying to have one side without the other. Alternate darkness and light flickered over everything like the weather.

Most of all, even more than the stories and the songs, Kate enjoyed the early morning talks with her cousin Brenda with whom she shared a room. This was the time when the two of them discussed everything – school, work, politics, marriage, careers, happiness, unhappiness, friends, parents and grandparents. Kate's visit coincided with her sixteenth birthday. They woke early that morning and started to talk. They discussed how fifteen might differ from sixteen and even, ridiculously, how sixteen might differ from sixty. They spoke, as usual, about happiness and what exactly it might mean for them. Could they ever get enough of it or would they, sooner or later, fall back into the flat, grey routine where most of their elders seemed to live? 'Some people,' said Brenda, 'think that happiness comes from living absolutely and totally in the present moment – not looking backwards nor forwards.' She insisted it was a business of taking the last drop of sweetness from these moments. On the other hand, happiness might be one instantaneous flash that lit up a whole day, a week, a month or, with luck, even an entire year.

At that instant the milk-van went past the window. It was an old horse-drawn van which Kate, every morning of her visit, had come to dread. She knew by the frenzied clopping of hoofs and the clatter of the milk-cans that it was being driven at the usual breakneck speed up the steep, cobbled street. Always it went so fast that a trickle of milk would escape from the rattling lids while the van would appear to rock precariously from side to side. The horse was a broken-down old nag with a white froth dripping from its lip and a raw patch on one shoulder. Its neighing was like some dreadful high-pitched coughing, most horrible to hear. Kate knew this for a true nightmare and no mistake – an early morning nightmare which would be repeated day after day till the end of her visit. 'I wonder if that horse will drop down dead one of these mornings,' she said over her shoulder to her cousin who was still in bed. 'And I'm not the only one who's seen it,' she added. 'There are people across the way watching from doors and windows. No-one's doing anything. Is *this* the present moment you're wanting me to keep?' At the same time she thought how weak and cowardly it was that she had never run down into the street herself, never called out or gone to the police about the driver and his whip. She had made no move at all. Now she could hardly bear to see her face in the mirror, the pink and white coward that she was!

'Well, never mind,' said Brenda from her bed. 'You can't always choose. Sometimes the present moment isn't good. But look again soon,' she added slyly. 'Maybe it will look better.' Kate couldn't help smiling even while the clattering hoofs still sounded in the distance. The holidays in this part of the world didn't exactly match those back home, and sure enough, two schoolboys from the top class were walking past on their way to a nearby school. Coming from distant farms, they had a long way to go, but every morning they contrived to go more and more slowly as they walked under the window of the girls' bedroom. Sometimes they would walk so slowly they almost stopped. Then together they would look up like two eager, wary young animals, all eyes. They were tall, long-haired youths, sporting sideburns and showing chins and throats that would soon be dark. Their hands were strong and bony with wrists too long for their sleeves. Both appeared to move in awkward mockery of their outgrown gear, at the same time instinctively raising their arms a fraction towards the window in expectation of some future state. For Kate these were the most romantic moments of her visit. She felt the leap of joy as she leaned far out, revealing a soft curve of lace around the sill as the boys stared up. It seemed they stared, steadily, endlessly, totally absorbed and almost vacant-faced in their intentness, as if their cheeks had been wiped blank by a full sponge of milk.

'So you've forgotten about your horse,' said Brenda softly from behind. She was up and standing back in the shadows of the room.

'No, no, I have not!' cried her cousin, 'and if it happens again . . .'

'What then?' asked the other girl.

'I'll do something about it, of course.'

Her cousin said nothing, but smiled to herself as she dressed. It was hot that day. When they went out they found the wet garden steaming. Cascades of drops fell from the bushes as they brushed past. In the morning they roamed about in the woods behind the house, went up the hill with a picnic tea, and in the early evening came down to watch Brenda's father dealing with his swarm of bees which hung from the low branch of a lime tree. Later when it was cooler he gathered the sizzling, brown bundle down into a basket and took them to the hive where he knocked them out cautiously onto the threshold. They knelt down to watch the regiment of bees move slowly up into their furious-sounding retreat. Then they went inside for supper – a rich fish pie with herbs from the garden. Brenda's father was a handsome, heavy, easy-going man who laughed a lot. He talked about the history of the district, he talked about bees, about flowers, sunshine and honey. Late every evening he'd go off to drink, always returning, benign or belligerent by turns.

'What about winter when there's no more honey?' Kate had asked him before he left.

'In the winter I make a special syrup for my bees,' he replied. 'I make great cans of the stuff. It keeps them going till the sun comes out again.'

'Yes, it's the only time he's ever inside the kitchen!' exclaimed Brenda, laughing.

Her mother didn't smile, but with a serious face kept plucking listlessly at the tablecloth. She looked so tired that Kate was only too glad to get up and go off with her cousin again.

'Your mother doesn't listen to your father,' she said when they were outside. 'She doesn't really believe him.'

'No, she doesn't believe him,' Brenda agreed. 'She doesn't believe the honey, sunshine bit. I wouldn't know much about the early time, of course.' Her mother had married later than most, she said. And then she'd worked too hard. One child every twenty months or so had knocked some of the verve and strength from her life.

'I was told everyone helps everyone else here,' said Kate. 'Even the largest families. It goes right down through them all, and the oldest can help the youngest.' All the same, there were days, Brenda had replied calmly, when her mother didn't, simply couldn't get up – not for the life of her. Then, naturally, she herself took over. No, she didn't mind doing dishes, cooking, looking after the others. Not at all. But she didn't think she would ever marry, she added.

'That's rubbish!' said Kate. 'With your looks, your intelligence.'

'Absolutely nothing to do with it,' said her cousin. 'But it's true I've got some talent like my mother.'

She described how her mother had been a true craftswoman and had brought back some of the old Irish designs into her illuminated scripts and wall-hangings when she started to work on her own. There were tapestries too, unlike anything that had been seen here before. They had got into exhibitions. One or two had been sent abroad and made a good deal of money. That meant her mother could occasionally go away for longer, visit foreign galleries, sell her work more widely.

'Why doesn't she go on with it then?' asked Kate.

Her cousin laughed at the innocence of this question, or was it stupidity? Sometimes these were very close to one another, she thought, as she stared at Kate's placid face. 'You don't know much, do you? And you've seen absolutely nothing,' she went on, stretching herself as if the whole subject made her tired and stiff. 'And you're so romantic, it's positively cruel,' she added. Kate couldn't believe that cruelty and romance could ever be spoken about in the same breath. Cruelty was a horse with rolling eyes and froth on its lips. Romance was two boys staring up at a window, and the sound of bees on a summer evening.

'Sleep well then,' were Brenda's last words that night. 'And remember!' Her cousin was almost asleep and so full of the sound of bees, the melting honeycomb and the sun that she couldn't remember what this command might mean.

But in the morning came the cruel awakening. Brenda aroused her cousin with a shout and Kate ran to the window. The coughing, knock-kneed horse went shambling by, the tilting cans clattering. The driver was brandishing his whip. At the back of the room Brenda was sitting bolt upright in bed. 'Do something!' she cried.

'Stop that! Stop!' shouted Kate from the open window. The sunlight was already bright outside. A few shopkeepers were standing at their doors. Otherwise the street seemed unnaturally empty and as sharply focused on man and animal as a snapshot. It was silent too in the country beyond, so silent that every distant sound could be heard – even the early morning train taking people to their work in some far-out district. Kate drew in a deep breath. Oh, to be a brave actor in life rather than an observer! She leant out again. 'Stop!' she shouted down.

The driver looked directly up at the girl. A wide, tilted hat cast a sharp, black angle across his face, but his white teeth flashed a smile. He swept off his hat in a mocking gesture as he galloped past. He cracked the whip again. 'Sorry, sweetheart, but I can't stop today,' he yelled. 'This old mare won't let me!' The stumbling hoofs approached the corner. The frenzied animal went on and disappeared.

Kate sat down on her bed in tears. 'Well, you didn't do much, did you?' said her cousin. 'No use crying about it. Maybe you'll get another chance.' In a few minutes the schoolboys would be coming down the street. Even Brenda felt the anticipation of joy and tried to bring it back for Kate's sake. Now there was a faint whistling and laughter under the window. 'Your friends!' she exclaimed in an encouraging voice. But Kate still sat on the bed, shivering, as if a wintry gust had caught her in midsummer. All sweetness of the momentary romance had suddenly disappeared. Nightmare was galloping through the bright day. Under her window the innocent milk had been spilt around and was trickling slowly through the dust.

This was Kate's last morning before flying home. They spent it happily enough, and in the afternoon her cousin accompanied her to the station where she would catch the train to Dublin.

'Till next autumn then,' said Kate as her train approached. She drew near to kiss her cousin. Brenda seemed to draw back for an instant, cool and unsmiling. 'Next year's visit might have to be postponed,' she said. 'There

may be another baby in the family.' Kate was asking
questions now, smiling and looking eagerly into her
cousin's impassive face. 'I don't want to talk too much
about it now,' Brenda explained, 'in case something happens. My mother isn't strong, and she's not so young, you
know.' It was obvious Kate didn't know. There was a slight
touch of scorn in Brenda's eyes as she said goodbye. Her
cousin got up quickly into the train. A gap opened between
them now – a gap which was more than the dark, sharp-
edged drop between train and platform. For the first time
Kate experienced sorrow and fear of this wounding gash.
On the platform Brenda was standing very straight and still.
She looked suddenly thinner, harder and older as if she
came from a country more mysterious, unexplored, and
much more complex than her cousin had ever imagined.
When the train started to move Kate leaned out and waved
with a gentle, reassuring gesture. But Brenda held her arm
straight up without waving. Indeed it seemed a salute rather
than a wave and before the train left the station she had
turned swiftly on her heel and disappeared.